HERS TO CLAIM

-VERDANTIA SERIES BOOK FOUR-

PATRICIA A. KNIGHT

ISBN 978-1-950661-09-1
ALL RIGHTS RESERVED
Hers To Claim Copyright © 2014 Patricia A. Knight
Edited by Josephine Henke and Tracy Sebold
Cover design, digital and paperback formatting by LJ Stock
Electronic book publication September 2014

DEAR READER,

Thank you all for your fascination with my world of Verdantia. It warms my heart to know there are others for whom the Second Tetriarch, et al, are living, breathing characters.

I have heard your desire to know how to pronounce characters' names, terminology, and places as the author would like them pronounced, and to that end, I have included a Glossary Of Terms in the back of this book. Yeah!

If there is a term or name that I have left out that you wish to have defined simply drop me an email at:

patriciaknight190@gmail.com

Warm regards,

Patricia

ACKNOWLEDGMENTS

Wow, where to begin? This was a hard year for me. I ran into some of life's little bumps in the road, health-wise. I doubt *Hers To Claim* would have been finished, even six months late, without the continued support, input and, at times, merciless nagging, of my incredible critique partners. So to Marilyn, Elizabeth, Stephanie, Brenda, and Travis, my heartfelt thanks. I love y'all. You're the best. There is some of each of you in my books.

Thank you to my fabulous editors, Tracy and Josephine. I appreciate the fast turn-around and all those imaginative suggestions… even if I don't use them…and all the commas…even if I don't use them. LOL

Thank you to LJ of LJ Stock Designs for the beautiful remake and formatting of Hers To Claim. I'm still swooning over the cover. For those of you unaware, LJ is also a hella-good author with a series of books I highly recommend.

And finally, to my sweetie, my "go-to-guy" for gut checks on the repartee between my two bickering alpha males and so much else. As my heroine says, "I am yours, my prince—beyond time." Hel was born in your brain. I hope I did him justice.

PROLOGUE

Verdantia had no memory of Her own creation nor how long She had existed. She had always been. For millennia, She hung suspended in vast space, a sentience aware only of eons of solitude. Her tendrils of golden life and intelligence extended into the impenetrable dark, into the terrible aloneness, always seeking another—until them— until Her sons and daughters arrived.

They were ephemeral, these organic creatures who appeared out of the vastness of space and walked Her surface. Their life spans were fragile and fleeting but brilliant as a flash-burning supernova. They spoke with Her, and for the first time in Her eternal existence, She had a name, Verdantia, Senzienza, Mother. At last, She was known by another. She delighted in their brief but wondrous interactions with Her energies. They brought Her great pleasure, Her family.

Her connection to Her sons and daughters ran soul-deep. She endowed each individual with vast powers borne of Her innate energies. They became entrusted guardians of the sphere that housed Her sentience, Her soul. She loved them as a mother loves her own.

Her surface glowed with hundreds of thousands of their brilliant stars—until the time of terror—until the time of great death. Now, when only a handful remained, She needed Her children as never before. The possibility She had foreseen in Her early days of innocence loomed with ominous portent. Drawn by the tendrils She cast ages ago in Her quest for another, an evil from the darkest reaches of the void had found Her. Black corruption burrowed into Her with icy fingers of spreading darkness, desecrating and despoiling, but She had no defense. She had given those powers to Her children in the days of their beginning. She could only hope those beloved few of Her sons and daughters that still walked Her surface would feel the ravening blackness and act—before the spreading darkness consumed Her completely.

CHAPTER ONE

The nails in the worn heels of Prince DeHelios' boots clicked against the stone as Hel climbed the stairs, and then softened to a rhythmic thud as he strode the carpeted hall to the small corner of the castle still maintained as a residence. He looked neither left nor right and ignored the signs of prosperity dimmed—room after room empty and dark, rooms where laughter and love once abided. He stared sightlessly past the shrouded portraits of his long-dead ancestors, the first kings, and queens of Verdantia, now ghostly rectangles adorning a poorly lit hall. A melancholy sorrow pierced his heart when he passed the empty nursery—its fleeting pain as biting as the cold outside—but he shrugged it off with grim discipline.

"Thank the Goddess, you are back." A stooped, elderly man accosted Hel as he entered a cozy chamber where a fire radiated warmth and candles lifted the gloom. Heavy tapestry curtains covered the floor-to-ceiling windows and prevented any draft. From the bookcases lining the walls crammed full of leather-bound tomes, the room had served as a library or office in an earlier time. Now, the pale bodies on low pallets arranged about the room testified to another use—a sickroom.

"Bernard, give me a moment." Hel shrugged his steward off and nodded at an older woman attending one of those ill. "Sara, how is Rolly?"

She shook her head. "He won't last the night, my lord."

Hel disguised his pain at the news. The man was a friend. "I'll come sit with him. Give me a moment." He turned to Bernard. "I got your message. I came directly." Hel pulled one of the squat, upholstered stools close to the fire and sat holding his hands out to the warmth. The icicles in his heavy black beard dripped onto the floor as they began to thaw. Bernard hovered over him, radiating anxiety.

"We *must* have a skilled Medicus and more brite-weed. I am unlearned in the healing arts, my lord—all of us are. We do our best, but…" The elderly man closed his eyes and seemed to shrink. "We lost Edgar today—another good man who was hale and hearty two months ago. The perimeter you set last month on the western border has failed. I don't understand why. We could always count on at least eight months, but we will have no wheat fields come spring if the blight cannot be pushed back."

As if the burden of feeding and housing his people was not sufficient, an unfamiliar, insidious blight, a black sickness, seemed to affect both the animate and inanimate on his mountain. One by one, his people had succumbed to a disturbing affliction that sucked their vigor, their *anima*, until they surrendered any attempt to live and just *faded* into death. The same contagion that afflicted his people drained the life from his land. The blight attacked the very soil under their feet, rendering it putrid, barren, unable to sustain life.

Hel sighed and hunched closer to the fire. His shoulders bowed as if every word from Bernard's mouth added yet another weighty burden to their width.

His steward's voice faltered, but his recount of the latest catastrophes continued. "Julian Goodman asked for the makings for brite-weed tea today. He said his wife was sickening. I told him to come back later. I couldn't risk the panic should he learn we had none."

At the old man's words, Hel straightened and raised his eyes to Bernard. "Tessa? Tessa is *fading*?"

Bernard nodded.

Hel's body tightened when he remembered the woman's sweet, erotic surrender. *Ah, Tessa.*

Together, they had performed the sexual rites to clean Nyth Uchel of an ugly remnant of the Haarb wars, soul-wraiths—though Hel preferred the term 'leeches'. Warm, giving Tessa—he *could not* let such a gentle soul die. His thoughts went to that day in the windswept courtyard when he had requested a partner for the rites and Tessa had answered, over her husband's vocal protests.

Her gentle voice carried in the quiet of the courtyard. "Julian, please reconsider. Lady Athena is dead, and our Lord has no one else. I have enough aristocratic blood to be of use to him. It will save *all* of us. It is just the temporary use of my body."

Her gentle eyes had shamed her husband, and he'd turned away with a snarling, "Do as you will."

Julian avoided Hel from that day forward. With regret, Hel considered he had made a lifetime enemy of the man; but Tessa, sweet, sweet Tessa had been a revelation, such a contrast to his dead wife who was cold even in life.

Hel felt a presence at his back, and the woman tending the sick room quietly addressed him. "My lord, you best come now. I don't think he has long."

Hel rose and moved between the ill to a chair pulled beside the pallet where Rolly lay covered with blankets. Vivid, suppurating sores covered his scalp and face, and his flesh hung slackly as if melted onto his skull.

"Rolly." Hel sat, then bent over his former gamekeeper and spoke his name gently. "Rolly, it's DeHelios. I'm here with you."

The man moaned and shifted slightly but otherwise gave no sign he had heard. Anger born of impotence rose in Hel's gut. He wished there was *something* he could do for the man. Of course, he *wished* many things and thought again of Tessa and all those whose lives depended on him.

Breath rattled in Rolly's lungs, and then he fell silent. His chest no longer rose and fell. Hel listened intently and watched for any sign of life.

"I think he's gone, sir," Sara said.

The effort not to scream or pound his fist through a wall left him rigid. When he was sure he could control himself, Hel stood and faced Bernard. "My damnable pride, my refusal to ask the Tetriarch for help has brought us to this. We need the radiance of our sigil tower to blaze forth once again and kill this dark contagion. For that, I need a magistra. Tessa was an incomplete substitute for my wife. A tender, willing heart cannot replace the genetics and the schooling that make a magistra a true conduit for power. I have wasted precious time that might have brought an end to this nightmare."

"My lord, the corruption beset us on multiple fronts. You made the best decision at the time. You couldn't have known the blight would spread with such speed and devastation."

Bernard's words didn't lift his sense of guilt. "Tell the people I have gone to the new capital, Sylvan Mintoth. I will return with a magistra, a healer and more brite-weed. I will beg for charity on my knees if I must."

After a long week of arduous, perilous travel, Hel reached his destination. In a surge of force, he stiff-armed the immense double doors to Queen Fleur Constante's audience hall.

Boom! The thick, metal-strapped doors flew open and

rebounded against the walls of chiseled stone. The resonating crash silenced the hum of voices and pulled all eyes to him.

The only noise came from the papers fluttering down from overbalanced stacks on a trestle table flanking a throne-like upholstered chair elevated on a dais at the end of the hall. A group of half a dozen or so men and women clustered around a diminutive woman seated in the chair. Their conversation ceased, and their heads raised as if they were a herd of chital at a waterhole alerting to a predator.

His keen senses absorbed the vast chamber of polished stone floors and rugged walls before he took a second step into the audience chamber. In a subtle display of riches, massive beams of entire spice-wood trees supported and braced a roof rising at least thirty feet. Clerestory windows ranging the length of each long wall flooded the audience hall with natural light. As befitted the first noble house of Verdantia, the crimson DeHelios banner, *his* banner, with its rampant white stallion encircled by the rays of a sun, hung beside the purple and gold crowns of the currently ruling House Constante. Below them hung the banners of the thirty lesser noble Houses of Verdantia.

Unnatural silence descended as he strode aggressively down the center of the great hall. The mass of previous supplicants melted away in unconscious recognition of a superior force to allow him unfettered passage. He stopped a few feet from the steps to the dais. "I am Prince DeHelios of House DeHelios whose standard hangs by the privilege of rank beside your own. House Constante will provide me a skilled healer, a magistra of level five or higher, and ten pecks of brite-weed. Time is of the essence. My people are dying." In the eerie silence, his booming baritone carried his demands to the furthest parts of the audience hall.

Immediately, three men—and a woman dressed in battle leathers—stepped in front of the upholstered chair and screened the queen's person from him, a living barricade. Their hands rested on the pommels of their swords. Assorted palace guards hastened to encircle the queen in a ring of bristling weaponry.

Hel snorted. "I have not forgotten *all* civilized behavior. I come unarmed."

A man dressed with austere elegance in close-fitting black leather stepped forward. "I am High Lord Ari DeTano, Primo Signore of the Second Tetriarch, and Consort to Queen Constante. You may address your concerns to me." His bearing and commanding voice conveyed the expectation of obedience.

Hel casually examined the High Lord of Verdantia. So *this* man had led the forces that defeated the Haarb. "I heard the Constante queen had taken two lovers. My words are for our monarch, not the men who warm her bed."

DeTano stiffened, and his calm gaze became arctic.

A blond man with far too much physical beauty for Hel's taste moved to stand beside the High Lord. "I am Visconte Doral DeLorion and Segundo Signore of the Second Tetriarch—the *other* lover. Who in the seven hells, do you think you are?"

Menace laced the blond's quiet voice. Unless Hel was mistaken, the man had palmed a throwing knife into his right hand, poised for a lethal strike. Interesting. Hel suspected either man would prove formidable in combat, but something about the slender blond suggested the killing edge of a well-honed razor. He must be DeTano's assassin.

A third male crossed his arms over his chest and with a low rumble of laughter, relaxed his stance. "DeHelios. Ha! The last time I saw you, you sprawled unconscious in a shrub, leaving a lovely piece of horseflesh in need of an owner."

Hel studied the speaker. He knew that laconic drawl—but its owner was a criminal with no love for Verdantian nobility. What was *this* man doing here? "Ramsey DeKieran, you nefarious thief!

You owe me the price of that fine horse. You fell on me from a tree, you coward. I never had a chance."

Ramsey snorted. "*Still* an egotistical ass. You should be grateful I took only the horse. Your head is still nicely attached." He caught the eyes of the other two men. "Gentlemen, that tower of smelly fur is 'Hel'. You may know him by a different name. The Haarb called him *bás dtost*—the silent death." Ramsey rolled his eyes.

Hel raised his lip in a snarl at Ramsey's mockery. "Such illustrious company, DeKieran. Your status in the world seems to have risen—but then it could hardly have fallen lower."

Ramsey grunted. "Unlikely, eh? You may address me as *Lord* DeKieran, Fifteenth Earl of House DeKieran, and the striking redhead preparing to unman you from ten feet away is my wife, Lieutenant Colonel Steffania Rickard of the Queen's Blue Daggers. Be careful with your words, Hel. My vixen is wicked with a throwing knife and takes insults to me personally."

Hel arched an eyebrow in surprise and nodded at the glorious redhead measuring him with amused golden eyes. "Ma'am, my condolences on your marriage. I assume you had no choice."

The stunning mercenary stifled a bark of laughter.

"So the *bás dtost* was real. I was never certain," the blond assassin murmured to High Lord DeTano.

Hel swung his regard to the queen's second lover and snorted. "I'm real enough."

"I thought you dead on that pile of ice you call a mountain," said Ramsey.

Hel paused before answering. Many nights, alone with grief and tormented by dreams, he thought death might be a kindness, but he refused to take the easy way out. "A few of us still fight to survive."

A soft feminine voice caught Hel's ear. Behind the men

blocking his access to the queen, Hel noticed movement. A tall, handsome woman, a brunette with sharp, angular features, cocked her head as if listening, then bent down out of sight. Her warm brown gaze, alive with intelligence, locked with his for a tangible moment. A pulse of electricity ran down his spine, and his instincts jumped to alert. *By the Mother, who are you?* He casually lifted his head, hoping to catch a further glimpse, but she had retreated behind solid bodies. The women's whispered conversation carried just enough to hear.

"Adonia, with your height, what do you see? Describe it."

"A rather large man, Your Majesty. At least, I think there is a man underneath all the hair and pelts. A black beard and mustache obscure his face, and his hair hangs in ratted clumps down his forehead and back. The only thing I can tell with certainty is that he is a hulking lump with gray eyes and desperately in need of a barber."

Hel laughed inwardly. Yes, a *hulking lump in desperate need of a barber* probably described him well.

He heard a sigh and a creak from the upholstered chair then the lilt of a melodious voice. "Ari, Doral, Lord Ramsey, please move aside so I may speak with, ah…DeHelios."

With apparent reluctance, the High Lord and his assassin made an opening. Ramsey stayed where he was, arms crossed, but turned to allow Hel room to pass.

Hel climbed the steps of the dais toward a delicately beautiful blond woman, a mere pittance in the upholstered chair. Her weight barely dented the cushions in spite of her advanced pregnancy. The addition of a padded step stool prevented her legs from dangling. She arranged her arms across her belly as if somehow she would shield her unborn babe from danger. Pain at the thought she would consider *him* a threat to her child softened his aggressive stance. He paused several feet from her and gentled his manner.

"Your Majesty is with child."

Bright blue eyes held his, and her smile radiated joy. "Yes. It will be our fourth." She pushed up on the arms of her chair and shifted to another hip. "And she cannot come soon enough. I find the waiting a little…burdensome."

"My wife complained of the same. Four children? You are truly blessed, Ma'am. I wish you a trouble-free birth and a healthy babe." He softened his gruff tone and finished with a respectful bow. He had issues with a Constante ruler on the Verdantian throne, but the utmost respect for motherhood.

"Thank you." She studied him for a long moment. "House DeHelios—the first kings and queens of Verdantia. The First Tetriarch. Hmm. Your House and the mountain city, Nyth Uchel, are so revered by the common people that you are almost fable. All Verdantia grieved the loss of Nyth Uchel and the radiant Torre Bianca. We thought your line dead, and Nyth Uchel razed in the Haarb massacres. I give heartfelt thanks to know we are in error. What brings you down from your mountain, Sir?"

"Ma'am, it is a dire and complicated story. I suggest my tale is best discussed somewhere more comfortable for you."

The queen moved her gaze to her consorts, who stood protectively at either side of her. "Ari? Doral?"

High Lord DeTano nodded. "The children will be running riot in our apartments, but my office should be comfortable enough. I would like DeKieran and Steffania to join us—and Medica Corvus—attend the queen, please." His eyes caught the tall woman who stood behind the queen's chair, and the brunette nodded.

"All right." Queen Constante wrestled her ungainly body to a stand. "Shall we?"

Hel stepped back and held out his arm to assist her down the steps, but the beautiful blond man moved forward and swept the slight figure of the queen into his arms. The two exchanged a look of such love Hel felt he intruded on an intimacy. The young queen must have seen his discomfort. She reached out and touched his arm.

"Prince DeHelios, my Segundo dislikes seeing me 'waddle like a duck' and finds it too painful to watch my slow, ponderous steps. He says it is necessary to carry me, and I must confess—I rather like it." Her playful grin pulled an answering quirk of lips from Hel and an arched brow from Doral.

"My preference, my Queen, is that you forgo walking at all and stay in bed these last two weeks, but I am just a poor male whose wishes you blithely disregard." Doral descended the steps and carried his queen out of the audience hall followed by High Lord DeTano, Lord Ramsey and his wife, Steffania, and the woman called Adonia. Hel trailed all of them but clearly heard the queen's gentle gurgle of laughter.

"I just like the feel of your arms around me, my love."

Hel found it difficult to continue his dismissal of this sweet-natured, loving young queen as "that upstart Constante woman." Perhaps he should have come down from his isolated mountain sooner. He acknowledged with bitter honesty that he envied Ari DeTano and Doral DeLorion. They possessed what he yearned for—a warm, passionate woman to love and bear him children. He'd even settle for what he'd had before—a marriage of cold respect—if the nursery held children once more.

Light and warmth, the delectable smells of baking bread and savory roasting meats and the lift of happy voices had wafted through the palace halls. Hel contrasted the inviting interior of this palace with the silent, cold, gloomy elegance of Nyth Uchel. He promised himself, again, that he would labor until his city and his home reclaimed their former majesty and pulsed with vibrancy and life—no matter if it took him the rest of his own to accomplish it.

CHAPTER TWO

Adonia Corvus dismissed the peculiar agitation that had engulfed her body when she locked eyes with Prince DeHelios and followed Ari, Doral, and Fleur through the halls toward Ari's office. She pulled her soft wrap closer around her bony shoulders with a convulsive shiver. Until she had come to court, almost two years ago, she had known nothing but the searing heat of the Oshtesh wastelands. Even the temperate climate of Sylvan Mintoth chilled her tall, spare, twenty-eight-year-old body.

Doral murmured something to his queen, and she flashed a glance toward Adonia.

"Adonia, are you cold, again? The trees still hold their leaves. It is a warm fall day. However, did you survive last winter?" Queen Constante laughed at her healer's answering shudder and grimace. "You have been at the High Enclave for over a year. Your blood must have thickened a little."

"It seems not, Ma'am." Adonia schooled the tartness out of her voice. With two attentive lovers, Fleur would never know the coldness of isolation or lack the warmth of human contact. Adonia's eyes shifted enviously to the ice-bear pelts wrapping Prince DeHelios and sighed inwardly. *I could put those heavy furs to good use.* Drawn by some inexorable attraction, her eyes tracked upward, and the same hyper-awareness as in the audience hall sparked through her when she met his gaze. *By the Goddess! The man winked at me.* She hurried to stay even with Fleur.

"I had a high compliment about you, today," Fleur teased, craning her neck to meet Adonia's gaze.

"Oh?"

"Yes, from the Senior Medicus of the High Enclave."

"You did?"

Fleur laughed. "Yes, don't sound so dumbfounded. Elder Beckton said he'd never before had a student with such a voracious capacity for learning. He told me you'd flown through the basic and intermediate material on applying healing magicks and were well into the advanced uses." Fleur smiled as her head bobbed in time with Doral's steps.

"He's a good teacher." Adonia's voice fell to almost a whisper. "It is my heart's desire to be able to apply the magicks in my healing, but I cannot use the diaman crystals. My learning is all theoretical."

"You are an exceptional medica—even without the magicks," Fleur maintained stoutly.

Yes, but if not for my common blood, I could do so much more. Adonia dropped her gaze to the floor and shrugged. "Thank you, Ma'am. I do what I can."

She counted every day spent with the medicae of the High Enclave a blessing. Her skill with the healing arts had increased tenfold as she gorged her mind on the practical knowledge in the High Enclave's vast library.

Practical knowledge did nothing to assuage her obsessive fascination with the magickal rites—the *sexual* rituals the highborn with their prized genetics used to energize diaman crystals to power their working of the healing magicks. But, that knowledge was of dubious use to her. Elder Beckton had shaken his head in apology. *"Only the highborn need learn this. You waste your time with those books."*

Her innermost yearning could never be realized. She resigned herself to be an onlooker, never a participant. She lacked the inherited talents bred into the noble houses for over five hundred years. *Probably not a bad thing. The Great Rite is said to be arduous—dangerous to a woman's sanity. I'd likely wind up like that poor insane* magistra *whose cries filter through the hall near my rooms.* A tendril of fear snaked up her spine. *Still...I wonder...*

"Your practical skills serve well, Adonia, and I am grateful that Eric and Sophi were willing to part with you." Doral's low voice brought a flush to her face. She hadn't realized the Segundo took note of her existence. *I should know by now that nothing associated with our queen goes unnoticed by Ari or Doral.*

Her close friendship with Fleur exposed her to the indelible bond among the Second Tetriarch. At times she had to turn away, beset by want, overwhelmed by the love that flowed between the three. *I have love to give a man.* But two years ago, she'd buried those desires deep and had thrown herself into her studies. She gave her love to her patients. It was too painful to do anything else.

As the group settled itself into the comfortable leather furnishings of Ari's office, Adonia shook off her troublesome thoughts and composed herself to listen. A pungent smell stung her nostrils. She turned her head, sniffing, lifting her chin to follow the smell—and came eye to eye with the hulk who proclaimed himself DeHelios. She dropped her head and turned away at his observant grin.

"I've had no time for the luxury of a bath, Lady. I expect I'm rather ripe."

"More like something long dead and rotting," she muttered under her breath.

The hulk leaned over and whispered, "It must be the bear pelts you smell, Lady. Every part of *me* is alive."

He'd heard her! Adonia shot him a sharp glance then faced forward. Did he *flirt* with her? *Surely not. Unthinkable.* She snuck a peek out of the corner of her eye. *By Her light.* The grin had vanished, but his eyes still laughed at her above a face obscured by curly black hair. She fidgeted with the two-headed phoenix charm on the chain around her neck and concentrated her attention on Ari.

"State your business, Prince DeHelios. You said something about a magistra, a healer and brite-weed."

DeHelios stood and shrugged off his heavy outwear before he addressed the room, turning in a semi-circle as he spoke their names. "High Lord DeTano, Your Majesty, Visconte DeLorion, Lord Ramsey, Lieutenant Colonel…"

"Oh, by Her stars, Sir. Let's not stand on ceremony." Queen Constante interrupted DeHelios with a smile. "I am Fleur." Her arm gestured to her right and then to her left. "Ari and Doral. Ramsey and Steffania. My medica, Adonia. And you are?"

"Hel."

"Yes, yes, but your first name is?" Silence settled into the room. "Sir?" said the queen.

"Just, Hel."

"Your mother named you Hel?"

"Just call me 'Hel'." DeHelios folded his arms and scowled.

With a rueful shake of her head, Fleur conceded. "All right, *just* Hel. Continue."

The man gathered his thoughts for a moment then frowned. "I suppose it all began with the Haarb invasion of Nyth Uchel and the massacre of House DeHelios. Their armies took the city completely by surprise."

"I understand the Haarb attacked you early on in the war. At that point, most Verdantians were still unaware we had been invaded," said Doral.

"Yes. And our city-state is more isolated than most." Hel gazed off at some unseen horizon. "My younger brother, Tristan, and I had gone down our mountain to track and verify the rumor of war and invasion. We returned to discover that war and invasion had come to us." Hel walked to a window and looked out. Every eye followed him. "The Haarb looted the city and massacred the living. In the weeks that followed, survivors filtered back into Nyth Uchel, but at the time of our return, all we saw was death.

"For the first time in our history, Torre Bianca stood dark against the sky, her diamantorre shattered. Nyth Uchel palace and the city below lay in ruins. Partially consumed bodies lay everywhere, the wolves and other scavengers so glutted they had eaten only the choicest parts." Hel tapped on the stone sill while he spoke. "My younger brother and I buried our entire family—my older brother, his wife and their three children, my mother, my father, my wife and," Hel paused and took a deep breath, "my six-year-old-son and two-year-old-daughter."

Adonia ached at the heartbreak poorly concealed in his flat voice. With a tiny, almost inaudible moan, Fleur slipped her hand into Ari's. Her other reached up and found Doral's resting on the back of her chair.

Hel turned to face the room, his arms loosely crossed, his hip cocked on the window casement. He gazed unseeing at the floor. "In the years that followed, I haunted the Haarb patrols that trespassed onto my mountain and made them pay."

Doral spoke into the pause. "Throughout the war, I heard tales of the *bás dtost* —the 'silent death'—of Nyth Uchel, of Haarb soldiers, gutted and left hanging from trees by their intestines. We were never sure if it was a superstitious tale or fact. That was you."

Hel's eyes held Doral's and Adonia didn't think she'd ever seen a face so bleak.

"Yes. That was me. I thought that death befitting for it was what they had done to me. Their screams were poor compensation for my loss."

Another lull settled into the room until Hel gave a sigh and a shrug. "Finally, the Haarb stopped coming, and the news of their defeat reached even the isolation of Nyth Uchel. I returned to my shattered city, my people, and we tried to rebuild.

"It was during that time that I noticed..." Hel frowned and gave a puzzled shake of his head. "Dead zones in the forest surrounding Nyth Uchel—pockets of death where nothing healthy lived, no natural animal, no normal green growth. A foul blight polluted the soil. Strange mutations of creatures appeared on the outskirts of the city.

"Since that time, the areas of blight have expanded unchecked, and one now threatens the western border of Nyth Uchel. This unnatural contagion, which alters the soil and all that grows in it, is slowly killing my people. I don't know how it spreads, but the foulness attacks a person's soul, their spirit, their *anima*, feeding on their life force until the afflicted simply lose the desire to live and succumb to a pernicious rot. My people call it *fading*."

Fleur's gentle voice broke into his pause. "Is there a cure for this *fading*? Is there some way to impede the blight?"

"Brite-weed administered early and often can sometimes stop death, but it is an uncertain cure. Energized diaman crystals halt the spread of the contagion on the ground—confine it. We established a diaman perimeter around Nyth Uchel, but the contagion continually threatens. My warden tells me the blight has penetrated the western border."

Hel let out a weary sigh and closed his eyes. His head fell back. He half-sat, half-stood, propped on the window casement with his arms loosely crossed. The light from the window shone on a face gray with fatigue, the portrait of a man at the end of his resources.

The desire to help this beleaguered soul who had taken so much upon himself grew inside Adonia. This descendent of kings had stripped himself of all pride to obtain assistance for those dependent on him. She knew something about losing one's dignity. "You must care deeply for your people."

Hel straightened wearily and frowned at her. "I am House DeHelios." His statement implied an obvious answer to an ignorant question, and she felt the hot flush of embarrassment. With a slow exhale, Hel continued. "Our quarries labored night and day to replace Torre Bianca's shattered diamantorre. We heard of DeTano's defeat of the Haarb and then watched brilliance light the horizons as Verdantia's sigil towers regained life.

Now, I lack only a magistra to partner me in the Great Rite and the White Tower will once more blaze in Verdantia's night sky. I am hopeful, once re-vitalized, Torre Bianca's energy will combat the evil menacing Nyth Uchel."

Ari cleared his throat. "Would that we could help you, but the ugly truth is we have no magistrae—not of sufficient age to perform the Great Rite. Other than our queen and Sophi, Doral's sister, our oldest magistra is thirteen years of age. She lacks a decade of age and training to be of use to you." Ari nodded at Hel's appalled exclamation. "Yes. The Haarb repeated the massacre inflicted on Nyth Uchel throughout all of Verdantia. They learned of the crucial role our magistrae played in our magicks, and they targeted them. The Haarb's elimination of all our magickal practitioners was horrifically thorough. The surviving members of our noble houses number a mere handful."

"But, how did all the sigil towers…?" Hel faltered to a stop.

"We are a true Tetriarch," Fleur said. "Just as with the First Tetriarch—your ancestors, Primo Federago, Segundo Agentio, and Prima Isolde—Mother Verdantia has gifted the three of us with the ability to empower all the sigil towers on the face of Verdantia when we make love."

Comprehension dawned across Hel's face, and he scanned the room, his eyes setting first on Fleur, then Ari and finally, Doral.

"How did you think the towers were empowered?" Doral asked, his voice benign.

Adonia sat bolt upright and paid close attention. She'd heard that tone from Doral before, and it usually preceded something lethal. Ramsey and Steffania in their positions near the door had straightened also.

"I thought it done in the conventional manner; each sigil tower housed a magistra and magister who performed the Great Rite. I never considered the much-heralded Second Tetriarch a true triad. How could you be? You aren't of the DeHelios bloodline, and..." Hel's eyes swung to Fleur, and unease furrowed his brow. "There was the old debate about House Constante's legitimacy. I...thought our Constante queen hot-blooded, desirous of variety...perhaps, one lover insufficient for her..." His voice trailed off.

He extended a hand toward Fleur, but a low growl from Doral cut off what Hel might have said next.

The High Lord of Verdantia's eyes held heat, and his clipped words threw down a challenge. "The Senzienza called to us. There was no mistaking Her message. Once the three of us came together, there was no mistaking the authenticity of the Second Tetriarch."

"Stop it. Both of you. He didn't know. He meant no insult." Fleur's eyes lifted to hold Hel's with a slight frown. "You didn't, did you? Mean to insult me?"

Adonia could have hugged the young woman. Fleur's sweet nature defused a potentially lethal confrontation between three proud men.

Hel straightened and stood stiffly. "Your Majesty, I—"

He never completed his thought as Fleur's hands shooed him into silence. "Never mind. It's not important. Tell us how we can help you and Nyth Uchel."

Hel bridged his temple with his hand and rubbed. "I, ah, I need to sit down." He proceeded to collapse into the chair next to Adonia. "So…no magistra. My problem is more ominous than I thought." He dropped his face into his hands, and Adonia wanted to put a hand out to comfort him—but didn't. She didn't know if this proud man would accept her solace or embarrass her again by shrugging it off.

Hel exhaled in a forceful gust, sat up, and faced Ari. "As soon as the Haarb retreated from Verdantia, we rebuilt the shattered diamantorre. If you re-energized all of the sigil towers on Verdantia, then Torre Bianca should be lit like a star in the night sky."

Ari pursed his mouth in thought. "We have always regretted the absence of Torre Bianca's light in the eastern skies. Our planetary shield is weak in one-quarter of the western hemisphere without her. We assumed the white tower destroyed. We meant to send a party to explore why she remained dark, but…"

Hel nodded. "We are not easy to reach, particularly during winter."

"Your damned mountain is impossible during winter. A man on foot, perhaps, but not a work party," Doral murmured.

Ari grunted an agreement. "Since the coronation of our queen, the Tetriarch has performed the Great Rite at least once a month—barring those months when our queen's pregnancies excluded her. Torre Bianca should be as a star dropped from heaven. There is some other malignancy at work."

Hel sagged in the chair, his devastation apparent. He scrubbed his face with his hands for a moment and then stood, pacing to the window. "I still have need of a healer and brite-weed."

Adonia spoke before thinking. "I am a healer. I will go with him. I would like to see the storied Nyth Uchel and the celebrated

Torre Bianca. I would like to help in whatever way I can." She rose from her chair and stepped toward Fleur. "You have many skilled medicae to attend you, Ma'am. While not as advanced as some, I am a skilled healer, and I'm used to hardship. I have studied with all the medicae at the High Enclave. From the sounds of conditions, I'd give ninety percent of them a week, or less, before they retreated to Sylvan Mintoth—if they even finished the journey to Nyth Uchel."

"Are you sure, Adonia? It will be arduous and quite possibly dangerous." Fleur's delicate features knit with concern.

Adonia met Fleur's eyes. She would miss the young queen. Other than Sophi DeStroia, her former flight leader, this was her only woman friend—well, actually, her *only* friend in Sylvan Mintoth—but this opportunity was unprecedented. "My Queen, I was medica and First Arrow of Falcon Flight. I am a skilled archer and highly trained in mounted combat. We of the desert-dwelling Oshtesh fought in the last Haarb battle of Vergaza alongside several of those in this chamber. I have known the hard life of the arid wastelands and have traveled the long road from *Sh'r Un Kree* to Sylvan Mintoth. I am not afraid of the danger or the hardship. If Prince DeHelios will have me, I want to go." Adonia felt the weight of Hel's perusal and turned to face him. After a long, anxious moment watching him silently evaluate her, he lifted his chin and brought it down decisively.

"Yes. I will have you."

The peculiar, slow twist Hel gave to his words made Adonia wonder if he intended another meaning, but she shook the thought away as ridiculous. He couldn't want her *that* way. Klaran's damning words rang in her memory as clearly as if her lover had spoken them yesterday instead of almost two years ago.

"What is it you don't understand? I'm done

with you. You got me into service with Ducca DeStroia and out of Sh'r Un Kree—for that, I thank you. But, did you seriously expect me to stay with you when I had a choice? There is nothing womanly about you. From your body to your soul, you are a hard creature." Her former intended's furiously hurled words had stripped her soul bare, and the lush-figured, flagrantly-accessible female who'd replaced Adonia in his arms had loosed the killing shot. *"No man wants between the legs of a gawky, stick figure reeking of some vile concoction."*

Adonia had fled to Sylvan Mintoth under the guise of advancing her medical knowledge. The compassion in Eric and Sophi DeStroia's eyes when they released her from their service had been the ultimate humiliation.

"Lord Ramsey, I would like you to go with Adonia." Fleur glanced across the room to Ramsey DeKieran, and Adonia disguised a laugh with a cough when he abruptly straightened after a hard poke from his wife. While the rest of the party sat in the comfortable sofas and chairs around Ari's office, DeKieran and his new wife had remained to lounge, side-by-side, against the wall by the door. Adonia had caught the intense stares and occasional murmurs Ram and Steffania had exchanged throughout the past hour. From the blush that crept up Steffania's cheeks when Ramsey fingered her exquisite choker of beaten gold, Adonia doubted that either had heard much of what had transpired in the last few minutes.

"Huh? What? Um, pardon me, Ma'am. I didn't catch what you said."

From the mischief in Fleur's eyes, Adonia revised her

assumption. Perhaps she was *not* the only one to catch their interchange of heated looks and whispers.

"I wish you to accompany Adonia to *Nyth Uchel* and stay until she is ready to return. She will need an escort home, and I don't want her dependent upon Prince DeHelios or his people to provide one."

Fleur's gaze returned to Hel. "No disrespect intended, but should Adonia wish to leave at any time, I want her free to do so." The queen's gaze then found Adonia. "And Adonia, while you are most capable, you will travel through country with unknown dangers. It will ease my heart to know you have a strong blade at your side."

"So, Lord Ramsey? Will you go?"

"To *Nyth Uchel*?" Ram blinked several times. "With *him*?" The expression of incredulity on his stern features created a moment of levity.

Hel looked affronted.

Adonia had been paying very close attention, or she wouldn't have heard as Doral laughed softly and then murmured to Ari, "Would it be uncharitable to hope they will kill each other?" A grin split the High Lord's solemn face, and he threw a laughing glance at his lover.

Steffania whispered something to Lord DeKieran, and he performed a sketchy bow. "Ah, if you ask it, Ma'am." Disgust flashed across Ramsey's face and, with hands on hips, he turned to Hel. "I suppose you want your horse back."

Adonia could see the stars dotting the night sky through the windows of the sitting area in her rooms. *Diaman* crystal globes illuminated the spacious accommodations, and a bronze brazier filled with glowing crystals radiated heat enough to warm the space twice over. A small leather duffle sat in one of the chairs. It had taken little time to pack the few possessions she owned—a medica's robe and two changes of underclothing, a hairbrush, and some ties to bind her hair. Her closet contained many rich articles of clothing from the queen, but Adonia had never considered them more than loans. Her medicines took far longer, and she knelt on the floor as, for a third time, she ran through the inventory of medicinal herbs and compounds she intended to take. A sharp rap on her door jerked her upright. Who? At this advanced hour? Had someone fallen sick? She opened the door and drew back in surprise.

"High Lord! Come in, come in."

Ari entered with a bundle of plush black fur in his arms and stopped in the middle of her room. "We want you to have this." He held up the pelt, and the glorious item unfurled. Its silky hairs reflected the light in a thousand blue-black sparkling glitters.

Adonia exclaimed in wonder, "Mynx! By the Mother, I have never seen an entire garment of it." Ari held out a full-length coat of the exotic alien fur. "Sir! This fur is brought from off-world. One tiny *pelt* is impossibly expensive—to have an entire coat! It is far too valuable. I cannot take this."

Ari crossed behind her and placed the coat on her shoulders. The gossamer fur waved from just the passage of her breath across it.

"Put it on. Let me see if it will fit."

Adonia reluctantly put her arms into the sleeves and allowed Ari to snug the coat up to her neck and fasten the clips that held it closed—then he stood back and observed her. "Good. It is not too long. The shoulders are big, but that will allow for extra layers underneath."

She laughed at the four inches extending beyond her fingertips. "I suppose I could cuff them." Adonia held her hands to her face and nestled her nose and cheeks into the thick, black pile. She luxuriated in its extraordinary softness and then raised her face with a sigh. "Sir, I cannot accept this. This is a garment for heads of state—or those with enough money to buy planets. While I appreciate the queen's generosity, I cannot take it."

"It's not from the queen." The High Lord smiled, and his expression softened to one of pleasure. "I gave it as a gift to Doral. Since he is going nowhere for many months, he wants you to have it. He says you suffer from the cold more than most." Ari laughed at her expression. "The things he notices amaze me, also. If nothing else, consider it a gift of thanks for your tender care of our queen. She values your friendship. Because of her position, it is hard for her to have true friends. She counts you among the few." Adonia dropped her gaze and looked away, uncertain what to do. Ari snorted in mock irritation. "If you won't take it, *you* will have to return it to Doral. I don't dare tell him I failed in his errand." Ari leaned over and whispered, "He's a scary man. I fear to cross him."

Recognizing a blatant lie—Doral might be a *scary man*, but Ari crossed him with impunity all the time—Adonia addressed him with skeptical eyes. Of their own volition, her palms stroked the silky fur, and her fingers sank into its thick pelt. In this garment, she felt distinguished, like royalty, and it would be so *warm*. Nothing she owned approached it on any level. With a heavy sigh, wishing she weren't so weak, she surrendered to the temptation. "Thank Segundo DeLorion for me. Tell him that I'll borrow it and return it when I come back."

The High Lord's smile left his face, and he studied her in silence for a long moment. "*If* you come back. DeHelios needs a wife and, from the way he watches you, I shouldn't be surprised if he intends to keep you."

Adonia's eyes widened. "He is highborn, a prince of the first noble House of Verdantia. I'm an ordinary Oshtesh woman from the desert. He would never consider me for a wife."

The High Lord's eyes lingered on her. He wore the strangest smile on his handsome face. "Do you *really* regard yourself as commonplace?" But before Adonia could summon the courage to ask him what *that* cryptic comment meant, he bowed, wished her, "Safe journey," and left.

As she stroked the luxurious fur, Adonia considered his remark. She'd always taken comfort from the thought she was a common desert woman. She'd never questioned the rightness of her way of life with the Oshtesh until her encounter with Doral's sister, Sophi, and Sophi's now-husband, Eric DeStroia. After the cataclysmic events surrounding the battle of Vergaza, Adonia had realized prejudice and ignorance warped much of what she'd been taught growing up.

The small religious sect her parents belonged to had indoctrinated Adonia with a scornful contempt for the aristocracy, but in a matter of months following Vergaza, she'd shed their influence and opened her mind to a different way of thinking. She'd been wrong about many things. The realization had hurt, but she'd swallowed her pride, owned up to her prejudices and set about changing how she thought and behaved. Throughout her internal upheaval, she'd clung to one certainty—Klaran cared for her. She had a place with him. She was Klaran's betrothed, his future wife. She had lost her entire family and many of her sisters-in-arms to the Haarb, but she wasn't alone in the world. She would always have Klaran.

It had taken Klaran mere moments to obliterate her self-worth and years later, she *still* bled from the gaping wound. Klaran's words had done more than strip her of any sense she was desirable. His betrayal had obliterated her identity, her confidence in where she belonged in the world. When he'd rejected her, nothing remained of her previous life, and she'd no sense of her place in a new one. Maybe she would know where she belonged at the end of this journey. Nyth Uchel's healer? Yes. She could take pride in being Nyth Uchel's healer.

CHAPTER THREE

I am so stinking tired of this damnable horse. Adonia snorted. The operative word being "stinking." Nights on the ground, days of road dust and an accumulation of horse and human sweat created an unforgettable odor, and the ache in her bones was enough to bring tears to her eyes. While she would not have traded her days in the library of the High Enclave for anything, they hadn't done her riding muscles any favors. She stood in her stirrups to ease the chaffed skin of her thighs, but when her legs refused to hold her, she slapped down onto the hard saddle seat and yelped.

Steffania glanced her way at her outcry, and Adonia thought the woman laughed. Adonia had little time to visit with the redhead who rode beside her at a steady gallop. She envied the fit mercenary leader for more than one reason and thought back three days ago to their early-morning departure in the palace courtyard.

The High Lord had watched Prince DeHelios tie a packhorse to his mount's tail. "I regret we can't send more brite-weed with you. We emptied the storehouses."

"At this point, I'll take what I can get. It will have to do." DeHelios had looked up at a clatter of hooves as two horses trotted into the courtyard.

"You are late, Lord DeKieran, and why is the head of my Blue

Daggers with you?" Ari DeTano had stood, arms crossed, and eyed Ramsey with displeasure.

"She is my wife, DeTano. Where I go, she goes, and *vice versa*. I left her behind once. I'll *never* make that mistake again."

The two men had eyed each other in a contest of wills until DeTano had exhaled forcefully, placed his hands on his hips, and nodded curtly. "Take better care of her this time."

Adonia sighed, remembering. She imagined what it must feel like to be so valued—to be so loved that any separation was untenable. *Stop it, Adonia.* Such romantic imaginings were of little practical use. No one felt that way about her, and she had a duty to Nyth Uchel. Those people needed a healer. *A healer, remember that, Adonia.* Her thoughts drifted to Prince DeHelios and the strange attraction that seemed to be forming between them.

Last evening, like the evening before, Hel had helped her tend to her horse and arrange her bedroll before seeing to his own. "I've pushed you hard today, Healer. I will assist you."

At her silent nod, his gray eyes had lingered on her thoughtfully. While stripping her horse and laying out her bedding, his bare hand had brushed her arm. An electric tingle had slid over her body, prompting each hair follicle erect in an eruption of tiny goosebumps. Her nipples had hardened into tight buds.

It was not the first time his frequent, *chance* contact had caused this inexplicable reaction in her. *Goddess!* He could not be attracted to *her*? Could he? A stick of a woman with an ordinary face? Hard muscles covered her skinny length, and calluses dotted her strong fingers—fingers skilled in unfeminine, practical tasks, not seductive arts. Her mysterious arousal and attraction to Hel scrambled her composure. His studious silence compounded her confusion—and then there was the mystery of what he looked like under all that hair. She *had* to stop such thoughts. They paved the way to heartache. She deluded herself if she imagined a mutual attraction.

When all was in order, Hel had straightened and slowly smiled. "That should do for tonight, Healer. Rest well."

Hel never addressed her by name—only as "Healer." That was her identity to him—the healer—desired for her skills, not her sex. She needed to hold firm to that thought.

Those in front of her gelding slowed, and Adonia grunted slightly as her horse dropped down to a trot. Darkness had made the road a pale ribbon flanked by deep purple-black. DeHelios must know the region well because they turned down a break in the trees she hadn't seen. She prayed they were stopping for the night.

"Praise the Goddess," she muttered under her breath as the dark lane opened up onto a wood-shingled, whitewashed building tucked snugly into a grove of tall conifers. Its multi-paned windows glowed with cheerful light and illuminated a small wooden sign that read simply *Wayfarer's Inn*. For the first time since leaving Sylvan Mintoth, the evening accommodations would feature a bed and four walls. Adonia fervently hoped they also included a tub and some hot water. She pulled to a halt and sat her weary horse as she summoned the energy to dismount with some semblance of dignity.

"Is the pace too much for you, Healer? You aren't the type to complain, so I must ask."

Adonia started as Hel's hand wrapped her thigh, a look of inquiry on his face. While it was full dark, she must be more tired than she realized not to have seen him there.

"You needn't worry. I'll keep up. A year ago, this ride would have been nothing. My months in the great library have softened me, but I won't hold you back. My muscles will soon regain their fitness."

He took the reins from around her horse's sweaty neck and held out his arms to assist her in dismounting. Her dismount became a controlled fall as she leaned forward into his hold and let him pull her from her animal.

"Oh!" Hel caught her as her feet hit the ground, and her knees threatened to give out. The strong band of his arms held her securely against him, and she felt dwarfed by his sheer mass. Was this what being enveloped by an ice-bear felt like? "Thank you." She grimaced as she tested her legs. They would hold now. "I think I can manage from here." She smiled up at him as he released her.

"Our swift pace is for those in Nyth Uchel for whom the brite-weed means life. But I would not kill our healer, either. You must tell me if I push too hard." His hand strayed to her cheek and rearranged a wandering tendril of hair behind her ear.

His gray eyes locked on hers. Their message chased any thought from her head. All she could summon was a croak of affirmation and a nod, helpless before the magnetic pull of this larger-than-life man.

Hel grinned and turned, leading their horses toward the stables.

She realized with a start that she was standing alone in the yard, an arm held out as if to arrest his departure. She dropped her arm to her side. A fan of light falling onto the courtyard profiled Steffania DeKieran as she leaned out the red-trimmed door to the inn and hailed Adonia.

"Ramsey acquired three rooms. I'll bet they will furnish us with hot baths if we offer to pay. I don't know about you, but I'm tired of smelling myself." The redhead laughed as Adonia hurried to join her.

After a welcome bath, no matter the tub held scant inches, the small group dined on a thick, meaty stew and fresh, hot bread with butter and stickleberry jam—the whole dinner washed down with cold cider. Adonia thought it tasted as fine as some banquets she'd attended at the palace. Hel, Ramsey, and Steffania had excused themselves as soon as dinner had ended, but Adonia took a comfortable chair in front of the large hearth in the public room and sipped another glass of cider. A lone traveler shared the fire with her. After they'd sat in silence for some time watching the flames dance in golds and blues across the logs, he cast a brief glance in her direction.

"Do you and your companions seek the safety of Sylvan Mintoth?"

She frowned. "No. We've come from Sylvan Mintoth. We travel east to Nyth Uchel."

"East? You don't want to be going east. I left my farm not two days ride from here, and you'd think me mad if I told you the unnatural things I've seen." He shook his head, and a shudder ran through his lanky frame. Up-ending his mug in a long swallow, the farmer thunked it down on the floor and stood. "Take some advice from an old man, mistress. Turn around and go back to Sylvan Mintoth. Don't go east."

Adonia watched as he climbed the stairs and wondered at his words. Too tired to do anything as strenuous as worry, she sank back into the comfortable chair, the blissfully unmoving chair, sipped at her drink and gazed into the flames.

The hour had been late when she sought her room, and the bed felt exceptionally lush as she crawled between the sheets. She appreciated anew the luxury of being clean, well fed, and in a comfortable bed. A low moan disturbed her just as sleep started to relax her body. She sat up, and fatigue fled as she listened to the sounds coming from the room next to her—the room occupied by Ramsey and Steffania.

There! Again, a soft feminine moan and then a low masculine murmur in response filtered through the shared wall. A pause. More feminine groans, a quiet male laugh and then a pause. A choked-off plea, then Ramsey's deep voice clearly giving an order though Adonia couldn't make out the words. "Please! Ramsey, please! Let me…" *That* was definitely Steffania begging. Again, she heard Ram's low masculine laugh and more indistinguishable words uttered in his low baritone. A soft feminine wail answered. More male laughter and then a deep groan. A number of indeterminate sounds followed.

Adonia fell back onto her mattress with a whimper. *Sex.* They were newlywed, and from the sounds of it, enjoying a passionate encounter. She jerked the pillow from beneath her head and covered her face, holding it over her ears to stop the sounds. *Oh, Goddess.* It had been so long—over two years since her thighs had parted for a lover.

Arrogant eyes above a silky black beard flashed through her mind. She moved her legs restlessly, sliding them against the mattress and rubbing them together. One hand abandoned the pillow, rose to the small, hard bud of her nipple, and gently rolled it between thumb and forefinger. *Gods!* The pleasure of that soft touch exploded in her clit. A small whimper escaped her mouth, and she abandoned the pillow altogether as her other hand crept to the soft folds between her legs. The plumped flesh was already slicking with her moisture. She dipped her middle finger into her hot center and slid upward to circle her tender bud as pleasure coiled like a wound spring in her pussy. A firm pinch to her nipple and a faster circle of her clit, and her flesh spasmed into a series of contractions that shot pleasure through her in spears of sensation. Her back arched, and her legs split, thrusting her pelvis forward as though meeting the penetration of a hard cock. Her soft keen was lost into the pillow.

Gasping, she collapsed limply on the bed. She lay alone, solitary. No loving arms held her. No satiated male snored in her ear. No warm body cradled her, driving away the cold. The pillow still over her face, silent tears of heartbreak slipped down her cheeks, the hot wetness tickling as it ran into her ears. There was something so lonely and desperate about masturbation. Now she remembered why she rarely did so. It was province of the unwanted. It reminded her that she had no partner and no prospects of ever finding one. In a land of petite, softly curved women with sultry eyes and exquisite manners, no male could possibly desire the lanky, mannish body of an ordinary desert woman—particularly one who lapsed into incoherence when faced with an attractive man.

At sunrise, after a restless night's sleep, Adonia joined the group gathered for a hasty breakfast of hot kaffè and buttered bread, consumed standing up, while the stable hands prepared their horses. Hel speared a resentful glance at a relaxed-looking Ramsey and grumped between mouthfuls about sleeping poorly because of "cats yowling" throughout the night.

Ramsey swallowed and wiped his mouth on his sleeve. "I slept *very* well, thank you. I never heard a thing." He snaked an arm around Steffania, pulled her to him, and kissed her soundly.

Adonia stood apart, stuffing her mouth with bread, trying not to watch, trying not to feel hollow and diminished. *I am content with the rewards of healing people. My accomplishments define me—not some man's desire.*

She took her horse from the stable hand, tied her pack behind her saddle, checked her girth, and mounted. Ignoring the protest from bruised flesh as her body settled into the saddle, Adonia put her horse to the walk and left the others to follow.

The small track Adonia rode resembled a game trail more than a byway of commerce. To hold her seat, she wrapped her hand in his mane as her horse lunged up the steep, rock-strewn trail. In spite of the increasing difficulty in maneuvering the grade, the constant insults and rude comments volleyed between Ramsey and Hel lifted her foul mood with a growing sense of amusement. She heard the frequent cackle of Steffania's laughter and her taunting jabs at both men.

"Loyal to *you*, DeHelios? Ha! Your retainers only stay because they are frozen solid to that block of ice you inhabit. I should relieve your people of the burden of gazing on your flea-infested, hairy face," said Ram.

"Bring it on, dickless wonder. There aren't any trees for you to fall from to give you an advantage. Your wife inspires more fear in me. You aren't half the man she is."

"Oh, your death at my hand is all but assured, DeHelios. Only the knowledge it would be pointless stays my sword. The Hound of the Seven Hells would vomit you up as an indigestible hairball, and I'd be back at square one."

Adonia pulled her horse up and turned to face the two men. The absurdity of their exchanges had finally pushed her over the top.

At Hel's irritated, "What?" hilarity welled up inside Adonia until she clutched at her belly and then her horse's neck to remain seated. She finally abandoned the attempt and simply slid down and lay on her back on the rocky ground, convulsed with laughter. Ramsey a 'dickless wonder'? Hel an 'indigestible hairball'?

She registered Ramsey's, "I don't know. Something we said?"

She flopped her arm in the air to motion them on and was aware Hel and Ramsey continued past her. When she opened her eyes, she looked up at a mounted Steffania grinning down at her.

"They're well-matched, don't you think?" Steffania chuckled. "One might be fooled into thinking they didn't like each other."

Adonia could only blink and summon the strength to remount, still giggling from time to time. Her depression evaporated as if it had never been.

Hel spurred his horse past the healer as she lay on the ground, wrapped in helpless laughter, and a halting smile creased his face. For a moment, his vile mood lifted. He didn't know how she did it, but the healer both soothed and inflamed him. She was the only one capable of lifting his brooding worry about returning to Nyth Uchel without a magistra. He'd failed to acquire the one key element necessary to lift the black affliction that haunted his city. Only the healer possessed the power to make his thoughts dwell on something else ... on *someone* else. And when he touched her? By Her light...

His intense sexual reaction every time his bare skin met hers felt uncanny. He was beyond denying it. He'd tested it time after time. She felt it too. He was sure of it, and he wondered what it meant. It wasn't only her body he wanted. The totality of the woman fascinated him. Who was she? What moved her? Why did she offer to come? He'd sought her out in the evenings before they'd all collapsed into their blankets, though all he'd done was observe. What he saw pleased him. She was gracious and uncomplaining and ever ready to lend a helping hand.

With an annoyed grunt, Hel realized the healer had been the focus of his speculation since he'd first seen her in the audience hall. His ill-humor descended again with the knowledge that he had nothing to offer her but a city cased in ice. He sighed wearily. His thoughts returned to the fruitless rehash of what he might do to change that without a magistra to work the Great Rite with him.

Adonia squinted up into the mid-day sun as Hel pulled their group to a halt with a grim expression. He pointed to an area on the downward slope where a section of skeletal, rotting trees encroached on the trail ahead of them for as far as the eye could see. "It's the contagion I told you about—a growing stain of death on my lands. This mountain pass was open when I came down. We cannot risk the chance of infection by going through it."

"All right," said Ramsey. "We go around. Easy enough."

Hel shook his head. "The only other pass takes us through forests infested with soul-wraiths, leeches. They are a parasitic scourge that rode in on the Haarb and stayed when the Haarb fled. They prey on life-force and attack anything warm-blooded. They wait until daylight fades and then descend in lethal swarms of gray shadow."

"Yes. I know all about soul-wraiths." Ramsey frowned. "How did you avoid them in the past?"

"Set a perimeter of energized diaman crystal. That will keep them at bay." Hel smiled without humor. "I have the diaman crystal in my saddle pack. I lack a sexual partner to energize them. I had intended to return with a magistra, but a magister will work as well. Care to volunteer?"

"Only if I top," Ramsey snapped.

"You'd have to kill me first," returned Hel.

"With pleasure."

Steffania took a breath. Ram cut her off. "No. I don't share you, Vixen."

Fear of the unknown almost froze Adonia's tongue, but she was the obvious answer. She could do this. The opportunity would never present itself again. "I'll be your partner."

At her faltering words, three pairs of eyes swung to Adonia, and she shrugged. "I am the solution. I've always wondered about the 'mystical sexual rites' of the aristos. Now I'll know, firsthand."

In spite of her heart's attempts to pound itself out of her body, she produced a wobbly smile. A momentary pause stretched into a lengthy silence. Her smile faltered and humiliation at Hel's failure to respond swamped her. "I suppose I'm not your idea of womanly appeal but, hey, I'm less deadly than doing Lord Ramsey." She chuckled weakly. No one laughed. *Goddess, please open the earth and let me disappear.* Perhaps her common blood made her too distasteful? "That is unless you need someone highborn."

"No. Though it's preferable, I don't need someone highborn for *this* rite. I accept your offer, Healer. Thank you." Hel's head jerked in a curt nod, and Adonia was left wondering if Hel might have preferred Ramsey after all. How depressing.

Adonia followed the three riders in front of her in silence. *What have I done?* The insane ranting of Sylvan Mintoth's mad magistra haunted her. It was said the Great Rite drove the woman into a catatonic state for weeks, and when she awoke, she had lost her mind completely. *Will I go crazy? No, DeHelios won't risk his healer. Would he?* It would only be sex, and by the Goddess, she could stand a little of that. *I'll be that much closer to knowing those mysteries.* Still, she wished the evening closer at hand so she wouldn't have so long to dwell on unknown terrors. *I wonder if we'll do this in front of Steffania and Lord Ramsey? Goddess!* She'd never considered that possibility. She straightened in the saddle when Steffania reined in her horse and took up a position beside her.

"You look a little shaken. Are you going to be okay?"

Adonia smiled faintly. "Yeah. Better this than dead."

Steffania smiled in return. "Yes. And I'm sure looks are deceiving. I mean, he looks rough, but DeHelios must have some finesse. The diaman crystals absorb energy from *your* sexual arousal. If he cannot make you feel for him, then it's pointless."

"Thanks," she said dryly. "If I don't get aroused sufficiently for Prince DeHelios to complete the rite, we die. No performance anxiety here. Nope. None at all."

Steffania burst into laughter. "Oh, Adonia. I'm sorry. I'm

certain you have nothing to worry about. Verdantian noblemen are formally trained in this sort of thing. You could comb the galaxies for star years and not find men more skilled at arousing women."

Adonia looked at Steffania sideways. "Ah, what if...what if." She let out a gust of air. "Shit. What if he sees me naked and can't, uh...can't..." She vaguely gestured toward her groin. "What if his...doesn't work?"

Steffania pulled to a stop and aimed an incredulous look at her. "What *do* you see when you look in the mirror?"

"I don't look in a mirror if I can help it," Adonia muttered.

Steffania snorted. "Let me assure you that is *not* going to happen."

Adonia kept her mouth shut and her eyes straight ahead. She'd already embarrassed herself enough for one afternoon.

They worked their way steadily up the mountain trail and an uneasy foreboding built within her as distressing signs of the wraiths' predation appeared. Game animals, whose contorted bodies displayed the agony of their death, dotted the area they rode through. Even their travel-weary mounts sidestepped and jigged anxiously in reaction to the aftertaste of evil that lingered to taint the very air. When the group stopped at a small lake to water and calm the fear-lathered horses, Adonia fought hard to control her nausea at what she glimpsed by the water's edge.

"Oh! Goddess! A man," she called. "Just beneath the surface." Beside her in seconds, Hel and Ramsey dragged the poor soul to the shore. A heavy stone was tied to his neck with a rope. The men undid the water-swollen knots and turned him over.

"He hasn't been in the water long. He still has a face," Ram remarked. "Do you know him?"

"Yes, he is a shepherd who came to Nyth Uchel from time to time." Hel's features were set in a rigidly severe mask.

"What happened? Who would drown such a defenseless

person? He cannot have had anything of worth," Adonia said.

"He drowned himself," Hel murmured. "He must have known the leeches would get him when darkness fell, and rather than suffer the torture of that death, he drowned himself." Hel sighed heavily. "I don't have the tools to give him a proper burial, but we can at least cover him with rocks to keep the predators from his body."

Adonia wondered what sort of monsters they would face that evening to make death by drowning preferable.

They had been leading their horses for some time, roaming in seeming circles through an area dotted with trees, tall up-thrusting boulders, and thick grass. The late afternoon light began to turn hazy when Hel hollered back, "I've found it. We will camp here tonight."

Adonia let out a slow breath. The time had arrived. She could blame fatigue for her trembling legs—but she'd be lying. She stripped her mount of gear, hobbled him and turned him loose to graze. Apprehension-induced weakness flooded her, but she resolutely walked up to DeHelios.

She examined the third button on his coat—he would lose it soon if not sewed on tighter— and shoved her hands into her pockets. "What do I do?"

His massive hand tucked under her chin and raised her head until their eyes met. "I chose this place because hot springs reach the surface there." He nodded his head. "And there is another behind those trees. The thermal pools provide a natural spa." Adonia thought he smiled. With all the facial hair, she sometimes guessed at his expression. "Ramsey and Steffania are going to use that pool. I would like for you to bathe with me in the other."

"All right. I have a request, also."

"Yes?"

She wondered if she dared ask. "Will you shave?"

His eyebrows rose. "Shave?"

She dug her hands deeper into her pockets and looked down at her feet. "If I am going to be intimate with you, I want to see your face." She glanced up at him through the fall of her hair.

"Huh." He pulled off his cap and scratched his head, considering, then turned. "Ramsey!"

"Yo!"

"Lend me your razor…and a knife."

"By the Goddess, what are you going to do to the poor woman?" Ramsey walked up and slapped a blade and his razor into Hel's outstretched hand.

"Not her. This." Hel flipped his beard.

"Good. It won't change your uncouth behavior, but you'll look less of an animal." Ram shot Adonia a glance. "Steffania and I won't be far. If you want me to hold him down for you, just call."

Adonia dared a smile at Hel's growl in response. Ramsey just chuckled and walked away.

"Come on. It's this way."

Adonia followed Hel past a tall stand of trees and up to what looked like the vertical face of a cliff. A small split in the sheer rock face, just enough for a person to squeeze through, ran up to the sky. The claustrophobic press of stone on either side of her body made for tense moments as she followed Hel through the gash. What lay on the other side was worth it. A pebble-strewn shore along an aqua blue pool beckoned them. Some god had stretched his hand down and scooped out a portion of rock, leaving an irregular basin filled with hot water. Steam rose from the pool and wafted off on the breeze that flirted with the water's surface. A slight sulfurous smell tinted the air, and the temperature in the grotto was noticeably warmer.

Hel turned and studied her for a moment before sighing. "You look as if a touch will shatter you. We are simply going to bathe together, and you will help rid me of this beard." Adonia felt his rough hand cup her chin, and his thumb moved over her mouth in a caress. "I know this is awkward for you. Do you want me to go first?"

"Why don't we do this together?" She smiled tentatively and began to undo the buttons to her coat.

"Agreed."

Each of them undressed. For Adonia, the slow disclosure of the body underneath Hel's bulky clothes was a revelation—as if a sculptor slowly removed the drape covering a masterpiece in white marble. When Hel stepped out of the last of his clothing and stood nude before her, she stood transfixed, holding a shirttail in her hand, only partially undressed. He cocked his head, and his smile turned to a chuckle deep in his chest. She realized he'd caught her staring. "Uh, sorry."

She never looked at him again and made quick work stripping down to her skin. She ooched on tender soles across the tiny pebbles and submerged herself up to her neck in the hot water of the pool, her arms clasped about her breasts, her hair loose and floating on the water. The temperature bordered on too hot but worked miracles on her tight, cramped muscles and chafed skin.

She closed her eyes and revisited the vision of blue-veined alabaster skin, lean rippling muscle, impossibly broad shoulders, chiseled pectorals, abs, and a sculptured waist—no extra flesh anywhere. She could count the man's ribs. A fine swirl of dark hair made a tee on his chest with a narrow line down the middle of his abdomen, past his navel to his groin, and below, ah, below... Goddess preserve her. In every way, he possessed a terrible beauty. She had expected from his height and width that he would be crude and bulky, perhaps hairy. No. He stood tall and wide, but every part of his height and width held proportion and refinement. Shit. Even his gods-be-damned feet were pretty. Who had pretty feet?

A touch on her shoulder brought her swirling around with a gasp. "Easy, Healer." Hel's gray eyes found hers, and he offered her the knife, handle first. "I think we take most of the hair with this and then use the razor. Yes?"

"Umm, yeah, yeah. Okay." She smiled tentatively and took the knife. With a deep inhale, she grasped a thick hank of his beard. His hair felt luxurious and silky. She raised her eyes to his and positioned the keen blade against his Adam's apple.

"Ready?"

"Always. Don't take more than hair—hmm?" She thought he teased her, but only his eyes broke rank with the solemnity in his face; amusement lurked in his clear gray gaze.

She sawed at the hank and whacked it off in an irregular swipe. She opened her fist and watched as the long strands floated for a moment then sank slowly in the aqua water. "Too late to change your mind now."

"Mmm. I haven't changed my mind about anything." His eyes twinkled at her and pulled a wary smile from her in return.

They still spoke of hair. Right?

His broad hands gripped her hips, his thumbs resting on her hipbones, his fingers wrapping her buttock cheeks. She tried not to stiffen. Inexorably, he pulled her to him—one step, then two. "You need to be closer. Your arms will tire if you stand so far away." He raised his eyebrows as if seeking her agreement.

"Ah, right."

Adonia worked steadily for the better part of thirty minutes—first with the knife and then with the razor—and his hands remained on her hips the entire time. She became so intent on her task, she forgot she was nude, standing between his legs, mere inches separating them. Scraping the hair off his face resembled watching him disrobe. As she removed the stubble from his cheeks, the face that slowly appeared from underneath the masses of silky black beard matched the body she had seen on shore. Chiseled. Elegant. Refined. When she finished, she laid the razor next to the knife on a stone ledge and crossed her arms. With a deep sigh, she studied his face. "I knew it."

The corner of Hel's mouth quirked. "What did you know?"

"You are prettier than I am. By Her light, you're prettier than Visconte DeLorion, and that's saying something."

He released her hips, leaned away from her and chuckled. "Oh, I think that's a matter of opinion, don't you? I doubt DeKieran would agree."

Adonia shrugged. "No, he'd agree with me."

Hel snorted then traced a wet finger across her upper lip. "It doesn't matter what he thinks, does it?"

Droplets from his finger balanced on her lips, and she licked them off. His eyes followed her tongue. Hel again pulled her to him with tempered strength, watching her face. She didn't know if she had a choice, but she stepped into his embrace, sliding her arms around his torso and nesting in between his thighs.

"No, it doesn't matter," she whispered to his collarbone. Her heart, unaccountably, had lodged in her throat.

"I think you undervalue yourself, Healer." He pulled her abdomen against the hard length of his fully erect shaft. "As I am sure you are discovering, I find you most attractive."

"Oh," she whispered.

"Yes." Hel tilted her face to his and angled his mouth to fit over hers in a feather-light press of warm lips. "Very attractive." Then he kissed her again—not at all feather-light—a kiss of demand with nips and a tangle of tongues—a kiss that consumed her—a kiss that she rose onto her toes to follow as he pulled back.

"Oooh," she moaned when he allowed her breath, and she

sank back flat-footed.

"Put your legs around my waist and your arms around my shoulders."

He cupped her buttocks and lifted her. Adonia did as he ordered. It never occurred to her not to. It was in his voice, in his actions—the unstated imperative, "I am your master. Obey me." He snugged her to him, sliding his thickness between her soft folds. His engorged flesh slid along the pouty cleft between her legs where she was most tender. Adonia sucked in air and flashed a glance at Hel when the crown of his cock bypassed the entrance to her warm interior and nudged firmly against her clit.

"Good?"

"Yes," she whispered.

His broad hands and long fingers cupped the cheeks of her buttocks and skirted her anus. A simple dip of his finger would penetrate her there. It tickled.

"Move," Hel ordered. "Show me what pleases you. I will hold you."

Adonia looked up and held his gaze as she slipped her center up and down the outside of his shaft, adding a sliding friction to the pressure and then circling her hips to roll her clit around the ridged crown of his erection. At first, his hands merely followed her actions, but when he caught the rhythm of her undulations, he added his own pressure, helping her move more freely. She pulled her hand away from his shoulder and rolled her pebbled nipple between her thumb and forefinger. The water made lapping noises as the waves from her movement hit the rock ledge of the pool.

The combination of firm male flesh between her legs and the streaking pleasure flooding down from her nipple to her clit tore a low groan from her. Her eyes slid closed to concentrate on the building sensation. More, *more*, **more***!* Without thought, she paused at the top of an undulation and dropped her hand to position his cock at her entrance.

"No."

Hurtling toward sublime ecstasy, she smashed against an invisible wall. Adonia's eyes flew open as Hel pushed her away gently, shaking his head.

His eyes were kind, but his firm words denied her absolutely. "No. I say when. I wanted you warmed, relaxed—more easy with me. I think I accomplished that."

Adonia's laugh was helpless. "I am at your mercy, Sir. Tell me what to do."

Hel's lips curved in a slight smile. "Get out. Dry off. I'll take it from there."

A shiver ran through her in reaction to the message in his eyes. *Goddess.*

Adonia used her shirt to dry herself and tried not to betray her fascination with Hel. She failed miserably. Every time she threw a guarded peek his way, he caught it. He answered with a stare that normally would send her running. His was not the look of shared passion. It was predation, ownership, plunder, and there was nothing gentle in it.

He held up his fur coat and delved into its deep pockets, tossing six *diaman* crystals the size of his fist onto his shirt. He then spread his coat out and pointed to its center.

"Here, lie on your back. Spread your legs. Put your arms over your head."

The way her heart thundered in her chest made her breath unsteady. She was certain Hel could hear her shuddering inhales and exhales. While she no longer doubted he would arouse her, the exact mechanics of this rite made her uneasy. "What are—"

"Don't talk. Answer me when I ask you a question but otherwise, don't speak. Understand?"

"Yes."

"Good. Lie down as I told you."

She lay down on her back, her legs spread and arms extended over her head. Hel laid a diaman crystal in each palm of her hand and closed her fingers over them. The remaining four he placed on either side of her wrists, two for each wrist.

"You need to hold tightly to those crystals and don't move your arms. It is necessary for the crystals to remain in contact with your skin for the entire rite. Do you understand me?"

"Yes." He might as well have bound her arms over her head. *Well, you always wanted to know what went on in those barbaric sex rites. Now you're going to find out.* She didn't think it possible for her heart to beat any faster. It did.

Hel's face was a study in solemn intensity as he knelt beside her. He started with a feather-soft stroke that began at her forehead and wandered down over her eyes and lips, then to her collarbone and shoulders and then around each small breast, avoiding the hard nipple that sat atop each like a plump raisin. His lips mouthed silent words while his fingers soothed the gooseflesh on her stomach and traced circles on her protruding hipbones. He left trails of ghostly figures on the insides of her thighs, especially the tender crease where thigh met abdomen. Hel repeated these patterns all over her body until her sensitive skin shuddered under the slightest of contacts, until she was hypersensitive, almost rising into each feathering touch. Her eyes fluttered closed, and her breath came easily, her senses hypnotized by the feel of him.

"Don't move," he warned.

"I won't," she murmured, lost in the gossamer sensation of his stroke.

Pain from a hard, twisting pinch to her right nipple sent another kind of sensation lancing through her. "Oh!" Her eyes flew open.

"Don't move."

Her breath came in pants, but the pain dispersed, and she had managed not to move her arms.

Again he stroked her with gentle, titillating slides, this time moving over her pubic mound and down between her legs in the lightest of touches. Again her breathing slowed to deep, relaxed inhales. The most delicate of strokes feathered on either side of her labia, in the tender crease of her buttocks and then straight up her swollen center, slipping readily in her moisture.

"Don't move."

Her eyes flew open, and this time when he pinched her nipple, the streaking pain caught her less by surprise.

Once more he returned to light brushes over her labia and clit, over her pubic mound and the tender inner crease of her thighs. He drew delicate circles behind her knees. The strangest thing was happening. Adonia felt as if every hair on her body was a nerve alive to the slightest motion. Her inner lips swelled and became slick. Her inner core felt heavy, and her lower groin ached. The nipple that Hel had abused throbbed with life and registered the merest shift of breeze across it. She waited with tense anticipation for his fingertips to trace over her clit, and it was all she could do not to arch into his touch for an increase in pressure when the stroke finally came. She must have moved in that exact fashion, for his hand suddenly pushed her hip back to the fur.

"None of that." His gentle finger slipped between her swollen folds and into the entrance to her body. His broad thumb moved up to her clit and rested beside it then circled ever so gently. She closed her eyes and bit her lip to stop a moan. *Goddess!* It felt beyond good. His harsh, guttural whisper sounded in her ear. "This may be *your* body, but your orgasms belong to *me*. It is for *me* to decide what is done for you and when. Adonia, look at me. Tell me you understand this. Tell me you agree to these terms."

She turned her head and stared into gray eyes that branded her, possessed her, and demanded her obedience. There were no half-measures with this man. At that moment, she made a decision she suspected would change her life. Her voice came out in a whisper. "I want this. I agree to this."

"Good. From this moment forward, this flesh—" he circled her clit gently, "—and this flesh—" the finger inside her stroked the front of her inner walls— "are to be touched only by me or at my direction. Understood?"

She nodded slowly. Considering her complete dearth of sexual stirrings the past two years, that would not be a problem. "I understand."

He grunted and withdrew his hand from between her legs. She couldn't prevent a slightly restless shiver of her hips at the loss of the pleasurable sensation. Hel glanced toward her hands, and a smile ghosted across his face.

"Good girl. You didn't disturb the crystals. My sweet Nia, they glow amber, but we need them stronger to protect us all night." He moved between her vee'd legs and knelt. "Carefully, put the soles of your feet on the fur and arch up. I want to slide your lower body onto my thighs."

She did as he asked, arching up while he slid underneath her buttocks. His use of a nickname she'd left behind in childhood surprised her, but she liked it coming from his mouth. She *felt* like a woman/child with him.

Again, his hard shaft nestled in the valley between her swollen lower lips, slipping in the slickness from her arousal. Now he used both hands and starting at her shoulders, ran gossamer touches across her collarbones, her breasts, her ribs, down to her hips, and across her inner thighs. From time to time, her ears caught an esoteric word whispered under his breath. Every time he rocked forward to reach her shoulders, for an instant, his hard cock slipped across her clit in an explosion of pleasure. The glancing contact teased her most brutally. As her arousal built, her pants sped up, and it was all she could do to remain quiet under him, accepting of whatever he gave her. If he would linger a fraction longer...

"Don't move."

This time he pinched both of her nipples, and the intense pain was as if a blanket smothered the fire of her arousal—not extinguishing it, just snuffing the flames and banking the glowing coals in preparation for the rekindling of another fire.

"Arch your hips. I am going to slide away." She did as he asked, and he slipped his body from underneath her and then knelt upright. His rigid cock slapped at his belly. Clear fluid dangled from the slit in its mushroom-shaped head, now purple with engorgement. She could see his heartbeat pulse in one of the large veins standing out along its length. His balls had pulled up close to his cock's thick base, where silky black hair formed sparse coils. Even there, the Goddess had favored him with beauty. Her pussy wept tears of anticipation, and she splayed her legs wider to make room for him.

"How close are you to coming?"

"Very close," she murmured.

"Hmm." He frowned, and she watched him spit into his hand. He took that glorious cock, the cock she ached for, the cock she'd beg to have penetrate her, and he stroked. Up. Down. Up. Down. A little faster. And faster, yet. With clenched teeth and a grunt, he came, his body jerking with every pump of cum from his cock. Breathing heavily through his nose, after a moment, he staggered upright.

"You can get up now. Put your clothes on."

She lay stunned. Tears of frustration, disappointment, and shame welled, but she refused to allow them to fall. Was her common Oshtesh body not good enough for his highborn cock, his aristocratic seed?

Adonia released the now, hot, glowing crystals, letting them roll to the side, and pushed herself to her feet. Her groin ached with heavy, fierce arousal. Her gut roiled with nausea. *I will not cry. I will not.*

"I don't understand."

Hel paused in his dressing and turned to her. He cupped her face in one large hand, and his eyes lingered on her. "No. I don't suppose you do, Sweet Nia." He stroked her face gently and then released her. "The diaman crystals pull energy from sexual arousal. Male, yes…but mostly female. You provide it. I direct it. This deadly trail we travel? We must do this every night to restore the crystals. It's why I didn't want this route. Tomorrow and the day after and the day after that, we won't have the luxury of relaxed, private foreplay, nor a hot thermal pool to soothe tired muscles. We will be exhausted, cold, wet, pursued by who knows what unnatural terror. You must be slick and desirous at a heated glance, a tweak of your nipple—orgasmic at the swirl of my tongue over your clit. You are the glowing ember who becomes the blaze that defends us. Understand?"

Yeah, she understood, but understanding didn't quell the heavy ache in her groin, soothe her hyper-sensitive nipples, or the quiet the needy pulse of her swollen clit. *This* was to be her state each evening for the next few weeks? Adonia struggled to swallow her frustration-fed anger. She had agreed, after all.

"Am I never to be allowed an orgasm this entire journey?"

"I'll let you come, Nia, but I decide when. Until then, I want you to burn." Hel turned away from her and resumed dressing.

If he wanted her to burn, he'd excelled at his task. She threw on her clothing. Buttons remained undone—ties, untied. She simply wanted coverage. She felt naked now when she hadn't a moment before. She still wondered if he failed to finish in her because he found her common blood repellent, but she lacked the courage to ask. When she'd put everything on, Adonia pulled her clothing tighter around her and strode off to the split in the rock.

In all her years with the Oshtesh, Adonia couldn't remember a time of prolonged sexual frustration. But then, her energy had always been focused elsewhere. If she searched her memory, she vaguely recalled occasional complaints from Klaran about her lack of interest. She'd never been a sexual creature, but then Klaran had never pulled her as this man did. Klaran had been... safe? DeHelios was anything but. *What will I be at the end of this journey? Someone different, I suspect—and very, very needy.*

CHAPTER FOUR

While Adonia jerked her clothes on, Hel gathered the radiant diaman crystals that lay discarded on the pelt and wrapped them in a scrap of cloth he'd brought for that purpose. When she had volunteered to serve as his partner, his immediate response had been frustration and anger. He'd tried to hide it but, from Nia's obvious misery, he'd been unsuccessful. A sexual rite was *not* how he wanted to begin with her, and Adonia's frustrated hurt gnawed on the raw discontent he hid. He snorted silently. He wanted to *woo* her. He wanted privacy, a bed, and all the other trappings of comfort necessary to submerge both of them in prolonged erotic pleasure. If he'd had any option, he would have declined her offer to partner him tonight.

For the first time in a decade, a woman sparked his intellectual and physical interest. Adonia was a rarity in his world, a creature without artifice. There was no pretense or falseness in her. She had no mask. Her face displayed every emotion. He couldn't explain his physical attraction, but he'd felt its magnetic pull from the first time they'd locked eyes in the palace hall. In another world, in an earlier time, he would have won her to him with the attention a woman of her high caliber deserved.

Their first time together should have been in a warm room on a soft bed where time had no meaning—not on the rough, rocky ground in a rushed rite he'd performed mechanically, knowing their lives depended on the outcome. He would have enticed her into the erotic world his particular carnality demanded and reveled in the passionate responses he knew he could draw from her. He would never have subjected her to the frustration of denial— not at first. He never would have demanded her obedience and submission as he'd done today. He would have seduced her until she offered both willingly.

Sadly, that world was not his any longer. Brutal practicality stripped his relationships of any niceties and turned sex into another duty performed for those who looked to him for protection. He had done his best to make Adonia's first time with him easy for her. He'd gone hours out of their way to find the thermal springs. It was the most he could offer her now. His present situation infuriated him. It was as if their Great Mother decreed he could have nothing for his own. He hurled the thought away on a silent snarl. *I am going to keep this woman.*

He scanned the area to find her and was immediately disgusted with himself. He had to repair the hurt he'd inflicted. The tall brunette had almost reached the split in the rock. "Adonia, stop." At his barked order, she stopped and stood, head down, arms wrapped around her waist as if she held the pieces of herself together. The glorious, walnut brown fall of her hair hid her face. He strode toward her and held the radiant diaman crystals in front of her, cupping the cloth with two hands.

"Look at this, Nia. This is *your* doing. The four of us and our mounts will sleep protected tonight because of *you*." He closed one hand around the neck of the cloth and reached for her. "Adonia, look at me." She tilted her head up and gradually brought her velvet brown eyes to meet his. "Nia…" He shook his head at the confusion and hurt he saw there. *Damnation, I hate beginning like this.* He wanted to share with her his own desires and frustrations, but it was too soon. He would frighten her more. "A healer's first duty is to save lives. You have done that. Hmm?"

She took a shuddering breath then straightened. "Yes. I did." She looked thoughtful for a moment, and if possible, more somber. "Yes, I am a healer. I just performed my duty. Thank you for reminding me."

"Yes …well, we'd better get back to the others. We must set our perimeter before dark falls." She nodded readily enough, but somehow, he felt he'd taken another wrong step with her.

Ramsey was tethering three of their horses to a high-line strung between two trees and looked over his shoulder at them when they emerged from the split in the rock face. A smile began, then broadened into a white-toothed grin. The devil danced in Ramsey's eyes. "Hel, you'd make a stunning woman. With that face, I'll cheerfully top you."

Hel gestured obscenely but silently thanked Ram for lightening the mood when Adonia gave a soft huff of amusement and threw him an I-told-you-so glance. Steffania walked up with the other three horses and handed them off to Ramsey. As Ramsey secured each animal to the line above, he threw a question at Hel. "What else do we need before nightfall?" His eyes scanned the horizon. "I'd guess at twenty minutes of daylight left."

Hel lifted the improvised cloth sack. "I'll take three, and you take three. We'll arrange them in a circle around us. Walk off a radius of about forty paces from the center. Use our bedrolls as center."

Adonia watched as Hel and Ramsey marched off their protective circle. Steffania came to stand beside her. "He's very pretty without the beard, isn't he? From the brilliance of those crystals, I'd guess there was no failure to rise to the occasion?"

Adonia choked back a mortified laugh. "Ah, no...no failure."

"I told you. Was it what you thought it would be?"

Adonia struggled for words while Steffania watched, a smile growing across her face. "It was nothing like I thought it would be." Adonia flashed a look at Hel and Ramsey. She had a few more moments before the men joined them. Typically, she didn't discuss intimate sexual details, but she was floundering, and Steffania seemed a woman of the world. "Is it common not to, ah, consummate the rite?"

Steffania's eyebrows rose. "You didn't have intercourse?"

"Ah...no."

"Did you climax?"

"He did. I didn't."

"The radiance and color of the crystals indicate significant arousal. He could not have lacked skill."

"Ah...no. If he'd been any more skillful, I think I'd have perished from frustration."

"So, you could have come?"

Adonia raised and lowered her chin in one, slow nod.

"He took you to the edge and left you teetering there?"

Adonia nodded—once.

Steffania drew back and covered her mouth. Her eyes shown with sympathy and amusement. "You poor thing. You must be frustrated as hell. Ramsey does that to me all the time. He's a real son-of-a-bitch."

Steffania's astonishing comment surprised a bark of laughter from Adonia, which she quickly suffocated behind a raised palm.

"Yes. Yes, frustrated as hell describes it perfectly. I suppose I should get used to it. He told me not to touch myself, not to seek orgasm through self-pleasure. Apparently, my orgasms are his to provide—or withhold. Is that normal?"

Steffania leaned over and hugged her. "For men like Hel and

Ramsey, yes. Come on. They want us to join them." Steffania threw a significant glance at Adonia. "I'll explain later."

Adonia was glad to see the four bedrolls aligned together—the men on the outside, the women in the center. She had zero experience with soul-wraiths. The desert of the Oshtesh was too bright and too hot for the monstrosities Hel called 'leeches.'

The shadows from the mountains purpled, and then, like a candle snuffed, darkness closed around them. The six, diaman crystals glowed brilliant yellow-amber, and a faint glow connected the individual stones. Gentle light illuminated the entire circle and cast shadows from the horses and the trees. All of them sat cross-legged on the bedrolls and distributed the water and food they'd brought with them.

"Have you ever seen leeches, Adonia?" Hel broke a piece of bread apart and ate it, chewing slowly. His gray eyes, blanked of expression, held hers. Adonia slowly shook her head.

Steffania shuddered. "Imagine a ravenous, foul miasma. Add intelligence, blood-red eyes and a round maw of jagged teeth, and you have a soul-wraith. It envelops its prey in a gray fog, and when it departs, nothing remains but a desiccated corpse. They prefer human flesh, but they'll feed on anything warm-blooded."

"Their victims sound as if their souls are being torn from their living body, hence the name soul-wraith. I encountered them on the battlefield of Yarudda during the Haarb wars." Ramsey took a swig from his water bottle then raised it in a mock toast. "To the Haarb for gracing us with soul-wraiths and fell wolves." Ram filled his mouth, rinsed it, then spat the contents onto the ground.

The horses stirred, uneasy on their picket line.

"And the leeches have found us," Hel murmured without looking up.

Adonia glanced toward the horses and froze as horror snaked down her spine. Ghosting around the perimeter of the diaman crystals were swarms of gray shadows and multiple pinpoints of red. Occasionally an amorphous shape would charge the light barrier, only to dissolve and reform. "So many of them."

"Yes. Soul wraiths like the cold and the long nights in the upper elevations. I'm not sure how we can kill them. I had hoped that re-energizing Torre Bianca would eradicate them. They cannot live in our Mother's light, but now…" Hel shrugged. "I don't know."

Steffania stared at the perimeter, her arms wrapped around her legs, her chin resting on her knees. Her casual manner reassured Adonia—until she spoke. "Those wraiths scare the shit out of me. A mission went wrong, and two of my men and I floated on a raft in the Topaz Sea on the planet Aquarion. Great, thirty-foot, megaton sharks circled us for days, their black fins slicing the water mere feet from our raft. Cortez fell asleep, and his foot trailed into the water. They dragged him under in seconds." Steffania shook her head and looked away. "Poor bugger. I can still hear his screams—see the bits of flesh and body parts come bobbing to the surface. I feel like I'm back on that raft." She shuddered convulsively.

"Vixen." Ramsey held out an arm to her.

She stood and moved to sit between Ramsey's legs. Ram wrapped his arms around her and snugged her close. He nuzzled into the hair behind Steffania's ear and said something in a low baritone.

Adonia didn't know what Ramsey murmured to Steffania, but the woman's whole demeanor changed. She gave Ram a look of such love that Adonia's heart ached. The red-haired mercenary relaxed into her husband's arms, laid her head against his chest and closed her eyes. *Goddess, to have someone whose words would banish all fears? If only I could possess that. I would give anything to be so loved.* She sighed. *Anything.* Her gaze strayed to the ravening leeches testing the limits of the diaman border and tried to suppress her fear. It would be a difficult night.

Adonia sat up in disgust and almost accused those sleeping around her of shifting every pebble and stone to beneath *her* bedroll. After what seemed hours of non-productive tossing and turning, and determined not to disturb the other three, she stood and gathered her blankets together to move. She glanced toward the perimeter. Ravenous eyes stared back. A flurry of shadows hurled themselves at the diaman crystals' barrier only to fall back, dissipate and attack once more. She shuddered in fear at their relentless pursuit.

"Healer."

At her feet, Hel lay on his side, an arm holding his blankets open in invitation. "Don't look at them. Your fear incites them. Come here."

She paused for only a moment before crawling into the shelter he offered and settling along his length.

He lay back down and covered them both. "The diaman crystals will hold them at bay. The wraiths' evil finds the pure energy of our mother planet abhorrent. Trust me. I won't let anything happen to you. You are too valuable to me."

As a healer and partner in the rites. For some reason, just as in the grotto, the thought did not satisfy as it should have. She lay snugged to his body, listening to the regular *thump-thump* of his heart. Its dependable rhythm finally lulled her to sleep.

Adonia craned her head and turned in a circle, trying to encompass the stunning landscape of a valley lush with grass divided by a clear, broad, swiftly moving stream and framed by towering, snow-capped mountains. They had startled a herd of graceful, lyre-horned chital grazing in the early morning light and, after handing off the packhorse and extra mount, Hel and Ramsey had given chase. Dismounted, she and Steffania stood and let their animals graze, waiting for the men to return.

Adonia watched the horses pull up fat mouthfuls of long green grass, clods of dirt and roots hanging from the sides of their lips. Bit by bit, the dirt and roots fell away, while the good grass remained. A horse's ability to separate the dirt from the edible green always amazed her.

Steffania glanced over at her. "Did you get any sleep last night?"

Adonia shuddered, remembering. "After I curled up next to Hel, yes."

Steffania grinned. "The big louts are good for making a woman feel protected." Her grin broadened. "Among other things."

"What did you mean yesterday? When you said 'for men like Ramsey and Hel'?"

Steffania wrinkled her brow as if replaying their conversation. "Oh! You'd asked if it was common for—"

"Yes, that question," Adonia interjected. She didn't want to hear it voiced again. She'd felt awkward enough the first time she'd asked. "You are ferocious—a deadly fighter. You command a mercenary squad of elite killers and yet…" Adonia lifted her shoulders helplessly.

"Ramsey controls me sexually."

For long moments, the loudest sound was the *crunch, crunch* as the horses cropped grass. Adonia studied the movement of the waterweeds streaming out in a straight line as the creek ripped past. "Yeah." She straightened. "And you like it."

Adonia turned to find Steffania still watching her.

Steffania nodded. "Yes. More than like it, I need it—and that puzzles you."

"Yes."

The redhead sighed. "The Blue Daggers consider me a ball-buster. As their commander, they fear and respect me, and that is how I want it." Her voice softened. "There is also a part of me that yearns to be known in a different way—desired as a female who sexually completes a male—a feminine being who surrenders herself to serve him."

"And that is what Lord Ramsey sees? The submissive female?"

"Oh, he sees the other, too, and we butt heads." Laughter filled her eyes. "The miracle of Ram is that he respects the warrior yet still sees the soft female. His dominant sexuality liberates that woman, and the more I abandon myself to him, the more he gives of himself to me. It's a delicious contradiction. He is never more wholly mine than when I am under his total control, in complete service to him."

"In complete service…" Adonia's memory leaped to the night in the inn and the deep male murmur of command, the female moans and pleas that filtered through the shared wall. Her imagination supplied scenarios that brought a flush of heat to her lower regions. "And you don't mind when he leaves you frustrated?"

"Oh, I mind." She grinned then sobered. "My reward with Ramsey is not in the many orgasms he gives me, but the knowledge that he cherishes and protects my surrender. We fulfill each other." After a moment of quiet, Steffania shrugged and laughed. "Besides, he knows what I need. He never leaves me wanting for long."

"But…" Adonia let her voice die, her question unspoken.

Steffania shot her a quick look. "It's like being a healer in a way. Do you do it for money?"

Adonia shook her head. "No. I would be a healer even if I

were never paid."

"Exactly. There is something in you that *must* heal people and the satisfaction from the service itself is your repayment."

Adonia shrugged and nodded. "Okay." She had not looked at it that way.

"For me, it is the same, with one difference. In all the universes, there is only one person I trust enough to give my true self to, and that is my Lord Ramsey." Steffania gave a soft chuckle. "Everyone else can go hang."

Adonia listened, head down. There was only one person in all the universes for Lord Ramsey, also. She had seen it in the palace courtyard when he refused to be parted from Steffania. Adonia desired what Steffania had—not Lord Ramsey—but someone who *saw* her and valued what only she had to give. She wanted that fiercely. A long moment stretched between them as the horses grazed. "Do you think Prince DeHelios wants that from a woman, too?"

"I think DeHelios demands it. DeHelios and Ramsey are two edges of the same sword."

Adonia turned Steffania's words over in her mind. Did part of her want to serve Hel sexually? He was delicious to the eye. Why *was* she so interested in DeHelios? Compassion and desire for knowledge, yes. *Well, that and a healthy dose of self-preservation.*

She had witnessed healers use Her power to perform astonishing cures. She wanted the ability to do that with a passion that bordered on obsession. She had thought the rites required a certain genetic key bred into the noble houses. From her experience last night, that wasn't always the case. Could she partner Hel in the more advanced rites? Or would her ordinary blood make the highborn prince discount her? Obviously, Mother Verdantia worked in ways beyond her understanding.

There was something else Adonia didn't understand, and the

woman with the answer stood two feet away.

"Steffania, do you ever wonder why you are still here?"

The Blue Dagger looked toward her, her brow quirked. "I live here. Verdantia is now my home."

Adonia closed her eyes and shook her head. "Two years ago, the battle on the Plains of Vergaza, when She channeled staggering power through Sophi and Eric. You were there that day."

"Yes. We all discovered what She meant by *the power of the two*." Steffania chuckled. "Eric still glows—how he hates that."

"You saw the roiling golden cloud that erupted from Commander DeStroia and swept the battlefield bare of all who lived. Only those born of Verdantia remained standing."

"Yes." Steffania's unfocused gaze seemed to see that day over two years ago. "Hard to forget that." Steffania abruptly straightened. "Oh! I see what you are asking. I'm not Verdantian born. Why do I still live?"

"Yes."

"Beats the hell out of me." Steffania chuckled. "I'm just glad She wanted to keep me around."

"Perhaps all your years on Verdantia have changed you, and our Mother considers you one of Her own."

"That would mean She has altered my genes, somehow." Steffania's face became thoughtful, then she shrugged. "I've seen too much crazy shit on this planet to doubt for one moment She could do it."

Hel crooned and ran a calm hand down the sweat-streaked neck of the animal underneath him. "You've ruined him, DeKieran." He urged his fretting, anxious horse across the creek and halted in front of Adonia. He leaned behind and undid the leather ties holding a dead chital across the rump of his lathered horse. The dead animal fell to the ground, and Hel's mount slid sideways, eyeing the body with a loud, rolling snort.

"It's the rider. Your hands are like stumps. I've seen bricks with more feeling." Ramsey leaned back, released his kill, then swung his leg over the neck of his horse and jumped, landing on both feet. He handed a rein to Steffania. "Should have taken you, Vixen. You're a better shot, and don't whine when you miss." Ram dragged his kill toward the packhorse and didn't see the baleful glare Hel threw at him.

Hel handed his reins to Adonia and dragged the second chital carcass toward the packhorse.

"Your hunt was successful," she said.

Hel looked up. "Yes. I hated to spend the time, but we need the food. Mount up. I want us out of this valley."

Something aberrant lurked nearby. His horse's behavior was a dead giveaway. The ordinarily dependable animal had been easily spooked, snorting and blowing at insignificant nothings all morning—the flight of some autumn leaves or an off-colored rock on the trail. He had blamed it on DeKieran, but Hel knew better— and so did DeKieran.

"Keep your eyes open." Hel caught Steffania and Adonia's gaze. "Something out there left enormous clawed footprints. Make certain your crossbows are to hand and your quiver flaps open."

As they mounted, Steffania asked, "How big?"

"Think the size of a fell wolf." The quiet warning in Ramsey's voice alarmed more than a shout.

"Was it? A fell wolf?" Adonia asked Hel quietly.

Hel shook his head. "I wish it had been. I know how to kill a fell wolf. I've never seen a track like this."

This time when they set out, Hel didn't tie the packhorse to his mount's tail. His horse was simply too fractious. Instead, he tied the lead line around the pack animal's neck. The horse's desire to stay with the others would keep him from straying.

As they climbed out of the valley, Hel's eyes tracked the horizon while his horse curveted and sidled beneath him. Nothing he did calmed the animal. That, more than anything, kept him alert. Something lurked, unseen, its smell enough to unsettle his horse.

In spite of their vigilance, they were taken by surprise.

Ramsey's hoarse shout, "Hel! Behind you!" broke the quiet.

From waist-high grass, a mammoth creature leaped at the trailing packhorse and took it down. The monster's hind claws raked massive gouges in the horse's underbelly, exposing viscera and bowels. A front claw laid the defenseless animal's neck open from throat to shoulder while the creature's slavering jaws closed on the doomed horse's head and worried it back and forth. After that, all Hel could see was flailing legs and a mass of muddy gray fur. All he could hear were the screams of the dying horse and Ramsey shouting at Steffania to get back.

Before Ram could maneuver for a shot, Adonia slid from her horse and launched a cascade of arrows, nocking and firing in a continuous flow of movement. The miss-shapen monstrosity rose up on its hind legs, towering over the downed horse and turned its blood-red eyes to Adonia. It sprang. Adonia continued to place arrow after arrow in the creature.

"No! Nia!" Hel spurred his horse forward, but the hysterical animal reared and refused to close.

With a shudder and a trailing snarl, the grotesque hulk fell dead, its shoulders and face a quill of arrows sunk deep. A pale but composed Adonia stood and looked at the dead monster splayed at her feet. "What is it?"

"Fine shooting, Healer." After his clipped words, Hel dismounted. When the grotesque creature had sprung at Adonia, he'd had a gut-wrenching moment. Everything had happened in a split second that lasted a lifetime, and his fear morphed to outrage.

He suppressed it. "It started life as a dervish-devil or a wolvertine, but it mutated. I have never seen anything quite like this."

They both looked down at the monster. Hel could not cleanse from his mind the picture of a disemboweled woman lying dead near the moaning packhorse—*his* woman. He would *not* lose this bright star before he even had a chance with her. Adonia reached for the fletched end of one of her arrows and started to pull it free. While outwardly calm, her unsteady fingers betrayed her inner turmoil and distress.

His hand encircled her forearm. "No. No, don't. Leave them. They have the creature's blood on them. This mutant is a result of the dark blight that plagues us. It would be dangerous to expose yourself to the contagion."

Her face blanked, and she looked at him dumbly, but she made no further effort to retrieve her arrows.

"I have rarely seen such skill with the bow. You stood as if aiming at straw targets, not facing oncoming death," Hel said.

"Pure reflex. For years I fought the Haarb as part of a *flight* of women archers under the command of Sophi DeStroia." Adonia shrugged. "I just acted without thinking."

"I've seen that woman hit shots I thought impossible," Steffania said. "She is not simply a skilled medica. Adonia is a deadly fighter."

"Again, I learn an unexpected thing to admire about you, Healer," Hel murmured.

Ramsey knelt by the head of the packhorse. "This poor fellow is done for." With a quick slice of his blade, he put an end to its pain.

"Come, we must help Ramsey," Hel quietly commanded, holding Adonia's gaze. "We need to shift the brite-weed and the two chital to the other horse. And keep your eyes open—all of you. That twisted creature may have friends."

Before he bent to the task of redistributing the items packed on the dead horse, his eyes scanned a full circle. As the black corruption invaded further and further down his mountain, the land that he had known and hunted on since birth had turned perilous and unfamiliar. *What else waits out there for us?*

CHAPTER FIVE

Hel rode beside Ramsey with the women trailing. He couldn't shake the feeling that something shadowed them, unseen, and he pulled up to allow the women to close. "We should not get too spread out." After hours of riding in tense silence, his eyes hyper-vigilant, his ears straining for sounds, his voice sounded particularly loud.

Ramsey spoke while his eyes continued to examine their surroundings. "Yes. I've glimpsed flashes of something in the undergrowth. We are not safe. We are being stalked."

In silent testimony to Ramsey's words, Hel's mount shifted uneasily beneath him. The animal's ears flicked nervously back and forth, his head raised alertly, his nostrils testing the air. Hel ran a soothing hand down the animal's neck and murmured words of calm. "Flesh eating mutants by day and soul-sucking wraiths by night." Hel scrubbed his face. "Those wraiths—I wish our safety didn't rest entirely on the healer. It's a heavy burden for her to carry."

"My schooling with the High Enclave was—abbreviated—but I'm competent through third level. Give me the words to your rite and the stones. I'll see what Steffania and I can do."

Hel raised an eyebrow, surprised Ramsey had volunteered. He knew the Haarb war and some scandal had cut short Ramsey's formal education, but Ram's disclosure of ignorance was rare. Those the High Enclave trained were usually too self-opinionated and overconfident to admit any lack of knowledge or aptitude. Hel shrugged. "Your skills are not really the issue. The Blue Dagger is not Verdantian born."

Ramsey stared straight ahead, his gaze intent on the horizon. "Steffania thinks our Mother might have altered her genetic structure. I understand the reasons for her thinking. I'm curious to see if she's right."

Curious, indeed. Hel wasn't in a position to refuse any help, no matter how tenuous the source. He shifted in the saddle, untied the sack holding the diaman crystals, and tossed them to Ramsey. "Repeat after me…"

They rode side-by-side as Ramsey parroted back the words. "I don't recognize the language," said Ram.

"No surprise. It's ancient *Engalian*, the original language spoken over five hundred years ago by the first colonists to make planet-fall on Verdantia. By tradition, this language has always been used by House DeHelios to focus a man's arousal and prolong the rite." Hel shrugged. "At this basic level though, the words don't have to be perfect."

"Yes, I could be reciting the recipe for… say… gamekeeper's stew as long as I concentrate on moving the energies into the diaman crystals." Ramsey shot him a sardonic glance.

Hel managed not to smile. "It's a time-honored mantra, DeKieran. DeHelios men have always used it in this rite." *A recipe for gamekeeper's stew.* Hel snorted inwardly. *If he only knew.* He slid a glance sideways and caught Ram eyeing him narrowly. Hel fought to present a face stripped of all emotion. "You and Steffania hang back. Find a place with some privacy. Adonia and I will ride this track for another thirty minutes and find a place to set camp."

Hel faced forward, expressionless, while Ramsey's gaze

searched his face. Apparently, he saw nothing to further his suspicions. The man grunted then surveyed the sky and position of the sun. "I'd guess at two hours before sundown."

Hel nodded. "You have half that time. If your experiment doesn't work…"

"Yes. You'll need time with Adonia."

"Oh, and, Ram…guard yourself."

The man snorted. "I'm touched that you care, DeHelios."

Hel scowled, and Ramsey turned his horse and rode back to his wife. From the look on Steffania's face, Hel didn't foresee requiring anything from Adonia tonight other than some mutual pleasure. He swiveled in his saddle and called. "Adonia, come ride beside me."

She moved up to his side. "What's happening?"

"Ramsey and Steffania will attempt to energize the diaman crystals. For some reason, Steffania believes Mother Verdantia altered her genes. We will ride ahead a little way and establish camp."

"Oh." Adonia's voice faltered. "I put that idea in her head. It was the only explanation for the aftermath on the Plains of Vergaza."

He looked at her sharply. "Explain."

"The condensed version: on the Plains of Vergaza, six hundred of the Haarb sandwiched a small group of our people—Steffania and her Blue Daggers among them—between opposing forces. From a high cliff, miles away, I watched an enormous golden cloud rise hundreds of feet into the desert air and sweep across the battlefield. When it dissipated, only the Verdantians and the Daggers remained. Everything not of Verdantia had been absorbed into the cloud. The Blue Daggers have been on Verdantia for years, since the beginning of the Haarb wars, plenty of time for…" Adonia spread her hand out.

Hel thought about her words. He lived magick. "It's possible. I would never set limits on what She can do."

"So you won't need me for the rites, tonight?"

Was she happy or disappointed? It didn't matter. He wanted her. He wanted far more from her than a rough coupling on the hard ground. If he couldn't have her *properly*, he could still feel the satin slip of her skin under his fingers. He could still hear her breath quicken with arousal, feel the slick moisture that would welcome him into her. He could still ensure, when the time came for him to take her, she craved him. "DeKieran may not be successful." He caught and held her velvet brown gaze. He saw the moment she realized his intent. "We'll set up camp first."

Adonia worked beside Hel establishing their camp, such as it was. He had chosen a small clearing by the trail and strung the high-line for the horses between two trees. Now they stripped their tethered animals of tack and supplies.

"Lay out the bedding over there." Hel nodded at an open area a few steps away from the horses. "While you do that, I'm going to suspend these carcasses where wild animals can't get to them. The diaman crystals will repel the leeches, but they won't deter a predator on four legs."

While she lay out their bedding for the night, the pit of her stomach roiled with nerves, as if two playful kits wrestled inside. She'd forgotten about this evening. The monster's attack had driven everything but vigilance out of her head. Now, it was impossible to think of anything but Hel.

She'd thought her near-death by mutant beast and the knowledge that some deviant life still stalked them had banished her libido to the darkest depths of the eternal abyss. Wrong. That beautiful man only had to look at her, his gray eyes hot with expectation and the previous night's arousal roared back. The tight buds of her nipples rubbed her shirt as she arranged the bedding for the evening. Extraordinary how such a small portion of her anatomy could generate such titillation. She'd never paid much attention before, but then she'd never reacted to any man as she did to Hel.

Adonia looked up from where she bent over arranging the blankets and then straightened. The man occupying all her thoughts stood watching her, legs spread, arms crossed on his chest. All thought fled and her tongue clove to the roof of her mouth. Her heart joined the two kits jumping around her insides, and she found it hard to draw a steady breath. Her gaze interlocked with Hel's.

He strode toward her and stopped at the edge of the blankets. He carefully placed his heavy sword and fine throwing blade within reach, then his hands went to the fastenings on his clothing. He methodically undid them and slipped first his coat, his tunic and then his shirt off his upper torso. She stood frozen, mesmerized by the fluid interplay of honed biceps, triceps, deltoids and abdominals underneath blue-veined, porcelain skin. When his hands rested on his hips, Adonia jerked to life.

"Oh! Ah…guess you'd like me to join you. Ah, yeah, yeah." Her fingers flew to her buttons and clips, and she frantically worked to undo them with clumsy haste—until Hel's huge hand settled over hers and stopped her.

"I'm glad you enjoy the sight of me. I would do the same with you."

"There is nothing to see. I'm mannish—all muscle and bone. I—"

"Hush." He put a forefinger across her lips. "It is true you are more lean elegance than luscious curve, but there is no uncertainty in my mind you are a desirable woman." He took her hand and placed it on the loose material between his legs. She could feel him grow and harden. "No confusion at all."

He smiled at her and plunged her emotions into a familiar state—chaos. This man—what he did to her! If chaos were a physical place, she'd qualify as a guide.

His big hands went to her clothing and those buttons and fastenings that had eluded her slender, nerveless fingers seemed to open magickally for him. First, her coat dropped and then her tunic slid off. Hel stopped, leaving her in boots and loose trousers. His eyes wandered her face and shoulders. His fingers traced her collarbones from her sternum toward her shoulders. Her raisin-brown nipples puckered in the cold air, and she brought her arms across her chest, hugging herself. In truth, she felt her nudity more than the cold. He must have guessed.

Hel tucked a finger under her chin and raised her gaze to meet his. "None of that. Drop your arms."

He spanned her waist with his hands and examined her leisurely. "You are lovely, Adonia." He leaned forward and nibbled warm kisses just below her ear. "Anyone who says differently is blind."

She leaned into his kisses, no longer cold but still in chaos. She had never heard the words, "you are lovely," with her name attached. "I have no breasts, no hips. My hands are hard with calluses. My nose hooks…"

"I forbid you to say anything else disparaging about your appearance at risk of punishment." He kissed a line up to the corner of her mouth and spoke against her skin. "Do you want to be punished?" He took her mouth with firm lips and an invading tongue before she could answer.

When he pulled back, the best she could manage was a breathless, "No."

"Too bad," he murmured, nibbling kisses against her neck. "Lie down."

Too bad? A shiver of unexpected anticipation surprised her. What did Hel consider punishment? Might she enjoy it? Should she risk disobedience? *No.* Adonia lay down on the blankets and looked up at him. He looked like a god from any angle. Why was he with her? *You are not 'with' him. You are a healer and a female partner for the rites,* not *a lover*, a voice in her brain supplied. Another part of her answered, *I don't care. I will enjoy him for as long as this lasts.*

"Hand me your left foot." He stretched out his hand and held her foot as he pulled off her soft hide boot. "Right, please." Off came the right. He knelt between her legs, unfastened her trousers and stripped her of those. She lay nude as an autumn breeze played across her bare skin and raised gooseflesh everywhere.

"Superb, lithe grace…and you are cold."

"A little."

Hel moved the saddles so they formed an upright support and spread his coat over them. He sat splay-legged and motioned to her to sit between his legs. "Bring some blankets, too."

She settled into the vee formed by his body. At her shoulders, she felt the heat of his chest. The hard bulge of his arousal pressed into the small of her back. The rough pelt of the ice-bear cushioned her bare buttocks and the fine weave of his trousers rubbed at each thigh.

"Put your legs over my knees."

She obeyed. The position spread her wide, and she was thankful when Hel swathed them in blankets. "You're not removing your pants?"

He laughed softly. "Someone needs to keep an eye open."

"You're going to tease me again." She started to rise. *What happened to, 'I'll enjoy this for as long as it lasts?'* her brain mocked. His arm locked her to him.

"Stop. Put your legs back where they were and don't move.

Nothing has changed from an hour ago. DeKieran may not be successful."

"Oh." She'd forgotten. *It must have been the kisses and the compliments. They didn't feel like ritual.* Adonia let out a long breath and relaxed back into him.

"Put your arms behind your back and don't move them."

Adonia slipped her hands behind herself, almost sitting on them. With feathering, brushing touches, Hel's fingers began to trace scrolls, and what she imagined to be arcane figures, on her bare skin. Despite her desire to control her arousal, his touches on the outside and inside of her thighs, on her intimate flesh, up her abdomen and around her breasts, ricocheted lances of sensation throughout her. It was as if his fingers contained some magickal spark, some magickal pulse. Wherever he left his tracery, nerves sprang to acute awareness. She lost all sense of time. His touch became her world.

A soft moan slipped from her lips when he rolled her nipples and then pinched hard. As before, she stiffened but lassitude recaptured her mere moments later as his delicate touch made her forget the momentary pain. Slipping easily in her moisture, his index finger lazily circled the little bud at the apex of her sex and then slid to ring the opening to her inner heat with a tickling promise of penetration. As if compelled by that faint touch, she couldn't stop the circling of her hips.

His hands traced back to her breasts and teased her nipples, then pinched hard and returned to between her legs. The third time he did this, her nipples continued to throb with life, aching for further touch, hypersensitive to every movement of the blanket across them, even though his fingers had moved on. Between her legs, his touch became lighter and slower, pushing her closer and closer to climax before retreating. She arched her hips to follow his elusive touch.

"Please." She whispered the entreaty in a mindless state of arousal.

"No." The low rumble tickled her ear. A broad palm wrapped her wrist and pulled gently.

Sanity rushed in, and she realized that her hands awkwardly wrapped Hel's bare cock as her body writhed in reaction to his touch. At some point, she had undone the opening to his pants. His hot length filled and wept in her grasp. In response to his silent instructions, she released him.

He shoved himself back into his garment with a grunt and shifted to close his pants. "If we must work the crystals tonight, I will allow us to come." Hel's hoarse words brought a groan of thankfulness from her.

Behind them, the horses screamed in fear and strained at their ties. Hel jerked his head up. Suddenly she sprawled, naked, on the bare ground. Hel thrust to his feet with a hissed curse and seized his sword and knife. He stood in a low crouch in front of her, every muscle tensed in readiness. A low growl vibrated in his chest and a snarl pulled at the lips of his mouth.

The sight that met her eyes froze her blood, and her hands scrambled uselessly for her absent bow. Two wolvertines, twins to the one she had slain earlier, slunk in hissing menace toward them. Insane intelligence gleamed from eyes that swung intently from her to the only thing standing in their way of an easy kill—Hel.

The creatures separated. Silently, one charged Hel. Adonia had no time to arm herself. She stood before the second prowling monster, nude. She jerked up the heavy leather saddle and used it shield-like as the second creature crept toward her. Saliva dripped off curved fangs. Malevolent intellect in insane yellow eyes dismissed her threat. Certain she saw her imminent demise, Adonia clubbed the mutant on its tender snout with the hard seat of the saddle. The beast paused for a moment, shaking its head with an angry snarl.

She must have made some sound of fear. With a pirouette of incredible agility, Hel broke off his combat with the first creature. In a tremendous sweeping slash, he brought his heavy sword from high above his head and decapitated the mutant beast facing her. Blood arced into the air from his ferocious strike as he spun to re-engage the first beast, impaling it upon his enormous blade. Only the hilt was visible as he thrust into the creature's gut; only the tip emerged between the beast's mighty shoulders. In silence, his face distorted in rage, Hel hurled the monster through the air and off his sword.

Adonia heard its spine crack as it hit a boulder and the creature fell motionless in the dirt. Hel poised over the mass of bloody, gray-tan fur, sword uplifted for another blow, a spectacular portrait of primal male supremacy. Adonia stood stunned, overwhelmed by the strength and unrestrained violence of the man before her. Hel more than matched those deviant animals in lethal ferocity. He surpassed them. Her eyes had borne witness to the emergence of the persona the merciless Haarb had so feared. Gone was the controlled prince of Nyth Uchel. Here, before her, radiating brutal, feral wrath stood *bás dtost*, the silent death. He stole her breath away with his magnificence.

Slowly his tense body relaxed and *bás dtost* morphed into the normal countenance of Prince DeHelios. His sword dropped to his side. He walked to her and handed her some blankets. "Are you hurt? Did those monsters touch you, break the skin?"

Adonia could only shake her head numbly. It was one thing to know intellectually Hel was a lethal adversary. It was quite another to witness it. Previously, Doral or Ramsey had topped her list of most deadly. She had fought beside them. Now? It was Hel.

"Thank the Goddess. Wash any blood off you immediately and cover yourself. I hear horses."

Moments later, Lord Ramsey rode in. He led a rider-less horse. A half-lidded Steffania snugged into his lap with her arms wrapping his neck. His eyes roved the carnage. "What in the name of the Mother?"

"The beasts that have stalked us since this morning, I think. They waited until we split up and then moved in."

"Anyone hurt?"

Hel shook his head. "Well? What did you discover?"

Ram murmured something to Steffania. She smiled up at him then held out a lazy arm. Dangling from the end of Steffania's fist was the pouch Hel had tossed to Ramsey. She opened her fist and it dropped to the ground. Light blazed from its open mouth.

"It looks as though you will not need me tonight," Adonia murmured. In spite of the animal attack or perhaps heightened because of it, sexual need tortured her.

Hel stepped to her, blocking her from Ramsey's sight. "Mmm, I want to taste you, Nia. I want to sink into your warmth and forget all responsibility," he returned quietly. "We are both frustrated in our desires." He pressed a brief kiss on her ear. "I will make this up to you," then she felt a light pat between her legs. "Remember. Mine." He left her in a swath of blankets, holding her clothes while he ran water over his blood-flecked torso and hands and then pulled his shirt and tunic on over his head.

Frustration mixed with a sense her life had become entirely too unpredictable. A nod was all she could manage. She pulled on her trousers and shirt while Hel assisted Ramsey and led the horses to the high-line. Her groin ached, and the flesh between her legs wept. Every time she moved, the friction of her shirt against her erect nipples tortured her.

"I want to sink into your warmth and forget my responsibilities." Did Hel see her as something more than a healer and a female source of energy? He'd certainly defended her

ferociously. And what about his whispered, *"I will make this up to you."* Did that mean what she thought? Or was she engaged in wishful thinking again? Unsteady legs took her to help Steffania. She wanted to *do* something to take her mind off what had just happened—and what had *not* happened.

Adonia jerked the girth loose and yanked the saddle from Ramsey's horse.

"You are the picture of frustration, Healer." Steffania cast a languid smile her way as she leisurely stripped her horse of his tack. Relaxation and supreme contentment permeated Steffania's features and movements.

"And you're *not*." With the heavy saddle balanced on her hip like a child and the saddle blankets trailing in the dirt, Adonia stomped away toward their pile of bedding then stopped. Her shoulders slumped. "I'm sorry."

Steffania joined her with her own gear held in her arms. "I understand. Do you want to talk about it?"

"No!"

The woman shouldered her lightly with a chuckle, and they both began walking.

"You were right about my…" Steffania thought for a moment, "…change in status, I'd guess you'd say."

"Does it make any difference in what you experience with Lord Ramsey?" Adonia had always wondered if the rites heightened pleasure. She had taken several steps before she realized Steffania wasn't beside her. She turned and smiled at the lost-in-lust look on Steffania's face. "I'll take that as a yes." She waited until Steffania caught up again and they fell to arranging the bedding.

"It's as if something magickal awakens each nerve in my body to his touch." Steffania spoke while she knelt and removed fruit and the last of their bread from the packs. The redhead paused and went limp. "And climax is…" She looked at Adonia and crossed her eyes with a comic drop of her jaw.

Adonia snorted softly and sat cross-legged beside her. "I know what you mean about the touching. When Hel touches me, unfamiliar parts become alive to the slightest pressure." She gazed at the tethered horses without really seeing them.

Steffania crunched into a tart, green mela fruit and addressed Adonia with a crooked smile. "When he finally lets you come, I hope you aren't somewhere you must be quiet."

"Doesn't matter. I'm not a screamer."

Steffania huffed then stated flatly, "I screamed myself hoarse." She examined the mela, took a bite and spoke through a mouthful. "But then Ramsey does that to me anyway."

"Does what, Vixen?" Ram walked up and sprawled, loose-limbed, next to the women. Hel followed him and sat next to Adonia.

"I'm not going to tell you. It will only go to your already swollen head and god knows you don't need encouragement."

Ramsey picked up a piece of fruit, bit into it, and chewed thoughtfully. "Ah. You were talking of my superlative sexual skills." He continued to consume his mela.

Adonia ducked her head and smiled at the gagging noises coming from Hel.

Steffania shook her head in mock sorrow. "I've heard it said people never grow up. They merely learn how to behave in front of others." She leaned over and whispered loudly, "Ramsey has done neither."

Ram arched an eyebrow at her comment but continued to munch on his fruit.

Is it too much to ask, to sleep through a night? Is it too much?

Adonia lay awake and stared at anything other than the paired pinpoints of malevolent red that tested the circumference of light. She thought of Steffania's circling shark analogy and shuddered. The Blue Dagger slept with Ramsey curled protectively around her. Hel reclined against a nearby boulder, his bow across his lap, his sword at his feet and kept watch. How could those three remain so composed when sure death circled and probed mere feet away?

"Adonia, come." Hel's low voice broke the quiet. She propped up on an elbow. He stretched a blanket-draped arm in invitation to her. "I know you don't sleep, and I would enjoy your company."

She grabbed a blanket and rose to join him. The heat of his body felt good against her chilled skin as he cocooned them in companionable warmth. With a wiggle, she snugged herself into his side. "How do you do it—sit here so calmly while a few steps away, death waits to devour you? Aren't you afraid?"

He shrugged slightly. "Of course I am afraid, but fear and I are familiar opponents. I turn death away every day. If it is not the leeches, it is the blight or a mutant beast. If not the blight, then the villagers need food or wood to burn in their hearths. Few will risk the unknown horrors in the forest, so I go. And always, a dark Torre Bianca rises into the sky in silent accusation." His murmurs held infinite weariness.

Does this man ever put down his burdens? "When I was a little girl, my father used to tell me stories of fabled Nyth Uchel and her shining white tower, Torre Bianca." Adonia rested her head on Hel's shoulder. "Were they ever true? Or were they just stories a father made up to entertain his daughter?" Hel remained silent for so long Adonia gave up waiting for an answer. His voice roused her from a half-sleep.

"Shall I tell you about the Nyth Uchel I knew as a child?"
"Please."
"As a boy, I played in a castle filled with light and life and joy.

Abundance graced our noble family and all those in our demesne. My brothers and I ran through streets in the city below which teemed with commerce and prosperity, with people going about their business, happy and whole. Hardship didn't exist. Poverty was unheard of.

"As we matured, my older brother and his wife, and later I and my wife, assisted Mother and Father. We performed the rites established by Federago DeHelios, he who founded the original *Tetriarch* and built the first and greatest of Verdantia's sigil towers, Torre Bianca."

Hel's head fell back against the boulder, his eyes full of warm memories. For the first time, Adonia saw the lines around his eyes and mouth smooth, devoid of care or worry. Hel freed his arm from the blankets and extended his hand in a sweeping arc. "Above all of this richness, the shining white tower of Torre Bianca blazed. She cast a radiance that held even winter at bay. Our Mother graced Nyth Uchel as a place of eternal spring. The city had been so since the First Tetriarch of my forefathers. For hundreds of years, House DeHelios fulfilled its sacred duty to Torre Bianca and Nyth Uchel and all who dwelled within as befitted Verdantia's first capital and Her most favored city—until now."

Adonia watched the worry lines around his eyes and the brackets around his mouth return and deepen. "The glorious city of our history is not the Nyth Uchel we travel to. A dark, empty place locked in seeming endless winter awaits us. My people die of a fading disease and an unknown blight afflicts my land and kills my animals. Nyth Uchel and all that surrounds her is dying or corrupted." He laid his head back against the boulder and squinted his eyes closed—as if closing his eyes would halt the images running through his mind. Adonia felt his ribs lift and fall in a heavy sigh. "I fear what we combat is not of this world. A skillful sword and careful management cannot overcome it. We must fight this darkness on the metaphysical plane. I just wish I knew how."

They sat in silence. Adonia considered Hel's words and the man who spoke them. She couldn't imagine the dark thoughts he entertained, the responsibility he shouldered. She started when he spoke again.

"The stories your father told you were not fables, Nia. I have vowed, before I die, Nyth Uchel and Torre Bianca will be as they once were—the best and brightest of Verdantia. I will *not* be the DeHelios who allows them to fall."

Adonia regarded his elegant masculine profile outlined in the soft gold light of the diaman crystals and spoke her heart. "I admire your goal and, of all the men I have ever known, I consider you the most worthy paladin. I would be honored to help you in whatever way..." Her voice died as she heard herself. How pompous and ridiculous she sounded. What could a prince of Verdantia need from an ordinary woman of the Oshtesh? Other than her skills with healing medicinals, she had nothing to offer him but a well-used bow.

Hel didn't reply but his arms held her tighter and closer as some prowling menace screamed its hunger into the night.

CHAPTER SIX

Adonia shrugged lower into her rain-sodden coat and allowed her mare to follow Hel's however she would. Their party climbed steadily. From time to time, Hel stopped and surveyed the area as if determining their location. He would find some landmark and their lurching trek would resume. She was tempted to ask if he knew where he was going; they followed no trail or path she could decipher.

Adonia shifted in her saddle with a squelch. The cold rain that had started as heavy mist that morning now fell steadily, whipped into stinging needles by a blustery wind. The wet mass of her hair dripped frigid water down her neck. Raindrops pelted her face and dribbled off in rivulets. Her nose had lost feeling, and she suspected it ran in an unflattering fashion onto her upper lip. Hopefully, the rain would wash the snot away. Her ears hurt with the cold. The only positive thought amidst all her misery was hope the poor weather had sent any beasts stalking them to their dens.

Hel remained silent. Ramsey and Steffania seemed enveloped in a world that needed no one else, so Adonia suffered her misery alone. Her mynx coat, bound firmly to the back of her saddle, teased her with its promise of warmth and dryness but she resisted. The cut and design of the coat would not accommodate an equestrian. She would do nothing that might damage the irreplaceable garment. She pulled the saturated lengths of her long coat around her with a convulsive shudder and bent her face away from the pelting rain.

"Nia." Hel's voice roused her from her miserable slump. He had pulled his horse up beside her and held his furred cap in an outstretched hand. "Put this on."

"Do you have another?" She saw the answer on his face. "No. You will have nothing."

He swung off his horse. Before she knew what had happened, she was standing on the ground facing him as he jammed the fur cap on her head, pulled it down snugly and jerked the strings of the earflaps into a knot under her chin. She yelped when he swept her up and replaced her on her mount.

His gray gaze stabbed up at her. "It was not a request, Healer." He remounted, and they resumed their tedious climb.

All right. She had no memory of ever being handled so effortlessly—as if lifting her bony length over his head was insignificant. A part of her liked it. A part of her liked it very much.

Sized for a much larger head, the fur cap obscured her vision. It was also deliciously warm and protected her face and neck from the cold wind-driven rain. Her ears warmed and throbbed painfully but no more frigid water trickled down her neck. As the hours dragged on, she admitted she felt vastly warmer simply having her head, neck and face protected. When her horse stumbled to a stop, she struggled with the ties under her chin and then gave up and shoved the cap back on her head.

They were at the door of a small stone dwelling. Cheerful light illuminated the windows in a welcoming contrast to the gloomy day, and a lazy lick of gray smoke climbed out of the chimney. A tidy barn rose behind the house, its doors open as if in welcome. Shaggy ponies cropped brown grass in expansive paddocks fenced with raw timber. An orchard of naked fruit trees stretched skeletal fingers to the sky.

A withered, elderly man poked his head out of the arched entry door and snapped, "I expected you yesterday. Stop dawdling. Stable your animals and get out of the wet." Then the door slammed closed again.

Hel stiffened in his saddle before shaking his head and motioning them toward the barn.

All four rode through the open doors of the barn, dismounted, stripped their horses of their tack and turned them in to the empty stalls bedded deep with fresh straw. Ram forked hay to the horses while Hel poured each a measure of grain.

Ramsey shot Hel an appraising glance. "This is your country, so I suppose you know we are at least twenty miles further east than we should be."

"I must speak with the man who lives here. A'rken is a mystic with 'the sight'. He has powers of foretelling and connects with Her in a way I've never comprehended. A'rken foretold the Haarb invasion and other events in the past. Some malevolence attacks our soil and perhaps our Mother, Herself. If anyone has insight into how it may be fought, I hope A'rken will."

"A mystic? How fascinating," Adonia said.

Ramsey snorted. "Don't get your hopes up, Healer. 'Mystic' is simply a kind way to say the man is a lunatic—bat-shit crazy. We won't understand one word out of five."

"Even lunatic ravings are preferable to listening to you, DeKieran," Hel muttered and stalked out of the barn toward the house. Adonia ran to catch up to him.

"We are expected?"

Hel sighed. "Not to my knowledge. I decided only last night to seek him out."

"How did he know we were coming?"

"I don't know. He's a *mystic*," he snapped.

She recognized ill-humor when she heard it and shut up.

Adonia followed Hel as he ducked through the door to the snug cottage—and ran right into a bush of low-hanging, dried herbs. Sputtering, she pulled Hel's hat off her head so she could see where she was going and brought dried vegetation raining down on her. A shriveled bush of some sort followed, and she caught it in her hands. From rafter to ceiling, herbs and shriveled creatures hung by cords—packed together, filling the open attic space. Adonia shuddered at the sightless, beady eyes staring at her, the twisted clawed feet reaching for her, and glanced toward the old man. He hunched over a steaming pot of something. It smelled heavenly. Honestly, at this point, she was hungry enough to gnaw on one of those dead things hanging from the roof.

The door opened to admit Ramsey and Steffania. They stomped in and began peeling off wet garments that they threw over pegs by the door.

Steffania looked at her and snorted. "You have green bits stuck all over you."

Adonia presented the shrub as if holding a bouquet.

The aged seer rose from his stool by the steaming pot and shuffled to her. He cocked his head sideways and peered up. Through multiple folds of skin, and masses of wild gray hair, his milky, swamp-green eyes studied her face. "I'll have the worm-wood back now, miss." A withered hand extended from his voluminous hooded robe, and she handed him the end of the shrub. He took the proffered plant, but never ceased his intense scrutiny. Adonia shifted her half-frozen feet back and forth in her soggy boots and shoved her hands deep into her cold, clammy coat pockets. Was she supposed to say something?

"You've the look of her, girl. The first one." The old man tapped his pursed lips with a thick yellow fingernail and nodded to himself. "Could be. Could be." With a, "Harrumph, careless idgit," he tossed the dried herbs into a corner of the room and returned to his simmering pot.

She looked toward Hel for help. He gave her an "I'm-as-clueless-as-you" shrug.

"A'rken, you said you expected us?" Hel assisted Adonia in stripping out of her water-laden outerwear but studied the old mage as he did. Ramsey and Steffania had pulled chairs up to a rustic table and relaxed, watching their interchange.

A'rken sniffed and cast Hel a withering glare. "*She,* the *Senzienza,* told me to prepare. *'The white horse heralds the raven,'* She said."

Steffania frowned. "A white horse and raven? We ride bays and a black and we have no bird."

The mystic paused in his stirring and turned. "You, girl." He pointed a gnarled finger bent by age at Adonia.

"Sir?" She pointed at her chest. "Me?"

"Your name?"

"Adonia."

"Your surname," he snapped.

"Corvus...Adonia Corvus."

"Ha!" The old man threw a triumphant look at Steffania and stabbed his finger repeatedly at Adonia as if that explained everything. Steffania shrugged and shook her head.

The old man grumbled something under his breath. Adonia couldn't distinguish the words but the tone was unflattering. His clouded eyes, brimming with accusation, sought and held Ramsey's gaze. "She said nothing about the gryphon and his off-world mate."

"We were bored. We decided we needed an outing," Ramsey drawled.

The old man erupted in a cackle of laughter. "An outing, ha! She summons all Her sons and daughters to *war,* gryphon. But this one," his shaky finger again singled out Adonia, "this one is the key."

Adonia stood bewildered. The other three must have been equally perplexed for the only thing accompanying their exchange of glances was silence.

The mystic jerked upright and muttered, "Food. We must have food." He scuffled to the hearth and, using multiple folds of his robe, lifted the pot from its hanger and plunked it down in the middle of the table. "Bowls and spoons on the shelf." He pointed. "There. Bread in the towel next to the spoons. Serve yourself."

"What do you suppose is in this soup?" Ramsey muttered as he picked up two bowls.

Hel glanced at the distorted, desiccated remains of unidentifiable shapes suspended just inches above them. "I don't really want to know."

Ramsey followed his glance. "Point taken."

All of them filled their bowls in pregnant silence. When they sat, Hel looked across the table at the mystic and voiced what was on the tip of Adonia's tongue.

"A'rken, Adonia is the key to *what*? And what's this about being called to war?"

The old man straightened and his gaze became unfocused, farseeing. "When Belarus mates with Cirrus in the northern sky. Stones…stones…written on the stones of the tower. Look to the wisdom of your forefathers. Blackness…death devours our Mother. Only the corvus can call them. The corvus is the key."

As all at the table sat aghast, expression faded from the mystic's face. His head sank toward the table and landed with a wet *plop* in his soup. The bowl tipped and its contents crept in a languid spill across the table. His eyes stared at nothing.

"Oh, Goddess!" Adonia leapt up and began to blot the spreading liquid with the towel used to wrap the bread.

Hel slammed his spoon down. "Rouse him, Ramsey. He can't nod off *now*!"

Ramsey rolled his eyes and commented to the room at large, "I warned you. Not one word in five." Ramsey jostled the old man, and then fisted a hank of the mystic's tangled bangs, lifting his head and peering into the seer's face. "He's not going to rouse. I'd say he's in a trance." Ram released the old man's hair. The ancient mystic's head made a soft *thunk* when it hit the table.

Adonia didn't blame Hel for the string of invectives that spewed from his lips. She had a few of her own to add. Hel wasn't the only one with questions. She cleaned A'rken up as best she could then sat back down as the words began to fly.

"I figure Ramsey is the gryphon and I am his mate—not difficult as the gryphon is the symbol for House DeKieran. You are the white horse, DeHelios?" Steffania looked at Hel.

"Yes. Our house symbol is a white stallion rampant."

"So, that makes Adonia the raven?" Steffania's words trailed off in question.

"In the ancient *Engalian* form, 'corvus' means raven," Hel supplied.

"I never knew corvus meant raven. Huh." Adonia sat perplexed.

Steffania snorted. "Good. I'm not the only one in the dark at this table."

"Well, assuming I *am* the raven, I don't understand why I'm the key?" Adonia rubbed her head, trying to dispel the feeling that straw had replaced her brains. "From what A'rken said, this dark blight is killing Mother Verdantia. And what did he mean when I came in? 'You've the look of her, girl. The first one.' I don't understand that at all. The first one, who?"

Hel shook his head. "I don't know. 'When Belarus mates with Cirrus in the northern sky' is an astrological arrangement of stars that occurs in late spring. That reference I understand. We have a few months to work this out, apparently."

"What about the 'words written on the stones of the tower'?" Ramsey arched a brow and looked at Hel. "Do you understand that reference?"

Hel scrubbed his face in frustration. "No. I've never seen any inscriptions on Torre Bianca."

Their exchange of one possible theory after another continued deep into the night. All the while, the comatose body of A'rken remained slumped on the table. His eyes stared sightlessly. His lips garbled unintelligible words.

Adonia's frustration at the lack of tangible information grew apace with her fatigue until she simply folded her arms in front of her, laid her head on the table and closed her eyes. "I can't do this anymore," she mumbled. She heard Hel stand and then felt his arms lift her up and cradle her. Adonia wrapped her arms around his neck and snuggled into his chest. She never opened her eyes. She simply didn't care what he did with her.

"There is a bed in the other room. I am taking it," Hel stated. "We are safe with A'rken. He has some sort of unnatural protection. No need to keep a guard. Rest well. It will be the last time we are safe until we reach Nyth Uchel. We leave at mid-day."

"Should we do something about the old man?" Adonia registered Steffania's voice, but lost track of any answer as words became incomprehensible sounds.

The next thing she was aware of was lying on a bed, fully clothed while Hel removed her boots and socks and then pulled off her damp trousers. She heard his muttered, "This is wet, too," and felt her tunic being lifted over her head. In only her half-shift and underpants, she shivered and curled into herself. He lay next to her then covered them both with a quantity of blankets. She turned and sought his warmth and he pulled her into him. His bare skin warmed her better than a hot fire. She tucked her frozen feet against his calves. *Goddess the warmth!* Wrapped in his embrace, warm, dry, fed, she knew no more.

A gentle hand sliding under her shift roused her from sleep. *No! I don't want to wake up. I am warm and this bed is comfortable.* She cracked open her eyes. In the dim light, she made out Hel's intent gaze mere inches from her face. His hand cupped her breast and massaged while his thumb passed repeatedly over the tip of her left nipple. Her back arched involuntarily and she drew a sharp breath. His sober expression remained but his eyes flared with satisfaction at her response. Hel leaned forward and placed warm nibbles and lingering kisses behind her jaw, her ear and the side of her neck while his talented fingers tickled and tweaked her nipple into thrumming sensitivity. She lay as one dead, too relaxed and contented to move. As if borne by her bloodstream, bubbles of sensation flowed throughout her and popped with bursts of exquisite pleasure. A low moan of gratification escaped her parted lips. The stubble on his cheek scratched as he nuzzled into the space where her shoulder met her neck—even that felt good.

The windowless room they occupied gave no clue as to the hour. "Mmm, must we rise?"

At her whisper, Hel stopped nibbling. "No, it's still early." His low voice vibrated in her chest and his hot breath tickled her ear. He resumed his kisses. His hand left her breast to attack the buttons on the placket of her shift. In no more than an instant, he had them undone.

How does he do that? His skill with fastenings is unnatural. Adonia was too sleep-drugged to move. Hel pulled her shift open and slid down to cover a nipple with his hot mouth while his hand resumed its previous play. She sank her fingers into his thick hair and grabbed.

"Ah!" Adonia bit her lower lip to stifle her cry before it reached full strength.

"Hush," he murmured. "The others still sleep."

His tongue swept over her nipple. His lip-covered teeth gently rolled it and then he sucked with a low groan of enjoyment. His right hand continued its teasing of her other breast, and she arched greedily into the feeling. The fingers kneading his scalp became more frantic as sensation piled upon sensation. She blamed the days of teasing denial for the speed with which Hel aroused her.

"Mmm," she choked. "Good, good."

With a last strong pull, he came off her breast and captured her mouth. His lips seduced and inflamed with feather-light glances. As he slid half of his heavy body on top of her, Adonia could feel the hard press of his erection against her thigh. She opened her mouth to welcome him and his tongue met hers in an aggressive invasion. A warm cushion of mobile lips pressed against hers in a firm surge and retreat of light nips and sucks.

His left arm swept behind her, and he cupped the back of her head in his broad hand while his right played a tickle of touch down her bare abdomen. Her skin shivered like a horse shaking off a fly. Wide-splayed fingers raked through the glossy black curls on her pubic mound. Four fingers curved over to play between her legs, then cupped her. He trapped her clit between two long fingers and began a gentle circling press. Had he moved down another inch, he would have found her ready for more than fingers.

Goddess, this man knows his way around women. Adonia moaned into his mouth. Steffania called it when she said Verdantian noblemen trained for proficiency in sexual arousal. Adonia would gladly be his practice partner if he would let her come occasionally.

The hand cupping her head twisted and trapped her hair,

tugging her scalp just short of painful, anchoring her head to the bed, preventing any evasive movement. His kisses deepened. The hand working below her waist circled, stoking the fire burning in her inner core. The flesh between her legs grew fatter, and she could hear the liquid click as Hel worked her. The hand circling stopped for a brief moment, and two fingers ran down the center of her lower lips to the entrance of her pussy. The fingers cupped, capturing the lubrication her body produced and stroked up in a feathering circle. Meanwhile, the assault on her mouth never stopped.

She groaned into Hel's mouth and then arched into him as the fingering of her clit brought her closer and closer to that long-denied orgasm.

Hel pulled away from her mouth just long enough to center himself between her legs. Both hands reached for her panties and made short work of pulling them off. He flipped her left leg over his hip, then returned to kisses that consumed her soul. The heavy weight of his thick shaft slid between her lower lips, slipping through her folds to her clit. He settled into place, bearing most of his weight on his elbows and began a circling motion with his narrow hips. His hands captured her wrists and hair. Adonia rocked her pelvis back and forth, trying to capture the head of his elusive organ with the entrance of her channel. She didn't realize she did so until Hel's weighty hand on her hip stopped her.

His mouth left hers for a brief moment. "No."

His kisses resumed. The pelvis-to-pelvis massage continued. He stopped and threw his head back with a low curse. He reached down and took himself in hand, centered on her opening and pulsed gently, entering her in tiny increments before pulling away. Each pulse sent him further and further into her but never more than an inch or two with each thrust. The opening to her inner sheath convulsed around him as if lips on a mouth closing to retain a favored treat. She knew better than to try to deepen his penetration, no matter how she craved it. He would simply stop her. The tight pull on her hair allowed her head no movement, and she melted into the sensations assaulting her. She'd never had a lover who controlled her so completely. With another insight into parts of her she'd never known, Adonia realized that she reveled in the feeling.

Hel surged into her and she whimpered at the painful stretch. He stilled, fully hilted. She felt overfull, stuffed beyond comfort, but the painful bite promised to morph into pleasure beyond her experience.

Hel groaned as if in pain, and his tortured gaze found hers. "Do. I. Hurt. You?"

"No." Yes, he did hurt her, but she would say nothing that might make him stop. A sudden thought burst through her flaring arousal. "The crystals. We need the crystals."

His breathing labored, and he hung his head almost touching, forehead to forehead. "No crystals. This time—for you." His breath hit her face in bursts as he spoke. He half groaned and half laughed. "And me." Then his mouth descended on hers once more, preventing speech, preventing thought.

He lay on her fully and propped his upper torso on his elbows. Again, his hands captured her wrists and held them over her head, catching her hair into his grasp. The hurtful stretch in her hot core morphed to impossible sensitivity. As he slid in and out slowly, Hel contracted his abdomen and rolled his hips, stroking her clit with his thick shaft each time he drove in and pulled out. Adonia had never felt anything approaching these sensations.

"Your legs," Hel grunted. "Around my waist."

She promptly obeyed and found the stimulation to her clit increased, as did the pace Hel set for his sliding penetration. She whimpered at the mounting pressure within.

"Close?" Hel gasped.

She managed a nod. *Oh, Goddess, if he stops now...*

A low animal growl came from deep in his throat and his rhythmic breach of her lost cadence. The bed shook as he pounded into her. That was all it took. Her keens became a hoarse scream that echoed off the stone walls of the room as ecstasy detonated within her core. Her climax swept through her body in ever-expanding ripples. When she ran out of air, her cry died—but her mouth gaped in a silent scream for long moments. Her back arched into Hel. The impossible sensations stiffened her fingers into rigid spikes, straightened her legs and pointed her toes. She couldn't say how much time elapsed before the ecstasy released her. Awareness returned when she sucked in a gasp of air and crumpled into the bedding.

Hel collapsed on her, partially supporting himself. His forehead rested on hers. His hot gasps washed her face. He stayed there until his breathing became normal. Adonia felt the warm slide of fluid from her pussy and then the retreat of his cock. His hands unclasped their tight grip on her wrists and hair. He opened his eyes and smiled.

"Good?"

The relaxed glory of his features silenced her. He gazed at her with such emotion, such warmth, as if she was more to him than just a "healer." She examined him with wonder. "I...I...I..." She stopped and shook her head. She lacked words. His smile stretched to a grin and pleased amusement shone from his eyes. Her smile turned brilliant and warm laughter rolled from her spontaneously. "Beyond good," she whispered. Hel favored her with another smile and a kiss then rolled to his side and pulled her to him.

"Go back to sleep, Nia. I'll wake you when we need to rise."

She glowed inwardly with happiness, snugged herself into Hel's big body—and passed out.

Hel listened to Nia's breathing become deep and regular. He felt her body relax against his. When he had penetrated her hot depths, the stunning explosion of pleasure ambushed him, and banished his exhaustion. His brain would not stop reliving the tight grip of her pussy—so tight he wondered for an instant if he had just taken a virgin. But, that couldn't be true. At her age—he put her in her mid to late twenties—Adonia would have had lovers, wouldn't she? *One more mystery to add to the pile.*

Initially, he had roused Nia to satisfy his desires, yes, but more to give *her* pleasure. The beast attack had probably erased his words from her mind, but the night before he had said he'd make it up to her when he'd teased her and left her frustrated—again. He hadn't planned on the experience overwhelming *him*, however. *That* hadn't happened in… well… he'd been very young. He'd count the minutes until he could take her again.

Somehow, Nia lifted the bleak sense of mindless duty off his shoulders. He could lose himself in her. She lightened him. For the first time in what seemed forever, he imagined another life for himself with a different wife—not the frozen, formal submission of the marital partner he'd had before—and please, Goddess, children. Nia's warm surrender was the furthest thing from the frigid duty Athena performed for protection and procreation. But standing in the way of his longing for her warmth was the evil that plagued his beloved Great Mother.

He'd thought the corruption contained on his mountain. The spread of the dark pestilence disturbed and horrified him, and his growing sense of unease gnawed at his gut. Nia stirred and with a kitten-like purr, rooted into him. Ah, Nia. Hel banished his troublesome thoughts and allowed the pleasure of holding his woman to carry him into sleep.

CHAPTER SEVEN

"Nia, it's time to rise." Hel's low voice accompanied soft kisses around her mouth. "As much as I'd like to stay here, we need to speak with A'rken—if he is lucid. I hear Ram and Steffania stirring. So, up with you." His breath tickled her ear. His calloused hand ran up and down her flank, rousing her.

She didn't know how long she'd slept, but daylight shone under the door to their room. *Ramsey and Steffania.* She'd forgotten all about them. She wondered if they'd heard her in the night. *How could they not—and I told Steffania I didn't scream.* The heat of mortification flushed her cheeks. She sighed. *I'll live. So what if they know. It was worth it.* The heat in her cheeks increased.

Hel kicked the blankets off and crossed the room in a few steps. Adonia took the opportunity to prop on an elbow and study his superlative ass. He picked up her discarded clothes and turned. *Oh!* She looked down immediately.

A low chuckle rumbled deep in his chest. "I don't mind you looking."

When she raised her head, she got a face full of trousers, socks and tunic and she collapsed back onto the bed, softly laughing under the pile of clothing. The most bizarre feeling tickled through her. She felt all girlie, womanly and feminine—adjectives she had never thought described her. What was it about this man? She didn't know herself with him. She was beginning to wonder if she had *ever* really known herself.

In the brief time she'd lain on the bed, Hel had dressed. Adonia sat up, holding her clothes to her chest. "My, ah, underpants?"

Hel took a few steps and snagged her underwear from the corner of the room. The frayed, utilitarian garment, threadbare with age, dangled from his outstretched finger. He offered them back to her with a raised eyebrow.

"Thank you." She frowned, puzzled at his dubious expression. "What?"

Hel merely smiled and shook his head. Still puzzled but not wanting to pursue it, she stood and slipped into her worn garment, acutely aware that Hel's eyes followed her every move. Her feminine parts ached and warm fluid slipped out of her, dampening the crotch of her underwear. There was nothing she wanted to do about it in front of Hel. Adonia pulled on her clothes and wrestled into her socks and boots.

"I don't suppose you have a comb?" she asked hopefully. Her hair would make a suitable nest for a small animal. She hadn't combed it since yesterday morning.

Hel cocked his head and examined her. "Sit on the side of the bed." He sat beside her and picked up the matted clump of her hair in his hand. "Turn, please." She faced the wall to her right. She felt the tugs as he teased the tangled mass into individual hanks and then methodically set about ridding them of the knots caused by wind, rain and tumultuous sex. He had not set himself an easy task.

She turned back to him with a protest. "I can do that. You have other things more pressing. Please don't…" Her voice trailed off at his growl.

"Nia, let me take care of you. Turn around and be still. Nothing is more pressing for me at this moment than you."

She turned around, silenced. She didn't know where the tears came from. A First Arrow never cried. She caught the cuff of her tunic sleeve and pretended to wipe her nose. She didn't want Hel to see her tears. He might ask why she cried and the answer, "*Because for many years no one has felt the need to care for me,*" was too painful to voice.

After thirty minutes of tugging, the comb finally ran through easily.

"Do you want me to braid it?"

She turned to him. "You would braid my hair?"

A smile played at the corners of his mouth. "I used to braid my daughter's hair." He straightened with mock affront. "Don't look so surprised. I'm quite domestic."

Questions begging to be asked crowded into her brain like unruly puppies tumbling over themselves in haste. What am I to you? Do you have a lover at Nyth Uchel? Why do you care about me? Do you want another wife? Do you want more children? Instead, she answered his question. "Yes, I would like my hair braided." She smiled shyly. "Thank you."

"Then turn around so I can get it straight."

When she and Hel walked out of the bedroom, brilliant morning sunshine streamed in through the windows. Steffania and Ramsey sat at the trestle table, nursing steaming cups of kaffè.

"Kaffè?" Ramsey held up a pitcher. "The bread is gone but there are some eggs."

Hel grunted and set about scraping the contents of a pan into two bowls.

"How's the mystic?" Adonia asked.

Steffania craned her neck in the direction of the mound of cloth occupying a corner of the room. "Still down."

Adonia crossed the small room and bent down to examine A'rken. His long even breaths indicated he slept, though his eyes darted left and right beneath his eyelids.

Steffania drummed her fingers on the table and examined Adonia pensively. "Have either of you been outside?"

"No." Adonia frowned. "Why?"

Steffania exchanged glances with Ramsey.

Ram took a casual swallow of kaffè and looked at Hel from over the rim of his cup. "You both might want to, oh…," Ram pursed his lips in thought, "…check on the horses."

Hel's eyebrows rose and Ramsey shrugged. "Just a thought."

Hel stood and motioned to Adonia. "Let's go check on the horses."

Adonia followed Hel to the door and stood back as he opened it. He froze in the entrance, blocking her view.

"What is it?" she asked.

He stood to the side and let her see.

Her mouth fell open in wonderment. Halting steps took her further outside, and she turned slowly, her eyes feeding her brain images that strained belief. Hel, Ramsey and Steffania straggled out behind her. Everywhere Adonia's eyes gazed, it was the same. Yesterday they had arrived on a gray, sodden, autumn day of withered brown grass and skeleton trees. But if her eyes told her true, the area immediately around the cottage and halfway through the paddocks burst with a returning spring. Green buds burst with fresh leaves on the fruit trees. Small, white lilies-of-the-valley and purple hyacinth bloomed by the door. Emerald-green grass flourished in the paddocks.

She turned to Hel, speechless.

"And then there is this." Ramsey upended the leather sack containing the diaman crystals onto the ground. All four raised their hands to shield their eyes from the blazing white light.

Squinting in the radiant blaze, Ram picked up the crystals and returned them to their sack. He crossed his arms and leaned against the doorframe of the open cottage, the leather bag clutched negligently in one hand. "What did the two of you get up to last night?"

Hel looked at Adonia, allowing her to choose how to answer.

"We had sex," she offered. She looked down and fiddled with the hem of her tunic, running it through her thumb and forefinger. "Umm, rather… stellar… sex."

"Ah." A crooked smile raised one side of Ramsey's mouth. "Nice to know he's good at something."

"I thought you might have heard us." She peeked up through her hair at Ram. At his roguish smile, she dropped her eyes.

"I've heard female screams for a variety of reasons," Ramsey offered with a wicked laugh.

She couldn't *begin* to address what Lord Ramsey implied. "You think all this…" Adonia motioned vaguely about her, "…is because I had *sex* with Hel last night?" She felt the flush of blood heat her cheeks. She'd never considered herself overly modest. Healers dealt with intimate matters daily but it seemed she was still capable of embarrassment when it was *her* intimate details revealed to the world.

Ram examined her as if he was seeing her for the first time. "Who are you, Healer?"

Adonia scratched her head, bewildered by his question. "You know who I am, sir—a woman of the Oshtesh."

Ramsey slowly shook his head. "I don't think so."

Adonia turned to a solemn-faced Hel and held her arms out in confusion.

"Whoever you are, you're the furthest thing from common. This is evidence of it. I always wondered what was possible if I had a proper partner." Hel scrubbed his face with both hands.

Adonia thought he looked like a man under siege. Hel propped his hands on his hips and looked around. "We don't have time for this discussion right now. We need to get something to eat, speak with A'rken—if that's even possible—and be on our way."

Steffania stepped forward. "I'll start preparing the horses."

"Turn them into the paddocks. A'rken will care for them. We proceed the rest of the way on foot." At their surprised looks, Hel grimaced. "The going is too treacherous for horses. We can take a couple of the pack ponies, but that's it."

"Don't your people believe in roads?" Ramsey jibed.

Hel directed a look of immense irritation toward Ram. "We have excellent roads made unusable by the blight. We'll be traversing some rugged terrain on foot, so save your energy."

Adonia put aside her curiosity with great difficulty and went to help Steffania.

Hel trudged up another steep grade made slippery by loose scree and tried to stay out of the way of the pack pony lunging up behind him. Nia trailed him, then Steffania and Ramsey with a second pony. Hel picked at his discontent like a dog worries an open wound. He'd been unable to rouse A'rken, and Hel's questions battered his brain with relentless antagonism. The mystic had been quite clear. Mother Verdantia faced a crisis the like of which they had never seen. A'rken said She called all Her sons and daughters to war, but where and with whom? And however unlikely, it seemed Nia was at the heart of the answer to saving Her—which raised the next question.

Who was Nia? Not some simple Oshtesh woman as she would have them believe. The miraculous events outside A'rken's cottage indicated as much. His father had always told him that with the proper partner—Lady Athena had not been 'proper' in that sense—

any prince or princess of House DeHelios wielded immense power. Nia had to be highborn and of a *particular* genetic line. There was simply no other explanation.

As a child, Hel had spent hours reciting genealogy until he spouted it in his sleep and dreamt of heraldic devices. He'd never considered the time well spent—until now. He knew Adonia didn't feign ignorance. No normal person would carry in their head the five hundred years of "begat" and "born unto" that jam-packed his cranium. Perhaps his encyclopedic knowledge would give him a clue into Nia's lineage. He would bet good money there was nothing average about her.

The going became easier for some time and presented a good opportunity to talk. "Nia, come join me." Hel watched as her head came up and she caught his eyes and nodded. He waited until she stood beside him before moving on.

"You appear more comfortable today. I no longer worry you will shiver and shudder into separate pieces."

She looked disconcerted. "Yes. I'm deliciously warm. Thank you."

He smiled at her as she shifted in her mynx coat. He'd fought with her about wearing it. Adonia had wanted to pack the coat. She was "saving it for a special occasion."

He'd put it on her with a stern admonition. "I refuse to see you quaking with cold when you have a fine garment that will keep you warm. Since we are walking, I require that you wear it." She'd subsided meekly and allowed him to fasten her into the fabulous coat. That had been hours ago and from her free, easy movements she didn't feel the effects of the cold raw day. That alone, warmed him. Yesterday, he had suffered each of her stoically endured, body-shaking shudders as if they were his own, and it had eaten at his gut that he couldn't help her, warm her, lavish care on her.

"Tell me about your parents. Who were they?"

She gave a deep sigh. "I knew this was coming. I'll tell you as much as I know."

It took Hel an hour of probing questions to discover the first clue. "So your paternal great-great-grandfather was Alon Killion and his wife, Genevieve Brecht." He shook his head like a dog worrying a bone. "Killion... Brecht... Killion... Brecht... by the Goddess, I know those names." He racked his memory as they walked in silence. With a metallic screech, the mental doors to his encyclopedic repository of genealogy creaked open and he saw the exact passage in his mind's eye. "Yes! Alon Exeter DeKillion and Genevieve Loir DeBrecht.

They were in love and rebelled when the High Enclave decreed different partners for each. They disappeared without a trace despite an extensive search that went on for years."

Adonia shrugged. "If they were my great-great-grandparents, I can only guess they fled to the wastelands and hid...and the Oshtesh took them in."

"Interesting. I'm certain they dropped the aristocratic prefix and became simply Brecht and Killion. House DeBrecht and House DeKillion carry genetic elements considered antithetical to each other. Small wonder the High Enclave didn't sanction their pairing. And on your mother's side? Tell me what you know about that branch of your family."

As Adonia struggled to reconstruct her family tree, a picture slowly emerged that stunned Hel with its implications. He stopped and put his hand on her shoulder. "Nia, your father's line traces to *Prima* Isolde DeCorvus of the First Tetriarch and your mother's to Queen Constante's consort, Ari DeTano. How *can* you not know this? The High Enclave geneticists should have been hunting you like a chital. This is *not* the kind of genetic wealth that passes without remark."

"It doesn't?" She looked at him lost. "I... I..." She threw

up her hands in a gesture of hopeless confusion. "It never meant anything to me. I'm surprised I recalled this much. Our family dwelled in the desert with the Mother's Acolytes. They shunned anything that hinted of 'corrupt aristocratic taint'. We lived lives centered on service to our Mother Verdantia. My mother and father either hid or never knew our links to aristocracy. I certainly never knew."

"The High Enclave elders don't realize you exist," he said, still thoughtful. "Your remoteness in the wastelands is the only explanation. What quirk of fate brought you to Sylvan Mintoth?"

"I wanted to expand my knowledge of the healing arts. I wanted access to the medical library at the High Enclave. The stored knowledge there is such a gift." Her eyes flicked to his. "To watch a sick person mend because of my care gives me great satisfaction. I always feel a deep sense of connection—almost a bond—with our Mother while treating the sick. Healing has always been easy for me."

"I suspect with some training you will make an immensely powerful magistra."

Adonia bit her lower lip, her eyes filled with confusion. "Are you and I related?"

Hel jerked upright with a frown. "What? Related?"

"Your line descends from Isolde DeCorvus and Federago DeHelios…so…?"

He thought about her words for a moment. "I suppose we shared a common ancestor three hundred and seventy-five years ago, but I don't think that qualifies as being 'related'—at least not the way you meant it." A pleasing thought filtered into his brain. Perhaps her motivation for asking indicated a different concern. "Never fear. I'll be between your thighs as often as opportunity allows."

"Oh." A glorious flush crept up her neck, and she dropped her eyes and ducked her head on a mumble.

"What did you say?" He cupped her chin and raised her face. Her eyes remained downcast. "What did you say, Nia?"

Her glorious brown eyes flicked to his then away. She cleared her throat and straightened. "Good to know. I, ah, said it was good to know."

He released her chin with a soft huff. "You aren't the least impressed with that lineage, are you? I think you are every bit as well-born as I am. If I am right, you descend from two illustrious houses."

She simply shrugged. "Perhaps. I am still just me—the same person I was an hour ago." Her eyes dropped, and she scuffed the dirt with her toe. "I grew up thinking aristocrats corrupt and venal. All my life, until I came to Sylvan Mintoth, I was taught the highborn perverted Mother Verdantia's bounty for their carnal use. I have since learned that is not so, and I accept that the highborn work for the common good of us all—but you must realize it is difficult for me to consider *myself* one. I need time to wrap my mind around what you've told me."

He found her lack of pretense and shyness with him infinitely attractive. As his eyes roamed her flushed features, he found more than her shyness attractive. She dressed like a beggar. When she had donned all her clothing that morning, her drab, practical garments had hung from her frame like a war-torn pennant on the end of a battered battle-lance, and yet...she pulled at him on a purely sexual level. He imagined her garbed in elegant, feminine clothes as befitted her sex and station in life, and a picture formed in his mind of the closets at Nyth Uchel. They brimmed with rich garments, untouched since the death of his family. A smile pulled at the corners of his mouth. He added another reason to his growing urgency to get home.

"Why are we stopping?" Ram asked. He and Steffania drew

even with them.

"I think I have solved one of our mysteries."

Adonia looked as if she wished the ground would open to swallow her.

"Well?" Ram asked impatiently.

A strand of brown hair escaped her braid and whipped across Adonia's face. Hel caught it and smoothed it behind her ear. "It is my belief Adonia descends from Queen Isolde DeCorvus on her father's side and traces back to Ari DeTano's lineage on her mother's. Our raven is highborn."

Steffania smiled. "I'm not even a little surprised."

Ramsey snorted and started to walk off, jerking the pack pony behind him. "Fabulous, one more person to address as 'my lady'."

At his clipped comment, Adonia jerked upright. "No! No! Please don't. I wouldn't know to whom you were speaking. Lord Ramsey, please!"

Hel caught her fluttering hands. "Nia, it's the appropriate form of address for you. And it won't hurt that ill-begotten rogue to exhibit some manners."

"But…" Adonia began.

Steffania laughed. "He needs practice behaving like a civilized person, Adonia." She wrapped her arm around Adonia and gave her a hug. "Besides, Ram needs to remember he's a nobleman, too."

"Let's get going," Hel said. "We have a couple more hours of daylight."

Hel chose a level, sheltered campsite tucked into the side of the mountain. For the first time since they started their trek, he directed Ramsey to help him make a fire. Steffania turned a portion of the chital on a makeshift spit over the flames, and the smell of roasting meat flooded his mouth with saliva. He'd left one of the creatures for A'rken. The meat would pay for the care and board for their horses. Adonia sat withdrawn, huddled into herself. Only her head emerged from her fabulous coat. From the look on her face, her thoughts wandered distant lands. He didn't blame her. She had much to consider. For that matter, they all did.

"How much longer do we trudge up this mountain?" Ramsey sat against a rock in the fading light and methodically sharpened a wicked-looking blade. Fat from the chital hit the coals with a hiss. Ram's blade made a repetitive *swick, swick* against a whetstone. He held it up and eyed the edge before slipping it into the sheath strapped to his thigh.

"Two more days of steady travel. Three if we are slowed," Hel answered. No one asked him the obvious—slowed by what? From his seat against a boulder, Hel stared dourly into the darkness that lay outside the golden ring cast by the crystals. At least there the Mother had favored them. Those diaman stones from A'rken's cottage held enough energy to last for the rest of the journey. His sword balanced on his knees. His bow lay at his right hand. What new menace prowled the blackness stalking them? Did he lead them to Nyth Uchel…or to their death?

CHAPTER EIGHT

Eight days ago, in an exuberant cacophony of sound, every tower bell in Sylvan Mintoth rang out the joyous news of the birth of another royal princess. Now, following her formal christening, crowds waited quietly for their first glimpse of the new babe. The huge, metal embossed doors of the Great Hall swung open and the ruling Tetriarch appeared on the flagstone terrace. Ari DeTano carefully took the nude baby from Fleur and held his daughter aloft for all eyes to see. He had performed the same presentation for his son, Patricio, and, as it had that first time, intense feelings of love and the desperate need to shelter his children and their mother from all threat, ambushed him. His throat clogged with suppressed emotion and he blinked rapidly, holding back unmanly tears.

A murmur of amusement swept the crowd as Her Royal Highness, Principessa Lissabetta Constante, flailed her arms and legs and exercised a powerful pair of lungs, loudly objecting to the entire procedure. Ari lowered her, snugged her tightly in her blankets and handed the now squalling infant back to Fleur.

"Lissa has inherited your dislike of fussy ceremony, my love." Fleur laughed as she took her daughter back.

"Yes, well, I can't fault her for that," Ari said. His eyes lingered on Fleur and Lissa, absorbing the sight of his wife holding their daughter. He'd never wanted marriage or his high position. He had spent years running from the responsibilities and restrictions of the life he now happily embraced—though he'd not had a choice, he could not imagine sharing it with any other woman. *I've gotten very lucky with her.*

Doral, his lover and second in the Tetriarch, had expressed a similar sentiment when Fleur had given birth to Lilly, Doral's daughter and Val, Doral's son. Ari turned his head and examined the beautiful blond man standing at his side. *I've gotten lucky with him, also.* The object of his scrutiny raised an inquiring eyebrow. "Just counting my blessings," Ari murmured.

The elegant male who all Verdantia knew only as a matchless assassin smiled gently. "We are both blessed. I thank the Great Goddess daily." Doral's mouth tightened. "We must keep them safe," he said in an undertone.

Ari met Doral's eyes in common understanding, then turned and wrapped a protective arm around his queen. She cooed and bounced their daughter into only occasional hiccups of protest. He hated the words he forced out of his mouth. "As soon as Lissa gets settled in with her nurse, we need to return to the topic of our dreams."

Anxiety clouded Fleur's blue eyes. "You and Doral were not the only ones beset with distressing images. Eric said Sophi woke sobbing hysterically in the night some days ago. He didn't mention it until now because he didn't want to upset me so soon after birth, but apparently her dreams returned last night."

The three of them exchanged uneasy looks as they re-entered the Great Hall and the heavy doors closed behind them.

Doral threw a sheaf of papers on Ari's lap and then slouched into a chair next to him and murmured, "These reports are increasing in number. This is the fifth account in the last few days of a town with people torn apart by warped beasts, and we have lost another sigil tower in the western quarter to the encroaching black affliction."

Before Ari could respond, a sharp rap sounded on the antechamber door to their royal apartments. The captain of their royal guard appeared and announced, "The Ducca and Duchessa DeStroia, Your Majesty." Ari looked at his lover and sighed heavily. "I suppose there is no putting this off."

"Send them in, Edmond," Fleur called over her shoulder.

Ari observed his wife as she stood before an ornate sideboard laden with food and chose an assortment of delicacies until the translucent china plate she held disappeared under a mound of tasty edibles. He suppressed his amusement at her hearty appetite. For such a tiny thing, she ate like a horse, but he knew better than to comment on it. He would love her if she resembled a barrel, but his adored wife seemed to think otherwise.

A sandy-haired man with broad shoulders and a military bearing entered with a stunningly beautiful blonde. Doral stood and gave his sister, Sophi, a hug and nodded to her husband, Eric. Ari relaxed further into "his" chair and smiled a welcome at the two joining them.

"I don't think our little Lissa is fond of public engagements," Eric teased as he crossed and bowed to his queen.

"You caught that, did you?" Fleur laughed and motioned to the bar and sideboard. "Thank you for being present for her christening. Help yourself and Sophi to something to eat and drink and save me from the embarrassment of consuming it all. As for my sweet little daughter, Lissa merely did what I frequently wish to do and one of these days, when my counselors prove too tiresome, I probably will." Fleur sat delicately in an enormous chair and placed her heavily burdened plate on the low table in front of her. Ari's scoff of amusement joined that of the others.

"Just point out those who test your temper and I'll remove them, kitten," Doral offered with good humor.

"How will you remove them? By glaring until they flee in terror?" Fleur shook her head with a laugh. "Not on my account."

Ari snorted. "I've rarely seen a man get such mileage out of a lethal reputation."

"It's because they know it's true." Sophi kissed her brother on the cheek while balancing a plate in one hand and a glass in the other. "My brother is a fierce champion of those he loves, and we would not have him any other way."

Ari motioned to the others to sit. "Unfortunately, what we must discuss today won't be dealt with as easily as irritating counselors." He bridged his right hand, his thumb on his temple as his fingers rubbed his forehead. He had a premonition about the dream that had plagued him for the past few nights. He'd awakened in a sweat, his heart beating out of his chest—and Doral, Doral had had them too.

"The dreams," stated Eric into the silent pause.

Ari dropped his hand and propped his forearms on his knees. "Yes...the dreams. Fleur tells me now you and Sophi are experiencing unsettling dreams. Describe them."

Seated together on an overstuffed sofa, Eric and Sophi exchanged a long, silent gaze, fraught with meaning, before Sophi composed herself and began. "I had the first dream about four nights ago. I dreamt of golden orbs suspended in a star-filled space pulsing with joyous power. I was one of them." Sophi's eyes traveled to Eric, Fleur, Doral and finally, Ari. "Each of you was present, and multiple others whose life force I didn't recognize. Gossamer strands of brilliant energy connected us and pulsed from our Mother, a vast central sphere." Sophi spread her hands in a gesture of explanation. "Whenever Mother Verdantia chooses to interact with me these are the forms I see on the metaphysical plane.

"I became aware that threads of blackness infiltrated Her, formed a dark spider web across Her brilliance. The blackness ate away at Her as if the darkness was acid dissolving living tissue. Putrefaction crept down the strands of light that tethered us to Her. Talons of barren blackness raped my soul and spread a despair that ate all hope, all joy, all light. The dark corruption clawed each of us toward its ravenous maw." Sophi shuddered and closed her eyes. "I awoke sobbing, feeling the death of everything bright and beautiful—of our Mother and all life that dwells on Her surface." Her voice faltered, and Sophi opened aqua eyes awash with tears of heartbreak. Her gaze found Eric. "I know what it is to love beyond measure then suffer the desolation of its loss."

Eric pulled her to him and rested his chin on the top of her head. His arms tightened about her fiercely and then released her to hold her gently to him. "You won't lose me again, sweetling. We'll find a way to prevent this dark future."

Ari spoke to the small group. "Last night, Doral and I shared the dark omen of another dream. We beheld a vast, dark plane, dotted with the scattered remains of a once great city. The sky was void of stars and nothing alive walked the surface. Death and ruination blanketed a forsaken, desolate place of rotting trees and broken buildings." Ari paused. "I recognized the ruins. It was Sylvan Mintoth. Our Great Mother is in peril—attacked by some malevolent darkness, and She shows us the future if we cannot overcome this evil. But how do we fight this?" Ari rose from his chair and began to pace, his arms crossed over his chest. "I wish She spoke clearly to me. All I have are fragments of instruction and cryptic allusions." He stopped, planted his hands on his hips and gazed at the ceiling. *Great Mother, must your meaning always be clouded? Can't you, for once, speak to me plainly?"*

He walked to a small writing desk and removed a sheet of paper. "I wrote down exactly what She said, *When the raven takes flight, all must join with the first.*" Ari tossed the paper back onto the desk in frustration. "Once again, the fate of our world hangs on deciphering some obscure, metaphysical shi—" Ari bit the word off then nodded toward Sophi. "Sorry."

"We must trust that our Mother will make Her meaning clear." Sophi smiled gently. "No matter how obscure."

"I think we are meant to fight this plague on the psychic plane," Doral murmured. "It would seem She tells us to come together in some rite...though I don't understand the reference to 'the first'. Perhaps the elders in the High Enclave could be of assistance."

Ari paused for a moment and scrubbed his face. "The influx of people into Sylvan Mintoth has increased. They bring with them dire news of a black pestilence corrupting the soil, of newly dead rising from their graves and strange, warped creatures preying on them and their livestock. The dreams point us to an evil on the aetheric plane, but the effects are all too evident on our living, breathing world."

Ari caught Eric and Sophi's eyes. "It is early fall. I don't know how much time we have to discover Her meaning. Eric, Sophi, I ask that you stay in Sylvan Mintoth. I think we are all bound together in this, and we must work together to answer the Mother's calling." They nodded. "In the past, She has spoken to us most clearly through the Great Rite, I suggest that we three and the two of you, plan a working of it as soon as Fleur is recovered...say a month from now?"

"Yes," Eric agreed.

"Yes," Sophi said softly. "As soon as possible."

CHAPTER NINE

For the past two days, Adonia and the group had picked their arduous way across a white, frozen landscape of majestic, old-growth forests, picturesque dells with abandoned cottages and thundering waterfalls. Unseen menace snarled at them from deep in the undergrowth, making even the sturdy, impervious pack ponies skittish. Ramsey and Hel had shared duty keeping an uneasy guard throughout the nights, while the diaman crystal held the other demons at bay. Hel had not repeated the invitation to join him during his watch, so Adonia had shivered in her blankets, alone.

Adonia found herself in the unusual position of missing Lord Ramsey's acerbic comments and Hel's barbed retorts. Things were too quiet and the silence carried a strained, unnatural quality. As the group of four came closer and closer to the end of their journey, Hel retreated more and more into somber gravity. Adonia suspected he hid a deep grief over the state of his realm. Lord Ramsey also lapsed into taciturn remoteness, and Adonia caught him staring with severe intent at the frozen landscape they traversed. Not even Steffania could temper her husband's dire mood.

The quartet had broken out of a heavily wooded stand of trees into a valley clearing where, for the first time, their destination's up-thrust spires and rooftops rose distinctly out of the surrounding mountains. A broad stone-paved road marched straight toward a rise that blocked sight of all but the uppermost parts of Nyth Uchel and Torre Bianca. The width and composition of the road suggested a well-traveled throughway for commerce. The lack of a single soul on its immaculate stone-paved surface underscored Adonia's rising sense of a place locked in isolation.

"Adonia." Hel touched her arm and pointed toward an imposing spire swirling up through the clouds that wreathed the craggy, snow-capped peak where the tower perched. Hel stood and simply gazed at the gray tower for long moments, his face forbidding. She wondered what heavy thoughts weighed his mind. "There, Torre Bianca. Now you can see her."

"Yes...I see her. The rooflines below are those of Nyth Uchel? By the Goddess, the shingles really are mother-of-pearl."

Hel motioned with his arm in a sweeping gesture. "You see the rooftops of the outer city walls. The bulk of Nyth Uchel and the castle rests within." Hel's smile contained sadness. "And yes, the shingles are mother-of-pearl, but I'm afraid you are not seeing Nyth Uchel at her best."

Adonia was unprepared for the awe that swamped her. She sheltered her eyes from the brilliant evening sun with her hand. She wished her father stood beside her. How he would have reveled in this experience. Had he known the significance of her heritage all along? Had he re-spun stories passed down from *his* father as a way of preserving some part of their illustrious lineage—even if only in oral tradition? She wished her parents were alive to ask.

"We join the main road here. We should be through the outer gates in a couple of hours," said Hel.

Ramsey grunted. "Good. I'd like to sleep somewhere with a roof tonight."

Hel threw Ramsey a measured sideways glance and marched off, dragging the pack pony onto the broad, well-paved thoroughfare. Ramsey followed. Steffania and Adonia watched as Ramsey and Hel marched off. The two men exchanged sharp words, bickering over something. Steffania shook her head. "Like two brothers—always poking at each other—but at least now they are speaking."

Adonia fell into step beside Steffania as they followed the men. "I keep trying to imagine what this must look like when it's not locked in ice. It's incredible, now."

"Ramsey said this used to be a utopia of lush greenery and abundant animal life." Steffania's eyes lit with amusement at Adonia's arch of eyebrow.

"Somehow I can't place those words in Lord Ramsey's mouth."

Steffania chuckled. "Okay. Ramsey's actual words were, 'There used to be good hunting here and you didn't freeze your dick off when you took a piss.'" Steffania pulled her coat tighter about her. "This paradise fell when the Haarb invaded. I think both Hel and Ramsey mourn the loss." Adonia privately agreed and snuggled further into her exotic coat.

Either the ponies knew a warm stable was near or Hel had increased their pace. She and Steffania had to hustle to keep up with the men. In spite of the women's lengthened strides, Ramsey and Hel outpaced them and stood waiting atop of a rise. At least Adonia thought they waited. It could be they had stopped simply to absorb the splendor laid out before their eyes, although Hel must have seen this same sight when the picture was painted in far more glorious colors.

The valley dropped in a craggy vee. At the bottom, a tumultuous river created mayhem on wide banks of huge boulders. Spume splashing high onto the stony upthrusts froze in fabulous spikes of white ice. Spanning the valley, a vast stone bridge carried the road toward Nyth Uchel's alabaster white walls. Ornate arched columns extended into the raging waters and supported the structure. Similar arched columns above carried small, windowed turrets that might have once held great lights to illuminate the bridge when night fell.

On the other side, the road continued until it met the scrolled iron gates of the city. The highly wrought metal portal stood closed and Adonia wondered if they had enough muscle, even with the four of them, to open just one of those vast gates. They certainly were not getting in any other way. From her vantage point, it seemed the eastern side of Nyth Uchel rose into the heavens from the precipice overlooking the river. The tower, Torre Bianca, appeared to rise directly out of an immense waterfall that sent a torrent of water thundering into the river far below.

Hel rummaged in a pannier on the pack pony and pulled out an embossed, red satchel. From within, he pulled a curved horn of highly polished yellow metal. Putting his mouth to the horn, he blew a long fanfare of liquid notes that hung reverberating in the air. He stopped and allowed the echoes to die then repeated the call. From within the city, a brother horn answered with the repeat of the last three notes he had blown.

"Good, the townsmen will have the man-gate open for us." Hel strode forward, pulling his pony behind.

All three trailed him as he strode toward his city. As they crossed the extraordinary bridge, Adonia felt like the most raw of tourists gawking at marvels in a strange land. The silence and swiveling of Steffania's head consoled her with the thought that she was not alone in her feeling of dumbstruck wonder. The setting rays of the sun gleamed off the quartz in the diaman crystal walls and the iridescent mother-of-pearl on the roofs. She could not take her eyes from the incredible sight of a Nyth Uchel displayed as if some eccentric god or goddess had placed a great jewel in the fanciful setting of heaven-splitting peaks. She almost ran into

Steffania's back when they stopped on the other side of the bridge.

Hel cleared his throat. "If you can stand to wait a few more minutes, I would like to say some words over the grave of my gamekeeper. Rolly died the day I left for Sylvan Mintoth, and I would show a loyal retainer my respect." Hel motioned toward a graveyard just a short distance from the city walls. Adonia could see any number of fresh graves.

She took the lead of the pack pony from Hel. "Of course. We will wait." The three drifted after Hel as his long strides took him to the field marked with gravestones. Their markings were difficult to read in the growing purple dusk. Hel wandered to several before stopping in front of one marker and kneeling with bowed head.

Adonia, Steffania and Ramsey stood in silence beside other freshly turned graves.

"Oh!" Steffania jerked her sword out of its sheath and slashed downward, close to her foot.

"What?" Adonia asked in alarm.

"I...I..." Steffania shook her head. "No it couldn't have been. I must have imagined it."

"Imagined what?"

"Something wrapped my ankle and jerked. When I swung at it, it disappeared into the fresh dirt of the grave. It looked like a clawed hand." Steffania shrugged with a frown. "But that's ridiculous."

One of the ponies started kicking and jerked away from Adonia, snorting. The dirt on the top of the grave next to them roiled as if something alive dwelt just under the surface. When Adonia went to recapture the pony, the graves around them fountained dirt into the air and a foul stench assaulted the Verdantians. Gray snakes of putrid slime poured from two of the graves and attacked the women.

A tentacle of slime oozed around Adonia's legs, coalescing

into skeletal fingers, then clawed hands. Another tendril grew into a featureless face of needle teeth that snapped, sightlessly, writhing on the end of a stalk of gray slime. A slicing blade severed the snapping head and then the clawed hand that wrapped her leg. Lord Ramsey jerked her back, away from the grave. The severed pieces fell to the soil with a plop and returned to amorphous goo. The foul substance oozed back into the soil and disappeared without a trace.

"Healer, Steffania, get back to the road. Take the ponies," Ram snapped and ran to assist Hel. Multiple stalks of slug-like slime wrapped both Hel's legs where he knelt on the ground, trapping him. A third column of rotting flesh rose vertically before him, writhing away from his slashing blade. Atop the column, a human-like face with features more fully formed than that which had attacked Adonia snarled and snapped, attempting to get under Hel's sword. Ramsey slashed at the tendrils binding Hel's legs to the ground, and Hel lurched to his feet. In a clean motion, Hel severed the snapping head off the slug-like body and both men turned and sprinted toward the women. The graves on either side continued to erupt a foul gray slime that formed into humanoid shapes of nightmare-inducing appearance.

"Thanks," Hel gasped.

"Fuck! What do we fight?" Ramsey snarled.

"Don't know. Keep moving. Get to the gates."

Hel grabbed Adonia's arm and practically pulled her off her feet in his hurry toward the still closed gates of Nyth Uchel.

A villager stepped through a man-sized gate Adonia hadn't realized was there and waved aloft a crystal-lit lantern.

"Hurry, my lord, get within, so we can place the perimeter. The crystals will keep it away from the gate. It will retreat to the graves come daylight."

After the last pony struggled through the narrow gate, the

villagers slammed it closed with an echoing ring of iron on iron. Men holding glowing diaman crystals lined the base of the immense portal. When the last flurry of activity died, Hel turned and barked at an old, bent figure. "Bernard, explain why I just decapitated some abomination wearing Rolly's face."

CHAPTER TEN

"Somehow, the soil of the graves has been corrupted. The black evil animates the flesh of our departed. The dead act as one entity, with one driving will—to destroy the living," Bernard said.

"Start from the beginning. Give me the facts as you know them," Hel demanded.

The sudden horror of the last few moments slammed home and a choked-off sob died in Adonia's throat.

Hel paused and his angry eyes ranged Adonia's body. She didn't know what he saw but his next words to Bernard were, "First, the women need hot baths and some food. Prepare the family's old apartments. Open and air Lady Athena's rooms and notify the cook."

Hel snapped more sharp orders, and Adonia watched in a state of numbness as townspeople hustled the ponies away. He turned to the trio and his voice held apology.

"I must speak with Bernard, my steward, immediately. Follow this thoroughfare. It leads straight to the castle. Someone will meet you and show you to your rooms. I'll see you at dinner. Seven of-the-clock."

Bernard and Hel strode briskly in the direction of the inner city, Hel's head bent close to his steward's but his concerned gaze returned to them several times. The agitated voice of the elder gentleman carried back to them but his words were undecipherable.

Adonia's heart melted for Hel. It was obvious to her that his sense of duty to the people of Nyth Uchel and the need to care for his fellow travelers tore him in opposing directions. As always, this honorable man set the requirements of others in front of his own. Hel seemed driven to fix the broken and nurture those destitute. She wondered, not for the first time, who saw to his hurts? Who nurtured him? *I want to do that for him. Unlikely.* She closed her eyes against the ache in her heart.

Ramsey frowned at the backs of the two departing men, then turned to them. "Either of you hurt? Vixen? Healer?"

"I'm fine, Ram." Steffania cast a reassuring glance toward her husband, and his gaze turned to Adonia.

"Thanks to your prompt reactions, I'm just shaken. Thank you, Lord Ramsey," Adonia said.

Ram's head jerked in a curt nod. "I suppose we are safe—but keep your eyes open."

Adonia's eyes roamed across the avenues of what, in some past life, had been a scene of prosperity. Wide display windows gaped with jagged teeth of dirty, broken glass in shops fronting wide boulevards. The sound of the company's booted feet sent forlorn echoes into the deep shadows. Doors swung ajar or hung crooked on a single hinge—where a door existed at all. Tall, ornate street globes, now dark, marched in regimented single-file along the spacious streets. The black spears of their shadows crisscrossed the thoroughfares they were meant to illuminate. Here and there, smudged gray snow formed icy drifts against the buildings and a low wind moaned around the corners and past vacant windows that resembled so many sightless eyes.

And then Adonia saw the castle of Nyth Uchel. She tripped over her feet and stumbled to a halt. Steffania and Ramsey joined her, standing on either side.

"It is as if the Great Goddess fashioned a private abode and set it whole upon our planet," whispered Adonia.

Crystal walls of inconceivable delicacy soared into the heavens. Even in the evening dusk, their white diaman slabs luminesced, creating a half-light, bathing the immediate surrounds in soft, otherworldly radiance. Impossibly graceful towers spiraled into the air—towers of such ornate tracery it defied logic they stood at all. As backdrop to this unimaginable splendor, Torre Bianca soared heavenward, the upraised scepter of the queen of cities, eclipsing those impudent, over-reaching spires beneath her.

"Magnificent," Steffania breathed.

"Her walls still glow with the residue of ancient power. It must be what repels the ghouls and wraiths. Even in death, her brilliance defeats description," responded Ramsey, his voice bleak.

"Why did we ever move the capital to Sylvan Mintoth?" Adonia wondered aloud.

"There was a rift among the royal houses. Envy and gods-be-damned politics," snapped Ram. "Come." His derisive bark shattered the spell woven by Nyth Uchel and Torre Bianca, and the women dragged their reluctant feet after him with Adonia the last to follow.

"I understand why your people stay," Adonia whispered to the city—her heart breaking at the diminishment of Nyth Uchel's transcendent glory. *I, too, will do anything in my power to serve your prince and heal you.*

Adonia lay back and luxuriated in a steaming hot tub in frigid chambers of unimaginable wealth. She'd thought her quarters in the palace in Sylvan Mintoth luxurious—until now. When shown to her rooms, she had stood speechless as a platoon of men and women feverishly removed linens draped over furniture and bedding. Dust clouds erupted with each tug of fabric, revealing furnishings she believed only existed in the illustrated volumes she'd pored over in the archives at Sylvan Mintoth. Clutching everything she owned to her chest, she turned a complete circle, taking in the thick carpets, ornate diaman lamps of priceless metal and an elegant arrangement of seating now emerging from under the storage coverings. The chairs' upholstery was of such fine and costly material she doubted she'd be brave enough to sit in them. Sets of paneled doors led to a sophisticated bathroom and a spacious bedroom, set with several braziers of glowing diaman crystals that struggled to dispel the chill.

When the small army left her in the now immaculate suite of rooms, she'd carefully arranged her travel-worn belongings in a tidy pile nearest the door. She hoped her personal items, still bearing the dirt from her journey, didn't soil anything in these elegant chambers. She had slipped out of her mynx coat and carefully draped it across a chair. *This is the singular thing I own not out of place in these lodgings.*

At the rap on the door of the bathroom, she snatched at a nearby towel.

"Healer?" The head of a young woman peeked around the door and Adonia relaxed.

"Yes?"

"My name is Maddie. Prince DeHelios asked me to attend you and help you settle in. I hope you don't mind. I've taken your traveling clothes for cleaning and repair and hung up your coat. I've left you a gown and over-robe to wear until we can see to other clothing for you. I'll stay and help you into it and show you to the family's dining room." The young woman picked up garments Adonia had discarded on the floor. "I'll add these to the clean-and-mend pile."

"Thank you, Maddie." Adonia smiled. "It's not necessary for you to stay. I have always taken care of myself. I wouldn't know what to do with a maid."

The young woman smiled back. "I'm afraid you are stuck with me, Healer. I am to serve you by Prince DeHelios' command. It won't go well with me if I disobey him. Besides, you will need me for the dress."

Adonia grimaced, remembering a certain hat he'd instructed her to wear. "Yes. I understand. I'll be out shortly. Oh, and, Maddie, may I have the items you took for cleaning first thing tomorrow?" The young woman looked at her quizzically. "Those weren't just my traveling clothes. Those were *all* my clothes."

"Oh!" Maddie straightened. "Of course, Healer. I'll have them for you when you rise."

Sometime later, Adonia stood in front of a full-length mirror and tried to find herself in its reflection. The refined creature who filled its frame bore no resemblance to the Adonia Corvus she knew. Maddie had brushed out Adonia's dark brown hair until it dried and then pulled up the crown and sides in a neat, ornate braid twisted with a colored ribbon of pale lavender that complemented the gown and over-robe she wore. Jeweled barrettes secured the braid in the back where it joined the fall of the rest of her hair. A long-sleeved, violet gown with a high, flared collar at the nape of her neck and a low square neckline, hugged her upper torso and waist before flowing out into a full-length skirt. A belt with links of semi-precious purple jewels wrapped her waist with the excess hanging down onto her skirts. By some magick, her meager breasts appeared ample mounds above the deep neckline and her waist a mere hand span. The buff-colored toes of warm, soft boots peeked out from under the gown's hem and a cap-sleeve over-robe of deeper purple, heavily embroidered with rampant white horses and trimmed in white fur, topped all.

"Prince DeHelios selected the gown and belt. He has a good eye. You look very fine in those colors, Healer."

"Who is this woman and what have you done with Adonia Corvus?" Adonia could only shake her head.

Maddie laughed and clasped Adonia's hand, turning her away from the mirror and toward the door. "Come, Healer, I'll show you where the dining room is. I believe they are waiting for you."

Adonia followed Maddie down several long corridors to a door partially opened. Adonia could see a small dining room through the gap.

"And this is where I will leave you, Healer. Prince DeHelios said he would escort you back to your rooms after dinner, so I will see you in the morning." The young woman paused and smiled shyly. "Truly, my lady, it is an honor to serve you. All of Nyth Uchel are desperately glad you are here. Thank you for your courage in coming." Maddie smiled and left while Adonia stood awkwardly, searching for words.

She could hear the hum of voices and the smell of food tantalized her nose. Suddenly, she was famished. Adonia slipped through the door and took a step into the cozy room. All of her traveling companions sat around a large oval table with several townsmen. A simple meal of some sort of roasted meat and potatoes steamed in a large serving platter centered on the table. Hel and the elderly gentleman he had addressed as Bernard had their heads together, still deep in conversation. Lord Ramsey saw her first. His head rose as if a predator scenting prey, and his eyes warmed as she walked further into the room. Ram pushed his chair away from the table and stood with old-fashioned courtesy.

"Beautiful. Absolutely beautiful," Ramsey pronounced.

Steffania looked up from her conversation and met Adonia's eyes. For a moment, the redhead looked taken aback, then she grinned broadly and clapped her hands with an admiring whistle.

Adonia would have preferred Steffania not be so demonstrative. All conversation stopped and every eye turned to rest on her.

She felt hideously self-conscious and out of place. She was not pretty. Klaran had told her so often enough. She willed thoughts of him away. The skin on her weather-roughened hands snagged the finely woven, delicate cloth as she clutched together the over-robe. Perhaps Lord Ramsey merely admired the gown? He had an unerring eye for costly things. That must be it. "Yes, this gown is unusually lovely—a tribute to the weavers, designers and seamstresses who created it."

"He was not referring to the dress," Hel snarled and then scowled at Ramsey. Hel rose, crossed the small space and took her hand to escort her to the empty chair next to him. "He described the woman inside it."

She felt her face flame and for a moment, considered the idea they made fun of her—though it didn't fit with what she knew of Ramsey. Irascible—yes. Cruel—no. "Perhaps Lord Ramsey's eyes have suffered a strain," she murmured.

Only she heard Hel's snort. "You will cease to denigrate yourself. I forbid it. I will punish you if you demean yourself again. Consider this your second warning."

She had no opportunity to reply for Hel stood and addressed the room. "Gentlemen, this is Lady Adonia DeCorvus. She volunteered to come and attend us as our healer. Lady DeCorvus has endured a tedious and dangerous journey to reach Nyth Uchel. She deserves your respect and every assistance."

One by one, the men at the table stood and introduced themselves. The ancient man Hel addressed as Bernard spoke last. He examined her for long moments with a peculiar look then cast a glance toward Hel. "Has she seen? No, she couldn't have…ah…"

Hel cleared his throat sharply.

"Yes, sorry. It's just…" Bernard shook his head as if clearing his mind. "My Lady, I am Bernard Kelso, the Steward of Nyth Uchel. I serve Prince DeHelios, as I served his father. Please accept my profound thanks for agreeing to help us. As soon as you recover from your journey, I would ask you to look in on our sick. Your arrival has been highly anticipated, and it would cheer their spirits to see you in the flesh."

"If I might go to them after we eat?" Adonia looked toward Hel for approval.

He nodded. "Yes, I'll come with you."

"And, Steward Kelso…have I seen what?"

Hel flicked an impatient glance toward Bernard. "A painting. I'll show you tomorrow."

Hel stood propped against the wall of the sick room, his booted legs crossed at his ankles, his arms folded across his chest. From between hooded lids, he watched Nia move gracefully from patient to patient—compassionate and nurturing—no hint of the loss of composure she displayed around him. *I want her, and she is mine to take.* No surprise. What staggered him was the companion thought. *I want her to claim **me**. I'm done with a cold marriage of duty. I want her heart.*

She did nothing but smile and speak a few words of encouragement to each man or woman, but they seemed to brighten at her attention, at her easy and assured manner. He envied them. Nia had been awkward and diffident with him since A'rken's cottage. He could hardly blame her. Even he recognized he'd been difficult to approach. Even so, he'd yearned for an unsought touch or word from her to breach his formidable silence. Though he would never have asked, her attentions would have lifted the bleakness of his heart.

For the last two days, Hel's insides had felt as frozen as

the stark landscape they crossed. The rapidity of the worsening conditions shocked him. Each empty farmhouse petrified in frost and each leafless, barren forest encased in ice hardened the winter expanding inside him until he felt as brittle and easily shattered as the frozen land they walked. He would have welcomed a threat from any source—anything to draw his malaise outward. He needed to bury his heartache and worry in something tangible to fight. As it was, the stimulus that demolished his frozen interior came in the nightmare form of *Rolly*—or some corruption of the loyal man's flesh.

Worse, the abominations had imperiled Nia, and he'd been helpless to defend her. The rat-bastard DeKieran had rescued both of them. All the helpless impotence he'd felt at the loss of his family flooded back. He had choked on white-hot anger, unwilling to take it out on the innocent townsmen who'd welcomed his return. It took fortitude not to turn a blind eye at his steward's approach but he denied himself the escape. Instead, he'd listened attentively to Bernard's calamitous recitals.

The one pleasure he had taken for himself was selecting garments from his mother's and sister-in-law's closet to showcase Nia's slender elegance—and even there DeKieran had stolen the moment. *I should have been the one complimenting her appearance. I had planned my words, imagined her shy, pleased smile.*

He quite thoroughly hated the man. He built images in his mind of Ram plunging down a mountain crevasse, or off the bridge, or... *shit.* He sighed. He didn't hate Ramsey. He liked the rogue. *Even if he did steal my horse.* He saw an earlier version of himself in Ramsey—a self before the life of a majestic city and its people rested on his shoulders. Hel allowed his head to relax against the wall and closed his eyes as fatigue dragged at him.

"Hel? Prince DeHelios?"

Hel's eyes opened slowly. "Hmmm?" Nia stood before him.

"I have finished speaking with all the patients. I've been able to evaluate all of the sick and have a good idea what is needed. I'll begin to treat them in the morning."

He examined the lovely woman standing before him—the one radiant light in his dark life, the one balm to his burdened soul. She spread warmth around her like a sun, and Hel felt calmed and strengthened in her presence. "DeKieran is right," he murmured. "You *are* beautiful, and I want nothing more than to spend the next few hours sunk in your heat. I want it more than my next breath." Her eyes flew wide. He straightened and gently tucked her arm under his. "But, I promised to meet with Bernard. So, instead, I'll show you back to your rooms. For tonight, you will sleep alone."

Adonia dropped her head and refused to look at him as they walked the hallway toward her chambers. When they reached her door, he stopped, tipped her chin upward and pressed a gentle kiss to her soft, plush lips. "I'll take your silence as a sign of disappointment."

As he turned away, Hel smiled at the look of confusion she wore. No matter how bleak the immediate future, his Nia lightened his heart. *I'll find some way to ensure she stays.*

Hel, Ramsey and Bernard met around the heavy, wooden, dining table scarred from centuries of family dinners with active children. With a fingertip, Hel traced his initials carved in the surface—the result of a dare that left both him and his older brother unable to sit for a week. His father had strong opinions about defacing heirloom furniture. Hel missed the senior DeHelios and wondered, not for the first time, what counsel his father might have given him.

"Thank you for staying, DeKieran." Hel had asked Ram to

stay. Ramsey would be intimately involved in the decisions made in the next few minutes. Hel had included Steffania, but she'd demurred.

"I'm feeling strangely fatigued. I'll live with whatever this rogue decides." She'd retired after kissing her husband good night.

"We were at the point of despair until you arrived." Bernard regarded Hel and Ramsey from an upholstered chair that swallowed his aged bent form.

Ram sprawled in a large armchair pushed back from the table, one booted foot resting on his knee. "You say you have no more energized crystals to hold those graveyard horrors at bay?"

"None. Only Prince DeHelios can revitalize them. He'd left us enough to last during his absence, but he'd not anticipated the new threat. We have been doing without heat and light in order to protect the city from the undead that slither from their graves when night falls." Bernard grimaced. "We used the last of the diaman crystal to heat the water and warm the family quarters for you. Unfortunately, an equally dire situation has arisen on our western border."

"With Lord DeKieran's help, I believe we can deal with both the undead and the western border simultaneously." Hel looked toward Ram. For a moment, he wondered if he could put Ramsey and his wife in such peril—but he had little choice. *The bottom line is they can do it, and I can't be two places at once.* "Will you and Steffania reset the western border?"

"What is involved?"

"Replacing the caches of exhausted crystal. You will need to work the perimeter outward where the blight has encroached. Take some energized crystals with you to push back the contagion then work the lesser rite I gave you to restore energy to the spent caches."

"How will I know the border?"

"The dividing line between the cultivated fields and the forest is clearly defined. You should also see the collection of exhausted crystals. There are four to each cache. Each cache forms a small pyramid. These fields are the only arable land adjacent to Nyth Uchel that will grow the wheat and potatoes that keep us from starvation."

Ramsey's wolf-like eyes returned his direct gaze. "I understand your need."

"I must warn you. You can never relax your guard on the western border. The source of the corruption comes from there. As you know, wraiths swarm unchecked. Mutant creatures prowl the edges of the forest, their forms ever changing. You never know what will come at you out of the thick woods. And then there is the blight. The contagion will infect you with the fading sickness if your exposure to corrupted soil is prolonged."

Ramsey listened without visible emotion. "The danger to Steffania concerns me. I'd just as soon pass on this."

Disappointment crushed Hel. He'd counted on Ramsey's help, but he couldn't blame the man. The decision was bitter, but he'd have to consider abandoning the western fields. "Yes…I understand."

Ramsey sighed deeply, and, with a slow shake of his head, swore with descriptive, colorful vulgarity. "Steffania would alter my manhood if she ever discovered I'd withheld aid to Nyth Uchel because of her." A somber Ram drummed his fingers on the arm of his chair and slouched further into its cushions. Tense moments passed before Ramsey straightened and once again met Hel's eyes. "You and this gods-be-damned city. We will go."

"Thank you." The words didn't begin to express his feelings. Hel hoped Ram understood the depth of his gratitude. "Bernard will provide you with the stones to take with you."

Hel caught his steward's eyes, and Bernard nodded.

"I estimate a dozen or so should be adequate to start," said Bernard. "But the ones I have are lifeless. You will need to empower them."

With a return to his customary self, Ramsey chuckled. "I will begin the onerous task tomorrow morning. Leave the crystals outside our door along with a do-not-disturb sign and food and drink for the day." He rose and stretched. "I wish all my obligations were met this pleasantly. Until tomorrow evening." Ram's steps paused at the door and with a grin, he tossed, "Or the day after," over his shoulder.

Hel snorted in reply. He knew Ram's roguish behavior hid a brave heart just as dedicated to the salvation of Nyth Uchel as his. In many ways, he and Ramsey were brothers in blood. Nyth Uchel would always welcome Ramsey DeKieran—assuming the city still stood after this current crisis. When the door had closed behind DeKieran, he turned to his steward. "I don't understand why the border continues to fail. I set it just prior to leaving for Sylvan Mintoth."

Bernard shook his head. "I have no answers. I agree it is unusual and worrisome. I do wonder what Lord DeKieran will find."

Hel rested his head on the back of his chair and gazed at the ceiling. "I went to see A'rken. I didn't know who else to turn to. I'm not sure I trust A'rken's ravings, but he was right about the Haarb."

Bernard's bushy gray eyebrows rose. "Oh? What guidance did the mystic offer?"

"No guidance. He spoke a warning and a riddle. The darkness that we fight at Nyth Uchel is only symptomatic of a greater evil that attacks our Mother. Verdantia summons all Her sons and daughters to battle, and somehow our healer is at the center of it all."

Bernard groaned. "Could he be any *more* cryptic?"

Hel frowned. "Does this make any sense to you? 'Stones... stones...written on the stones of the tower. Look to the wisdom of your forefathers.' A'rken muttered those words from a trance." Hel waited while Bernard mulled over what he'd said.

"Aside from the obvious—something is written in the stone of Torre Bianca—no. It makes no sense and I don't know of anything written on her." Bernard shook his head. "I'm sorry, my lord, I'm of no help either."

"I suppose I can look forward to crawling on my knees over every inch of that tower." Hel sighed. "According to A'rken, we must act when Belarus mates with Cirrus, so we have some time." He sat lost in thought, plotting a systematic method to search Torre Bianca.

Hel dropped his forearms to his knees and hung his head, suddenly drained. He echoed his steward's palpable frustration. Life and death dilemmas demanded he find solutions but the answers spawned more questions. He longed for surcease from the crushing burden—but there was no one else to assume the responsibility. As ever, Nyth Uchel, Torre Bianca—Verdantia herself, it seemed—would live or die based on *his* decisions. *So be it.* He sat upright and squared his shoulders. *I am DeHelios. Our Mother has shaped me for this purpose. I will not fail Her.*

His steward's voice brought him back to the present.

"She is Isolde DeCorvus returned to us."

Hel straightened. "Adonia? Yes. I think so, too, though I didn't see the resemblance at first." The carefully chosen garments had done everything he had hoped and one thing he hadn't expected. The borrowed gown revealed the beauty Nia hid under her ragged, masculine attire. However, in her finery, Nia might have stepped out of the portrait of Isolde DeCorvus that hung in the family gallery. He shook his head. "I don't know how I missed it. A'rken says she is the key to something." Hel rubbed his tired eyes and slumped back in his chair. "Until four days ago, Adonia was ignorant of her heritage. She is special, Bernard. Our healer is another mystery—one I intend to solve as quickly as possible."

"Can she help you with the lesser rites? Can she take Tessa's place as your partner?"

A smile of satisfaction spread across Hel's face. Finally, something pleasant to anticipate. "Oh, yes. I believe she can be infinitely more than a replacement for Tessa. Our healer's training as Nyth Uchel's magistra begins tomorrow."

CHAPTER ELEVEN

Beams of sunlight lanced through tall, mullioned windows into Adonia's eyes. Blinking, she roused slowly from a profound sleep. Only the top of her head and eyes peeked from the crisp, white, down-stuffed duvet. The rest of her lay cocooned in delicious warmth. A tentative knock sounded on her door. Perhaps it was not the sun that had awakened her.

"Healer? Healer, it is Maddie. Are you awake?" The maid knocked again. "Ma'am?"

Adonia pushed the duvet back and struggled with her long embroidered gown before giving up and sitting with the duvet pulled across her lap. The room was surprisingly warm. The heat from the brazier of diaman crystals had dispelled the cold efficiently.

"Come in, Maddie," she called.

Adonia heard the door to the sitting room open and the tink of cutlery against ceramics. The young brunette walked into her bedroom carrying a silver tray with what looked like remnants of last night's dinner. Steam escaped from a pot of some brewed liquid.

"Put the tray on that table, please, Maddie. I want to get up and moving. I am neglecting my patients." Adonia pushed the bedcovers away then wrestled her sheer nightgown down from where it had bunched in a roll at her waist. Lower body sufficiently covered, she padded barefoot to the table and looked down at the food. A lonely piece of unidentifiable meat sat beside a finger-sized potato on a translucent plate of pearl white.

"I'm sorry we don't have better. This can't be what you're used to."

Amusement lit Adonia's eyes. "What I'm used to would surprise you. I grew up eating lizards and cactus."

The young servant chuckled. "Well, it's not lizard...that much I know."

"It will keep body and soul together; that is all that's important." Adonia pulled her gown out of the way and sat to eat. "Thank you for the nightgown. I assume you put it on my bed. It was nice not to sleep in my clothes for a change. Thank you for turning my bed down also. I don't think that's ever been done for me."

"You're welcome. I put more clothes in your closet last night while you were at dinner. I would be happy to help you chose a dress for today."

Adonia chewed a piece of meat and swallowed. "I'd planned on wearing the clothes I arrived in." From where she sat, she could see her neatly folded tunic, shirt and trousers. "Thank you for washing and mending them."

"You're welcome."

"I hear hesitation in your voice."

"Prince DeHelios seemed set on you wearing those dresses." Maddie's eyes swung to the closet. "I'm not certain, but I think he picked them out himself."

Adonia battled with the last of the dentally challenging meat then gulped a cup of what turned out to be herbal tea. "Where do they come from?"

"Most of them belonged to his brother's wife. She was tall and slender like you, but the one you wore last night was a favorite of Hel's mother."

"Mmm." Adonia considered the beautiful gowns for a moment and then sighed. "No. Those aren't for the likes of me. I would live in fear of soiling them in the sick room. Besides," her voice turned wry, "Prince DeHelios has more pressing concerns than what I'm wearing."

"It seemed important to him," Maddie murmured.

Adonia gazed up at her with a slight shake of her head. "No dresses."

"Then I will help you with your hair and take the tray back."

"It's wonderful to have such accomplished help in the sickroom. Thank you for all you have done to help me, Sara." Adonia smiled at the matron. "The people of Nyth Uchel are lucky to have such a capable nurse."

The older woman nodded with a genuine smile. "You are welcome, Healer, but I gladly surrender the direction of the sick room to you. If we're through here, I'll start brewing more brite-weed tea."

As Sara left the room, Adonia's gratitude to the woman welled to fill her heart. The morning had progressed into early afternoon as, one by one, Sara helped her evaluate the most critical patients and plan a treatment program for them. Sara had patiently explained what had been done—what worked and what didn't work—for those afflicted with the *fading*.

Adonia had some ideas of her own about magickal treatments she could try. A thrill of delight coursed through her at the thought and she blessed the days—days others had ridiculed her for—spent memorizing procedures she had never thought to practice. At last, an unlooked for answer to a hopeless prayer. *Adonia Corvus is going to work healing magick!* At least…she hoped so.

Unease rode the shoulder of her anticipation. She'd require Hel's assistance to empower the diaman crystals required in the magicks. *I must ask him for sex.* Her body warmed at the thought. Hel wouldn't say no. He'd do anything to assist his people. She just didn't know how to couch her request. It would be pure arrogance to simply demand—she cringed at the thought. *That will never happen.* And then there was her fear of the unknown. *I have book learning—not practical experience. At the end of the day, I have never done this.* Adonia redoubled her determination and straightened her shoulders. "I'll just ask Hel straight out," she muttered.

"Ask me what, Healer?"

Her eyes flew open to meet the glowering eyes of Hel. Where had he come from and why was he angry? He made an impatient sound. "Ask me what?"

She could only produce garbled words.

"Fine. When you regain your voice, ask. Until then, why are you dressed in rags? Didn't Maddie show you the dresses? I'll have words with that girl."

Adonia frowned at the vehemence in Hel's voice. "No. She did tell me. Don't blame—"

"Ah. So my first question stands. Why are you dressed in rags?"

Defensive indignation straightened Adonia's spine. "These are perfectly good clothes." She winced inside as she stroked the drab tunic with its mismatched buttons and frayed cuffs and hem. At its finest moment, she'd thought it an ugly, utilitarian garment.

"Do you dislike my choices?"

"No! It's just…" Her voice faltered. "They are dresses for the highborn and I'm a…"

"Enough! Healer, do you intend to defy me—flout my commands?"

Defy him? How could he think such a thing?

"Nia." His growl demanded an answer.

"I would never—"

"Then, why did you disobey me? I specifically told you—twice. You are forbidden to disparage or demean yourself."

"I hardly think wearing—" As before with the hat, one moment she was one place and the next moment another. One moment she stood, and the next she flopped, head down, over Hel's shoulder as he strode in ground-eating strides down the corridor to her rooms. "By the Mother! Will you let me finish a sentence?" They passed a wide-eyed Sara plastered to the wall as Hel forged by.

"Prince DeHelios! Put me down!"

"Silence! You will learn your value, Nia. You *will* learn not to belittle yourself."

Hel strong-armed the door to her sitting room and crossed in four strides. He stopped before an armless chair and dumped her on her feet before spinning to sit in the chair. He jerked her, facedown, across his left leg. In mere seconds, he had her tunic halfway up her torso, trapping her arms and hands over her head, baring her from the breasts down. One of his massive hands held her easily confined while his other stripped her pants down to bare her buttocks and upper thighs. His right leg trapped her bare ass against his left, effectively immobilizing her. It was only then it occurred to her to struggle.

"What are you doing?" she cried into the cloth now muffling her head.

Swack!

His hand descended on her right buttock cheek in a stinging slap.

"Ow! Stop it! That hurts!"

Swack, swack, swack!

Rapid slaps hit each cheek, growing heavier each time. Left, right, left. Brief explosions of pain jerked her in time to his spanks.

"Hel, stop! Please, stop!" He must be able to hear her.

"You. Will. Not." S*wack!* "Denigrate." *Swack!* "Yourself." *Swack!*

"Ooohhh!" Adonia couldn't control the writhing of her hips. Hel merely hooked her thighs and clamped down harder with his right leg.

"You. Will. Not!" *Swack!* "Say it, Nia. Say it."

"Wha..?"

Swack! Swack! Swack!

Fire radiated down her buttocks with every slap of his open hand.

Swack! Swack! Swack!

"I won't. I won't!" she yelped into her tunic.

"You won't what?"

Swack! Swack! Swack!

"Denigrate…denigrate…myself," she sobbed. Mortification jousted with the fire burning in her hind end. Mortification won the day, and her emotional turmoil buried the stinging pain. "Stop, Hel, please, stop."

His hand gentled, and his palm lay open on her right buttock cheek. The flesh underneath it burned. At his slightest movement, hot sensation streaked to a most unexpected place—her clit. To her chagrin, the little bud throbbed in time with the pulse of heat in her buttocks. The slickness she felt between her legs stunned and confused her. Hel slowly moved his hand in a light circle on her abused bottom. She moaned in accompaniment to the provocative touch. His fingers tickled at the seam of her inner thighs and the right leg that held her motionless loosened to allow her movement.

"Open your legs," he commanded.

"Wh…"

Swack!

With a yelp, she spread them as far as the hobble of her trousers would allow.

His long fingers traced down the seam of her buttocks and delved between her widespread legs. "You're wet," he murmured, and his index finger pressed into her slickness and spread it toward her pulsing clit with a swirling caress.

Oh…that feels good. Soft passes over those nerves sent a different kind of heat coursing through her. She arched her back and opened her legs further. "Mmm, please." She didn't care what it revealed about her. The hand teasing her flesh disappeared. Goddess, what had she expected? She slumped across his knee in resignation.

The arm that had held her torso and shoulders trapped released her. "Kneel up."

Hel pulled her tunic back to cover her breasts and abdomen, and she cast a wary glance toward him. The sensual heat in his eyes and the carnal gratification in his twisted grin caught her by surprise. "Now that we know what spanking does to you, sweet Nia, you can be sure I will do this more often." His grin disappeared. "I warned you I would punish you. Now, go to that closet and select garments befitting your station."

As she rose, Hel completed the baring of her lower body, stripping her underwear and her trousers from her legs as she balanced on one foot and then the next.

"My underpants, please?" Adonia held out her hand then dropped it at the look on his face. "I need them," she pleaded softly. "I only have two pair."

"No."

"No?"

"No panties under your dresses and no trousers unless you are sitting a horse."

She blinked. *Huh.*

"Now do as I instructed. Pick a gown from the closet and put it on. I will wait." He sprawled like a great, indolent cat in the armless chair and examined her through lazy eyes.

At least he doesn't seem angry any more. She gingerly pulled her tunic over her smarting derriere and padded into her bedroom, the womanly flesh between her legs almost as hot as her ass. A faltering smile played at the edges of her mouth. *I'm not certain I'd call that punishment.* She wondered what that said about her.

Hel watched Adonia gingerly cross the room to her closet, the hem of her threadbare top flirting with her cherry-red buttock cheeks. He adjusted his pants, loosening the fabric trapping his semi-engorged cock. These unplanned minutes with Nia had proved stimulating. His smile broadened—for each of them. A flare of satisfaction eclipsed the gnawing frustration and flash-fire anger that had plagued Hel all day. *Cathartic, but I shouldn't have lost my temper with her. She is not the source of my aggravation. Sweet Nia. How little she knows of herself.* He relaxed further into the chair and closed his eyes. His day had started early and promised to finish late.

Earlier that day, when the earliest rays of daylight speared between the craggy peaks surrounding Nyth Uchel, he had joined Bernard and a work crew at Torre Bianca. Methodically, the workers had examined Torre Bianca's exterior to the extent hastily constructed scaffolding allowed. Hel had left them to their work and searched the first two interior levels of the tower. The sun stood high overhead, well after mid-day, before he paused. Spills of light reflected off the vast interior of diaman crystal slabs and revealed only smooth, unblemished surfaces. Hel wondered if the men outside had fared better.

"What have you found, Bernard?" Hel walked out of the tower, dusted his hands on his pants and squinted into the bright mid-day sun. The radiance did little to remove the frozen bite of the air.

"Nothing, my lord. The workers have scoured the base of the tower since dawn. We've found nothing."

"Extend the scaffolding higher and keep looking." Choking back his frustration, he walked back inside. His eyes lifted to the soaring interior staircase of ornate worked iron and the mechanical lifts that stood on either side. *Searching this will take weeks.*

"I cannot fasten the gown. Will you please help me?"

Adonia's voice roused Hel from his reverie, and he straightened in the chair. Nia looked over her shoulder at him, offering her back. Standing, he moved into her and began to close the series of hooks on the long-sleeved, rose-colored gown. He had chosen the gown for its warmth and simplicity. In his eyes, cleanly tailored lines best suited Adonia's elegance. As his fingers closed the last fastening, he rested his hand on her waist and simply stood enjoying the warm, toned flesh under his palm.

"All of the gowns are like this." Nia turned in his hold and stepped back with a questioning expression. "I cannot manage any of them on my own."

"I'll help you with them." Hel enjoyed the uncertainty crossing her face.

"How? I can't…"

"It won't be a problem, Nia. You'll be sleeping with me from now on. My room adjoins yours."

He supposed it wasn't nice to laugh at her but the dumbstruck expression on her face was comical.

"With you?"

"Yes."

"Every night?"

"Yes."

Her arms wrapped her waist, and her gaze dropped to the floor. "We'll have sex?"

Hel nodded. "Yes."

"Every night?"

"Yes." He wondered how far down her neck the flush went. "And it will please me to serve as your maid, my lady."

Her eyes rose to his. The vulnerability filling them brought a pang to his heart. "It will please *you* to attend *me*?"

"Nia." He shook his head and pulled her into his arms. She went unresisting, her hands and arms gathered in front of her. "Everything about you pleases me."

She strained her neck back and stared at him dubiously. "You didn't feel so ten minutes ago."

He stifled a smile and raised a hand to caress her cheek. "Hmm. You are everything I have prayed for." The expression on her upraised face softened. "A healer, and once trained, a powerful magistra."

Her yielding body stiffened. She straightened out of his arms and turned away. Her shoulders sagged. "Of course."

He watched her withdraw into herself and an unfamiliar sense of inadequacy shot through him. *I've disappointed her somehow. What am I missing?* He set his personal thoughts aside with a sense of frustration. More pressing matters demanded his attention. "I have much to teach you. It is time to start your lessons in the Great and Lesser Rites. We'll spend our afternoons and evenings together, as much as your sickroom and my search for A'rken's engraved words will allow."

"Yes…I understand a magistra is needed. I'll do what I can."

Her gaze flicked up to his and she faced him, chin held high. "I need your assistance with the healing magicks."

His eyebrow crept up. "What do you need from me?"

She cleared her throat, and her hands clasped and unclasped. "Energized diaman crystals—to begin. Later, perhaps your guidance in managing the energies."

He nodded, and amusement at her attempt to be assertive brought a slight smile to his lips. "Gladly. Do you want to start now?"

Her eyes flew open then she dropped her gaze to the floor. "Ah, yes. Yes, I'd like to start… ah, now."

He chuckled deep in his chest. Her shy, artless acquiescence disarmed him—every time. "Then come with me to the storerooms. We need crystals."

She followed him through the door and waited as he closed it. "Down that hallway, turn left, second door on the right." He motioned with his arm. "After you, Healer."

Her spine straightened, and Nia did an excellent imitation of a soldier marching to a firing squad. Hel prowled behind and feasted on the swing of her slender form. An eagerness rose in him to feel that lithe body beneath him, those slender thighs wrapping his waist. It wasn't the only thing that rose, and he found himself adjusting his trousers again. *Patience, DeHelios, patience. You'll have her soon.*

CHAPTER TWELVE

H el smiled inwardly at the wonder in Nia's eyes as she examined the Chambre Cristalle.

"It's warm in here. I had thought it would be as frozen as the rest of the city," Nia said.

"Torre Bianca has a unique heating system. I'll show it to you after we have done what we came to do."

She jerked her head in acknowledgement and slipped off her mynx coat. She laid it by three tall woven baskets containing diaman crystal that rested against the dais. Rather than exhaust her with a physical climb, Hel had chosen to take one of the mechanical lifts and had transferred the baskets from the lift to the chamber while Nia moved slowly about the expansive room, her eyes busy absorbing the Chambre Cristalle as if sheer intensity of gaze would force the chamber's secrets from its walls. Nia stopped, seemingly arrested by the sight out one of the floor-to-ceiling windows. "Incredible. It's as if I'm a goddess surveying her world."

He moved to stand beside her. "Yes, these views have always inspired me." In the afternoon light, snow glistened off a vast panorama of jagged crags and peaks. Beneath, plumy falls of white water plunged hundreds of feet, the final terminus hidden from view. Enormous black forests of hundreds-of-years-old trees draped foothills as far as the eye could see. He frowned. The vista revealed a land locked in ice.

Hel wondered how the Chambre Cristalle appeared to Adonia as she saw it for the first time. Memories of his first glimpse of the room flooded back with sweet nostalgia. "I remember when I first climbed that spiral staircase to the upper-most level of Torre Bianca and walked into this chamber with my father. I was sixteen and just coming into full manhood. I stood where you stand now and marveled." Hel gestured with his arm. "My father stood in that doorway. 'This is the Chambre Cristalle,' he said. 'Your mother and I work the Great Rite here. When you are sufficiently schooled, you, your brother and the magistra*e* chosen for you will assist us.'"

Nia turned from the window to face him. Her face softened. "You did not choose your wife?"

Hel exhaled on a long breath and wondered if Nia would understand the restrictions and obligations placed upon the highborn. "No. Nor did I expect to."

He barely heard her whispered, "Did you care for her?"

As the Mother was his witness, he tried to keep the dislike from his voice when he spoke his dead wife's name. "Lady Athena fulfilled her duty, as did I."

He hadn't been in the Chambre Cristalle since the death of his wife. Seeking a distraction from the emotions Nia's uncomfortable question raised, Hel examined the eight-sided room with its tall, arched windows that ran from floor to ceiling. An enormous dais of roughly quarried gray diaman crystal occupied the center of a great circle engraved into the floor. Deeply chiseled rays radiated from the circle to all eight windows. The altar's top reflected the light off its highly polished surface. All other sides still bore the marks of the stonemason's chisel. A domed skylight in the center of the circular pitched roof cast a spotlight of sun upon the altar. Through the dust motes dancing in its beams, Hel could see the eyebolts sunk into each corner of the altar. Leather lashings run through the bolts hung loose.

In this place of austere and imposing beauty, he and Athena had worked the rite that empowered the atmospheric shield and held winter in abeyance. Here, driven to the edge of insanity by sexual arousal, he and his partner melded their spirits with their Great Mother. She'd use their bodies as a conduit for Her staggering power, a living channel to distribute Her vitality for the benefit of all.

Each time, wielding and channeling the tremendous forces unleashed during the Great Rite had pushed his mental and physical discipline to the point of failure. Each time, he'd found the inner strength to stand triumphant. Through the fiery gauntlet of the Great Rite, She had tempered him into a wielder of Her highest magick—an adamantine son, a paladin-prince steadfast in his service to Her.

Adonia's hand on his arm returned his wandering thoughts to her. "You must have been intimate with her daily. I cannot conceive of how difficult that was for you if you did not care for her," Adonia said.

Hel groaned inwardly. It had been difficult in ways he could never explain to Nia, but it had also been a journey of self-discovery. He closed his eyes against the rising memories. The physically brutal battles—the only way Athena could be aroused—had also aroused him. He'd acquired a taste for the carnal high that accompanied sexual dominance even if tempered by an antipathy for the extreme severity Athena had required. When he opened his eyes again, Nia's worried gaze met his. A half-smile pulled at his mouth. He cupped her jaw and ran his thumb across her lower lip. "Sweet Nia, certain methods for sexual arousal are not gentle, not always born from love. Some women and some men require…

different… stimulus to bring them erotic fulfillment. Sometime soon I will show you another chamber on the level below us." Her eyes widened and he bit back a chuckle. "I will enjoy introducing you to its pleasures."

She turned from him and stared sightlessly out the window.

Hel watched her for a moment. Her consternation amused him, and the dark feelings resurrected by her curiosity faded back into the past. He crossed to the baskets and began placing the crystals into the deeply engraved circle and rays surrounding the central dais. When he'd finished, he leaned back against the altar and let his eyes wander up and down Nia's slender form—fuel for the carnal fire that had lain banked since A'rken's cottage. "Nia."

With a deep inhale, she turned. "Now?"

"Now." He held out his arms. "Come to me."

She took halting steps toward him. Fine tremors shook her body. "Now that the time has come to perform a Lesser rite, formally, on a dais—in the Chambre Cristalle—I'm a little bit afraid."

He smiled gently, his arms still extended. "Yes, I know. I will deal with your fear. Come here." He enfolded her into his arms with a soothing murmur and ran his hands in gentle strokes over the bony planes of her back. He didn't mind her leanness, but it spoke to him of deprivation or disregard for her own wellbeing. He wished he could stuff her with finely prepared meals and opulent desserts and add some softness to her spare body. He waited long moments until her shudders stopped. "Have I told you how brave I think you are?"

She shook her head buried in his chest. "Not brave—a scared, fluffy-tailed hopper."

He made a low sound of comfort. "There can be no bravery without fear. The soul's triumphant fight over what's most feared is the definition of courage." He caught her chin under his knuckle and raised her gaze to his. "That makes you one of the bravest people I know."

She snorted. "Why, because I'm afraid of everything?"

Gentle amusement filled him. "Are you always so painfully truthful?"

"I'm not afraid of the physical act… well… maybe a little. I think you aristos have out-of-the-ordinary tastes." She rubbed at her behind and choked off a laugh then once more pressed her cheek to his chest. All he saw was a wealth of fine brown hair, and he had to strain to hear her. "I'm more afraid of the aftermath. I have a fatal habit of associating sex with love. I cannot seem to divorce the act from the emotion, and my thoughts already dwell too often on Nyth Uchel's prince."

Fierce satisfaction filled him at her forthright words. Perhaps he hadn't blundered as badly with her as he'd feared. Perhaps when all had been set right—*if* all could be set right—Adonia would choose to stay with him—not for Nyth Uchel or her people, or because of the dictates of a genetic match, but because of *him*. He hid the heady joy of that thought in a secret place in his heart.

He couldn't ignore the brave vulnerability she displayed to make such a statement. Though he doubted Nia would believe him, he'd tell her his honest feelings.

"Adonia DeCorvus, you have drawn me from the first moment I glimpsed you. From the first day in High Lord DeTano's office, I've considered how I might persuade you to remain in Nyth Uchel. Every moment I've spent with you since has reinforced that desire."

He tipped her face to his. He needed to see her eyes, judge her reaction to his words. He sighed. Patent skepticism was not the response he'd hoped for. He leaned in and kissed her gently on her parted lips—a kiss hinting at his passion and desire. "I would welcome your love."

She gazed at him for a long moment, expressions fleeting across her face. He wished he knew her thoughts. Finally, she took a breath and spoke.

"I will tell you my greatest nightmare; I'm not what you and A'rken seem to think I am. I will fail you in your time of greatest need."

"I understand your fears, Nia, and I share them. Not that *you* will fail...but that I will."

"No. You cannot doubt yourself." She pushed away, and her gaze blazed with fire. "You are splendid and steadfast. You carry the weight of Nyth Uchel on your shoulders like the mountain upon which this city is built. Immutable. Your people look to you for their salvation and their trust is well-placed." Her eyes fell and her tone softened. "Your only weakness is in those upon whom *you* depend."

Hel doubted words would persuade her. Acts and time would show his Nia her value—make her understand what she was to him. This moment would be one of many he could use to demonstrate what they were—together.

"And I will prove to you there is no weakness." He pulled her up into a passionate assault of lips and tongue. His hands tangled in the fastenings on her dress. The taste of her mouth and her generous response affected him like a potent brew and he lost himself, intoxicated by her. Many minutes passed before he slipped the rose gown from her shoulders, picked her up in his arms and laid her on the dais.

"Stay on your back. Hands above your head."

He stripped quickly. Her heavy lidded eyes never ceased their scrutiny. When he lay down beside her, he could feel the thudding of her heart against his chest. Her ribs rose and fell in quick pants, but to her credit, Nia remained pliant against him.

"Open your mind, Nia. Relax your body. Close your eyes.

Concentrate on the rhythm and cadence of my words, the touch of my fingers and warmth of my tongue."

A faint smile answered his directive.

He briefly considered tying her wrists and ankles. *I wonder how she'd react?* No. For this first time, he'd keep things conventional. *Perhaps tomorrow I will show her the playroom below.*

Without thought, he fell into the familiar words of the lesser rite for heat and flame. The pads of his fingers passed across the satin of her skin in feather-light swirls. His concentration became so intent the merest hitch in her breathing registered. He started at her forehead, then traced her face to behind her ears, under her jaw, down her neck to her collar bone.

"I am going to cover every inch of your body like this."

A soft moan answered him.

By the time he got to her delicate navel, goose bumps peppered her entire body and Nia's nipples were hard buttons on the tips of her breasts. With a quick lick of his tongue, he latched onto her right nipple and flicked his tongue back and forth.

"Ah!" Nia arched into the air. Her hands grabbed at his hair and she curled into him.

"No…no. Flat on your back, Nia."

She rolled her head in protest but complied, never opening her eyes.

"Lie flat and accept the sensations. Submerge yourself in the arousal. Feed it with your mind."

Hel resumed the cadence of the chant. With light tracery, he outlined her hipbones and then the small concave of her belly. His fingers tickled into the groove separating her thigh from her mound and then tangled in the hairs of her pubis.

"Spread your legs, Nia. Whenever I touch below your waist, you will spread your legs to their fullest extent and keep them that way."

Hel watched as Nia obeyed and veed her legs His cock gave an unruly jerk. He contemplated how, in the days to come, he would educate her on how wide she really could open them. For now, this would do. Hel picked up the chant again and resumed the tracery of his fingers on the outsides of her thighs, behind her knees, down her calves to her feet and then back up the insides of her legs. He disciplined his breathing to slow, regular inhales and exhales. The twitching of his painfully hard cock was not nearly so disciplined and cool spills of precum escaped the tip.

He worked his fingers up the insides of her thighs. Now the flesh at the apex of her legs glistened with her arousal, the swollen pink lips a target for sensual play. As he slipped his fingers up and down the seam in the lightest of teases, Nia groaned and writhed her hips. More fluid leaked from her plush flesh and he caught it on his knuckle. A slight swipe of his tongue transferred the heady taste of Nia into his mouth.

Not enough, not nearly enough. The warm diaman crystal slab pressed his hard cock into his abdomen with almost cruel pressure as he slid his shoulders between Nia's legs. He rolled slightly onto one hip to relieve the strain. His thumbs separated her moist lower flesh to reveal the prominent nub of ruby red at the apex of her sex. He lowered his face between her legs and feasted. With a feminine cry, she boxed his ears with the inside of her thighs.

"Spread them and keep them spread, Nia, or I will tie you." Hel's ears rang from the resounding blow of her legs, but he resumed his erotic kisses. With a helpless growl turned whimper, her thighs spread wide. He pulled her clit into his mouth and suckled. With soft swirls of his tongue, he teased the hard nub. Periodic convulsions in her pussy alerted him to the height of her arousal, and he slipped a finger into her. With firm strokes, he thrummed the fleshy pad on the front wall of her slick pussy, just opposite the bundle of nerves he teased with his tongue and lips.

Her sharp gasp signaled him in time to prevent his ears being boxed again. "Next time I am tying you," he muttered. The chamber thrummed with a low sound, as if a deep-toned bell were ringing...but that could have been the result of the blows to his head.

"Please, oh, please." Nia's head thrashed back and forth. Her palms and fingers massaged her hard nipples. "Please...in me...please."

Intent on the cadenced rite and on arousing Nia, he'd missed when the glow had begun but there was no missing the pearlescent luminosity of the dais, now. The entire chamber held a soft brilliance that rivaled the sunlight streaming in the windows. The low chiming wasn't a result of a box to his ears. The dais, itself, hummed with life. As he drew back and absorbed the changes, he bared his teeth in a snarl of victory. Damnation, it was good to be right. Nia would be a powerful magistra.

"Please, Hel."

"Yes," he growled and plunged into her slick center, sliding her up the smooth stone with the force of his entry. "Yes." *Too much heat, too much pleasure, just...too much.* The firm, slick walls of her pussy sheathed him tightly. With his every withdrawal, her inner walls tightened further as if to hold him within.

The timbre of the altar's vibrations tormented him on another level. All the pleasure centers in his body pulsed. Perhaps it was the anticipation, perhaps it was the four-day hiatus but he did something he hadn't done since his teens. When the convulsions of her slick channel signaled Nia's climax, he allowed the reins of control to slip through his fingers. He retained only enough awareness to channel their energies into the diaman crystal they lay upon. Like some great beast unleashed, he pounded into the woman underneath him and gloried in his savage possession.

Climax detonated in his brain, and the explosion wiped all conscious thought.

Adonia's muscles and bones had turned to warm honey. She would have slipped from semi-consciousness into sleep, replete with satisfaction, but a heavy weight pressed her with uncomfortable firmness into the diaman slab. Her shoulder blades and tailbone complained—each a point of pain. *Hel.* She had no sooner thought it than the pressure lightened and the weight lifted. Her thoughts drifted in dazed euphoria and strolled a wandering path to the present.

"Nia." Hel relished her lips in a lingering kiss.

I must ask him to do that more often.

"Nia, you must rise. We are not finished. There is something I want to show you."

Unwilling, she opened an eyelid and caught Hel's gray gaze, his face scant inches above hers. Soft gold light haloed his head. The effort to keep her eyelid open was too great. "Mmm." She nodded her head a fraction. "Mmm-hmm. Moment."

His deep chuckle vibrated in her ears. "Open your eyes, Nia. You'll want to see this."

"Can't wait?"

"No," he murmured and pressed another soft kiss on her mouth. "Put your arms around my neck."

He slid an arm behind her shoulders and another under her knees and lifted her limp body from the dais. She sighed a protest as he placed her on her feet. "Sadist. I don't have the strength to stand."

He stood with his hands on her hips until she steadied. "Open your eyes."

"Oh! The tower walls are glowing." She looked at her

bare feet, planted on warm, golden stone. "The chamber floor is glowing." She turned. "Hel! The dais. Oh, my stars…" The formerly cold, gray, crystal block radiated with amber brilliance. Within, an occasional streak of white lightning blossomed then faded. "The diaman platform is pulsing!" A frown creased her brow. "Tell me it always does this?"

His sultry smile widened as he slowly shook his head. "Normally this lesser rite for heat and flame generates only enough energy to empower the small crystals on the floor. I've never seen it make the walls and dais glow. I've always wondered what the rites would be like with a powerful partner." He cocked his head and those gray eyes of his seemed to look into her soul. "However uncomfortable it makes you, you have an exceptionally strong link to our Mother. With even minimal schooling, you will be an exceptional magistra." He bared his teeth in a predatory grin. "I'll enjoy every lesson."

His eyes lit as he examined her, and she remembered she stood before him nude. She couldn't hold his gaze and dropped her eyes. The pattern engraved into the floor finally registered. "The lines form a sun with flaming rays. I hadn't noticed before."

"Yes. Our House is DeHelios. In the old form it means, 'of the sun' or 'bringer of light'."

"Ah. May I have my dress, please?"

"I prefer you naked."

"Ummm." She reached and gently tugged her gown from his loose grasp. While she slipped her dress over her head and settled it on her shoulders, Hel stepped into his pants. He gathered the rest of their clothing and her mynx coat and laid it across the dais.

"Let's get these baskets filled and to Bernard. I told him to meet us on the first floor chamber. Turn, I'll fasten you." His warm hands did a few hooks at the nape of her neck, then at her waist. When she pulled her hair over her shoulder, he nuzzled a kiss below her ear. "I'm not doing all of your hooks. I'll have this dress off you again, shortly."

What did he have in mind? More sex? While the idea wasn't without its appeal, she needed a little more recovery time—and a bath. At bare minimum, she needed a wash cloth. The results of their last encounter bathed her thighs. *I wonder if I could get pregnant?* She straightened. *Why hasn't this occurred to me before?* Probably because she hadn't had sex in over two years and her courses had been irregular to nonexistent in the years prior. *I'll need maiden's clover.* The thought of using the contraceptive herb brought a heaviness of heart. *I would like his child.* Strange—she had never had those thoughts with Klaran.

"My lady, my lord." Bernard's deep bow greeted them as they stepped off the mechanical lift. Echoes of "magistra," uttered in reverent voices accompanied his. Several of the townsmen stood alongside Bernard and began to remove the baskets filled with glowing crystal from the lift.

"I cannot describe my emotions when I saw the gray walls of the Torre Bianca gleam amber." Bernard seemed almost giddy in his happiness. "For the first time in years, you give us hope, Lady Adonia. Goddess, bless you, you give us hope."

Confronted with his fervent, joyous face, Adonia searched for an adequate reply. Her eyes sent an appeal toward Hel, but he simply stood and grinned like an idiot.

"Ah...glad to help," she stuttered. *Gah...glad to help? Great Mother.* Well, no one would accuse her of a polished tongue.

"I'm taking Nia to the subterranean grotto." Hel wrapped a warm hand around her upper arm and began to draw her away.

Bernard's eyebrows shot up. "Could she? When Lady Athena failed?"

"Yes, I believe so." Hel nodded and continued to lead her toward a small arched door at the far end of the chamber.

The indigo painted door opened onto a narrow stone stairway that wound down into darkness. A humid gust of hot air brushed her face. Two small lanterns hung on brackets fixed to the wall.

"Here." Hel handed her one lantern and kept the other for himself. He placed an amber diaman crystal inside each. Amplified by mirrors inside, each lantern cast a circle of light. Slipping past her, with a murmured, "Follow me," Hel began a descent into darkness.

"Remember the hot pool at the beginning of our journey? The small grotto?" Hel's voice and the scrape of their shoes on the steps echoed hollowly off the diaman crystal walls.

"Yes." I remember every second, every word, every touch...

"I am taking you to another. It is also the source of the heat in the tower. Torre Bianca sits on a thermal feature. Her walls have ducts to vent the rising hot air, though in the past they were little used."

As they descended further and further into blackness, the temperature rose. Condensation dampened the walls and slicked the steps. Soon moist tendrils of hair adhered to her cheeks and Adonia reached back to hold her hair off her neck. "It is hot down here."

"Yes…and we're here."

She followed Hel around a corner. An exotic and incredible sight spread before her. A huge lake of clear water covered the base of a vast natural cavern that extended beyond sight. Radiance filtered up through the water and played across the stone walls in ripples of green and gold. The walls themselves shone here and there with a luminous glow as if nature herself refused to hide her glory in darkness.

"Ohhh…Hel…never, I've never…" She had no words to

describe the splendor.

"Staggering, isn't it? Grotta D'oro is one of Nyth Uchel's best kept secrets."

Hel set his lantern on the rock floor and pulled Adonia into his arms. A gleam lit his gaze—one she had seen last in the Chambre Cristalle.

"What?" She eyed him suspiciously.

His busy hands freed her gown.

"I think you need a hot bath."

She nodded and pulled her dress over her head. "Umm-hmm. Is that all?"

"Perhaps. Probably. We'll see." Suddenly sober, Hel stepped back and started shrugging out of his clothes. Adonia didn't think she would ever tire of seeing his nude body. He entered the water and held a hand back toward her.

She stood on the shore and eyed his extended hand. "Perhaps. Probably. We'll see? Somehow, I'm not reassured."

He simply smiled. "Come."

She obeyed and took his hand.

"Mmm, the water feels wonderful." Though she stood waist-deep, she could clearly see her feet outlined in the green-gold light. "Where does the light come from this far underground?"

"Organisms live in this lake that interact chemically with the natural mineral deposits."

Adonia had lived her entire life in an arid desert. This much water was an unknown to her. The unknown made her uneasy. In a body of water this large, her brain suddenly produced images of flesh-eating aquatic snakes or acid-squirting mollusks. "Um, animal life or plant life?"

Hel walked further into the water and sank to his neck. "A little of each, I would imagine. Come here."

"Ah…I'm good, thanks."

His hand beckoned. "Nia."

With a grimace, she part walked and part dog-paddled her way to him. *It should be safe. He's the one with the dangly bits.*

Hel sat on a natural rock ledge and pulled her onto his lap, facing him. Inches from her face, his gaze lingered on her. She didn't trust the glint in his eyes. It didn't matter. The kisses he pressed to her mouth soon destroyed her ability for logical thought. She could feel the lips of her pussy grow fat with arousal. The bumps of his hard cock between them teased her with his desire. His mobile lips paused then drew back, and she opened her eyes. She turned her head to see what had captured his interest.

"Oh, no, no, no, no!" She flipped on his lap and tried to tear out of his arms. Just under the surface of the water, a brilliantly colored flutter signaled the approach of a living organism.

"Be still. You're frightening them."

"Them! I'm frightening *them?*" she squeaked, her legs and arms thrashing.

"The *miku amar* won't hurt you. Quite the opposite. Stop your flailing."

Hel's arm bound her back to his chest like an iron band. She'd little choice but to watch as two aquatic creatures, one indigo blue and the other fuchsia pink, bobbed in their direction. The size of Hel's fist, the brilliantly colored organisms propelled themselves through the clear water with contractions of multiple tentacles and ripples of delicate frilled edges. The pair floated in the water just out of reach, their intertwined tentacles waving in the subtle current.

"Be still and let them approach, Nia. They won't hurt you. Look." Hel extended his hand, palm up, and held it motionless. By slow increments, the iridescent blue creature approached and hovered over his palm. A tentacle dropped to wrap around Hel's thumb as others explored his fingers and wrist. With a shivering ripple, the creature lowered to fill his hand, the frills around its circumference fluttering rapidly. At Hel's low groan of pleasure, Nia tore her eyes from his hand to peer at his face. He wore an expression of relaxed bliss. "I'd forgotten how good that can feel." Hel nodded his head to the brilliant pink creature still holding in place just out of reach. "Hold your hand out. Invite her to you."

"No, thank you."

"Nia."

His tone brooked no disobedience. She extended a trembling arm and opened her hand cautiously. Long moments passed and the small pink *thing* floated, neither closer nor farther, its tentacles waving as if it were tasting the water.

"It won't come to me, Hel. Can I put my hand down?"

"It's not an *it*, Nia. That beautiful, delicate organism is a *she*. Give her some time. They are empathic creatures. She's literally as frightened as you are."

"Oh." Adonia relaxed against Hel. "Poor thing. If she's as frightened as me, then she's pretty scared." Somehow, that realization made all the difference and Adonia could feel her apprehension vanish. "What did you call them?"

"*Miku amar*. In the old *Engalian* form, their name translates as 'companions in love'. The pheromones we give off during arousal attract the *miku amar*. This pair has been here since I can remember."

With her arm extended to its fullest, she gently waved her fingers at the small creature. "Come here, pretty one. I'll try not to be frightened."

Slowly, with one tentative bobbing swoosh after another, the creature drew nearer and nearer until Adonia could feel the soft touch of a tentacle at the base of her thumb. The tickling pleasure was intense. With uneasy astonishment, she realized the impressions turned sensual. One after another, magenta pink tentacles feathered down onto her palm and traced lines of erotic thrill across her skin. The arousal her fear had killed rushed back. A yearning rose in her mind for a more intimate contact, for a complete *knowing*. As the female *miku amar* settled into the sensitive flesh of her palm, Adonia realized that the feelings emanated from the small creature.

"I thought she'd be slimy. She is delightful—petal soft and she vibrates. I think she's purring." Adonia couldn't help the smile that crossed her face. "You'd never believe where I feel it." Adonia glanced up at Hel.

He shook his head at her with a soft laugh. "I'd believe you. She experiences what you feel and shares those emotions with her mate. Through him, I know exactly what you are feeling. The blue male formed a life-bond with me when I was young. His female should have life-bonded with Athena. To her vast irritation, my wife never could entice the *miku amar* to her."

"Why do you suppose?"

"I don't know, Nia. The *miku amar* are telepathic empaths. Perhaps something in Athena repelled the female." Adonia saw all warmth leave Hel's eyes. The soft ripples of the male's frills stopped, and Hel stroked the back of the small creature with a gentle fingertip. "I brought Athena here twice when we were first joined. After the second time, my lady wife refused to return. She said she'd be damned if she'd have her character judged and found wanting by a primitive invertebrate."

Adonia felt a wave of melancholy. Were those Hel's feelings?

"I returned my male to this cavern. I would never separate him from his female. To live without the warmth of a mate is a lonely existence."

Adonia got another glimpse into the life Hel had lived. No matter that he'd had a wife and children, this man had known prolonged loneliness. "The *miku amar* can live out of the water?"

"Yes. They are symbiots. They need a human bond to complete their reproductive cycle. When your empathic bond is complete, your female can live on your life force indefinitely—in or out of water."

"What completes the bond?"

The wicked gleam sparking in Hel's eyes put Adonia on guard.

"Your orgasm. Specifically, your orgasm with the human her male has life-bonded to."

"You."

His teeth nipped delicately at the crook of her neck. "Umm-hmm. Me. Turn around, Nia."

CHAPTER THIRTEEN

Hel rocked back in his chair at the dining table and smiled at Nia. Her shy smile in return was the first overt emotion she'd displayed since leaving the grotto and a stunning second round of sex.

"To experience your partner's emotions, to feel their pleasure combined with yours, adds intensity to sex. Now you know why we prize the *miku amar*, and keep them secret," Hel said.

Amusement lit her eyes. "Yes, the entire population of Verdantia would storm the Grotta D'oro if they knew." She ducked her head and shifted in her chair. Her hands rubbed her upper arms. "I found the experience somewhat...overwhelming. I hope no one heard."

Hel dropped his head back and laughed. His delightful Nia was a screamer, and the cavern's acoustics amplified all sound. He could reassure her they were too far underground to be heard, but he wasn't certain that was the truth, and he would hate lying to her.

Had it not been for his *miku amar*, he would never have guessed at the roiling emotions that seethed beneath her diffident exterior. Surprise, confusion, inadequacy, hope—all cycled through her mind as companions to an overwhelming sense of curiosity. *No fear. That's good.* He wondered what she felt from him through her fledgling bond with the pink female. *Hopefully, immense satisfaction with my healer.*

Warmer than body-temperature, the gel-like *miku amar* cradled his cock and balls in a gentle tease of an embrace. Always a seeker of heat and attracted to Hel's sexual pheromones, the blue male had entwined itself about his genitals and anchored itself with tentacles that wrapped his upper thighs, buttock cheeks and waist with elongated, paper-thin tendrils of immense strength. It was disturbingly comfortable. Hel laughed inwardly at his mental image of his cock and balls suspended in a bath of warm, supportive gelatin—definitely a pleasant feeling. Athena had snorted derisively at his constant semi-arousal—as if that male family trait was a curse. If blessed with a welcoming partner, his insatiable libido was a boon. Hel grimaced. One more reason he'd returned his *miku amar* to Grotta D'oro in years past. Athena's perfunctory cooperation never qualified as welcoming, and he'd confined his interaction with her to the minimum required by the rites. Shifting in his chair, Hel considered Nia. *I wonder what part of Nia's anatomy her female has chosen to nest on?*

"We wait for Lord Ramsey and Steffania? I've not seen any sign of them all day. Where have they been?"

"I asked Lord Ramsey and Steffania to re-establish the western perimeter. That required they empower a number of diaman crystals prior to leaving. I... Ah, here they are now."

Hel congratulated himself on assigning Ramsey the rooms furthest from the family living areas. Otherwise, he was certain Nia would have heard them. Ramsey and Steffania enjoyed a robust— and vocal—intimate life. A wry smile fleeted across his lips. Before he finished with Nia, she would be making similar sounds.

A boneless Steffania oozed through the door and molded into a chair with a slight wince. Through half-lidded golden eyes, she regarded them with a somnolent smile and a nod. Ramsey followed close on her heels and sprawled, loose-limbed, into a chair next to her. Hel watched with amusement as Ram picked up one of Steffania's hands, kissed the back of it and lowered it to his lap. Her wrists bore the marks of a rope.

"So DeKieran…do you leave in the morning or do you require another day?"

"We applied ourselves. We leave in the morning," Ram murmured, deadpan. "I ran into Bernard, and he promised to have supplies enough for two weeks packed for us. He seemed to think it would be sufficient."

A light rap on the door announced the entrance of a servant bearing a small haunch of some animal and more potatoes.

"You can leave it on the table; we'll serve ourselves," Hel instructed. With a nod of respect, the servant did as he requested and left the four of them alone in the dining room.

Ramsey eyed the platter suspiciously. "That bears an uncanny resemblance to lunch and lunch bore an uncanny resemblance to breakfast. I'm going to come away from here hating potatoes." He helped himself and Steffania to small portions.

Hel snorted softly. He shared Ram's feelings. "If you get lucky, you will find some game to supplement your diet."

He served Adonia and then himself. As they ate, he and Ram discussed the trip to the western border. Neither woman uttered a word.

Ram swallowed a long draught of brew and placed his mug back on the table. "Well, at least the drink is palatable." The old chair creaked as Ram rocked back and straightened his booted legs, crossing them at the ankles. Hel wondered what went on behind those wolf-like eyes that examined him so thoughtfully.

"Did you discover anything written on the tower?" Ram said.

The sour taste of frustration filled Hel's mouth. He shook his head. "No. When I left to find Adonia, the men had scoured the first two outside levels and were extending the scaffolding further.

I met a similar lack of success inside."

A crooked smile tipped Ram's lips. "And what did you do to exhaust our lady healer?"

Hel followed Ramsey's gaze. *Ah, the poor girl.* Nia's cheek rested in the crook of her arm on the table next to her plate with her left hand closed loosely around her fork. A slice of potato dangled precariously from a tine. Her eyelashes curved in black commas above the sharp edges of her cheekbones and her rib cage rose and fell on soft inhales and exhales. Hel pushed his chair back from the table and rose, as did Ramsey. "I think this is a signal for an early night. I'll see you in the morning before you leave."

Hel slipped the fork from Nia's hand and picked her slight body up easily. She never roused—not even when he stripped her and laid her in his bed. A smile tipped his lips, and he traced a caress over the pink *miku amar. I thought you'd nestle there. She's not going to like that, you know.* He climbed in next to Nia and pulled her into his arms. The intimacy of bare skin on skin soothed his soul and the quiet of Nyth Uchel settled a blanket of strange serenity over him. Wry amusement tugged at his mouth. Nia would, no doubt, disbelieve him, but he couldn't resurrect a memory of a time his bed had held an adult woman. Athena had insisted on her own quarters. Once his younger self had shed his disillusionment about their marriage, he'd welcomed the solitude.

Memories of his daughter and son's little bodies nested against him in this bed returned him to happier days, and, for the first time in years, Hel welcomed the bittersweet recollections with a faint smile. His children would have adored Nia. It seemed irresponsible to picture a life with her when the whole of Verdantia faced an unnamed darkness—and yet the woman in his arms promised more than simple survival and a loveless future. His eyes wandered the face of the precious being snugged tight against his chest. "You were wonderful today. You are my touchstone for hope tomorrow will be better. I haven't felt so in many years." Of course, she gave no response. "We must defeat this encroaching darkness. I will have that tomorrow with you, Nia." Hel closed his eyes and allowed sleep to claim him.

Adonia jerked the material of her long gown out from under the ball of her foot and mentally castigated the gods-be-damned alpha male who had sentenced her to impractical dresses—though her little-indulged feminine side secretly preened at the glorious clothes. The moss green and gold ensemble Hel had laced her into this morning, which her meager breasts threatened to fall out of, befitted a woman of leisure—not one whose long strides tangled in the sweeping skirts and imperiled her at every turn. Only her excellent balance and the sudden presence of Hel's strong hand under her armpit prevented a stumble on the stone steps leading to the portrait gallery. Hel strode down a marble hall lined with loosely swathed paintings hung on walls paneled in exotic woods. Hoisting up her damned skirts, she tromped after him. He stopped before a massive picture hung high on the wall. Its storage drapery lay on the floor, folded into a neat square.

Hel gestured with his arm. "The first Tetriarch of Verdantia, Isolde DeCorvus, Federago DeHelios and Agentio DeLorcha."

Adonia examined the life-size portrait. Framed in ornate, heavy gilt, the lavish interior of a library or private office held the figures of two handsome males in antique dress standing protectively behind a seated woman. The physical features of Isolde DeCorvus duplicated those Adonia had seen in her mirror this morning—with one difference. The regal woman's fierce gaze could command armies. The skill of the artist or the vibrancy of the woman herself imbued the two-dimensional artwork with her force of character. The subject in the painting looked as though she'd never had a moment of hesitancy in her life.

"I agree we have the same features," Adonia murmured. *That's where the similarity ends.* "But, I don't understand why you show me this."

"You hold yourself too cheaply. After seeing this portrait, you cannot doubt your aristocratic heritage. You descend from the first of Verdantia's powerful queens. Your will commands vast energy—energy that up until now has lain quiescent. I want you to become comfortable with the thought of using that power. No more hiding from who you are and what you are capable of."

Hel's words resonated within her and challenged the uncertainty buried deep in her heart. Presented with convincing proof of her lineage, Adonia set aside the last residual of the Mother's Acolytes' indoctrination and embraced *who* she was. *I am not an ordinary Oshtesh woman. I am highborn, a descendant of **the** Isolde DeCorvus.* Nascent pride swelled within and she stood taller and straighter. She examined the portrait of her ancestor more closely.

"You need the confidence and sense of self that attend the knowledge of your lineage. When we work the Great Rite, it is easy to become lost in the swamping arousal and overwhelming presence of the *Senzienza*. Unless you hold fast to your identity, the tempest will consume your mind."

He'd surprised her. "The Great Rite? You are going to work the Great Rite with *me* as your partner?" The insane cries from the magistra in Sylvan Mintoth, the one whose mind had lost her anchor, echoed in Adonia's memory. Fear robbed her legs of their strength.

"Yes. Just as soon as I familiarize you with the lesser rites." Her face must have revealed her thoughts. The corners of his mouth tipped and his knuckle brushed her cheek. "We will work up to it."

Her shoulders sagged and relief almost collapsed her knees. "Yes," Adonia said. "We have until spring, after all." *Months. Half a year…no need to panic. I have months.* Even so, her heart threatened to pound out of her chest.

"I will have you ready in two months. We will attempt the Great Rite then." Hel's gaze caught and held hers.

"Two months." Her knees deserted her and hard wooden panels lifted her dress to bunch at her waist as she slid down the gallery wall.

"Nia!" Hel caught her up against his hard body before she reached the floor. She buried her face in his chest. Each hand clutched a fistful of material at the back of his tunic. She sucked in air in needy gasps. Hel cupped her face and raised it to his. "So we skip a few steps. I have faith in you. You can do this." For a fleeting moment, his gray eyes warmed her with the confidence shining from them. "You faced down a mutated horror on foot and sent arrow after arrow into its face as it leapt to devour you—you can do this."

She stared at him. *It isn't the same thing at all. It takes seven years to achieve the status of* magistra—*not two months.* His faith in her was misplaced—again. From his frown, the doubt invading her heart appeared on her face.

"I am House DeHelios. With *me* as your partner, you can do this." He shook his head impatiently at her continued blank expression. "House DeHelios has never boasted of the intimate link those of our genetic heritage share with our Mother, but it is well-known and an undeniable truth. Suspicion and envy of our unique bond with Verdantia created the original schism between Nyth Uchel and Sylvan Mintoth. The other noble houses envied and feared us, afraid that by having both the rule of the planet and an intense connection with our Mother, House DeHelios held too much power. We narrowly avoided a civil war." Hel traced a finger across her cheek. "By the High Enclave's scale, my strength as a magister cannot be measured—none of the men and women born of House DeHelios could be calibrated. I agree with those who name me arrogant because House DeHelios has always been something other, something *more*. Beauty, with me at your side, you need not fear the Great Rite, and must I remind you that you and I share the same lineage?"

Her brain fought for comprehension. That *he* was some uber-powerful magister, she could believe—but *her*?

"You said you wished to try some of the healing rites on those afflicted with the *fading* this morning. Do you still want my help?" Hel raised an eyebrow.

Adonia barely registered his question. Her eyes left his face to stare sightlessly down the hall toward the sickroom as her mind labored for coherent thought.

Hel caught her attention with a murmured, "Nia?"

"Umm?"

"My time to attend you in the sickroom is limited. If you want my help, we need to start." Hel opened his arm and indicated their direction.

Adonia nodded and followed him mindlessly. She shook off her paralysis of thought when they entered the sickroom and Sara greeted her. *Finally, a place where I am comfortable...where I am confident of my skill, more or less.*

"My lord, Healer, good morning. Maddie brought a number of diaman crystals for your use. Shall we begin with the rites or would you prefer to start with the more conventional treatments?"

"We will begin with the rites, Sara." Adonia nodded briskly and moved to sit next to the woman she and Sara had agreed was most in need.

Hel rested his hand on her shoulder. "What do you require from me, Nia?"

The tempest of emotions swirling through her calmed as she ordered her thoughts. "I know what is supposed to happen. I will open my mind to our Mother and using Her connection to all living things on our planet, I will direct my energy into my patient, locate their illness and repair their body. If I need more power, I draw from the diaman crystals."

The slight smile never left Hel's face and he nodded. "Yes, that is what I understand, though I've never used the healing magicks with any great success. It's not an aptitude I have."

"But you can help ground me on the meta-physical plane?"

Adonia sighed with relief at the slight smile on his face.

"Yes. That I can do."

She couldn't help returning his smile and confidence flooded her. A gift from Hel through their *miku amar,* she thought. "Thank you," escaped on a rush of breath. "It helps to know I am not alone in this."

His forefinger traced her upper lip then fell to his side. "I will always be here for you, Nia." He pulled up a chair next to her and placed a large warm hand on her thigh.

She pulled a deep breath into her lungs and released it at a measured rate, setting a rhythm she maintained, as thought by thought, she purged her mind of extraneous ideas. The words of mantras she'd memorized but had never thought to use marched forward in disciplined precision, as if soldiers arranged in lines of battle. Her sense of the present evaporated. At last, she severed the final tether to her physical self and floated, pure spirit, bathed in a luminous atmosphere of golden light. The possibility threatened that she could be lost on this plane. Her aetheric being cried out in panic and Hel was there, strong and steadfast, her anchor. Her panic subsided as she reaffirmed her purpose. *I am a High Enclave medica. I have dedicated my life to the healing arts and for once, I don't need to stand on the sidelines reduced to herbal remedies.*

The malaise suffocating the life from her patient below revealed itself graphically. Dark threads of corruption smothered three of the body's seven centers of life. The woman's throat, heart and navel appeared as pustulating balls of disease with spears of darkness spooling outward into her veins.

The central darkness drew Adonia inexorably, and she laid the palms of her hands on the corruption obscuring her patient's heart. A deluge of despair, desolation, hopelessness and anguish ravaged Adonia's soul, eating all joy, hope, and health. The ravenous hunger consuming the woman beneath her opened its maw and engulfed Adonia in malevolent blackness.

"Daughter of our blood, hear us. Our foe is strong but you are stronger."

A pure golden sphere centered itself on Adonia's forehead and blazed a radiant message of love, compassion and courage into the spreading darkness. The face in the portrait seared through Adonia's mind and for an instant, she knew with certainty Isolde DeCorvus spoke to her through centuries of time.

"Daughter of our blood, have courage. The Great Deceiver cannot abide the light of love. Armor yourself in its truth, and you cannot be overcome."

Warm memories flooded her. The smiling face of her father appeared before her child-self. The memory of evenings spent wrapped in his loving arms halted the chill eroding her soul. Her mother's kisses as she settled Adonia into bed and the laughter of her friends and companions as they practiced their archery, the wonderful sense of belonging and companionship, began to repulse the corrosive desolation enveloping her.

"Look to Her own for strength. Above all others, we will not abandon you to the darkness."

'Look to Her own....' Adonia's metaphysical being reached for Hel. Immediately, his masculine presence of steadfast strength surrounded her. Courage filled her, and she confronted the black corruption boiling out of her patient. She hurled a challenge into the darkness. Hopeless emptiness swarmed in answer, and Adonia clutched fiercely to images of joy and love and light. She fired the emotions into the darkness as if arrows from her bow, but her weapons fell harmlessly against the black void that advanced to rend her very soul. She screamed her agony into the nothingness.

"Stand behind us, daughter of our blood."

For an eternal moment, a blazing sphere of warm gold light shielded her from the ravening dark. Its warmth strengthened her, and armored in its light, she rose on trembling limbs and strode forward into the fearsome blackness.

She faced the dark onslaught for countless eternities, certain any second she would fail under the relentless attack. For every rebuff she dealt the corruption, the darkness rebounded with redoubled ferocity. For time without end, she clung tenaciously to one speck of light—a beachhead shining through an ocean of despair. A lifetime passed before she felt a weakening in the furious assault, a withdrawal of the avaricious hunger.

Adonia looked down to see that radiance shone through the fingers of her hands where they pressed to her patient's chest. Satisfaction blended with an exhaustion of soul. Much more needed to be done before the fight to save this woman would be won—and the woman was but one of many in dire need. Adonia withdrew her battered spirit and, following the anchor Hel created for her, she settled back into her physical body.

The body she re-entered no longer sat on a chair. Hel's arms supported her and cradled her, childlike, on his lap. The *thu-thump* of his heart beat rhythmically into her ear where it rested on his chest. When had he picked her up? Had she collapsed? She had no knowledge of it. She opened her eyes. His concerned gaze softened to an emotion much warmer when she managed a weak smile.

"Thank you. Your strength filled me when my need was great. I would have been lost without you."

The corners of his mouth lifted. "You're welcome." Hel's eyes studied her face. "You are the answer to a prayer, Nia. Your strength amazes me."

She shook her head slowly. "I had…help." For the moment, she felt compelled to keep the other presence to herself. It seemed too bizarre. Perhaps she had just imagined a long-dead queen strode into battle beside her.

Adonia straightened by degrees, soaking in the comfort and safety Hel's body offered. Long moments passed before she could put together the words she wanted to say. "We don't fight normal disease. Our foe is a ravenous void. It seeks to engulf all life, and its strength is dreadful. Your conjecture was correct. We don't fight for the bodily health of our people. We battle for their *anima*, their spiritual essence." A shudder ran through her. "Cold. I'm so cold."

She wrapped her arms around Hel's shoulders and held him tightly, trying to thaw the ice piercing her soul with the warmth of his body. The nature of the horror she had come face-to-face with shattered her. She couldn't prevent her soft keens and the steady roll of tears. "I think we battle for *Her* soul—for Verdantia."

"Yes. I suspected as much." His broad hand caressed her back with soothing, repetitive strokes. "Don't bear the horror alone, Nia. Speak to me."

"I am shaken on a profound level. I cannot bear to confront that abomination again, but I must. I am more terrified of the consequences if I don't."

"I know." The tips of his fingers raised her chin. His thumb wiped the tears from her cheeks and in his gray eyes she saw infinite weariness and recognition. He did know her fear. For years, Hel had faced this malevolence alone. She had confronted the darkness once and was ready to flee.

"I'm such a coward." She ducked her head back into his chest and tightened her hold.

He hummed a low disagreement. His broad fingers ran through her scalp in a gentle massage. "You are one of the bravest people I know."

She shook her head vigorously.

He sighed and then straightened. "You are particularly vulnerable to this enemy due to the astral plane on which it attacks. A good medica is hyper-sensitive on a psychic level, and you are an exceptional medica. I wish I could do this for you. I can't…but know everything I am is at your service. Simply ask."

His generosity of spirit unraveled her. How could she give this man anything but her utmost? Adonia compelled her trembling to stop and straightened in his hold. She forced a smile of pure bravado. "Then there is no force on this planet that can stop us."

Adonia slid off Hel's thighs and stood on wobbly legs. A cascade of spent diaman crystal bounced to the floor. Hel must have put them in her lap. Another thing she hadn't noticed. She had pulled the stored power from them as well. The rough surface of the gray crystal weighted her hands as she gathered the scattered hunks, and the meaning of the pattern of shadows on the floor registered. She had come to the sickroom with Hel that morning. From the light shining in through the western windows, afternoon advanced into evening. "I've been here for most of the day! I'd not realized the passage of time."

"Yes." Hel cast her a significant glance. "You waged a fierce battle, Nia. I felt the repercussions of the onslaught on the aetheric level, but look at your patient."

Her patient's skin had turned to a healthy pink. Gone was the sick yellow pallor. The woman drew easy, regular breaths. Adonia bent down to examine her further, and with the thrill of accomplishment, lifted her face to Hel. "She looks better."

"Better? I'm certain she will make a full recovery. I couldn't have said that before."

Adonia felt her cheeks pink with pleasure at the approval in Hel's direct gaze.

"Do you have instructions for Sara before we go to Torre Bianca?"

"Torre Bianca?"

"Yes, your schooling in the lesser rites begins now. I know you are weary, but we must make use of every moment we have. I'll try not to make it too onerous."

Adonia recognized the implication in Hel's heavy-lidded gaze and crooked smile. *Sex.* Masculine admiration mixed with sexual arousal and impatience flooded her—Hel's emotions. Distinguishing his feelings from her own was becoming easier. His emotions tasted masculine. The pink *miku amar* softened and purred in reaction, and Nia's nipples hardened in response to the tease.

Adonia wished the little female had settled somewhere less titillating than directly between the petals of her labia. While Hel looked on with barely suppressed hilarity, she'd tried that morning to coax the delicate creature into moving somewhere less intimate—with no success. She supposed the *miku amar* enjoyed the pheromones and other physical results of Adonia's bodily arousal. It would explain the animal's amorous behavior. One elongated tentacle nursed her clit ever so gently, and the cilia on the female's underbelly provided a continuous minute tickle on the most sensitive of her flesh. Adonia could feel the lips of her sex swell and slick—the same condition in which she awoke this morning in Hel's great bed. Adonia hoped the dear little creature had not endured the desolation of spirit that had devastated *her* for long hours today. Regardless, the female now thrummed happily in a warm nest between Adonia's legs—a distraction she endeavored to ignore.

Adonia motioned Sara over and conferred with the nurse for some time before turning to the commanding figure standing patiently at her side. "I'm ready."

"I hope so." Hel took her arm and escorted her from the sickroom, a basket of spent diaman crystals held in his other hand. Adonia's mind shied away from the implications of his statement.

CHAPTER FOURTEEN

Hel turned the heavy metal key in the door lock of the chamber he euphemistically referred to as "the game room." A gentle push swung the ponderous arched door fully open to reveal several stout bondage frames placed throughout a spacious area devoid of any sort of decoration—unless one considered the whips, floggers, spreaders, hooks and harness that covered one windowless wall decoration. He heard Nia gasp at the revelation of the room's contents. Elaborate cupboards lined another wall and held smaller items like dildos, butt plugs, gags, blindfolds, cockrings and clamps, but Nia couldn't know that. One of the cabinets also held his copy of the *Libre de* Diamantorre, the great book containing the Great and Lesser Rites. He had come for the book, though Nia's reaction to the room's interior intrigued him.

He turned to his wide-eyed partner. "Do you have any experience with sexual discipline?"

Nia stood silently for so long it was on the tip of Hel's tongue to repeat his question. Finally, she lifted her chin in a defiant gesture. "I lived among everyday people with simple tastes. I have no experience with anything other than man on top, woman on the bottom."

"Your lovers were not adventurous."

She slid him an uneasy glance. "Lover. Not lovers. One lover…and then not often."

He cocked his head in surprise at her answer. "How long were you together?"

"Over ten years." She spoke her soft answer to the floor. "When I left Sh'r Un Kree, Klaran came with me. We were betrothed."

"You left him?"

"No. He left me."

"Then he was a fool."

She jerked her head up. "It wasn't Klaran's fault. I, ah, I…" She inhaled deeply. "I'd always been preoccupied with my medicines, and then we fought the Haarb…" Nia closed her eyes and her voice came out thready. "Klaran said I was hard and unwomanly."

"No." A flash of fury blazed through him at the forlorn acceptance in her voice, and he pulled Nia into him violently, trapping her wrists behind her with one hand and holding her face up to his with the other. She closed her eyes, but otherwise didn't resist.

"Look at me, Nia," he snapped. When her brown eyes met his, Hel stared as if he could ingrain his words in her mind with the force of his gaze. "You are not hard *enough*. You care too much for everyone but yourself. You risked your soul today for a patient to whom you've never spoken. As for womanly?" He ground the thickening length of his erection into her soft abdomen. "You are woman enough for the Prince of Nyth Uchel."

Nia gave a sob and caught her lower lip between her teeth. Her gaze slid to the side.

"Do I need to punish you again to remind you of the consequences when you question your worth?" Her eyes flared and, for a moment, her body softened against his. *I think I do.*

A soft laugh escaped his lips. "So that's how it is. All right, my beauty. You will get what you're asking for."

Hel hauled her over to a square frame set waist high. "Bend over. Lie face down on the supports. Spread your legs."

He could feel his cock getting harder as he fastened each slim ankle to a corner of the block with a padded cuff and then did the same with her wrists above her head. She watched him without sound until he stood behind her and gathered her long skirts over her waist to expose her bare legs and ass.

"Are you going to whip me?" She had craned her head over her shoulder and met his eyes. Those brown glimpses into her soul held more curiosity than fear.

"No, Beauty. I am going to spank you with a paddle until your buttocks are as pink as the *miku amar* nestled between your legs, and then I am going to take you to the Chambre Cristalle, tie you spread-eagled on your back and fuck you until all Nyth Uchel hears you screaming my name."

Hel selected a broad, smooth wooden paddle from a cabinet behind him.

A long shudder ran through her body. "I read the entire *Libre de* Diamantorre. I don't remember a lesser rite starting like this." Before Nia hid her cheek against the platform, Hel saw her lips twitch.

Smack! "Impudent girl." She yelped, and he smacked her twice more where the cup of her buttocks met her thighs. *Smack! Smack!*

"Oh!" She twisted her hips in an unsuccessful attempt to evade his next three paddles. *Smack, smack, smack.* "Please, Hel, please."

"Please what, Beauty?"

"Stop. Please, stop."

"No. I don't think you want me to stop." He slipped a broad finger through the moisture glistening between the swollen folds hiding the entrance to her hot interior. Hel had tickled the female *miku* into moving up to rest on Nia's lower abdomen. The hard nub of Nia's clit slipped back and forth as the pad of his finger slowly pressed and circled, lubricated by her generous arousal.

"That doesn't mean anything. I've been like that all day. It's the *miku amar*. She does...she does...she...she...aggh! Why wouldn't she move for me?"

The needy moan echoing off the diaman walls and the quivering globes of Nia's red buttocks went straight to his painfully hard cock tortured by the blue *miku's* rhythmic massage of his balls.

He knew it wasn't kind. He wasn't feeling kind. He baited her. "She does what, Nia? What does she do?" *Smack!* "Nurse your clit? Bathe your soft pussy in warm caresses that never stop?" *Smack!*

"Yes," she sobbed.

"Do her tentacles enter your most private places and tickle you?" *Smack!*

"Stop, Hel," she whispered.

"If you meant that, I would—but you don't, do you? I think you like receiving discipline as much as I like administering it." *Smack!* "The pain feeds some masochistic part of you that whispers, *'you deserve it'*." *Smack!* "Bad girl." *Smack!* When her only response was a muffled groan, he laughed, low and wicked. "It definitely satisfies me to deliver it."

Nia yowled and jerked her hips in time to four more rapidly delivered strikes of the paddle. Her breaths came in heavy pants. "Ohhh, Goddess, I need to come," she groaned.

Hel grunted and threw the paddle down next to her head. *Poor girl. She sounds desperate.* After the day's earlier events, combined with what he knew was to come, it would be cruel to provoke her further. It was the work of moments to unhook her gown to her waist and un-cuff her ankles and wrists. He pulled her lithe form into his arms for a punishing kiss then murmured against Nia's lips, "Fly up those stairs. Get rid of the dress and lie on your back on the dais."

"Where will you be?"

"Right behind you. And, Nia…you don't want me to catch you."

With wild eyes and a chirrup of alarm, Nia gathered her skirts and fled, taking the stairs two at a time before disappearing into the Chambre Cristalle. Hel pulled the *Libre de* Diamantorre from its cupboard and held it under one arm while he closed and locked the 'game room' door. With a snarl of desire, he loosed the predator that always lurked just beneath his veneer of domestication and vaulted up the steps after Nia.

She was climbing onto the dais as he prowled through the door, her dress a puddle of color on the chamber floor. "Fasten those corner cuffs around your ankles then lay back." He watched her as he laid the diaman crystals in the grooves around the center slab. She hissed when her brightly colored buttocks contacted the cold rock, but otherwise she obeyed him exactly. He stripped his clothes off rapidly, leaving them in an untidy pile and strode to the head of the dais.

"Your cock and balls are blue." The brown eyes examining him widened further. "You've, ah, gained in…girth."

Hel barely restrained a snort of laughter. "Yes, and your pussy is hot pink and undulating. Like you, this gods-be-damned creature has had me semi-aroused all day. Are you beginning to understand why the *miku amar* are called companions in love?" She nodded silently. "Stretch your arms above your head, Beauty."

He cuffed one wrist to each corner of the dais and pulled the ties taut. The bindings allowed Nia little movement. With a satisfied grunt, he moved to kneel between her outstretched legs.

The hard stone bit into his knees but he welcomed the distraction from his over-eager cock. The ill-behaved organ jerked and wept in anticipation of plumbing Nia's moist inner core. "Now, your first formal lesson, the fourth level rite for kinetic power. Repeat after me…."

Adonia found concentrating on the words shaped by his delicious lips impossible. Perhaps the wild light in his storm-gray eyes promising forbidden wickedness shattered her focus—or the throbbing of her buttocks spread-eagled on the dais. Always, his sculptured body fascinated her. But, all of those faded into nothingness when the plush head of his heavy cock began a slow repetitive stroke from her clit to the entrance of her wet sheath— and then the real torture began. The pink *miku amar* elongated impossibly and slid between the cheeks of her ass. Its gentle probe of her anus morphed into full penetration from a rubbery, pulsing tentacle. Several more crept into her moist channel, creating an insidious tickle.

"Hel, I can't hold on. It's too extreme."

"Concentrate, Beauty. I promise whatever you feel now only intensifies as we delve into the more complex rites. Master your body. Control your arousal. And, Nia…don't climax without permission."

Adonia shuddered at the expression on Hel's face. She'd seen the same on great hunting cats as they closed on their victim. She'd become prey. Gathering the shattered pieces of her self-control, Adonia choked out the phrases Hel snarled into her face for what seemed an eternity. She managed to keep her climax at bay—until he penetrated her.

The sear of her over-full sheath stretching to receive his *miku*-enhanced cock knocked her arousal down just enough to prevent instant climax. The tissue of her inner channel throbbed in protest to his invasion. Hilted inside her, Hel stilled, his face mere inches above hers. His eyes, framed by a thick fall of almost black hair, burned with demonic light. Regular explosions of his breath washed her face with his hoarse enunciations of the rite.

Then, the *miku amar* made her presence known. Within Adonia's sheath and back passage the creature's rhythmic pulsations intensified. A tsunami of sexual sensation swamped her, a combination of both hers and Hel's. Suddenly, every nerve in her pussy, clit and anus quivered with electric excitement. If Hel moved—at all—she was gone. With a vicious growl ripped from his gut, Hel withdrew and slammed home—and she lost it.

"I can't...coming! I'm coming!" In her extremis, her back arched and strained against her bindings, lifting both their bodies from the surface of the dais, holding them suspended for untold minutes. She barely recognized when Hel's guttural cries combined with hers. Pleasure unlike any she had known, raped her mind of conscious thought and she blacked out.

"Nia?" Warm lips pressed to hers. *Hel.* "Nia? Come back to me, Beauty."

Disoriented, she fluttered her eyelids. Bright light flashed through. She kept her eyes closed, unwilling to abandon the maternal cocoon enfolding her mind. The motherly presence slipped away as awareness infiltrated her senses. "Mmm-hmm."

Adonia lay in Hel's lap, his arms wrapped about her. The fine material of his clothes caressed her bare skin. *I am nude.* She didn't care. She wrapped her arms around his torso and snuggled into the velvety softness of his tunic. *He's become my shelter from the storm.* The thought wandered into her mind as she lay against his hard body, her own rising and falling with his breaths. *I would willingly spend a lifetime with this man.* The deep thrum of his throaty laugh tickled the ear she pressed to his chest.

"I know your connection with our Mother is unusually strong; so, I tell myself, each time, to expect the extraordinary. Even so, the results of our pairing continue to astonish me," Hel stated on a laugh.

"Mmm-hmm."

Hel's arms tightened around her as she burrowed deeper into his hold. Again, his chest rumbled in her ear with low amusement, and he shifted her in his arms. "Get up, Healer, or I'll dump you on the unforgiving stone floor currently wearing a hole in my ass."

His words penetrated her comfortable haze. "Better yours than mine," Adonia mumbled under her breath and opened her eyes. She blinked, and then shielded them with one hand until she could adjust to the radiant light. Everything in the Chambre Cristalle glowed—the dais, the floors, the walls and the chunks of diaman crystal—especially the chunks of diaman crystal.

"Is this lightshow typical?"

In an effortless show of strength, Hel picked her off his lap and deposited her butt onto the shimmering floor. Her tender flesh objected, and she struggled to rise. In one fluid movement, Hel stood and held a hand down to assist Adonia to her feet. "No. Nothing associated with you is normal."

I'm abnormal? Maybe trained magistrae didn't pass out every time they performed a rite. Maybe they weren't as… enthusiastic, or as loud? She didn't know. The *Libre de* Diamantorre gave only the words to the rites. It didn't go into behavior during them. Embarrassment colored her face, and Adonia suddenly felt her nudity where she hadn't a moment before. Well…nude, if you didn't count the *miku amar* nested between her legs like a vibrant pink thong.

"Hey." Hel gathered her into his arms and raised her face to his. He pressed a warm kiss on her. "Unusual in the best possible way." Interspersed with nibbles on her lips, he murmured against her mouth, "You are a gift from our Mother, and you could not have arrived at a better time."

Adonia sighed inwardly at his reassurance and melted into his hold. "I am glad I please you."

"You do please me, but…" His low growl burst her bubble of contentment. "You disobeyed me. You came without permission. Don't think it escaped my notice."

"I couldn't hold on any longer."

"Then I need to motivate you to try harder."

Nia clamped her mouth closed on the retort that flesh could only bear so much. She couldn't do any better, no matter the motivation. Hel picked up her folded dress and held it open for her. She placed a hand on his shoulder for balance and gracefully stepped into the full skirt. When Hel had seated the gown on her shoulders, he gathered her hair and draped it forward over one shoulder before beginning to close the fastenings. She tipped her head slightly to catch his eyes. "What sort of motivation?" she asked cautiously, thinking of the many foreign instruments in the chamber just below.

Hel must have recognized where her thoughts led her. His arms wrapped her, and he pulled her close to him. His teeth nipped at the hollow where her neck met her shoulders, then his tongue and lips soothed the bite. "Shall I tie you to the X-frame and see how many orgasms I can give you before your legs collapse? Perhaps then it will be easier for you to endure the arousal that accompanies the rites."

Adonia gasped. "I'm not…I don't think…" His nips and kisses around her shoulders and neck sent chills down her spine and she could feel her nipples harden. "I can't possibly come again this soon."

His low laugh did nothing to reassure her. "Did I say it would be soon? You have something to look forward to tomorrow… or the day after… or the day after that."

Adonia didn't respond. What could she say? She acknowledged silently that her heart and body belonged to Hel to do with as he wished. She didn't mind. The uncertain future now offered her a place, and someone to whom she might finally belong.

CHAPTER FIFTEEN

Adonia took the glowing lantern Hel handed her as they left the Chambre Cristalle and stepped into velvet darkness. The chamber's radiance had obscured the fact that night had fallen.

"I have a favor to ask." Hel's deep voice reverberated off the diaman walls.

"You must know I'll do whatever you ask of me." She offered him a shy smile with her soft reply.

"And that knowledge makes me weigh my every request." His eyes studied her and then his arm surrounded her waist to hug her to him. She felt his rib-cage expand and contract in a long sigh, and he rested his chin on the top of her head. "Goddess knows you've done enough today, but I need your help in searching the upper levels of the tower for those engraved words A'rken referred to. I cannot waste a single day."

Adonia pulled back enough to see his face. "Of course, but it would seem the more eyes the better."

"Hmm, yes. Bernard and several townsmen and women are searching the lower levels again and more yet search the walls outside, but the Chambre Cristalle and the three floors below have always been off-limits to all but family. I would prefer it remain that way. There is enough coarse speculation about what goes on up here without revealing certain… ah…" Hel grimaced.

Adonia swallowed a sputter of laughter. "Yes. I understand. The *room*. Certainly, I will help you. I'm glad you consider me family."

Hel snorted softly. "With reservations. I don't feel at all brotherly toward you."

At his wry comment, she threw a glance at him. His infectious grin captured her and flooded her with warmth—not the heat of arousal or the physical warmth from his large body—rather, an inner glow of shared camaraderie and friendship the like of which she hadn't felt since her days with the Oshtesh. She felt included and necessary and, oh, *valued*. Yes, she'd use that word. Her mind shied from the term love. *He feels something for me. I know he does…but what?*

"Follow me, Nia, and mind the stairs. They are worn here."

She and Hel descended six long flights of steps separated by spacious landings. Human voices and activity on the lower floors of Torre Bianca filtered up faintly from the central gallery separated by the railing that surrounded the landing. Hel set his lantern down on the stone floor before another huge, wood-paneled door set into the stone on heavy metal hinges, the door a match of the two above. Turning an ornate key into the heavy lock, tumblers clicked and he swung it open. Impermeable blackness met her eyes.

"Wait a moment. Let me see about some light," murmured Hel.

Before her eyes, a mammoth library gradually revealed itself from out of the blackness as Hel placed glowing diaman crystals into translucent, cream-colored wall sconces engraved with fantastical creatures from eons ago. Adonia identified dragons, wyverns and a phoenix rising from ashes. She recognized the rearing stallion from the DeHelios standard. Other mystical beasts, she could put no name to.

The fixtures cast pools of soft light upon myriads of thick books in priceless bindings and collections of haphazardly bound papers. The dusty tomes leaned in disordered stacks on shelves that spiraled upward on a cluster of pillars rising two stories in the center of the room. It was as if a forest of books sprang from the middle of the noble chamber. On the perimeter walls, groups of couches and upholstered chairs arrayed themselves around low tables. On one table, a book lay open, its pages gray with dust. A discolored ribbon carefully marked the place where some long ago reader had abandoned it—obviously with every intention to return. *I wonder what happened to prevent it.*

"It's nothing when compared in size to the great library at the High Enclave, but the *Initium*, the chronicles of our peoples' first interactions with Verdantia, are here as well as the collected wisdom of past ages. The Haarb destroyed much of Nyth Uchel, but in their ignorance they left one of her greatest treasures intact." Hel spoke from Adonia's right where he placed a radiant diaman crystal in the final wall sconce. "I hope, someday, to set this archive of our first beginnings as a race to rights. If you wish to explore all that is House DeHelios and early Verdantia, spend some time here."

"I love libraries like this," Adonia murmured. "It is as if the learned voices of all those who have passed come alive again and unveil their secrets to you."

"Yes. Unfortunately, we must save that exploration for another day. This evening we need to concentrate on the walls and floors of the room." His eyes followed one of the columns of books to the ceiling high above. "If you will concentrate on the lower floor, I'll work on the second level. It's all up and down stepladders and catwalks."

Adonia nodded with a genuine smile. "Thank you for giving

me the easy part."

Hel returned her smile. "Let's get started."

Adonia began on the walls of the great chamber and then moved to her hands and knees to examine the floors. She pulled her long skirts between her legs and tucked the hem into her belt, all the while silently muttering to herself about impractical dresses. When she had scoured the last inch of stone, she gingerly transferred her weight from her aching knees to her tender hind end and leaned back against a column of books, legs akimbo. Her sore bottom protested her position but physical exhaustion muted its complaint. A well-stuffed shelf provided a headrest and Adonia's eyelids grew heavy and then closed. With a gurgling complaint, her stomach reminded her she hadn't eaten since breakfast. She couldn't bring herself to care. All she wanted was a bed. Hel collapsed beside her sometime later, rousing her to awareness.

"Any success?" she murmured, never opening her eyes.

"None. And you?"

"Nothing."

She felt him wrap her hand in his. "You've been wonderful today, Healer."

She felt his warm lips press a kiss on her knuckles. For years, she'd been proud to be called "healer". Now she'd give anything if the word never again passed Hel's lips. She wanted to *be* more, *mean* more, to him. With a soft sigh, she opened her eyes.

"You're welcome. You've been wonderful, too. Thank you for your help in the sickroom this morning." Shudders vibrated through her at the memory. Her gaze fell to her slender hand enveloped in his and she straightened. "I would like to return as early as possible tomorrow and try again. I don't think I can do it without you. Will you help me?"

Hel stood and assisted her to her feet. Again, she felt the warm press of his lips against the back of her hand. Sober gray eyes held hers. "For you, Nia—anything."

Adonia dreamt a roiling cloud of hideous desolation sought to swallow her alive in a gaping orifice of death. As it slithered its inexorable way toward her, she could not move, each limb frozen to the ground. It was upon her! The horrible pain as it sucked her into nothingness shattered her soul. She awoke screaming.

"Nia, by the Goddess, you are freezing. Get under the covers, Beauty."

Hel's strong arms wrapped her and pulled her into him, covering her with his warm body. With a cry of inexpressible gladness, she burrowed into him, pathetic sobs still escaping her lips. The soft gleam from a single small diaman crystal dimly lit his bedroom and cast a false sense of normalcy.

"Did you dream of the blackness?" he murmured.

"Yes." Her whispered response cracked on a shuddering inhale. "Do you have such nightmares?"

The hand stroking her paused then resumed. "Yes."

"Hel, what do we do if we cannot figure out the puzzle A'rken gave us? Even if we do…what I came face-to-face with today? I drove it from one person. I didn't begin to defeat it. How can I treat all those in need if it takes me this long with just one?"

"We will solve the puzzle, Nia, and it may be that we will not win. I believe our Mother has given us the weapons to oppose this enemy; and I will not surrender to the *fear* of the encroaching dark. I will fight until my soul is physically ripped from me."

In the quiet that surrounded them, turbulent emotions swirled through Adonia and she lay awake for a long time sorting them into some semblance of order. She examined the residual terror from her nightmare and fought to control her lingering panic. Part of her said to dismiss A'rken's ravings and flee Nyth Uchel. Return to the relative safety of Sylvan Mintoth. Leave the psychic combat to those more experienced.

No. In spite of the almost overwhelming attraction of fleeing for safety, that option was closed. The strange interaction with the entity she thought was Isolde DeCorvus hinted at powerful assistance and truth behind the mystic's ramblings. Maybe Adonia *could* make a difference. But underlying all of these considerations, no matter how much she quailed in abject terror at the thought of the looming confrontation, she couldn't live with the idea she'd diminish herself in Hel's eyes by leaving. Adonia wanted to believe she would battle the corruption to restore Nyth Uchel to its former majesty or to save her sentient planet, but, after the confrontation this morning, self-doubt consumed her. She was not that self-sacrificing, not that…noble. But, because *this* man asked it of her, she would screw every smidgen of backbone she possessed to the sticking point. She'd stand before the black void defiantly even as it ate her soul—for it surely would. She would face the terror of the dark void for *him*.

One of Hel's arms lay heavily across her waist. His breathing came even and regular. Adonia thought he slept. Just as well. She couldn't remember when she'd felt such uncertainty about what she intended to say, but she needed to tell him. For good or bad, her painful honesty drove her to speak the words that revealed her changed motivation.

"I am in love with you."

There. Her breathy whisper was hardly a resounding declaration, but she'd given vocal life to the feelings of her heart. Hel shifted slightly and his breathing pattern changed. His sleep-heavy rumble disturbed the hair across her cheek.

"I love you, too. Now, get some sleep." He snugged her closer to him.

Dumbfounded, she lay inert while her heart darted to and fro in her chest like a herd of startled chital. *He. Loves. Me.* She'd little doubt Hel meant what he said. *He loves me.* Other men were careless with their words—not this man. *He loves me!* She wanted to spring up, to shake him and insist he explain how he meant for them to go on. She didn't. Adonia gnawed on her thoughts and stared at the opposite wall until fatigue beat her undisciplined, extravagant emotions into somnolence.

She's mine. She has claimed me, and I will never let her go. The predator within Hel roared in triumph and a violent surge of possessiveness rocked him. *Mine.* When her screams had awoken him, he'd meant only to soothe her fears. The words that had slipped unplanned from his lips in response to her whisper of love had been sincere even though spontaneous. *She is mine.* His mouth curved in a satisfied smile. Now, more than ever before, he must ensure they remained alive. He had a future to fulfill—with her.

CHAPTER SIXTEEN

When Adonia awoke, the sun stood high in the sky; a bedside tray bore a cold, congealed breakfast, and she was the lone occupant in Hel's great bed. *He loves me.* The warm, golden joy of that thought licked lazily up her insides and curled around her heart like a purring cat. As Adonia sat up, the figure of her maid roused from a chair in the corner. Maddie laid aside the book she'd been reading and stretched.

"My lady, let me help you get dressed. Prince DeHelios said he would join you in the sickroom after you rose. You are to send word for him to Torre Bianca."

This time as Adonia stood in front of her closet, a strange feeling accompanied her examination of each elegant article of clothing. What style of gown set off her mannish shape? What color flattered her? Her ignorance about such matters left her vulnerable. With a soft huff of embarrassed appeal, she turned to Maddie and held a rich gown of lilac shot through with golden thread and deep violet trim against her body.

"Will this one favor me? I…ah…I want to look…" Adonia dropped her eyes to the floor. "I want him to…" Her shoulders fell. The arm holding the luxurious garment sagged. "I don't know how to begin to do this." She looked up when Maddie placed a warm hand on her forearm.

"You will look like a delicate sylph in that dress, my lady. You will pull every male eye in the city—*especially* his. There is a lovely set of topaz and amethyst hair clips that will complement the gown and if I may suggest some light cosmetics? Your skin is so clear it needs very little...but perhaps a berry lip-stain and some enhancement of your beautiful eyes?"

Adonia put herself in Maddie's capable hands and blessed the young woman for neither laughing at her pathetic desire to look pretty—if such a thing were even possible—nor asking who "him" was. When she rose to leave a mere half hour later, she stopped and gave the young woman a hug. "Thank you. You have managed to transform a gawkish stick figure into something approaching a lady."

Maddie returned her hug and drew back, shaking her head. "You *are* a lady, mistress—and I transformed nothing. We merely gave you a proper setting."

"Well...ah...thank you."

Maddie nodded and grinned as Adonia walked through the door and turned down the hall toward the sickroom. *The sickroom.* For a brief moment, her nightmare returned and her steps faltered as fear of a second confrontation with the dark corruption threatened to unnerve her. Memories of the past night banished that fear, however, and replaced it with a steady serenity based on one miraculous thought. *Hel loves me.* So armored, Adonia calmly walked down the hall to join Sara.

She spent her time tending the everyday ailments among her patients as she waited for Hel. Her results with the young laborer with a broken hand from a poorly aimed hammer blow reassured her of her competence. Withdrawing onto a level of metaphysical plane more shallow than that she'd achieved with her patient stricken with the fading, Adonia readily identified the broken bones in his hand. Using the power within the diaman crystals she'd placed around him, she entered his body as spiritual energy and then temporarily blocked the nerves that sent signals of pain to his brain. With a surge of thought, she pushed the bloodstream to rush healing nourishment to the area.

Using physical energy, she straightened his fractured metatarsals and prompted his body's cells to accelerate the healing process. When she had done all she could to speed his recovery, Adonia returned to herself. His face swam into her consciousness, and she was once again in Nyth Uchel's sickroom with Sara hovering anxiously.

"I've set your bones but keep your hand still while Sara wraps it in a cast." Adonia glanced toward Sara and she nodded in understanding. "I'm afraid you won't have use of it for about six weeks. Come see me in another two weeks and let me check on your healing. How does it feel?"

Her young patient flexed his hand cautiously and waggled his fingers. "Her blessings on you, my lady." The tow-headed young man nodded with a thankful expression. "It feels marvelous. Very little pain."

"Good. You will tell me if that changes." She directed a steady gaze toward the young man.

"Yes, my lady."

Adonia smiled at her patient and then turned toward the doorway where Hel stood propped in careless masculine splendor. His black hair hung down his back past his shoulders. She was glad he hadn't cut it. He had continued to shave—though at this time of day a dark shadow covered his chiseled jaw. His elegant features never failed to start her heart racing.

The corners of her mouth tipped up shyly. She'd known he was there. She'd felt his presence several minutes ago, but didn't want to distract herself from her patient.

This man loves me, but what does that mean?

Words of welcome died unborn. Thoughts crashed against her mind like waves in a stormy sea of uncertainty. She'd thought she had the confidence to accept that Hel could love her...but then those damn insecurities from her past washed ashore like so much jetsam and once more she fought doubt. Perhaps she should take her cue on how they would go on from him. If he chose to ignore the whispers exchanged in the night—so would she.

She ran sweaty palms down her dress and then straightened and walked to him. His gray eyes told her with silent honesty how desirable he found her. Adonia blessed Maddie for her skills. She almost felt beautiful—almost. "Thank you for coming," she murmured. "I'm sorry I took you from your search of Torre Bianca."

"A welcome interruption of what I am coming to believe an exercise in futility." His knuckle stroked her cheek gently as his eyes considered her. "You've taken extra care with your appearance today, Beauty. I approve."

Heat flooded her face and she examined her toes. For some reason, she found it hard to catch her breath and her statement came out more breathy than she'd planned. "I would like to see what can be accomplished with two of our most sick. Like the woman yesterday, they suffer from the *fading*."

"Nia."

She shifted and wrapped her arms around her waist. "Umm, yes?" she whispered.

His arms enveloped her and pulled her into him. "Look at me."

Her head fell back, and her eyes met his.

"I wasn't asleep. I heard you quite clearly." His expression softened and his voice lowered to include only the two of them. "When you face the void, the brutal desolation...remember, you are the beloved of DeHelios. No power, natural or unnatural, can stand against us. Use that as your lodestar."

"Oh!" Joy catapulted her onto her toes, and she kissed him with all the passion and exultation in her heart. He returned her kiss and the firestorm of their joined heat wiped all thought from her mind—until he drew back with a low chuckle.

"I think we've scandalized the sickroom, Beauty. We should probably tend to business now." His eyes held apology and humor. His whispered, "Later," contained a promise.

Adonia dropped from her toes with a thud and cautiously scanned the room from over her shoulder. Sara looked on, beaming approval, but those others who still maintained their mental faculties wore expressions that ranged from bemusement to shock to disapproval. Heat flushed her cheeks.

She surreptitiously dabbed at her mouth with the back of her sleeve. "Ah, yes, yes." Standing straight, she took one of Hel's hands and led him to chairs placed next to a pair of pallets laid side-by-side. This time, as she mentally chanted the focusing mantras that would take her to the high aetheric plane necessary to delve deeply into her patients, Adonia felt a presence join her. As she slipped the final tether binding her spirit to her physical self, the aether around her shimmered luminous and golden. A star-bright sphere pulsed in Adonia's awareness.

"Daughter of our blood, beloved of the light-bringer, we greet you."

"Who are you?"

"Isolde, the first of the greatest. My most-beloved Agentio stands beside me."

"I doubt my sanity. You are long dead."

"None who live through our Great Mother die."

"You shielded me from the worst of the horror. Thank you. How is it that I can speak to you?"

"We are linked through the ages by blood, daughter of my daughters. There used to be many but now, only you."

"Will you help me again?" Already Adonia could "see" black corruption pulsing in the bodies of the two men below her—not as formidable as that which had enveloped the woman of yesterday, but still frightening.

"You have the ability to unite and draw upon vast powers, daughter. But the enemy now knows its opponent and its strength is building. We will hold back as much of the dark as we can."

Adonia reached out and placed a hand above the breastbone of each man and, as before, frozen bleakness enveloped her. As it had done the day prior, the pulsating blackness sucked Adonia toward it as if it were a black hole absorbing all light. With a shrill cry of agony, she relived each hurtful moment of her life, every mean and spiteful word cast at her, every humiliation and physical pain. She wallowed in the helpless grief and sense of abandonment she'd felt at the death of her mother and father. She relived the horrendous evening she had parted from Klaran.

His mouth pulled back in a sneer. "I am done with you."

"What are you saying? You love me. We're to be married in two months."

"Mere words. I never cared. Your dried-up cunt served a

purpose." Disgust dripped from his lips. "Really, Adonia, look at yourself. You are a pathetic excuse for a woman."

"I am a warrior, like you."

"You are unnatural. There is nothing feminine or soft about you. From your body to your soul, you are a hard creature. Why would I take such as you for a wife? No man will want you. No man will ever love you. You will be alone until you die."

Alone. Never loved. Always alone. It seemed she drowned in despair for an eternity. Somehow, the words spitting from between his lips were distortions—twisted untruths—not what he'd really said. She kept telling herself this memory was a lie. Klaran hadn't used those words. He'd been hurtful but not…not like *that*.

A sliver of light pierced through her blindness. A shred of memory tugged at her consciousness. Gray eyes held hers. *"…remember, you are the beloved of DeHelios."*

She clutched at that memory as a drowning man clings to a lifeline and clawed her way toward an ever-expanding brightness. With a ferocity she hadn't known she possessed, Adonia smashed against the encroaching desolation, shattering the cancerous entity into motes of black pustulence. With a guttural scream from her soul—"I am not alone. I am the beloved of DeHelios! Love is the truth! Death is the lie!"—Adonia blazed, a ball of golden light, her radiance consuming the diseased particles in bursts of living flame.

As showers of burning specks fell about her, Adonia sank back into her physical self. Again, she returned from the aetheric plane to find herself on Hel's lap. Her eyelids fluttered open and she raised a limp hand to his face. He turned his face into her palm and kissed it.

"I am loved. I am not alone," she whispered, then lost consciousness.

The fine sheets and warm blankets of Hel's bed were tucked up to her chin. Maddie sat bedside and read by the light of a diaman lamp. The soft golden radiance lit the chamber. Full dark had fallen.

"What time is it, Maddie?"

The young woman looked up. Relief and gladness filled her features. "You're awake. Thank the Goddess. I was worried." She glanced across the room at the timekeeper. "It is eight and one-half of the clock, ma'am. Can you eat something? Drink something? How do you feel?"

Adonia pushed up to a sitting position. Her arms trembled, barely able to hold her. Someone had put her in a sleeping gown. Now that Maddie suggested food, her mouth watered at even the thought of another potato. "I'm fine. Something to eat, please! And Maddie...where is Prince DeHelios?"

Maddie poured her an elegant tumbler of amber drink from a lavishly engraved decanter. "After he put you to bed, he stayed for some time but then left to continue his search of Torre Bianca. I assume Prince DeHelios is still at the tower. He issued orders you are to drink all of this."

Adonia took the glass and wrinkled her nose at its contents. "Orders?"

Maddie lifted her eyebrows and nodded once. "Orders."

With a shudder at the smell, Adonia took a large gulp and after a tortured inhale sputtered in a coughing fit. "By the Mother...what *is* that?" She sipped cautiously, wincing each time the burning liquid passed her tongue.

Maddie grinned. "*Pottsdim Likor* from off-planet. It's the prince's private reserve. He said it would raise the dead."

With asthmatic heaves, Adonia wheezed, "I agree. Was I that bad?"

"Yes, my Lady. We knew you weren't dead—you still

breathed...but he *was* quite concerned. Let me call for a tray and then I'll help you dress."

With an audible clunk, Adonia put the now empty tumbler on her bedside table, swept her coverings off and rose. She stumbled the few steps to her closet, pulled out the dress she'd worn earlier that day and then stripped off her nightgown. She threw out an arm and braced it on the wall to steady herself. "I feel like I've fallen down the gallery stairs."

Adonia had satisfied her hunger and then announced she would take Hel his dinner, eager to thank him for his care of her. *Actually, you are just eager to see him,* the painfully honest part of her had corrected.

"Hel, I've brought your dinner." Adonia peered cautiously through the doorway, past the open "game room" door. As her eyes searched the softly lit chamber for Hel, her eyes consciously avoided the racks of implements on the walls. "Over here." His deep baritone preceded his massive shape emerging from behind a row of cabinets. He moved to a low table, pulled out a chair and sat. His eyes fixed on her as she entered. The welcome in them filled her with quiet joy. She crossed the room to the table and emptied the basket of its contents. She pulled up a chair beside him and began to sit.

Hel reached over and clasped her wrist gently. "No. Here." She followed the steady pull until she sat on his lap. Her gaze met his and she held it for as long as she could before she had to drop her eyes overwhelmed by the blaze of emotion in his steady stare.

"How do you feel?" A broad hand swept the hair off her cheek and cupped her jaw.

She leaned into the pressure and closed her eyes. In spite of her rest, exhaustion wrecked her and she couldn't shake a persistent, inner chill. "I feel like someone dragged me by my heels down the hall to the bed, but I know you must have carried me." At his small snort, she opened her eyes and lifted both arms around his neck. "I'm fine, really. Just tired."

His forehead descended to rest on hers. His warm breath washed her cheeks. "I'm pushing you too hard. Asking too much of you."

"You don't request one-half the things of me that you demand from yourself. I want to do this. I *can* do this."

He pulled back and his eyes searched hers. "I hope so or I'm no better than the corruption that we battle. I'll have destroyed something beautiful and fine."

His words did much toward dispelling the chill that permeated her, but she dropped her eyes shyly. "I'll say again...what I give is given freely."

"I know, Nia. I know. But I think, without speaking a single word of protest, you would allow me to empty you of all life."

At that, she lifted her eyes to his and considered his words. "Yes." A small smile tilted the corners of her mouth at the worry and concern she saw there. She lifted a delicate shoulder in a slight shrug. "If that is what you need."

"Oh, Nia," he groaned. "You are so precious. Our need is desperate, Beauty. Of that, I am certain. But I'm equally certain that a future without you is of little value to me. It seems as if I tempt fate, but, Nia...you have given me hope for a life I thought lost to me...children...a home...a loving partner. When this evil is driven from our planet, stay in Nyth Uchel—as my wife."

An upwelling of emotion sealed her mouth as effectively as if he'd gagged her. He read her answer in her mute nod, the soft sheen of tears she couldn't prevent and the trembling smile on her face. He gathered her to him, and his arms wrapped her in a painful constriction—which she endured gladly.

"Please, Beauty, you must have a care for yourself. Promise me." Hel cupped her face and breathed soft kisses on her mouth. "Promise me, Nia. This is important to me. Promise."

When he would allow her use of her lips, she whispered, "I promise."

"And still I have no doubt you will give yourself up without a moment's hesitation, as you did with the mutant beast...as you are doing with our sick."

She felt his ribs rise and fall and heard his heavy exhalation of breath. In the lull, she considered his words. She considered how *she* would feel in a world that didn't contain those strong arms that now encircled her. She drew back slowly until she could see his face. Her hand rose to trace his elegant cheekbone, his strong jaw, and then slid back to his shoulder. "I'll make a pact with you. Promise me that you will guard yourself and I will promise you the same. I would not choose a life without you, either."

His storm-gray eyes held hers steadily. "Pact."

Adonia supposed if she were most women she'd spend the next few hours extracting heartfelt vows and romantic plans for the future from Hel. While she'd no doubt he meant his words, their future together looked so uncertain she didn't want to spend any time investing emotion into things that might never be. She'd done that with Klaran. The pleasures of this moment would serve her very nicely, thank you very much. The knowledge that she belonged to this man, that he wanted her as a wife and mother to his children was glory enough. For a fraction of a moment, she missed Steffania. The red-haired warrior would have celebrated with her, she was certain.

Adonia relaxed into the shelter of Hel's embrace, and her mind wandered to another issue that had troubled her throughout the last night and day. "Hel, I'm afraid for the female *miku*. I'm worried exposure to the black corruption has fatally traumatized her."

Hel shifted her in his arms, and Adonia felt the full force of his intent gaze. "Why do you think that?"

She lifted one shoulder and turned troubled eyes to him. "The little creature has withdrawn into silence. I sensed nothing from her for the past day, at least—perhaps longer."

"When I put you in your sleeping gown, I noted she had left her nest between your legs."

A hot flush of blood crept up Adonia's neck. In theory, one of these days his casual handling of her naked body wouldn't disconcert her so—though she'd not give long odds on that happening any time in the immediate future. "Yes. After the last session in the Chambre Cristalle, she moved to wrap my waist, and has not left that position. As a delicate creature of empathic bond, I fear the ordeal of my battles on the aetheric plane have damaged her."

Hel leaned back in his chair, placed a portion of meat in his mouth and chewed thoughtfully. Another mouthful replaced the one he swallowed and still he didn't speak. Slowly, the dinner she had brought disappeared. Adonia waited in patient silence, content to simply be—to absorb the intimacy and sense of safety this man seemed to impart effortlessly.

Finally, Hel cleared his throat. "There is one other possibility. Gestation."

Adonia straightened in his arms and pushed back, turning her face to his. "Excuse me?"

His expression softened and pleasure lit his eyes. "She could be pregnant with young. That would be a very good thing, as I believe this pair is one of the last of their kind." Hel stood, cradling Adonia in his arms as he rose and then placing her on her feet. "The pair could have mated during your instruction in the fourth level rite for kinetic energy. The *miku* require human intercourse to complete their own reproductive process and, if memory serves, they were particularly active when we coupled. The female could have shut down afterward to protect her developing offspring from empathic overload."

"What do we do?"

"Are you up for a hot soak? We need to return the pair to the Grotto D'oro. Come."

She took the hand Hel offered.

As before, they descended the narrow, spiraling stairs deep underground into an increasingly humid and warm environment. As before, the display of flashing gold and green that illuminated and gilded the vast cavern walls and deep lake mesmerized Adonia with its fantastical splendor. When they stood on the white sand shores, the bath-temperature water of azure blue and chromium green lapping at their bare feet, Hel turned to her and lifted her heavy hair to her back. His hands rested on her shoulders. "I thought I could be content simply to soak in the grotto's warm waters. I thought I could stay away from you for one night. Allow you rest." She watched as his expression made a lie of his words. He scoffed in self-derision. "I want you. Goddess help me, but I've wanted you from the first moment I saw you. I will never have enough of you."

Shivers of anticipation raised gooseflesh on her skin, and Adonia felt her nipples harden to pebbles as he bent and with warm sips of lips and tongue, covered the bare skin of her neck and collarbone. "So sweet, so fine. I'll try not to ride you too hard, Beauty."

The warm, humid air of the cavern caressed the bare skin of her upper torso and then her tender buttocks and slender thighs as her dress fell away and puddled at her feet. When had he unfastened her gown? One powerful hand banded the soft nape of her neck while his thumb raised her chin to allow him to plunder her mouth. The other hand engulfed a tender buttock cheek and ground her hips across his hardening groin. She melted into him in willing surrender. He separated from her just long enough to shed his clothes then silently walked her backward into the hot water of the thermal lake.

When Hel had finished with her some long time later, the two *miku amar* bobbed intertwined, glowing with incandescent brilliance in the warm waters of the Grotto D'oro, and he had to carry her insensate body to their bedchamber.

Adonia marked that evening as a turning point in her relationship with Hel. From that evening forward, he rarely left her side. She reveled in the luxury of effortless companionship and intimacy with Nyth Uchel's prince that day-by-day repaired her shattered self-worth and replaced it with serene confidence and a deep sense of belonging—and the greatest miracle of all, the unassailable knowledge that Hel loved her.

Hel's physical use of her never slacked. If anything, their private understanding freed some constraint within him and with increasing frequency, he pulled her into a private alcove or hidden niche in the castle and drove her to orgasmic frenzy with his lips and tongue and driving cock. Her lessons from Hel in the Chambre Cristalle grew in occurrence, as did her familiarity with the game room and the use of its multiple implements. His demands that she learn and practice her arts never diminished.

There was nothing tame about Hel's love, but rather than beat her down, his aggressive masculinity and severe, exacting focus strengthened her, empowered her, and she gloried in the woman she was becoming. Steffania's incomprehensible words—words that seemed to have been uttered in another lifetime—echoed through her thoughts with regularity. *"....the more I abandon myself to him, the more he gives of himself to me. It's a delicious contradiction. He is never more wholly mine than when I am under his total control, in complete service to him."* A knowing smile tipped her lips. The next time Adonia saw Steffania, she'd have to tell her that now, she too, understood.

CHAPTER SEVENTEEN

A shockwave of unceasing, clarion blasts from the watchtower's horn jerked Adonia from sleep. The pink light of dawn flirted with the gloom in their chamber. She pushed off Hel's chest and looked toward the window with an impatient swipe at the itinerant locks of dark hair obscuring her face. Hel, his warrior instincts bringing him to full wakefulness at the first note of the horn, flew out of the bed, swathed his nudity in a heavy robe and then helped Adonia into hers as she staggered out of the covers on unsteady feet.

"There is some crisis. Stay here and keep safe. I'll be back." Hel kissed her swiftly on the mouth and strode across the chamber. His sword blade hissed as he jerked it from its scabbard. He pulled open the door and disappeared.

Adonia stood at the side of the bed where Hel had abandoned her and blinked owl-eyed at the open door. "I'm a First Arrow. I don't stay and keep safe." She'd no more tottered across the chamber to the door when Ramsey DeKieran staggered past her, cradling his wife in his arms. Hel followed on his heels. Adonia blinked, then made an about-face.

"Put her on our bed, Ram."

As gently as if Steffania was spun of sugar, Lord Ramsey laid his wife on the bed that she and Hel had just left and turned a distraught face to Adonia. "Lady DeCorvus, help her. She is not far from death."

His words slapped her into complete wakefulness.

"Move! Let me see her." Adonia pushed at Ram with frantic hands and peered down at her friend. Purple lips in a chalk-white face laced with spidery veins of black met her eyes. Adonia's trembling hands sought Steffania's pulse points, and willed her fingers to feel the beat of a heart in a body that gave every indication of death. *There.* Faint. Irregular. But still beating, thank the Goddess. Gently, Adonia lifted an eyelid and almost cried in horror. Black film blinded the expressive golden eyes that normally invited the world to share with her in laughter. Death looked out of them, now.

"Tell me she is not dead. Please, tell me you can help her." The grating words sounded as if ripped from Ram's gut.

She is so far gone. Panic threatened to send all her newly found confidence scattering like so many wild birds. *I can do this. I must do this!* Adonia straightened and slowly inhaled then turned to Lord Ramsey. She caught one of his hands between hers. "She is not dead and, yes, I can help her." Her gaze rose to where Hel stood grimly watching. "I need your assistance." Her lips tipped slightly at his silent nod.

"How can I help?" Lord Ramsey whispered. "Give me a task."

Adonia surveyed the gaunt man who stood before her. His hollow-eyed expression of despair shattered her. She feared for him should Steffania die. "Steffania lives. Where there is life there is hope, and I have come to know this enemy well. As for a task? You do the most difficult of all, my lord. Wait. Rest. Eat. Pray. She will need you strong. You are welcome to return to this chamber, though I must ask that you remain quiet. I need to calm and center myself...and then I, with Hel's assistance, will fight the ugly war for her soul."

Hel arranged Adonia's exhausted body next to Steffania and tucked warm blankets underneath both women's chins. His beloved's eyes fluttered open. She saw him, smiled and closed her eyes again with a soft sigh. He noted with some concern that his own muscles quivered and lacked strength. It had been three excruciating days of hard fought advance and agonizing setback. Ultimately, the great blackness corrupting Steffania's body had withdrawn, driven out by Adonia's remorseless assault. Hel had suffered the tortures of the damned watching his Nia drain herself almost to death, but she refused to save herself at the cost of losing Steffania.

When he was certain that his beloved healer slept comfortably, Hel rose and crossed their bedchamber to stand in front of a large chair holding the slumped, sprawling figure of Ramsey DeKieran. He leaned over and put a quiet hand on the man's travel-stained shoulder. In spite of Adonia's periodic urgings, Ramsey had not left—not even to change his clothes, bathe or eat. He'd remained in their bedchamber with his wife. He'd occupied that chair with all the fury of a caged *fell*-wolf, but as Adonia had requested, Ram contained himself. The man's silent agony was another form of torture for Hel to watch; *he'd* sent Ramsey and Steffania to the border. He felt responsible.

Hel placed a gentle hand on Ram's shoulder. "DeKieran."

With a start, Ramsey sat upright and dropped his arm into his lap from where he'd thrown it over his eyes.

"Go find a bed," Hel murmured.

"Find a bed, you say." Blood-shot gray eyes ringed in indigo blue met and held his. "My wife?" the man rasped.

"Will recover." A smile tugged at one corner of Hel's mouth. "She just needs time."

"Goddess be praised." Ramsey rose and moved to stand beside Steffania's sleeping form. His normally erect posture waved unsteadily, as if his balance was an uncertain thing. Methodically, he began to strip, dropping his clothes at his feet. When nude, the man pulled the covers to the great bed back and slipped in beside his wife. Hel didn't have the heart to stop him, though any other time he'd have quantities to say about a naked Ramsey DeKieran in bed with his Nia. The expression Ramsey wore bared his soul. Hel doubted Ramsey knew Adonia shared the bed with his wife. Ram saw no one but Steffania.

Exhaling a fervent, "Vixen," Ramsey pulled her into his arms and settled his face into the masses of her red hair. "DeHelios." Hel listened intently to Ram's barely audible words. "As I breathe, if Lady DeCorvus ever has a want within my power to cure, be it great or small, tell her to make it known to me and it will be done."

"I'll tell her." Hel wasn't certain Ramsey had heard him. The man had passed out.

Hel understood the elevated status and intimate connection with their Great Mother that House DeHelios enjoyed came with a price. Oh, how he knew. In his life, he'd paid handsomely and never begrudged it. He'd bedded a cold wife to ensure the Great Rites continued. He'd risked his body for loyal subjects whose lives weighed heavily on his conscience as he fought for their safety. He had sacrificed his basic humanity for years as the *bás dtost* vanquished anyone—anything—that had dared to threaten Verdantia. But now? She had finally bestowed on him the one gift he would *not* sacrifice—the one price he would *not* pay—Nia.

He'd watched Ram almost lose the love of his life. The thought the same could happen to *him* was not to be born. To watch Nia nearly empty herself of all life for Steffania, well … Suddenly the bedchamber closed in with claustrophobic threat, and his lungs labored to draw air. *I've got to get out of here.*

He didn't know why his feet brought him to the old nursery door. His aimless wandering had taken him to the one room in the entire castle he hadn't entered since he'd buried his small children. Perhaps with the knowledge that, by the grace of the Great Mother, more little heads would occupy these cradles, more tiny hands would reach for these stuffed toys, his frozen grief had finally thawed enough that he could face the memories held within these walls.

Tentatively, almost reverently, he pushed the door open and entered, on guard against the recollection of the gruesome past. He tipped the nose of a rocking horse, his young son's first mount, and watched it nod up and down. His forefinger stroked the battered pile on a one-eyed pink hopper: the ever-present companion of his precocious little daughter, and slowly, he relaxed. The ghosts inhabiting this chamber now had smiles instead of sightless eyes.

The corner of his mouth lifted slightly as he imagined his future daughters and sons, those beautiful children he could have with Nia, filling this empty room with laughter and gaiety, with hours spent reading storybooks and campaigning toy soldiers. It could happen. But what if he lost Nia? An upwelling of the same emotion that forced him from their bedchamber drove him to his knees. He sank, clinging to the bars of a dusty crib and buried his head between his bent forearms. His throat thickened. His eyes burned with unshed tears—and he begged unashamedly. "Please, Great Mother, as you love me, keep her safe. Allow me this future."

He knelt there for a long time before he could master the unvoiced sobs that shuddered through his great body.

"Nice place."

"The library of Torre Bianca is one of the few places in Nyth Uchel where I am assured of privacy—normally." Hel watched DeKieran's intent gaze evaluate the white tower's fabulous library as if casing the room for valuables. Pure force of habit, Hel thought. He felt relatively certain Ramsey no longer needed to steal. Ramsey prowled into the spacious chamber, holding a carved crystal decanter that looked suspiciously like his carefully horded *Pottsdim Likor* in one hand and two tumblers in the other.

Trust the scoundrel to find the outrageously expensive *Pottsdim*. While Ramsey's red-rimmed eyes still appeared sunken and his cheekbones stood out too prominently, the man wore clean clothes, smelled of Nyth Uchel's costly spice soap and had lost the aura of glacial despair. Hel leaned back in his armchair, closed the book he had been paging through and set it on the low, elegant table in front of him. He gestured in invitation toward one of several chairs placed in a comfortable arrangement around the table. "Our women?"

With a solid *thunk*, Ram set the decanter and tumblers on the table's glossy surface and threw himself into a chair across from Hel. Ram poured both of them a finger of *likor* and shoved a tumbler across the table to Hel. "Lady DeCorvus rests comfortably. I moved Steffania to our bed. No matter how pretty, yours is not the face I wish to awake to."

Hel arched a brow. "A shared sentiment."

"Your maidservant said she would sit with Steffania and send for me if she wakes." Ramsey rested his forearms on his knees and leaned forward. He leveled his uncanny gray eyes on Hel. "We need to talk."

"Yes. What happened on the western border?"

"Nothing was as you described. The caches were gone. Steffania and I searched for days but could find only three or four crystals. In the end, there were not enough stones to set the boundary again. Those diaman caches were deliberately scattered. Someone in this city works against you, DeHelios."

"The same thought has occurred to me. Though I have cudgeled my brain, I cannot think of anyone who would be so insane as to threaten the entire city of Nyth Uchel simply to attack me." Hel pulled the tumbler toward him and ran a fingertip around its lip. "How did Steffania become infected?"

DeKieran raked his hands through his hair. "I don't know. She doesn't know. It could have been a dozen different ways. That living nightmare you sent us to..." Ramsey stopped speaking and exhaled through pursed lips, swearing softly. "Fuck." He tossed the contents of the glass down his throat. The decanter clinked on the rim of Ram's tumbler as he poured another. "The infection overtook her with such virulence I feared she would succumb before I could return to Nyth Uchel."

Hel rubbed his jaw and blew out a heavy breath. "Ram...I don't know what to say. If that had been Nia? I'm sor—"

"Don't. I don't blame you. I should have been able to protect her." A small silence settled in the room. Ram swallowed the second glass in a single gulp and poured another. He motioned to the volume in front of Hel. "What do you search for in these scratchings of the long dead?"

"I've pulled the old architectural drawings of Torre Bianca. Perhaps there is some hidden room, some place lost to time. Our inspection of the tower walls found nothing." Hel sipped at his drink, rolling the *likor* around in his mouth before swallowing.

Ramsey rocked his chair onto its back legs and drummed his fingers on its arms. "You have examined every bit of exposed stone?"

"Exhaustively."

Long minutes passed.

"When was the tower built?"

Hel frowned. "Nuovo Terra Solar 4142. At the start of the First Tetriarch."

"So…over four hundred years ago."

"Yes."

"Enough time for many layers of dirt and debris to build up and obscure Torre Bianca's original foundation stones."

Hel straightened in his chair. "Damnation, I'm a blighted idiot."

"I'll drink to that." With a crooked smile, Ramsey raised his glass in a toast and tossed the contents down his throat. This time, Hel joined him.

Hel nodded at Maddie as she entered the comfortable sitting-room attached to his and Adonia's bedchamber the next morning and immediately regretted the action. Some overly-ambitious drummer beat a timpani inside his head. Movement quickened the pounding from one-quarter to triple time. His and Ramsey's drunken stagger from Torre Bianca back to the castle in the wee hours of the morning had required a joint effort—each held the other upright. Hel hoped Ram's head punished him worse than his own. "Madelyn, Lady DeCorvus still sleeps. The Goddess willing, she will sleep all morning. How is Lady DeKieran?"

"She woke briefly last night when Lord DeKieran returned but still slept comfortably when I looked in on her this morning."

"Tell Lady DeCorvus I am at the tower. Send her to me when she wakes." At the maid's nod, Hel left a peacefully sleeping Adonia. The cold outside air helped to clear his head and the sight of Ramsey, Bernard and a work party of men grouped with shovels and pick axes at the foot of Torre Bianca cheered him. He held only the vaguest memory of directing Bernard to do *something* last night. It had been years since he'd worked his way to the bottom of a decanter of *Pottsdim* and, from the pounding in his head, many years would pass before he tried it again.

As he strode toward the group, Ram and Bernard stood to the side in close discussion. Ramsey looked Hel's way with something less than a welcome on his gaunt face. "How's your supply of bootblack?"

"What in the seven hells are you on about?"

"Bernard tells me your time-honored rite, those ancient Engalian words I so carefully memorized, you know—the ones to *save Verdantia* and your *gods-be-damned way of life*—are nothing more than a list of—"

The smile on Hel's face broadened at the ill-disguised annoyance in Ramsey's voice. "You said it yourself. On that basic level, the words don't matter as long as you concentrate on the desired *result*. Rest assured it *is* my favorite formula for bootblack. I didn't part with it lightly."

"Entertained by that thought, were you?"

"I find my amusements where I can."

Every muscle in Ramsey's clenched jaw worked but he never shifted from his casual, cross-armed stance.

Hel finally tamed his ear-to-ear grin and pointed to the work party. "Backing out?"

"Not when you are in such dire need for *results*." Ramsey grabbed a pickaxe and rested it on his shoulder. "How's your head?"

"Never better. How's yours?"

"Just fine."

Hel thought he heard a groaned, "Fuck!" when Ramsey's blade bit into the hard-pack soil but his own head hurt too much to jibe at the man.

After several hours of intensive labor, Hel and Ramsey leaned on their picks and watched as the final course of stone began to emerge from the hard scrabble packed at the tower's base. Both men's gazes sharpened when deep cuts in the thick building blocks turned into chiseled cursive script and the crew of men worked with renewed frenzy.

Ramsey snorted. "Of course, it's in Engalian. Another ancient recipe for bootblack?"

"No…by the seven hells, man. You were right."

"Hurt to admit that?"

"Actually, yes. But, it happens so rarely I'll survive."

As the broad swirls and angular cuts into the stone revealed themselves, Hel read them aloud.

> *Beneath her feet the raven finds them,*
> *the mighty asleep from ages gone.*
> *High in her keep the raven binds them;*
> *to evil's bane and a new light's dawn.*

Hel turned to Ramsey. "Adonia. Now."

"My lady, there is a messenger for you. Julian Goodman urgently requests your attendance on his wife. The messenger awaits your return with him."

Adonia looked up from the remains of a small breakfast she had consumed, un-tasted. Nothing on the plate seemed to warrant more attention than mere consumption. Adonia had looked in on Steffania; she rested peacefully, no signs of the *fading*, thank the Goddess. Now, she intended on joining Hel at Torre Bianca. The crisis of the last three days had intensified their connection, and she felt the loss of him the moment she awoke alone in their bed. "Julian Goodman? Is he someone important to Hel?"

Maddie nodded. "Not Julian, so much as his wife, Tessa. Tessa Goodman partnered Prince DeHelios in the rites to re-energize the diaman crystal after the death of Lady Athena. If not for Mistress Goodman, all that remained of Nyth Uchel and those who lived within her would have perished to the soul-wraiths. It is impossible to overstate the debt our people owe her."

An upwelling of an unwelcome emotion ambushed Adonia. She'd never before felt the cutting edge of *this* sharp blade, but she knew the pain immediately for what it was. Jealousy. "So Mistress Goodman would take precedence over my finding the prince at Torre Bianca?"

"I would think Prince DeHelios would want every courtesy extended to her, my lady."

"Is Mistress Goodman pretty?"

"Surpassing."

"And she partnered him for over three years? Exactly how close *was* the prince to Mistress Goodman?" Adonia mumbled under her breath.

Maddie's observant eyes softened. "Oh, my Lady…nothing like what you are thinking. He never took her to the Chambre Cristalle. He never showed her Grotta D'oro, and he certainly *never* insisted she sleep in his bed nor picked out dresses for her. Theirs was a working relationship of mutual respect, but that is all."

"I cannot imagine any woman who received the attentions of Prince DeHelios could remain unaffected." Adonia busied herself with her tea.

"Perhaps on Tessa Goodman's part warmer emotions grew. I can't say. The prince was never more than pleasantly courteous. I never saw him look at her the way he looks at you—as if dawn has broken an endless night and you are the rising sun."

"He looks at me like that?"

The young servant smiled tenderly. "It brings joy to all of us who witnessed his suffering. For years, he was as frozen as the land."

Adonia shoved her teacup and her unbidden jealousy away. "Tell the messenger I'm coming."

CHAPTER EIGHTEEN

"**L**ady DeCorvus, you came...and alone. I didn't think *he* would allow it. I am Julian Goodman." Adonia nodded at the unkempt, blond-headed man who opened the door at her knock and ushered her into the neat, isolated home some distance from the castle. The warmed air held the sour smell of corruption. "Sir. Of course I came. All Nyth Uchel owes you and your wife a great debt."

"A debt that can never be repaid."

The bitter tones of the man's voice alerted Adonia and she stopped her examination of the well-appointed dwelling with a frown and returned her attention to Julian Goodman. He had closed the sturdy entrance door firmly and turned a key in the door, locking them in. Of middle height and weight, the man's red-rimmed eyes held something akin to hatred or madness as he turned and faced her.

A thread of disquiet niggled at Adonia as Goodman removed the key from the lock and tucked it in his pocket. "Where is Mistress Goodman? Will you take me to her?"

"She's through this hall. Come." His beefy hand closed around her wrist, and he strode across the room, jerking Adonia forcibly behind him.

"Please! Mister Goodman, you are hurting me. Such force

isn't necessary. I'm coming." He didn't release her nor lessen his grip.

With a growl, Julian opened a door at the far end of the hall and shoved her into a frozen bedroom. Condensation from her breath created white mist in the air. The stench of the chamber stung her nostrils and lungs. Even in the frigid air, there was no mistaking the reek of someone dead several days. The filtered light that made its way through closed draperies revealed the figure of a woman on a bed, and Adonia immediately went to her. Her cursory glance at her patient confirmed her thought.

"I don't understand. Mister Goodman, your wife no longer draws breath, nor has for some time it appears. I'm afraid there is nothing I can do for her."

"Oh yes, she is quite dead. May she burn in the seven hells. *He* inflicted his twisted lusts upon her and perverted her—made her crave his sort of warped usage. Did he think I would touch her polluted flesh?" Insanity stared at Adonia out of Goodman's wild eyes. "No one, not a single soul in this vile city voiced a protest at his actions. They didn't care about his defilement of my wife as long as *they* were safe." Goodman's voice hissed a whisper of menace. "Well, I'll send them all to the seven hells right along with that whore. It's too late for him to stop it."

A horrid sense of unease assaulted Adonia. This entire situation was…off. "I don't understand. I am sorry for your loss, but why did you summon me?"

"Because I am going desecrate you as he did Tessa, and then I am going to kill you."

Adonia bolted for the bedroom door. She got as far as the main room before he tackled her to the carpet.

"Lady DeCorvus went with Julian Goodman's messenger, Sir,

perhaps thirty minutes ago?"

Hel stiffened at the name. "Goodman...Nia took Sara with her?"

"No, my lord...she went alone." Maddie frowned. "Why? Should she not have gone? I thought—"

"Too much has happened to ignore. Someone within Nyth Uchel betrays us. I don't like the timing of this, and Julian Goodman bears no love for me." Hel couldn't move fast enough. "Find Lord DeKieran. Send him to Goodman's." He sprinted out of their bedroom, praying he was wrong, cursing the debilitating hangover that weakened his limbs.

It took him far too long to get to the Goodman home. His fist pounded on the entry door while he worked the handle. Locked. He heard Adonia cry out. With a roar of anger, Hel ran at the generous front window and, in a burst of shattered glass, fell into the front room of the house. The sight that met his eyes fulfilled his worst imaginings. The unkempt form of Julian Goodman struggled on top of a frantic Adonia, tearing at her clothing, snarling curses. He had her bared to the waist. Julian raised a burly fist to strike her. Spittle and obscene threats spewed from his mouth.

"No! Goddess curse you, no!" Hel sprang at Goodman and threw him off Adonia, then turned on the sprawled man in fury. The much smaller Goodman was no match for him. Hel pummeled the man mercilessly, reveling in each heavy thud of his fists meeting flesh until bones broke and blood flew from Goodman's disarranged features. Mindless anger drove his hammering fists.

A hand fisted the collar of Hel's leather tunic and jerked him away from the beating he ferociously administered. With a roar of rage, he turned on whoever had dared interfere.

Ramsey slammed him hard to his back. "Stop it. You are killing him. Get a hold of yourself."

Hel lunged at Ram, rabid with fury, and the two men wrestled.

DeKieran's heavy weight pressed him into the hard wooden floor while he twisted and turned.

"Damnation, man! Stop fighting me. I'm not your enemy. See to your lady."

Goddess, Nia. Hel went limp. "Fuck you, you pestilent bastard. Get off me."

Ramsey ground Hel further into the floor and growled, "Fuck *you* for not protecting her, you arrogant, self-righteous, prick. She's worth ten of you." Ramsey cautiously released his hold and, with a final shove for good measure, rose. Hel rolled to his feet and went to Nia leaving Ram to deal with a moaning Goodman prone on the floor.

Adonia sat slumped against a wall, holding the torn pieces of her dress to her breasts with a blank expression on her face. Hel couldn't name the emotion that shredded him. He didn't like it. He never wanted to feel it again. Hel sat beside her and lifted her into his lap. With a sob, she wrapped her arms around his neck and clung to him. He couldn't stop stroking her, checking for physical injury. She felt slender and desperately fragile. *Damn you, Julian Goodman.* "Ah, Beauty. Did he hurt you?"

"Bruises. I tried to fight back, but he was insanely strong. I don't know what I would have done had you not come."

The stifled sobs that Nia bit back tore his insides into a seething mass of white-hot rage, and his gaze returned to the bloody pulp of Julian Goodman's face as Ramsey lifted the half-dead man to unsteady feet. "Deal with him, DeKieran. If I get near him again, I will kill him."

Ramsey jerked his head in a curt acknowledgement. "I have some questions to put to him, then feel free to finish what you started."

Hel watched until Ramsey half-dragged, half-carried Julian Goodman through the now open door and out of his sight. He dropped his nose into Adonia's thick, sweet-smelling hair. "Beauty, I'm so sorry. I'm so sorry." He tipped her face to his and kissed the tears from her cheeks. "I knew he despised me, but I never realized the extent of his hatred. Goddess," he groaned and gathered her to him gently. "I cannot find the words to say how sorry I am this happened."

She wiped her eyes with the heel of her palm and sniffed. "Don't listen to Lord Ramsey. It's not your fault. How can anyone predict the behavior of a mad man?"

Ramsey. The parallels between himself and Ramsey were too similar to be ignored. The outside world viewed both of them as hardened warriors, apex predators with only a superficial gloss of civilized behavior. Little did the outside world know that two fragile women cradled the lives of those two primal males in their delicate hands. Hel refused to dwell on the outcome should he have arrived a few minutes later. Desolation and rage would have ruled him. "You've made another champion for life, Beauty. After the miracle you worked with Ramsey's wife, the rogue would give you his left nut. I'm supposed to tell you that."

Adonia's shoulders shook gently with amusement, and she snuggled further into him. "And what would I do with Lord Ramsey's left testicle?"

Hel wrapped his arms tighter and murmured into her hair, "He might have been a little more eloquent than that. Something about whatever you need for as long as he breathes. Should something happen to me, remember that."

"Mmm. Then don't let anything happen to you." She pushed away slightly, and her concerned brown eyes found his. "Goodman said something that worries me. He said he would bring down all of Nyth Uchel, and it was too late to stop it. What did he mean?"

Hel lifted her off his lap and then stood and helped her to her feet. "I don't know. But I suspect Ramsey will find out." With a heavy sigh, he regarded her ruined gown. "I suppose your mynx coat will cover you. I can't take you through town like this, and there is something I want you to see. Are you really all right?" He peered at her intently.

Adonia straightened, head held high. "Of course."

A smile tugged the corners of his mouth at her tart response. Nia might yield to him, but there was nothing wilting about his beloved.

An hour later, Nia stood beside him, gazing at the base of Torre Bianca. "What does it say?" He read the passage aloud.

> *Beneath her feet, the raven finds them,*
> *the mighty asleep from ages gone.*
> *High in her keep, the raven binds them;*
> *to evil's bane and a new light's dawn.*

Hel glanced at Nia's solemn face when he'd finished. "Now we merely need to decipher its meaning and translate that into practical action."

"I should tell you something." Nia dropped her head. Her voice sounded diffident as if she was not sure of his reaction. "When I heal people stricken by the *fading*, I do so with the aid of Isolde DeCorvus and the First Tetriarch. They come to me on the metaphysical plane and add their strength to mine. It is the only reason I did not succumb to the darkness. I have grown much stronger since. I could probably stand on my own now, but..."

"Nia...say that again." He grasped her shoulders and turned her to face him.

She peered up at him with a tentative smile. "It sounded so crazy when I said it in my mind. How could I expect you to believe I spoke with a dead queen?" She chuckled softly. "And not recently dead...dead for over four hundred years...and not *any* queen...the greatest of all our queens, Isolde DeCorvus." Nia closed her eyes and let her head fall back. "She calls me, *daughter of my blood*. I suppose that resolves any question of my lineage." She opened her eyes, and her gaze held his with growing wariness. "Every time I began to say the words, I imagined *that* look on your face—the one I see right now."

"What is it you think you see on my face?"

"Incredulity. Disbelief."

"No, Beauty. See admiration, amazement. See hope. Explain to me what you experience on the aetheric plane..." Hel glanced upward and frowned. "Night is hard upon us. I must get you back to the castle and safety. The situation within Nyth Uchel is deteriorating. Lacking the diaman perimeter Ramsey went to set, we've had reports of mutant beasts and soul-wraiths threatening our western approach. The gatekeepers tell me ghouls swarm the eastern bridge. They've yet to penetrate the city proper, but I cannot risk you." Hel traced a finger down Nia's face and pulled her mynx coat tighter around her. "Have you eaten since rising?"

Amusement lightened her dear face for a moment. "I think so. It is hard to remember..."

"Yes," he snorted. "Nothing to distinguish one meal of stringy meat from another. Cook does her best, but she has little to work with."

He clasped her hand in his and they walked toward the main entry of the castle. Shadows fell across their path and the glimmer of stars began to dot the black heavens. They were about to leave a narrow alley, only a few short steps from where it opened onto the main thoroughfare, when Hel noticed a moldering, stale odor and looked intently into the darkness ahead of them. The blackness undulated.

Nia slowed. "What is that stench? It smells of a charnel house."

He dropped her hand—instead filling his with the hilt of his sword and withdrawing the blade with a slow hiss of steel against hardened leather.

It rose out of the blackness with no warning, a hideous mishmash of gelatinous ooze and human parts, blocking the narrow alley. One side of its head dripped ooze while the other had two ears and a lipless mouth pasted below a single eye. A black void filled the space where a nose should have been. A foul miasma emanated from it, and its numerous lower limbs bent at unnatural angles. One side of its form had one arm, while the other carried two. It was a wholly unnatural construct—part human and part... other.

The aberration lurched toward them with an ominous hiss.

"Run, Nia. Back the way we came."

As they turned to flee, more dark shapes obliterated the light entering the alley from the other end. The undead mutations listed in inexorable pursuit trapping them in the narrow alleyway.

With a vivid curse, Hel heaved his weight against a door fronting the alley.

The ghouls closed remorselessly on them, low moans and hisses echoing in the dark.

"Nia, help me. Put your shoulder to this door!" Both of them slammed against the wooden door. With a splintering crack, it spilled them inward.

Hel slammed the door behind them and leaned his full weight against it. Complete darkness enveloped them.

"Can you see anything?" Nia's voice came from no more than an arm's length away, yet Hel couldn't make out a thing.

"Give me a minute to adjust to the darkness, and then we must barricade this door and find the front entrance."

At that moment, a heavy jolt against the door almost moved Hel from his stance. "Damnation! Another heavy slam rattled the door on its hinges, and Hel cursed again. "We must find something to brace this door. Nia, help me." Another slam shoved both of them forward, and they groaned with the strain it took to close the door the few inches that the ghouls had opened it.

"Won't we be missed? Surely someone will note our absence and look for us," Nia panted.

"Probably...but I fear not soon enough to preserve our skins."

Hel peered intently into the gloom of the building. He could discern the shapes of worktables and multiple stoves. Now, he knew where they were—the kitchen of *The Half-Witted Sister* across from the entrance to the castle. "This is a grill house, Nia. One that used natural gas for fuel, not diaman crystals. I want to let the ghouls in and light the gas."

He could feel Nia's nod. "And where will we be?"

"Running like the seven hells, straight through that doorway." He pointed. "There is a small dining room on the other side with a large display window. Be prepared to dive through the window. Tuck and roll and come up running for the castle entrance."

"How do we ignite the gas?"

The door suddenly jolted and their feet slipped against the hard floor as they again fought to keep the door closed. The moans and hisses on the opposite side became more agitated.

Hel thought for a moment. "The kitchen grills have spark igniters for their burners. We'll turn on the gas to all the grills, allow the gas a moment to accumulate in the air, then hit the igniter spark on our way out and just hope the explosion takes out the ghouls."

"We can't stay here much longer, that's a certainty," Nia stated. Hel could hear the physical strain in her voice as she leaned into the door.

"Yes. Quickly, Nia, the stoves. Turn the surface units on full. The far left knob on each grill is the spark igniter. I'll flip one as we leave."

"And hope we don't blow ourselves up as well as the ghouls,"

Nia muttered as she hustled to do as he'd ordered.

"Yes...there's that. I'll try not to blow us up."

Nia moved hastily from stove to stove in the gloomy kitchen, peering at the controls from inches away. "Okay...I think all the burners are on high."

"Ready? Here we go." Hel leaped away from the alleyway door. As soon as his weight no longer restrained the door, it smashed open to admit one of the lurching monstrosities. As the creature fell through the door, Hel paused at the stove and flipped the igniters, then careened through the open doorway into the dining room, propelling Nia in front of him.

A thunderous detonation obscured his scream of, "Jump!" Hel felt his feet leave the floor. The force of the explosion thrust both him and Nia through the large front windows of the eatery, flinging them into the middle of the street beyond. Ears ringing, head whirling from the explosion, shards of glass raining from his body, Hel crawled crabwise toward Nia, cast into the street like a rag doll. She stirred.

"Up. Get up." His hand closed around her wrist, and he half-dragged, half-carried her in a stumbling run toward the castle.

They had gone only a little way before a welcome sight met his eyes. A dozen diaman lanterns carried by townspeople spread out in a phalanx and progressed down the street. Their escort to safety had arrived.

Hel wrapped Nia in his arms and held her tightly. "Are you in one piece?"

She straightened but clung to him. "Yes. I'll have bruises on my bruises, but I'm whole."

"By Her ruby red tits, Nia! This must stop."

"Goodman was your saboteur."

Hel watched Ramsey sheath a stiletto he'd been cleaning and throw the bloody cloth onto a dining room table that still bore the remnants of a meal. Ramsey slouched, limbs sprawled, in an armchair pushed away from the table. Steffania reclined on a chaise nearby, all but her head obscured by plush pillows, blankets and Ramsey's cloak. She smiled brilliantly at Nia as Hel ushered her into the family dining room.

"Did you discover the extent of his tampering?"

DeKieran pulled a small blade from his belt and began to clean beneath his nails. "Goodman repeatedly broke apart and scattered the cache-stones on the western border. He contaminated the graves on the eastern side with polluted soil and threw hundreds of energized diaman stones into the river." Ram raised eyes of cold dispassion. "Damnation, man, what happened to the two of you?"

Hel jerked his head sharply. "Later."

Ramsey shrewdly eyed him then shrugged. "Goodman was too smug, DeHelios. He gloated about some mischief as yet uncovered, but deteriorated into mindless drivel before I could get details out of him." Ramsey returned his small blade to his belt. "Be on your guard."

Hel stood rigidly and fought to master his rage. He suspected he and Nia had already encountered some of Goodman's mischief. "Where *is* Mister Goodman?"

Ramsey sat forward and met Hel's glare but responded with the same lack of inflection with which he had enumerated Goodman's crimes. "I'm not certain. He met with an unfortunate accident—a fall from a watchtower. His body broke on the boulders at the base of the wall and the river washed his remains away." The first hint of emotion entered DeKieran's uncanny eyes. "But he suffered before his...mishap."

Hel's face twisted with fierce satisfaction. "Thank you."

DeKieran cocked his head with an almost imperceptible nod

and studied Nia. "I'm glad to see you more or less in one piece, Lady DeCorvus. I would have killed DeHelios personally had his negligence resulted in your—"

"I suffered no permanent hurt, Lord Ramsey. Thank you," Nia interjected, glancing at Hel.

By Her light, the rogue knew how to taunt him. Hel owed Ramsey, but right now, he'd gladly take his fists to the man. Only Nia's pleading gaze held him immobile.

"Adonia, thank you. A thousand times, thank you," Steffania declared, also stepping into the breach. "This one won't say…" she nodded at Ramsey…"but I'm certain I owe the two of you my life."

Nia shrugged modestly. "The important thing is that you're recovering. How do you feel? Are you sure you should be out of bed so soon?"

Steffania groaned. "Not you, too. I just fought that battle with Ramsey. I feel fine." She glared at Ram who studiously ignored her. "You didn't need to carry me. I was perfectly capable of walking!" Her gaze returned to Adonia. "One more moment lying in bed and I would've gone crazy." Her eyes laughed at the wealth of cushions and blankets piled on, over and around her. "And as you can see, no pillow or blanket has been spared to ensure my comfort."

Hel pulled out a chair and seated Nia when servants entered with hot food. "You will eat," he said pointedly. He watched Nia until she raised a fork to her mouth and began to chew.

A commotion in the hallway drew his attention and a townsman burst through the door.

"My lord! Soul-wraiths! Soul-wraiths and ghouls swarm the eastern entrance to the castle. The men you set at the doors are barely holding them at bay. We need more diaman crystals and every available sword."

The undead already prowled the streets—and now soul-wraiths. If a horde of wraiths attacked the castle, they were also elsewhere in the city. The news was devastating. There was no possible way Nyth Uchel's occupants could repel a swarm of ghouls and soul-wraiths for the long hours of every night for months to come.

Only one hope for salvation occurred to him. His mind stuttered in horror. He wouldn't ask it of any unschooled woman, let alone the woman he loved beyond reason. With almost crippling despair, he realized he'd little choice. He must attempt the Great Rite with Nia.

Hel barked orders to the stunned servants attending them in the dining room. "Unlock the armaments room. Distribute weapons to every able-bodied person in this castle, women and children included. Send them to the western doorway. One of you get to the storeroom and bring all the lanterns and diaman crystals available. Now! Be quick about it." Hel turned. "Ramsey, meet me at the west castle entrance. We must ensure everyone is suitably armed with a weapon and a quantity of diaman crystals. We are abandoning the castle."

Ram glanced at his wife, who was flinging pillows and wraps to the floor in a flurry of urgency. "Change to your battle leathers and arm yourself, Steffania. We need to assist DeHelios in getting to the white tower and then buy him as much time as we can."

Goddess bless the man, DeKieran had guessed what Hel proposed to do.

"What does he mean, Hel?" Nia stammered. "Buy you time for what?"

Hel could have screamed to the heavens at the anguish that ravaged him, knowing what he was about to demand of her. She needed more time. She needed more training. She wasn't ready. The bitter realization that he could very well lose her to madness cut bone deep. But it was Nyth Uchel's only chance—it was *Nia's* only chance—of remaining alive. "We are going to the white tower and perform the Great Rite. Ramsey, Steffania and as many others as possible will hold the ghouls and wraiths at bay, away from the Chambre Cristalle. Nia … please don't look at me like that. The monsters are only active during the hours of darkness. The odds are not in our favor, but this is the only way we have a fighting chance. Beauty…it is *our* only chance."

She shook visibly. Bruises from Goodman's attack and their encounter with the ghouls colored her body in hues of purple-black and exhaustion was apparent in her stance. "We are to work the Great Rite? Now?"

Hel could read the terror in Nia's eyes. A twin to it dwelt in his heart when he considered the real possibility he might gain Nyth Uchel yet lose Nia. With her loss would die any hope for Verdantia, but that scarcely mattered to him. If she was gone, he wouldn't care to live. With gut-churning desolation, he silently repeated his nursery prayer. *Great Mother, as you love me, protect her.* "We cannot wait if we are to save our people. We must act now."

CHAPTER NINETEEN

donia considered their flight through the dark to Torre Bianca, surrounded by armed townsmen holding aloft diaman-lit lanterns, as the stuff of pure terror. Shrill screams echoed through the city streets—cries of townsfolk dying hideous deaths—the folk of Nyth Uchel who'd fallen to the invading nightmares. Every step she took brought her closer to her ultimate dread, the Great Rite. It was yet another terrifying step into a mystical unknown—a step for which she was grossly unprepared—and failure would exact a horrifying cost.

She and Hel had ascended to the Chambre Cristalle, all the while hearing the shouts of Ramsey ordering the perimeter placement to defend the entrance to the tower. Her heart wept at the thought of those close to her who might die to give them this chance. In addition to Ramsey and Steffania, Maddie and Sara, and others from the castle who had become a part of her, guarded the defensive perimeter.

When they entered the chamber, Hel had cupped her face, his own a study in pain. "I can't do this. For the first time, I believe She asks more of me than I am willing to give. I think I would rather die than extinguish your bright light with madness. You are too dear to me. Say the word and we will look for another way."

Adonia could not have wished for a more profound statement

of what she meant to him. At that moment, she wanted nothing more than to be the person he thought she was. "If we perform the Great Rite successfully, then all in Nyth Uchel might live. Yes?"

Hel nodded slowly. "It is my hope, my belief, the rite will cleanse the city of all pestilence."

"Then I am asking you to perform the Great Rite with me. This is my choice, my decision. I understand the risk. I wish to take it."

His great hand cupped the back of her head, and he lowered his forehead to hers. Hel rested there for a long moment, eyes closed. "Dearest Beauty, never again tell me you're not brave."

Hel crossed to a low sideboard and removed a stopper from a cut crystal decanter. He poured a liquid into two massive goblets of crystal banded with bejeweled precious metal.

"This is cinnagin-spiced wine." He held one goblet at eye-level and studied it. "Cinnagin, both our greatest curse and most profound blessing. This aphrodisiac brought the scourge of the Haarb upon our heads, and yet, it provides our sole wealth in interstellar trade. The pinch of cinnagin in this goblet would purchase a hyper-light star cruiser." He swallowed the contents of one goblet in several long pulls and handed her the other—but stopped Adonia as she raised the cup to her lips without hesitation.

"Wait. Before you take this irreversible step, there are things I must tell you about cinnagin. The dried concentrate of this aphrodisiac enables and enhances an intense electro-chemical bond with *diaman* crystal. This creates a neural-chemical reaction that hyper-excites your nervous system. Your craving for orgasm will push you to the threshold of insanity...and Nia, the sensations will deluge you brutally and without surcease. Do not come—no matter if you think you will die—do not come, not until I command it. That way lies certain madness."

Adonia remembered the soul-stripping cries of the insane

magistra in Sylvan Mintoth. She lowered the cup, placing it carefully next to the empty one. "We must use cinnagin?"

He stepped up to hold her in an all-enveloping hug. She felt the heat and solidity of his great body through her robe. She felt the deep vibration of his voice as he spoke. Somehow, it was impossible to continue to doubt with this man supporting her. "When I allow our mutual climax, a bond is formed with Mother Verdantia that allows me to amplify and focus all our combined arousal into the dais. The diamantorre absorbs the shockwave of our orgasms and converts it to greater magnitudes of energy. Somehow, during this moment, our Great Mother adds Her own inherent energies. Torre Bianca will blaze with the clearest of white lights, the *arcobaleno*. I pray that pure light will purify Nyth Uchel of the ghouls and wraiths that afflict us. Do not be surprised if you visit the aetheric plane for a time. Some women speak of interacting with *Her* during the aftermath, though it is uncommon."

She sighed deeply and pushed away, offering him a wobbly smile. "I trust you. So…I drink this and then what happens?"

The familiar wicked glint appeared in his eyes. "Within a short time, you will beg me to fuck you, and I will be exerting all my self-discipline not to grant your pleas." He grimaced. "Cinnagin has a side-effect. For a period following the Great Rite, you will need the presence of my semen inside you to orgasm." Hel traced a finger down her cheek. "We cannot make love until the cinnagin passes from your system or that dependency becomes life-long. You may have a few uneasy days. I want you to understand why I will not touch you afterward. I made a mistake with my wife and gave in to her pleading with bitter consequences. She despised her dependency—and me."

Afterward…he spoke as if an afterward was assured when they both knew it wasn't. Still … Adonia held his gaze for a long moment. She had so little she could give him. She'd never considered this within her power. "I am not Lady Athena. What if I *desire* to give you this gift?"

Unreadable emotions ranged across his face. "*That* is a consideration for another day." Hel leaned in and pressed his lips to hers in tender exploration. "Now ... drink that cup, Beauty."

As Adonia did so, the sounds of conflict, the shouts and shrill cries of combat, filtered through the chamber's windows and she sent up a prayer for those below.

It began as he'd said. An inferno of arousal washed through her system, in unrelenting wave upon wave. Nude and bound spread-eagled to the dais in the Chambre Cristalle, Adonia realized that forevermore, her benchmark for torture would be the Great Rite and its cinnagin-driven extremes—when she could think at all—when the detonation of sexual craving moderated enough for rational thought. Klaran had branded her cold and unwomanly. She'd believed him. Cinnagin transformed her into an insatiable succubus, and she forgot she'd ever been anything else.

"Remember, Beauty, stay with me." Fire burned in Hel's gray eyes as he knelt between her legs and scanned her body while she devoured his muscled elegance and prodigious cock. Then began hours of unremitting torment—or perhaps days—she couldn't tell anymore. Awareness of her surrounds faded, and she forgot who and where she was. Her vision fogged. Why she was in this place and who shared the chamber with her drifted from her rational mind. She only *felt*.

The very air across her body teased her in the most violent fashion. Her nipples contracted to stinging firmness and ached for any touch as her most private places swelled to the limits her aching flesh would allow and wept with her body's dew. Uncontrollable undulations stretched her to the limits of her bonds as she craved contact to assuage the wildfire that consumed her.

"Touch me. Goddess, please, a touch. Anyone...please."

A man's broad shoulders spread her already straining thighs further apart as his tongue moved in a well-lubricated slide across her swollen intimate flesh. He paused and circled her clit with the tip of his tongue. The muscles in her buttocks trembled, straining to press into his caress, to deepen the stimulation that merely taunted her with completion.

Her eyes found his, her neck corded with the strain to hold her head upright. For a moment, reality filtered through her mental daze. "Please, Hel...please..."

He raised his head enough to meet her gaze, his chin glistening with her wetness, his full lips swollen and red. "Please, what, Beauty?" His snarl should have warned her.

"I need you."

"You have me."

"Inside. I need you inside."

His eyes closed to mere slits and he slowly shook his head. That was when she began to hurl vitriolic curses at him. As time passed, her venomous curses turned to abject begging and then to mumbled incoherency as all conscious thought abandoned her, and she became a piece of needy, wanton flesh. In the background, almost obscured by her lust, the low bass rumble of sound and the increasing brilliance of the Chambre Cristalle filtered through her awareness.

At last, Hel's heavy weight lay on her. His hard length parted her swollen feminine lips and invaded. She grunted at the glorious satisfaction. He withdrew. She refused to breathe, all focus poised for the return of that singular sensation. Again, He probed, thrust and withdrew. A low growl built in her chest. "More," she snarled with guttural ferocity. Viciously, his thick cock pierced her and held deep, hitting the end of her channel, and then began rhythmic, punishing thrusts that pushed her to the precipitous brink of orgasm. Beyond coherent speech, she snarled hysterically when his rhythm slowed.

"Easy. Hold fast. The *Chambre* glows brilliant with our arousal. We are almost there."

She shook off the choked syllables of Hel's voice and strained upward to force a more rapid penetration. He retreated. She fell into a seething, ravenous silence. The tempo again picked up and again she climbed to the heavens.

"Nia, come. Come now!" Incapable of disobeying him, she exploded—ecstasy pulsing from her physical body in tsunami-like waves.

When the mind-wiping pleasure released her, Adonia floated bodiless in what could only be a dream world set on a vast metaphysical plane. The universe spread out before her like a velvet cloud. Joy swamped her as she recognized others around her—Hel, Fleur, Sophi and Eric, Ari and Doral—all displayed as brilliant globes of golden light, swirling in the plush blackness. She didn't question how she knew their individual identities—but she knew them. Just as she knew the vast, radiant intelligence was their Great Mother, Verdantia.

Adonia frolicked with childlike innocence among the others but her joy dimmed and horror invaded when her awareness stretched outward. A dark void had gained terrible inroads in its invasion of Her. Black veins threaded the whole of their mother and patches of pustulent corruption dotted her once pristine brilliance. In places, the darkness swallowed Her radiance completely leaving gaping holes of nothingness.

"Welcome, my beloved daughter."

An immeasurable sense of acceptance and love overwhelmed

Adonia. There was no question in Adonia's mind as to who spoke. Her. Their Great Mother. Verdantia.

"Bring them to you…all my bygone sons and daughters of the light…only you can call them forth."

"Great Mother? I don't understand."

"To save me, child, you must summon them. Soon."

Adonia reached out to Her in panicked question, but she was thrown back into the Chambre Cristalle.

Her body felt as if she'd turned for hours on a fiery spit, and her brain refused anything but the most fleeting coherence. She swam in and out of consciousness, trapped in a world of leaden flesh. Her spirit yearned for a return to the grace of the Mother. A dead weight kept her pressed full-length into the diaman-stone dais, and a blazing radiance pained her eyes. Adonia had no concept of how long she lay smashed into the brilliant surface before the weight stirred—a man. Her mind supplied a name—Hel. He lifted himself off with a groan and slid clumsily to his feet. She felt the stinging ties on her wrists loosen. Her struggles against her bonds had abraded her flesh leaving raw sores.

"Nia? Tell me you are all right. Nia?" Vague sounds became words that echoed in her brain, and she fought to comprehend their meaning.

As he freed her hands, he eased her upright on the dais, massaging her arms, and then pulling her into his body in a fierce embrace before attending to her feet. She could do nothing to assist him. She couldn't respond at all. It was as if all strength and will had drained from her.

Hel massaged and caressed Nia's limp form, trying to rouse her. Shallow breaths parted her lips but otherwise Nia showed no life—no cognizant life. His greatest nightmare had become a reality that he rejected with ferocious adamance. It was too cruel. He choked on a garbled cry at the anguish that tore through him. "No! Goddess, no! Great Mother, you cannot allow this. I refuse to lose her." His lips curled back in a snarl. "I reject this end for her. Do you hear me! This will *not* happen."

The force of the pain ripping him apart made it difficult to steady his trembling hands to touch her. "Nia...Beauty...talk to me. Please, talk to me. Your silence is destroying me."

Hel cradled her in his arms and sat them on a low bench arranged against one of the now radiantly brilliant walls and rocked back and forth in agony. "Sweetheart...please...say something."

The tortured despair in Hel's voice spurred Adonia to gargantuan effort. She waded through the leaden sludge that comprised her conscious thought and attempted to organize her mouth and lips to produce a lucid sound. Her throat hurt as if at some point she had screamed herself hoarse, though she had no memory of doing so. She draped heavy arms around his neck and lifted her head to meet his intense gaze. "Fa-fi...fine."

He closed his eyes and when he opened them again, their gray depths displayed vast relief and the corners of his eyes were suspiciously wet. His body shuddered, and he choked out an incoherent sound of reprieve. "Thank you. Now can we try for more than a one-word answer?"

"*She* spoke. *She* spoke," Adonia croaked. "To me."

His face filled with understanding, and he pulled her into him, wrapping her more tightly in his embrace. "I understand. The first time you discover our Great Mother is real and aware of each of us, individually…it robs you of speech."

Adonia nodded dumbly. "Also *what* She told me." Adonia squinted into the blazing light of the chamber and made a valiant attempt to master herself. "After the Great Rite, is it always this bright?"

Hel grunted softly. "No. As I am coming to expect anytime I work a rite with you, something unusual has happened. But first, what did our Mother say?" Hel stood and gathered their robes from the glowing chamber floor. After donning his, he helped her to stand and slip into hers. "Steady."

Adonia shivered at his touch and felt the remorseless heat of lust flare anew. She needed a respite, some time to gather herself mentally and physically. She doubted she'd get it. Her legs threatened to give way, and once more she sank onto the bench. "Our Mother told me to summon Her bygone sons and daughters— soon. She told me only I could do so." Adonia lifted her face to Hel's. "I don't understand."

Hel considered her words for a moment as he slid her bare feet into the slippers she'd worn to the chamber, then his brows rose. "It's a reference to the script from the base of the tower, Nia. It must be."

"That says I will find them beneath my feet." Adonia squinted down at the glowing floor and tapped the soles of her slippers against the stone as if testing its solidity. "The mighty asleep from ages gone." She shook her head and sighed. "My brain refuses to make any sense of the words. The incomprehensible has followed the fantastical so relentlessly I feel as if I sleep-walk."

Hel sat beside her and took her hand. "Understandable. The demands on you have been unremitting. I've not taken very good care of you, Beauty. I…by the Goddess…if I had lost you..."

She raised her eyes to his and placed a finger across his lips to stop his words. "Please, I am yours to use and glad of it. You were willing to sacrifice your city and your people for me." She shook her head. "I couldn't let you do that. I want a whole Nyth Uchel returned to you." She saw a light enter his eyes that warmed her weary soul. With an inarticulate expression, he gathered her into a tight hug for many long moments.

Hel broke the silence with an exhale of breath and released her. "Torre Bianca has a crypt where Nyth Uchel has buried four and a half centuries of kings and queens." Adonia pulled back from him and Hel held her gaze steadily. "The mighty asleep from ages past? The crypt is quite literally beneath our feet. I'll take you there after you have a chance to sleep and eat something."

"How long have we been here? In the Chambre Cristalle? I'm so befuddled."

Hel turned his attention to the nearest window. "I'm not clear on that myself," he admitted. "A day and a half, perhaps? I may have rushed a few steps. I feared…" He frowned. "I feared for Ramsey and Steffania and all the others." He stood and held out a hand to her. "Come. It is time to see what the Great Rite has accomplished...and if our friends still live."

As they descended in one of the mechanical lifts, the groundswell of noise filtering through the thick walls of Torre Bianca hinted that all was not as it had been—that and the scent and temperature of the air. Adonia smelled the green of spring and a warm zephyr flirted with her cheeks from the open door on ground level where a weary, sweat-stained Ramsey leaned, his arms wrapped around his equally disheveled wife. Intense joy pierced Adonia and a brilliant smile lit her face. An upwelling of emotion brought tears to her eyes. "You live. Thank the Goddess. And my maidservant, Maddie…and Sara?

Ramsey held her gaze steadily and gave an almost imperceptible shake of his head. Adonia inhaled an unsteady breath at the sorrow that replaced her joy. She swiped at her eyes but the tears overflowed and ran steadily down her cheeks.

Ramsey straightened. "Many died but their sacrifices were not in vain. Come, you should see the impossible magick you have wrought."

An incredulous sight met her eyes as they walked out the entry door into Torre Bianca's courtyard. It was A'rken's cottage revisited. Puddles of water stood everywhere and eaves dripped with melting snow. Green sprouts emerged from formerly barren flowerbeds and a warm breeze had replaced the bone-chilling cold. Even more astonishing, the very air shimmered with a silver luminosity, a reflection of the brilliance of Torre Bianca blazing like a white flame at their backs. Composed entirely of diaman stone, the tower's whole structure radiated an interior light of the purest alabaster white. The atmosphere teemed with life and vigor silvered by Torre Bianca's radiance.

Among the splendor were signs of its cost—women and men with grief-stricken faces, children crying for mothers and fathers amid rows of motionless bodies neatly laid out, their faces discreetly covered.

A mighty cheer had gone up from the ragged townsmen gathered in the spacious area when she and Hel emerged from the tower. Confusion reigned as everyone pressed in on them wanting to touch Adonia's body, her clothes, her hair. Adonia didn't want to push them away but it was overwhelming; the strength she'd summoned to make it this far on her own two legs drained out of her until she hung on Hel for support.

Finally, Hel, Ramsey and Steffania, Bernard and a few other attendants, forced the crowd back with sharp commands to, "Let Magistra DeCorvus through. She is exhausted and needs rest." In a blatant display of protective ferocity, Hel swooped her up in his arms and hustled her toward the castle as the townspeople fell back to allow her room to pass.

Cradled in his strong arms, oblivion closed in again and she surrendered to complete exhaustion.

CHAPTER TWENTY

As he restlessly prowled the sitting room adjoining his bedchamber, Hel's gaze flicked from the impassive features of Ramsey to the curious face of Steffania and then to the concerned frown of Bernard. He'd tucked an unconscious Adonia into their bed and had called the three to join him. He'd explained what the Great Mother had told Nia during the Great Rite when the events of the last forty-eight hours hit with the force of a tidal wave. His normal self-discipline abruptly deserted him, and the acid discontent roiling within him erupted into screaming rage. "I cannot protect her, and the thought is driving me mad!"

His feet caught on an ottoman and he stumbled. With a feral cry of frustration, he drew his sword and hacked violently at the footstool in his path. Fabric and feathers flew through the air and floated to the exotic carpet. Ramsey and Steffania exchanged glances of sympathetic concern, and Bernard hustled to a safe corner. When Hel's innocent, unarmed victim collapsed to the floor, a mess of shattered wood and upholstery, he grunted in disgust and threw his blade into the opposite corner. "Someone take that away from me. I just ruined a 300-year-old antique. I'm not safe with a weapon at the moment." Once again, he stalked the spacious room. "I cannot see a way to spare her. Worse, I must use her myself. Nia is critical to all Verdantia's survival."

Ramsey grunted rudely. "Come spar with me. Unlike the hapless furniture, I'll hit back."

Hel saw right through the man. Ramsey was *handling* him. He didn't care. Perhaps physical exertion would excise some of the impotent inferno raging throughout his body. "In my present mood, I might kill you, DeKieran."

Ramsey chuckled at his snarled threat. "Accomplish what the wraiths and ghouls didn't? You can try."

Hel stomped to where his great sword lay and picked it up. "The training circle behind the armory."

Ramsey grinned and opened his arm in a gesture. "After you." He nodded at his wife. "Care to referee, Vixen?"

Steffania demurred. "No, thank you. I promised to help Bernard inventory what remains in the armory." She raised on her toes, kissed his mouth and murmured as she pulled away, her arms still draped on his shoulders, "Be nice to him, *dominus*. No cheating."

Ram blinked at her ingenuously while his hands massaged the globes of her ass, and he pulled her tightly into his groin with a low groan of desire. Hel couldn't endure the intimate tableau. It reminded him too much of what *he* desperately wanted. "Any time you can *bestir* yourself, DeKieran." He whirled and stomped out the door.

Hours later and much the worse for wear—that gods-be-damned hell-spawn *had* cheated—Hel groaned as he sank into the tub of chest-deep hot water. The bath was already taking on a pinkish tinge from the fall-out of his bout with Ram. Multiple flesh wounds burned as the hot water penetrated his torn flesh, but the heat felt wonderful on his abused muscles. He submerged totally and gently washed the grime from his face, taking care not to press too hard on the left side of his jaw. DeKieran had dealt him a brain-rattling blow with the hilt of his sword that had ended their contest with both of them sprawled in the grit. Hel counted himself lucky he still had sight in that eye. But, he had given as good as he'd gotten and smiled at the thought. The information Ramsey had relayed about the state of Nyth Uchel and their immediate surrounds also cheered him.

As the two of them lay on their backs in the gritty soil of the practice ring, gasping like speared carp, DeKieran had described the magickal effects their working of the Great Rite had accomplished.

"There is the obvious. Torre Bianca blazes as the brightest star on the night's horizon, and the severe cold that gripped Nyth Uchel has turned temperate. We seem to be entering a new spring. You and Lady DeCorvus have also purified the land surrounding this city—though I don't know how far that purification extends. It seems the wraiths and the ghouls have been eliminated from the city or at least driven back." Ram groaned, and Hel turned his head and studied the man. Ramsey lay loose-limbed, eyes closed, his sword flat in the gravel beside him.

A grin pulled at the corners of Hel's mouth. "Ha! You look like a three-day-old kill, DeKieran."

"You should see yourself, you hulking mass of flea-infested idiocy," Ram retorted, lying motionless. "How Lady DeCorvus tolerates you in her bed is beyond me. She must like sleeping with a mutant goat."

"Hell-spawn."

"Repellent, pestilent asshole."

"Noxious carcass of flatulent gas."

Ramsey remained silent for a moment. "That's your fault. Serve something other than those gods-be-damned potatoes."

Hel blinked several times and then exploded in loud guffaws, joined quietly by Ramsey. Their hilarity attracted several townsmen who assisted them to their staggering feet.

"What have you done to yourself?" Nia entered the bathroom and knelt by the tub. Her anxious eyes scanned Hel's body and her hands reached for his face, gently turning his head and smoothing back his hair so she could look at the puffy mound of purpling flesh that used to be the prominent ridge of his left cheekbone. "Oh…Hel," she sighed. "Is this the worst of it?"

He cleared his throat, feeling like a five-year-old child caught in some mischief by his mother. "Yes. The rest are superficial cuts."

"Steffania told me you and Ramsey had beaten each other to a bloody pulp. I brought some crystals. I will heal this quickly."

He held her wrist when she would have stood and moved away. "No, I don't want you to expend any energy on my self-inflicted wounds. They will heal just fine on their own."

Nia kissed his battered knuckles and slid her wrist from his hold. "At least let me poultice your wounds. I have some plant extracts that will reduce the swelling and ease your pain."

"All right, Healer. Work your craft." He met her concerned gaze with a wincing smile. "And see to DeKieran, if you would."

"I have already seen to Lord Ramsey. He wouldn't allow me to heal *him* either."

Nia's exasperation made him smile. "Then I'll allow him to live one more day. How do *you* feel? Any after-effects of the rite?"

"Ah." She rose and wrapped her arms around her waist, dropping her head. Her hair fell in a velvet brown curtain between them. "Well…ah…" She shifted as though uneasy in her skin. "Yes…well…"

For the first time, he noticed a slight tremor that shook her slender frame. Hel knew well what his shy beauty hesitated to put into words. "It's that bad?"

The veil of her hair rippled as she nodded, but he still could not see her face. "The hot mineral waters of the Grotta D'oro have been known to temper the burn of cinnagin's arousal. Would you like to join me there? We can check on the *miku amar*, and the burial crypt is not far from the grotto."

She lifted her head with a smile. "Yes," she whispered. "I'd like that very much. I'll just go get my medicines…" She fled out the door.

With an amused shake of his head, Hel rose, stepped out of the tub and began the painful task of drying off. He'd enjoy a long soak in the waters of the Grotta D'oro, too.

On the white sand shore of the subterranean lake, Hel proffered a hand. "Come. The hot mineral waters will soothe you.

She'd placed her hand in his and followed him to an underwater ledge where she sat straddle-legged on his lap, back to his chest, and allowed the waist-high water to appease her overwrought flesh. "Look, Hel, the *miku amar*."

Adonia had no doubt the sweet creatures had sensed her as soon as she and Hel entered the grotto's waters. Repressed lust rattled Adonia's body. She must have projected pheromones to the deepest parts of the subterranean lake. They watched as the delicate creatures swooshed toward them.

"Look carefully, Nia. Tell me what you see," Hel whispered, his voice full of burgeoning excitement, and she strained to see what had provoked him.

There! Sheltered among their parents' free-floating tentacles and cilia were small blobs of blue and pink, tiny duplicates of their mother and father. She watched with growing delight as the pink female wrapped a delicate tentacle around Adonia's wrist and her tiny offspring bumped and bobbed against Adonia's belly. Laughter welled inside her at the antics of the tiny offspring. "Oh! They tickle. Sweet babies. There are so many of them. Do the little ones always behave like this?" Adonia wriggled on Hel's lap, giggling at the sensations the tiny *miku amar* made as they continually bumped into her abdomen.

Hel drew back and looked at her with the strangest expression.

"What? Oh, Hel, they tickle. I'm afraid to move for fear I will hurt them."

"The little ones are saying hello to my son or daughter." His voice choked out the words thickly and his eyes looked suspiciously bright.

"What?"

"Nia, you are pregnant."

"What!" she squeaked as Hel crushed her to him and straightened, turning them in dizzy circles in the warm waters.

"You wonderful woman! Oh, by the Goddess, Nia…"

Adonia saw the moment he recalled their circumstances and the unsurpassed joy filling his expression faded. He lowered them to the ledge and sat her across his lap; his great hands bracketed her face, and his gaze captured and held hers.

"You are pregnant with my babe." Hel said flatly. "Is that distasteful to you?"

"No! No, never. I'm…stunned…and puzzled. I have used Maiden's Clover without fail. It is a good contraceptive. How?" She saw sorrow flit across Hel's face and raised a hand to his cheek. "Don't misunderstand. I delight in bearing your child. This is just so...unexpected."

His lips quirked up on one side, and his eyes lost the pained look they'd worn moments ago. "Another benefit of the *miku amar*. It's known they cause ovulation in a woman if the *miku* are also breeding. It probably happened just before your female went dormant." Hel wrapped his arm around her middle and cuddled her closer to him with a slight chuckle at the tiny blobs of color bobbing atop the disturbed water then making small darts toward Adonia. "Since they are symbiots, the boost to a woman's ability to conceive ensures their own species continues." They both watched the tiny *miku* swarm around Nia. "You are certain you don't mind?" Hel murmured.

Adonia planted a long kiss on his elegant mouth. "I would have chosen a different time, but I am over-joyed to be giving you a new DeHelios."

Hours later, damp, cool air washed Adonia's face as Hel led her hand-in-hand through an immense underground space filled with marble statuary and tombs of the majestic rulers out of Nyth Uchel's fabled history. He stopped in front of a massive block of unadorned marble bearing a simple inscription.

Our beloved, Isolde,
eternal queen of our hearts.
We are yours in death
as we were yours in life.
Federago DeHelios & Agentio DeLorcha

"They outlived her by some years. When Federago died, Agentio followed soon after. Lore has it that their faces wore beatific smiles as they passed—as though they greeted their lost love. I've often wondered if she met them. It's a nice thought."

She thought so, too. Adonia's throat had closed, and her eyes threatened to spill the tears collecting in them. She cleared her throat and swiped at her face.

Hel drew her close. "Since she has come to you during your

healing trances, do you want to try to connect with Isolde first?"

"Yes."

Hel spread a thick blanket on the stone floor and sat cross-legged. He reached up for her hand and pulled her onto his lap, wrapping his arms around her waist and snugging her to his front.

Adonia spilled the glowing diaman crystals she'd brought onto her lap, took a deep breath and tried to relax her body. "This may take a while. I'm not sure of what I'm doing. I don't know what I'm supposed to find."

His lips traveled kisses along her jaw. "I wish I could guide you, but there is no precedent for what you attempt. Whatever time you need, Beauty. I'm here."

Adonia settled into the repetitive chant she'd found most effective for reaching the aetheric plane when healing those of the fading and despite her doubts, found herself in a familiar disembodied state within moments of beginning. She looked down on herself from above and could readily see the slim white stream of aetheric energy that tethered her to her physical body—a body safely enwrapped in Hel's arms. Thus reassured, Adonia began to quest mentally, expanding her awareness of the amorphous metaphysical plane, calling out for the woman she had come to think of as a protector in this altered existence. "Queen Isolde, it is Adonia. Queen Isolde, if you hear me, please make yourself known to me."

Adonia didn't know how long her spirit wandered in the crypt below Torre Bianca when she felt a masculine presence join her—a presence lacking the welcoming warmth she had come to associate with Isolde DeCorvus.

"Woman, why do you disturb the slumber of kings and queens?"

"I seek Isolde DeCorvus. I have a question I would ask of her." Adonia hesitated. "Is she known to you? Will you bring her to me? To whom do I speak?"

Again, Adonia felt the swirl of an intense male essence surround her with a sense of increasing threat until she felt distinctly imperiled—as if the aetheric presence somehow held the potential to harm her.

"Who are you, woman, that you dare ask the name of
a prince of royal blood, and presume to make him your errand
boy?"

Had her mission not been vital, Adonia would have fled on the spot, such was the weight of threat that suffocated her. "I am Adonia DeCorvus, daughter in blood to Isolde DeCorvus. The Great Mother tasked me to summon 'the mighty asleep from ages gone' to meet the great evil consuming our planet. I believe I am the raven referred to in the inscription at the foot of Torre Bianca." Tempest buffeted her spirit as if a great whirlwind whipped the aetheric plane.

"You are the raven?"

Scornful, angry laughter echoed through her mind.

"We shall see. The great deceiver makes lies seem like truth"

Adonia screamed with agony, and her earthly body writhed in Hel's arms as an enraged force shredded her aetherial self into a thousand wisps of scattered energy before withdrawing into a boiling cloud. Her essence gradually reformed, and she quaked with internal terror. If her task hadn't been so urgent, Adonia would have surrendered to hysteria.

"I am Federago DeHelios, my lady raven. You taste of our blood and bear the touch of our Great Mother. You are of the true light. I will bring my queen and Agentio."

"My thanks … Prince DeHelios … I am very grateful." She received no reply. She didn't wait long.

"Daughter of our blood, it is Isolde and Agentio. My beloved Federago says you've questions to put to me?"

Adonia mentally exhaled, glad beyond words she didn't face the spirit of Federago DeHelios again. "My Queen, my Lord Agentio," Adonia acknowledged respectfully. "Our Great Mother has told me I must summon *Her sons and daughters of light from ages past* to combat the great evil that consumes our planet. We think that means those illustrious dead from Nyth Uchel's history—those who are buried in this crypt. But I don't know how, and I don't know when, and I don't know what to tell them to do."

"Our Great Mother faces grave peril. We cannot foresee the ending. By the blood of the raven, summon all the bygone kings and queens of Verdantia by name to the aetheric plane but only when all your might is exhausted and defeat an imminent surety. The Great Deceiver is unaware of our strength and cannot be allowed time to marshal resources against us; then pray we will be enough to defeat this dark evil. I think we'll not meet again. Be vigilant. Have courage. Where the light of love burns, so does life."

Isolde and her lovers departed, leaving Adonia overwhelmed

with desolate bleakness. She awoke in Hel's arms, convulsed with terrible quaking sobs.

"Nia, ah, love, don't." He held her close to him and whispered, "Beauty, please, your tears cut me deeper than any blade."

Adonia scrubbed her face with her hands and tried to temper her shudders and slow her breathing. She couldn't explain to Hel her sense of despair and loss and her foreboding about the future. She had nothing solid upon which to base her feelings. They were just…feelings. "Don't worry. It's just exhaustion." She forced a smile. "I'll be all right."

"Did you get any answers?" Hel helped her to stand and then gathered the blanket.

Her smile wavered. "Yes. I know what to do now—sort of. I just don't know when. From what our Great Mother said, we must act soon." Adonia turned worried eyes to Hel. "But what is soon? I cannot escape the feeling an imminent disaster looms. I'm consumed by a need for haste."

CHAPTER TWENTY-ONE

H el thought about her concern. He didn't discount her feelings, but… "A'rken specifically said when Belarus mates with Cirrus in the northern sky. If he is to be believed, we still have months."

She shook her head. "I cannot explain my unease. I just…" She faltered to a stop. "I don't think we have months."

Hel wanted a reprieve for Nia after their recent crisis. By the Goddess, he wanted a respite for all of them—but especially his 'beauty'. "You have done so much these past few weeks. I want to see you rest and recover. I prescribe some relaxation and pampering for you and our child. I want the gray of exhaustion gone from your face. I want to lie next to you at night and know that your sleep is natural and not that of physical collapse. Come." He enveloped her hand with his and led her out of the crypt into a soft spring-like night scented with green things bursting into life and velvet black lightened to dusk by the shimmering glow of Torre Bianca.

Adonia paused for a moment on the entryway steps and gazed about her. "I don't think I'll ever become used to this magickal place. I wish my father could have seen it."

Adonia described her experience in the crypt as they walked back to the castle, particularly her run-in with Federago DeHelios.

"That was when your body writhed in my arms?" Those minutes were branded in his memory; he'd been helpless to aid her—not a feeling he relished.

"Yes. He was testing me, I think. I don't believe I'd have enjoyed meeting him in the flesh."

"Hmm. I understand that was the general consensus. History describes him as formidable."

Adonia's eyes met his briefly. "Like you, then."

He drew back. "You still consider me formidable?"

She tossed him a sideways look of skepticism. "*Bás dtost*? And when was the last time anyone said no to you? Even Lord Ramsey does your bidding."

He stopped and drew her to him, first cupping her face in his great hand and then gently running his fingers through the hair at her temple and tilting her face up to his. "You said no to me."

She cast her eyes down shyly. "And got a very sore ass for it."

Hel dropped his hand and his head fell back as he laughed freely then resumed walking. "Which you rather enjoyed. Ah, Nia, how you lighten my heart."

"The accomplishment I take the most pride in during these difficult times," she murmured with pleasure.

He warmed at her gentle disclosure and, with an arm around her shoulder, he drew her closer to him. "Of all the miraculous things you have done, you count easing my heart as the one you take most pride in? Not banishing the wraiths and ghouls and saving Nyth Uchel? Not dispelling a lingering winter or saving Steffania from certain death?" Hel felt her shrug.

"Of course I *should* count those as greater but you are a miracle more valuable than any of those other deeds. If I can lighten your heart? *That* is beyond price to me."

He stopped and turned to her. The extent of Nia's loving, giving nature stole all thought from his head but one. Though they could ill afford the time—there was a battle looming—he wanted to steal some precious moments to love her, cosset her, show her how dear she was to him. Lurking in the back of his mind was the thought he might never have another chance. "My dearest Healer, I wish to cosset you and attend you for the next few days. We are going to put aside our cares and anxieties temporarily and enjoy a brief hiatus from worry."

Her luminous brown eyes found his. A smile turned her lips. "I'd like that very much."

Hel raised her hand to his mouth and kissed the back of it. "Make sure you tell me when the symptoms from the cinnagin abate."

Hel heard those words two days later. During those two days, Hel and Nia took comfort in each other as their friends were buried; he held her in his arms while they shared intimacies about their life before the Haarb changed things forever on Verdantia—and he fell deeper and deeper into love with his self-effacing, giving 'beauty'. They spoke of children's names, and Hel nuzzled the satin skin of her belly before bed each evening, kissing the nascent life within her and telling the tiny DeHelios how longed for and loved he or she was. It was two days where his world narrowed to only Nia.

Soft half-light, what now passed for night in Nyth Uchel post-Great Rite, surrounded them as Hel pulled her slender hind end into his groin and pulled the coverlet over the top of them.

"I feel normal."

Nia's whisper galvanized him and her squeak of surprise accompanied his surge over her, flattening her on her back. Hel's hips and thighs demanded she spread her legs to cradle his quickly hardening cock, and his hands wrapped her wrists at arm's length over her head. His face hovered inches over hers. It had been exquisite torture to sleep next to her these past two days, his cock stone hard and aching with the knowledge she burned for him, too—and do nothing but hold her. Nia had offered him relief with her mouth or hands, but he'd refused. If she suffered unappeased lust, then so would he.

"Say again, Beauty. Did I mishear you?"

Her eyes gleamed with mischief as they held his gaze. Her head shook ever so slowly.

"You did not mishear me." She pulled a wrist free and her finger traced his cheek. "Be careful of your poor face. The swelling there is just now starting to leave."

"I'm sure you'll make me forget." A broad grin crept across Hel's face until his cheeks ached. "You have sealed your fate. I hope you're prepared to reap a whirlwind."

Her throaty laugh answered him. He held her gaze until her features blurred as he lowered his mouth to hers and closed his eyes to savor her plush lips. She opened to him immediately, and her tongue danced with his as he quested inward and sought her taste. She intoxicated him like *Pottsdim Likor,* and his brain reeled as if he'd consumed a decanter of the potent beverage.

Hel lost himself in the wonderland of Nia's mouth for endless minutes with the thought he had not kissed her nearly enough. Finally, he pulled back, dragging in air, and released her other wrist. His fingers sifted her hair at her temples. He held her gaze as his hips flexed and the head of his cock sought the wet haven between her thighs. "Can you take me?"

A siren's smile and half-lidded eyes accompanied her movement as Nia wrapped her long legs around his flanks and set her heels into his buttocks. Her motion opened her fully and centered his shaft at her gateway where, with a mere push of his hips, he could penetrate her. The steady pressure of her heels pressing him downward made clear her desire. He sank inward carefully and groaned as the slick, warm moisture of her inner flesh teased his greedy cock in a mind-blowing slide of pure wonder. He submerged himself in her, cleaving and joining with her, so lost to sensation that he no longer knew where he began and Nia ended. Hilted within her depths, Hel opened his eyes to meet hers. "Our future is uncertain. I don't know what fate holds in store. But this I know; until time ends, with my body and soul, I pledge myself to you, beloved."

Tears appeared in the corners of her eyes and she blinked. "I am yours, my prince—beyond death—even as Federago, Agentio and Isolde."

There was no expressing the emotion filling him with something as simple as words so he told her with his body, disciplining himself to hold back until he had brought her again and then again to climax—though he could have screamed at the agony of restraint as her hot flesh suckled his hyper-sensitive cock. When he finally slipped the leash of his self-control, his triumphant roar echoed against the walls of their chamber. Both of them lay shattered in the aftermath, their eyes locked, and the luminous joy he recognized in Nia's expression forged a bond between them Hel knew not even death could extinguish. "For eternity," he murmured.

"Beyond time," she whispered.

The warm breath of her soft sighs gradually became the regular exhales of sleep as her slender form relaxed beneath him. Hel prayed to all the deities known to him for the ability to keep her and their babe safe from the threatening cataclysm. He knew with certainty should Nia perish, he would shortly follow her into death—for life would hold nothing that could make him stay in a world without her. He arranged himself protectively over her and their unborn child but sleep remained elusive. He lay awake, guarding his beloved's rest, until daylight stole into their room.

"Rise, Beauty. I'm afraid our idyll must end."

Adonia opened her eyes to her prince stroking her sleep-styled hair away from her face. In spite of all the recent tragedy and all that still threatened, an elated wonder suffused her that she had captured the heart of such a man. She clung to her joy even more, knowing how short-lived it might be.

"Your bath awaits you, then we'll join Ramsey and Steffania for breakfast."

When Adonia entered the dining room at Hel's side, Steffania's bright gold gaze found her. "So … you two have finally emerged from the bedchamber," she teased.

While Adonia wouldn't have sacrificed the time she'd spent with Hel for any reason, nevertheless, her conscience gnawed at her for abandoning her responsibilities at such a critical moment.

"Are you well, Steffania? I'm afraid I've been a very poor healer. I should not have disappeared for days when so many must need me."

Ramsey grunted. "We managed. We knew where you were, Lady DeCorvus. Had there been a crisis, we would have found you."

Adonia turned to catch the exchange of speaking glances and nods between Lord Ramsey and Hel before Hel pulled out a chair and seated her; some sort of unspoken communication between males of a similar ilk, she supposed. She was struck again by the similarities between the two men and thought back to that seemingly long ago day in Sylvan Mintoth when Lord Ramsey had refused to be parted from Steffania and Adonia had wondered what it must feel like to be loved to such a degree. Her gaze sought Hel's and the message in his steady gaze confirmed her certainty that now she had that kind of love.

As they fell to eating, the men began discussing the current state of the city and plans for an excursion to Nyth Uchel's borders. With a casual glance at her husband, Steffania leaned across the table to Adonia and murmured, "You glow with an inner joy, Adonia. The change in you and Nyth Uchel is wonderful. It is like witnessing a rebirth." Delight brightened Steffania's expression until the woman beamed.

Adonia found it impossible to contain a return smile. "I know it sounds bizarre, but I don't think I remember being happier."

Steffania sat back. "Good. I don't know of anyone who deserves it more. Has Prince DeHelios asked you to stay, to make it official?"

Emotion clogged her throat, and Adonia could only nod with what she was certain was an idiotic grin. "And, I carry his babe."

Steffania returned a similarly ridiculous smile. "We knew it. Ram said the …"

Adonia never did find out what Lord Ramsey had said for just as Steffania would have completed her thought, a trumpet fanfare resounded distantly through the open windows. Hel stood abruptly, his chair toppling to the carpet. Another horn from within the city answered, with an elaborate run of notes. The whole repeated three times while the other three diners listened, frozen in place. When the last answering note had died, Adonia turned to Hel in puzzlement. "Were you expecting visitors?"

Hel leaned down and righted his chair. "Come, all of you—to the eastern courtyard. *That* was the royal fanfare. Unless the horns lie, Nyth Uchel is about to receive an historical first visit from a sitting Constante queen."

CHAPTER TWENTY-TWO

S tunned, Adonia stood beside Hel, Ramsey and Steffania on the castle steps and watched a phalanx of sweat-stained battle mounts, nostrils distended, manes flying, thunder through Nyth Uchel castle's eastern portal and swirl to a chaotic halt in the courtyard. Adonia assumed Hel and the others were as taken aback as she, for none of them had spoken a word.

The ringing commands of High Lord DeTano sorted the seeming chaos into order. That the Second Tetriarch had traveled fast and hard was not good—but more ominous—the ruling trio had brought their children. Foreboding crashed down on Adonia as she noted with alarm the small figures riding pillion with members of the Queen's Guard. Then she heard a well-loved voice lifting above the hubbub.

"Adonia! Here! Adonia!" Astride a slender desert mount, a spot of white amid the heavier, blacks and bays, sat her dearest friend, Sophi DeStroia, and helping her from her lathered gelding was her husband, Eric.

Adonia raised the hand not clasped in Hel's in a return wave. Neither they, nor the royal children, should be in Nyth Uchel for any but the most dire reason. Icy fear shivered down her spine, and she slid into Hel for support. "I don't like what this arrival portends."

"No. It cannot be good." Hel wrapped a reassuring arm around her waist and pulled her close. Adonia felt his half-turn as he looked over his shoulder at some of the castle retainers who'd joined them on the steps. "Prepare my mother's and brothers' apartments and air the nursery. Make sure the queen and her company have all they need. Alert the stables."

Hel's gaze returned to those filling the courtyard. "Why do you suppose *he* rides with them?" Hel's puzzled tones pulled Adonia's eyes from Sophi and Eric, and she followed the direction of his nod. Behind the royal trio advancing at a brisk walk, hobbled a shrunken, travel-stained A'rken.

Ramsey and Steffania stepped up to flank them, and Ram's acerbic voice drawled, "Perfect. The Tetriarch brought the lunatic. My joy is complete."

Adonia ran her gaze around a room in Nyth Uchel's castle she'd never known existed. Hel had called it "the receiving room." Covers had been hastily snatched away from the plush upholstered furniture in this spacious, elaborately decorated chamber to make them available for the four of them—Hel, Ramsey, Steffania and her—plus their royal visitors and the mystic, A'rken. As quickly as the cloth covers were removed, the chairs and sofas were occupied, and shortly very curious eyes exchanged glances with travel-weary ones that held far too much bleakness for Adonia's comfort.

Even more disconcerting was the ominous silence that fell when Hel dismissed the servants with orders to bring food and drink and sat back and observed those sitting opposite him. Adonia thought it the strangest of meetings. Not a word had been exchanged—as if not doing so would forestall whatever calamity had brought the Second Tetriarch to Nyth Uchel.

Abruptly, High Lord DeTano rose, crossed his arms and began

to pace behind the sofa where Queen Constante and Visconte DeLorion sat. "DeHelios, the corruption you described to us months ago did not stay confined to your mountain. Day by day, some unknown malignancy devours our planet in swaths hundreds of miles wide. Dreams of horrendous portent have tortured Doral, Eric, Sophi and me. Reports of sigil tower after sigil tower falling to this black plague accompany the refugees pouring into Sylvan Mintoth, bearing tales of misshapen creatures savaging their towns and villages.

"Not even our dead rest, as graveyards vomit up abominations of flesh and pustulence that overwhelm those living nearby." Verdantia's High Lord stopped his pacing, and his gaze locked onto Hel. "We have come to join our strength to yours, because it seems Adonia is the key to defeating this grim enemy, and we have little time to waste." DeTano's eyes sought out A'rken. "At least this is what *he* would have us believe."

The mystic's eyes darted feverishly around the room, unseeing. Repeatedly, his lips muttered, "Wrong. No time. Wrong, wrong. No time. Now, now." Adonia thought it probable A'rken's mind was elsewhere than in this room.

"You removed your children and the queen from the safety of Sylvan Mintoth on the word of that madman?" Ramsey stated with caustic incredulity.

DeTano's posture stiffened and he all but snarled, "Not the *mystic's* word only. *She* directed us here. To what purpose, it remains to be seen. We could not leave the children when their safety in Sylvan Mintoth without us was so uncertain."

"I am unhappily acquainted with events similar to what you describe," said Hel, his gaze seeking some far horizon.

"And yet, Torre Bianca blazes like a day star and the air is fresh with life. A far remove from the Nyth Uchel you described to us in Sylvan Mintoth," Doral stated quietly. "What accomplished such renewal?"

Adonia felt the weight of Hel's regard and lifted her face to his loving appraisal. A solemn smile flirted with his lips. "I attribute it to Adonia. It was she who worked the Great Rite with me—that which has seen Nyth Uchel returned to a portion of her past glory. Adonia has an unusual connection with our Great Mother."

The potent scrutiny of every eye in the room landed on her, and Adonia dropped her head to hide behind a curtain of hair. It was difficult to hold onto the identity she'd acquired in Nyth Uchel when so many from her past knew her only as a mundane Oshtesh woman skilled with herbs.

"Chin up, Beauty. You are as worthy as any of us," Hel whispered and then stood to address Fleur where she sat wrapped in her visconte's arms. "Your Majesty, you were ignorant of the great prize you sent to Nyth Uchel or I'm certain you would never have let her leave your side."

Adonia straightened in alarm. "Hel, no!" she whispered vehemently. "Don't—"

Hel opened his arm to Adonia in a sweeping gesture of acknowledgement. "May I present *Lady* Adonia DeCorvus, a descendant of our first queen, Isolde DeCorvus, through her paternal line and *your* distant cousin, High Lord DeTano, through her maternal line. My Nia is a healer of immense talent, a magistra of raw, unschooled power and every bit your equal in birth."

"Of elite aristocratic lineage…and you've performed the Great Rite…of all people," Eric mused with a soft shake of his head. "How surprised you must have been, Adonia." He smiled at her with a wry lift of an eyebrow—not unkindly, for Eric had never been unkind to her—but she still closed her eyes in mortification. She deserved Eric's gentle teasing. In her ignorance, she'd been simply awful to the man because he was highborn.

"Your Nia?" Doral's quiet voice fell into the small lull.

Adonia felt her hands seized, and Hel pulled her into his arms. His eyes met hers and softened when she half-smiled in return, her heart rejoicing in his public declaration of possession. "Yes, my Nia. She has agreed to be my wife, and I will value her as the treasure she is."

"Assuming we live another seven-day," muttered Ram.

"She dies. She dies!" screamed A'rken, suddenly standing in their midst. "No time. No time! Now. All Her sons and daughters. The corvus must call them now! It must be now!" His delirious rants continued, escalating in hysteria until only shrill shrieks and spittle spewed from his mouth as he scratched and clawed at his head, pulling clumps of hair from his scalp in frantic distress.

Sophi flew to him and captured his flailing hands, all the while murmuring soothing words. His frantic screeching abated, and he collapsed to the floor, rocking and moaning.

"And this is the learned counsel that prompts you to act?" Ramsey directed his derisive question to Ari. "Do you have a more reasoned support for your precipitous arrival?"

Adonia thought Ramsey courted death. Certainly Ari's reaction indicated the High Lord enforced the most severe self-control—his body so rigid it appeared stone. She didn't think he drew breath. It made his quiet murmur resonate in the room. "Dreams, DeKieran. Waking dreams afflict us—dreams of a horror that devours one's soul. She dies. Our Great Mother dies and, with her, all life on this planet."

Adonia gasped as memories of her recent nightmare invaded her mind and her eyes sought Hel.

Hel's arms tightened around her. "All of you, come with me. There is something you must see."

Hel led Ari, Doral and Eric around the base of Torre Bianca, deciphering the recently revealed words for them as they methodically examined the writing carved into the footstones. Fleur, Sophi, Steffania and Ramsey grouped around Adonia, and she explained the inscription to Sophi and Fleur.

"The words on the Tower are simple, and if we understand them correctly, straightforward in what I must do." Adonia went on to recount the events of the last few weeks. She felt their attention centered upon her intently and tried to ignore the part of her that would have deferred to anyone else. "In the crypt beneath this tower, I have spoken with the First Tetriarch. Queen Isolde told me that through the blood of my ancestors I can summon the kings and queens of ages past by name to aid us in this fight for our Great Mother."

The group clustered around her opened to include Hel, Ari, Doral and Eric. Hel immediately pressed her to his side and held her to him. "Both A'rken and High Lord DeTano confirm your desire for haste. The final battle is on us, Beauty. We must act immediately. We will perform the Great Rite in the morning."

The hum of the quiet background conversations fell away, and Adonia's attention narrowed to only his beloved face, his possessing strength. Every particle of her being rebelled at the thought of the possibility of losing him. Her inner self cried in anguish, *"No! I cannot do this! I cannot risk you. I cannot risk our growing child. I have just found you!"* It seemed self-centered of her to dread the loss of this man above all things when life to the smallest blade of grass could be lost to the encroaching horror.

Adonia knew from the expression writ across Hel's features that he saw her desperate fear and she watched as pain replaced the glow of love in his eyes. She couldn't stand the thought she added to his cares. For him, she could pretend to be brave and relieve his heart of a small burden. She closed her eyes and, when she opened them again, she let all the warmth of her true love and false confidence fill them. "As you told me some days ago, 'I am the beloved of DeHelios.' No power, natural or unnatural, can stand against us."

It helped mitigate the terrible ache in her heart to see his expression soften and some of his worry fade.

The group returned to congealed food and lukewarm beverages on the sideboard in the receiving room. After watching how quickly it was dispatched, Adonia didn't think anyone cared. All they could speak about was the inscription on Torre Bianca and its implications.

Ari's gaze swept the room. "We agree that we must fight this…" his eyes swung to hold Adonia's, "…what did you say Isolde called it—the Great Deceiver—on the aetheric plane."

"Yes." Adonia nodded. "But, High Lord, we cannot defeat this darkness. Its power is too immense. We can only weaken it, drive it away; we can only make our Great Mother, our planet, so unpalatable that consuming us is too costly."

"How do we do that, Adonia? Only you have any experience with this corruption." Doral's quiet voice pulled her eyes to his beautiful face. Another soul she bled for, a kind and gentle heart camouflaged by the severe trappings of an assassin. Would she ever have an opportunity to thank him for the gift of a mynx coat, but even more, for the unexpected validation of her worth at a moment when she'd been the most vulnerable?

She swallowed audibly. "Visconte, find that which you love most dearly and cling to it with all the tenacity and might you can summon, for the Great Deceiver will rape your soul with despair and desolation until it seems hope has fled the world and there is nothing for you but surrender to endless death. You will dwell in your greatest pain, your deepest loss. You will forget the pain ever ended. You must remember it is a lie." Adonia raised her eyes and looked at each person, holding their gaze for a moment before moving on as each face dawned with realization of the personalized horror they faced. "Find that which is good and true, and surrender your soul to it. It is the only way to survive being eaten by the dark. The abhorrence cannot swallow joy or love or truth." Adonia took a shuddering breath. "And then you endure. You cleave to the ephemeral reminiscence that once life held beauty and light—until the darkness consumes you or withdraws."

"Oh, Adonia, is that what you experienced each time you healed someone here?" Sophi's tender voice throbbed with anguish. "How could you bear it?"

Warmth flooded Adonia's heart, and she lifted her face to gaze at Hel. "I am the beloved of DeHelios. He is my lodestar. He is my truth." Hel's gray eyes studied her intently and the ghost of a smile hovered on his mouth.

A profound silence followed her words and, after a long moment, Adonia allowed her gaze to wander the faces of those surrounding her. Their images became blurred as tears filled her eyes, a reaction to the poignant exchange of embraces, kisses and emotionally wrought looks between Ari, Doral, Fleur, Eric and Sophi.

Hel pulled her to his side and wiped her tears away with gentle fingers. Leaning down, he whispered in her ear. "Am I imagining things or does Eric DeStroia glow?"

She clapped her hand to her mouth to stifle a surprised catch of laughter. Adonia thought of Sophi's dignified husband and smiled softly before pressing a kiss to his lips and murmuring, "It is a residual effect from a previous communion with our Great Mother. He hates it. It would be wonderful if you could simply ignore it." She wasn't sure how to interpret Hel's grunt.

Her attention was diverted from Hel when Ari sighed and

reluctantly disentangled himself from the embrace of Doral and Fleur. "I suggest that all of us rest, marshal our energies and come together in the morning to perform the Great Rite in a common ceremony, each of us with our established partners. It is easiest to access the metaphysical world and our Great Mother through this rite."

"I agree," Hel said. "I'll have the satellite chambers in Torre Bianca prepared for the three of you and Ducca DeStroia and his wife."

With a weary smile, Hel's gaze stopped on Ramsey and Steffania. "My best of friends, I cannot, in good conscience, ask you and your lady to join us in this rite, but will you again guard the door to the tower? I hope you'll not be challenged but these times are uncertain and it's critical we not be disturbed for what could very well be days."

At Ram's curt nod, Hel turned to back to Ari. "Please avail yourself of all Nyth Uchel has to offer. I'm sure you'll want to see your children and their nurses settled in." At the word 'children,' Hel's face relaxed. Adonia saw the yearning in it, and he dropped a lingering caress over her abdomen. "I should like to meet them if there's time," he said.

"We'll make time, now, Prince DeHelios," Fleur responded. "But be forewarned, they have no sense of restraint or due dignity and have never met anyone they didn't instantly consider a playmate. You'll be immediately drafted into whatever game occupies them at the moment."

As Adonia and Fleur looked on in the nursery, Prince DeHelios, descendant of mighty kings, sovereign-head of the fabled Nyth Uchel, spent a carefree hour as the trusty steed of a four-year old as they battled a terrible fell wolf, capably played by the High Lord of Verdantia.

CHAPTER TWENTY-THREE

A sense of desolation and loss, emptiness and despair, beset Hel. He stood in an empty void, face-to-face with the scavenger-picked corpses of all those he had loved. The empty eye sockets and desiccated facial features of his mother and sister-in-law mocked him while the rotting flesh of his father and brother clambered up from where they had been struck down, hissing, "You should have died with us. You don't deserve to live."

He stood in the nursery staring, as the tiny bodies of his children floated eye-level, looks of accusation written on their faces. Blood from the gaping slashes in their throats still glistened on their clothing; their heads tilted askew on their necks from the ferocity of the Haarb's blows. "Why did you let them kill us, Daddy? Why didn't you protect us?" Hel cried out in anguish and reached for them but his fingertips slid through empty air, and they slowly faded from sight, replaced by the snarling cadaver of his lady wife. With a strangled sob, he jerked upright. He was in his bedchamber in Nyth Uchel. "It's a dream. It's only a dream."

Next to him, Adonia stirred and propped up. She was wide awake. He must have worn his tortured emotions on his face for she threw the covers back and wrapped herself around him. "Night terrors?" she murmured into his neck.

He swallowed heavily and tried to discipline his breathing, to still his thundering heart. "Yes. A dream that used to haunt me regularly. I thought I was free from it. I've not had it since returning to Nyth Uchel."

"My prince, think of my love for you. Think of our babe. Our Mother's enemy seeks ways to undermine you. Don't allow it a foothold."

Hel closed his eyes and let the warmth of Nia's embrace and strength of her love wash through him. He thought of the promise of their unborn child. "You have named me your lodestar, Nia. You are my light as well."

They held each other until the soft half-light turned to true dawn—unwilling to sleep for reasons neither wished to discuss.

When Hel had gone to wake the others, he'd found the three members of the Second Tetriarch not in their bedchamber but in the nursery, awake and entwined in each other in silence, watching their children sleep. "It is time," he murmured and the three of them rose and followed him noiselessly out of the nursery.

It was a solemn, lonely procession that slipped away silently to Torre Bianca at the break of dawn. Hel gripped Nia's hand tightly, unwilling to lose the warmth of her living touch for even a moment. He noticed that Eric did the same with Sophi, and the queen held each of her consorts by the hand. Even Ramsey had pulled his wife into his side with an arm slung over her shoulder.

As they reached Torre Bianca, Ramsey and Steffania fell to the sides and took positions at the ground floor entrance to the white tower. It had been agreed that the purpose for this communal working of the Great Rite would be withheld from the town's population to avoid widespread panic. Only select retainers, Bernard and a few others, were told of its significance.

The members of the Second Tetriarch and then Adonia and Sophi filed through the tower doorway and Hel heard Steffania's low murmur of, "Her light be with you."

The last to enter, Hel and Eric paused and exchanged a warrior's clasp of muscled forearm with Ramsey and a nod of acknowledgement with Steffania.

DeKieran gazed steadily at both of them. "My vixen and I will hold this entrance until you emerge." His mouth twisted wryly. "Don't make us wait too long."

Hel gave a dry laugh. "We shall try to be brief." And then he closed the door on Ramsey's humorless grin and barred it behind him.

The group ascended in the mechanical lifts and grouped briefly on the upper landing. Ari paused for a moment, and his somber gaze swept their group. "As we agreed—though it cost us our lives—we must prevail. We attack as one blade, one thrust, but for Adonia. You are to be the last to engage the darkness. Do as Queen Isolde instructed and wait until you see no other hope. If you see us fall, summon our forbearers to the attack." He took a deep breath and blew it out slowly. "For our people. For Her," he said soberly.

"For our people. For *Her*," their low chorus of voices echoed.

Steely purpose filled Hel. They would succeed. They had to. He rejected any other outcome. Hel escorted the Second Tetriarch to their ritual chamber and then Eric and Sophi. When he closed the great arched door to the Chambre Cristalle behind him, he turned to Adonia. "Ready?" At her nod, he picked up the twin to the goblet Nia held, swallowed the contents and then disrobed.

Hel hoped that Nia was spared the bleak foreboding that continued to attack him—initial probes from their enemy meant to weaken him, he was certain. He could read nothing from her face or manner but confidence and love. As the cinnagin swirled through their system, he swept her nude body into his arms and laid her gently on the diamantorre slab. "I've given this some thought and I'm not going to bind you." At her questioning look, a poignant sorrow made inroads into his cold determination. "I don't know if I will be able to untie you, Nia. I cannot stand the thought of you surviving me, only to suffer a death of thirst or starvation bound to the dais."

She returned his solemn gaze. "Ramsey and Steffania would free me."

"If they lived. It is too uncertain for you and our child, Beauty."

"We will succeed." As he watched, Nia's lips curved in a smile of limitless devotion and her lovely eyes shown with love. "Beyond death, my prince."

Armored and strengthened by her confidence and love, he began.

It seemed the scorching heat of arousal tortured him endlessly, as sunk in Nia's hot depths, he struggled to concentrate on the words of the rite. Decades of self-discipline and years of ignoring the complaints of his body served him though, as through the endless hours of erotic agony he held firm and finally reached the shattering culmination that catapulted him into the metaphysical world.

For the first time in his life, he wanted to turn tail and flee—anything to escape the roiling void that blackened the surface of their Great Mother with an inky cloud of pustulence, extinguishing Her golden light, suffocating Her life. Tendrils of desolate blackness stretched from Her into the aetheric plane like skeletal talons and impaled upon each talon writhed a sphere of golden light being slowly drawn into the central mass. Hel could name them: Ari, Fleur, Doral, Eric and Sophi. By the Goddess, the golden spheres looked so small and the evil they fought so infinite.

Despair permeated his being. How could they prevail against this enemy? There was no possible hope. The dark was too vast, and they were too few. He gave a moment of agonized regret for his beloved Nia and their unborn child.

With a battle cry of, "Verdantia!" that resounded across the metaphysical plane, he plummeted toward Her surface and into the abyss.

Pain almost beyond endurance pierced him. An enormous force slammed him onto an arid, forsaken plane of bleached bones and ruined buildings where red winds of acid-filled clouds flayed the skin from his body and carried his tortured screams swirling into the distance. The bodies of Haarb, their intestines trailing like viscous ropes from their gaping abdomens taunted him, brandishing the lifeless corpses of his son and daughter impaled on their swords, and in his pain and despair, he forgot. He forgot who he was. He forgot *why* he was. He forgot that existence had ever held anything but anguish and hopelessness, and the howling wind seemed to fill with the gloating overtones of triumph.

In the eternity of his suffering, for the merest instant his despair receded, and a word flared in his mind like the flicker of a star in the deepest night. *Nia.* Hel recognized the power in that word *Nia.* The longer he held the word in his mind, the brighter the starlight glowed on the shadowed desolate plane, and Hel clung to that word as if it held his immortal soul.

Adonia surrendered utterly to the fires raging within her. Awareness of time fled before the all-consuming erotic heat of Hel's body working its magickal torture on her. When climax detonated within her, her consciousness burst into awareness on an aetheric plane much changed from when she'd journeyed there last.

She barely contained her cry of despair as she realized the roiling blackness consuming the aetheric plane blotted out the light of their Great Mother. The diseased, tornadic whirlwind on the surface of Her obliterated all illumination but six small specks, specks that Adonia realized to her horror were her beloved Hel, Sophi, Eric, and the Second Tetriarch.

One by one, the blackness ate away at the golden spheres until all light was extinguished, and she knew with certainty that she had witnessed the deaths of those she loved. She felt the tearing pain as first Ari, then Fleur, then Doral, Eric and Sophi fell. Finally, with a scream of inconsolable grief that echoed throughout the darkness, Adonia felt the rending of her soul as Hel vanished. It seemed the black boiled up in greedy exaltation, and pain and despair, the like of which she'd never known, eviscerated her metaphysical being. She almost succumbed, throwing herself into the black void, wanting nothing more than to join her beloved. But she held to the greater goal. *He* would not have acted so selfishly. In this, she could serve her prince as he would have wanted.

"Beyond death, my love, and in death I will join you. But first, I have a duty."

Adonia assembled her shattered heart and set aside her crippling sorrow, and sent a call into the aetheric plane. "By the shared blood of the raven, I call you, Isolde DeCorvus, First Queen of Verdantia, and with you, your consorts, Federago DeHelios and Agentio DeLorcha. I summon you to this plane and bind you to my will."

"We answer your summons, Lady Raven. What is your will?"

Adonia felt the distinct presence of Federago. "Help me summon those noble kings and queens who followed you. We go to war against the Great Deceiver."

"Call these names, daughter of my blood, and they will come."

And so, crying out the names that Queen Isolde gave her, Adonia began the roll-call of the mighty kings and queens of Nyth Uchel. Adonia had no room for more emotion. Hel's death, and that of the others, had stripped her of the ability for anything but heart-rending grief. Had she been able to feel, she would have been awestruck as each majestic personage appeared until the assembled host resembled a multitude of flaming suns gone nova.

For Her! For Verdantia!

In response to the battle cry from a voice she recognized as Federago, the assembly swelled into eye-searing radiance and streaked into the center of the roiling black invasion—and was consumed. As blackness swallowed their last hope, Adonia surrendered to the grief ravaging her heart. She had one final task to perform to honor her prince. Holding the thought of her beloved Hel in her mind, knowing with surety that she went to her death, she arrowed into the midst of the dark void and engaged the Great Deceiver in combat. As she lanced into the heart of the ravening darkness, the familiar assault of hopelessness and despair began.

For an eternity she lived the moments of her greatest heartbreak, and this time her enemy had a weapon of stunning power—Hel's death, Sophi's death, Fleur's death. Adonia watched and felt their life force being eaten alive and torn from her heart over and over again until the pain of their loss consumed her, and yet, she held fixed on her lodestar. *I am the beloved of the light-bringer.* The Great Deceiver could do its worst to her, but it could not corrupt that eternal truth. She seized and held that thought until she felt herself slipping into a vast nothingness and consciousness left her.

CHAPTER TWENTY-FOUR

wareness returned to Adonia with aching slowness. There was a dire reason she didn't want to wake, though she couldn't form an articulate thought. Leaden weight pressed her down onto an unforgiving surface. She lay on her side in a fetal position, and her shoulder and hip ached ferociously. She registered the physical pain and a niggling thought that some horrible grief waited in ambush. Her thoughts shied from wakeful recognition and retreated to the dark corners of her unconsciousness mind.

My beloved raven, you must rise. The white stallion needlessly sorrows for his mate.

"Great Mother?" Adonia was having such a strange dream. Torre Bianca. The Second Tetriarch in Nyth Uchel. Eric and Sophi. Hel. The Great Rite. Thoughts and memories crowded into her brain and suddenly she remembered the reason her heart felt as if it had been sundered from her chest. "Hel's dead. They're all dead," she whispered and curled tighter into a ball as uncontrollable sobs shuddered throughout her.

"Nia? Beauty? By Her light ...you live!"

Suddenly, she was lifted against a warm, well-muscled chest.

Broad hands wiped her hair from her face and lifted her chin. "Nia, open your eyes. Look at me!" Hel's dear voice sounded choked with emotion. "By all that is holy, Nia, show me you live," he demanded.

Still sobbing with uncontainable grief, she opened her eyes and looked into Hel's face mere inches away. Incredulous, she raised a hand and felt him. She shook her head repeatedly. "No. No. I don't believe this. You can't be real. I saw you...I *felt* you, die! My heart was torn from my body." She read the same emotions in Hel that were ravaging her—grief, disbelief and delirious joy. She was having a terrible time convincing her mind he was there. It was as if her grief had been so profound it would not release her. She couldn't stop the cries of sorrow wrenched from her gut, though the evidence Hel lived was inches from her nose.

"I didn't die; though it was a very near thing. You did it, you incredible woman. You did it." His eyes searched her face as she lay in his lap looking up, still not able to reconcile her memories with her present reality. She continued sobbing with grief-stricken inhales, and tears coursed down her cheeks in a steady roll. Hel snugged her tightly to his lap and continued to compulsively stroke her face. "You summoned them, Beauty, 'the mighty from ages past' and they came. They weakened the enemy tremendously, but the final strike was yours." He caught her up in her arms. "I saw you die, my love...but then it seemed you hadn't. I didn't know what was truth and what was the lie."

Adonia pulled in a shuddering breath and her precarious physical state stabilized from sorrow-laden convulsions to hiccups. "The others? Queen Constante? High Lord DeTano, Eric, Sophi? Visconte Doral? Ramsey and Steffania? Do they live?"

Hel shook his head. "I don't know, Beauty. I don't know. We'll have to leave this chamber to find out."

Nestled in his lap, Adonia wrapped her arms around his chest—his living, breathing chest—and her emotions got the best of her again. Her body shook with uninhibited sobs as she ran her hands over him, feeling every inch of bare skin to cement his reality in her mind. "I thought I had lost you, my prince." He held her and covered the crown of her head with gentle kisses until, gradually, after a passage of some time, she brought her grief-stricken keens under control. With a convulsive shudder, she hugged Hel and murmured into his chest. "My nose has run all over you. How unattractive. And I'm naked. May I please put my robe on?"

Hel pushed her away from him and, with a raised eyebrow, looked at his chest and chuckled. She scrubbed her nose with the back of her hand and joined him as he rose and set her gently on her feet, his arms hovering around her until she nodded.

She placed her arms into the sleeves of the ornate robe Hel held open for her and stood quietly as he tucked her into the voluminous garment and wrapped the sash several times around her waist before donning his own robe. "I'm afraid to leave this chamber. I'm afraid of what we'll find," she confessed as Hel opened the door for her.

"Yes. I share your apprehension. But we cannot stay here forever."

Hel took her hand, and they walked out to a quiet tower atrium. Adonia looked at Hel in question. "There is no outside noise."

"The walls are very thick, and we may be the first to leave. I'm uncertain how long we were in the Chambre Cristalle. Don't read too much into the quiet."

Nevertheless, when the lift reached the bottom floor, Adonia couldn't help but feel uneasy as they crossed to the entryway door. The bar that Hel had put into place when they had entered hung shattered in half and daylight shone through great gouges in the door itself. "What happened here?" she wondered out loud.

"Someone tried to enter. Unsuccessfully, from the unsullied interior of the tower's ground floor." Hel pulled the door open carefully. "Stay behind me until I know it is safe, Nia."

She grabbed the belt of Hel's robe at the small of his back and followed him through the heavy door to a courtyard scene of arrested activity. Every person in the spacious area, and there were many, had paused in whatever they were doing, their attention riveted on Hel and Adonia as they exited Torre Bianca. The low hum of conversation began to rise in volume as their voices called excited words of welcome.

Adonia noted with a cry of gladness the presence of all her dear companions. Fleur stood with her two lovers—their conversation paused—relieved smiles lighting all three of their faces. Eric watched as Sophi tended a battered and bloody Ramsey. An equally disheveled Steffania collapsed on a low bench nearby, her left arm bound in a sling and her right forearm wrapped in a stark white bandage. All but Sophi, Ramsey and Steffania started toward them and that's when Adonia noticed the piles of massive, misshapen creatures littering the courtyard.

She met Hel's gaze. "What happened here?"

He shook his head in silence and turned to look at the tower door they had just walked through. Deep gouges that could have been claw marks raked the door diagonally and fist-size holes marred two of the timbers making up the door itself. "Something, or several somethings, tried very hard to gain entrance."

They both swung their attention to where Sophi continued to dress Ramsey's wounds. "I suspect we owe that pair more than we will ever know. I'll ask, of course, but he won't tell me—not what really happened," Hel murmured. "Remind me of this the next time I want to kill him."

Adonia simply hugged Hel closer before they descended the tower steps to meet Fleur, Ari and Doral. The three ruling heads of Verdantia walked up to her and, for a moment, she looked at faces that held veneration and wonder. Hel stepped behind her and rested his hands on her hips. She appreciated the physical support. She had no precedence in her life for such open tribute from those she considered far above her. How did one behave when publically revered by the queen and her consorts?

Ari was the first to speak.

"I saw you die, Adonia." His gaze stopped at each person and returned to linger on her. "I saw each of you die. I have never felt such profound desolation. I lost who I was. Then, as if a mist cleared, I saw a different scenario. An immense blaze of light, like a newborn sun, seared through the darkness and began to dissolve the corruption eating our Great Mother and, suddenly, I recognized the despair that consumed me for what it was—a deceit, a dark lie, a curtain obscuring the truth—and I remembered my purpose." His eyes caressed his queen and his second. "I remembered those I loved." Ari swung his piercing gaze to Adonia and held her transfixed. "And then I saw you. I've had many interactions on the metaphysical plane. I've never seen anything as glorious as you. You radiated purity of love with the brilliance of a twined-star. Your light illuminated every dark crevasse and exposed every falsehood. There is no doubt in my mind. You determined our fate—individually and as a planet."

All those who stood around her murmured their agreement, including Hel. Adonia stood stunned, aghast. Such generous accolades from Verdantia's most elite left her floundering. She had no words. She'd done nothing noble. She'd had no altruistic motives. She'd simply tried to be a woman worthy of Hel. She had acted out of love for her prince. Her eyes fell. The High Lord's words generated absolute confusion within her. She reached for

Hel's hand and pulled his arm around her waist, confounded at the unqualified praise heaped upon her from a man she considered austere and formidable. "Not me alone. It was all of us."

The High Lord of Verdantia shook his head. "No. I arrogantly assumed nothing could take the surety of my love for Verdantia, my queen and my second from me; but when the corruption consumed me, I am ashamed at how quickly I lost my soul to despair." Once again, his eyes scanned the small group. "We all did. The sole obstacle, the one star blazing with an undimmed truth—a truth that forced the Great Deceiver to spit us out—was you. We might have provided a diversion, pulled its attention away for an instant, but the telling blow was you, Lady DeCorvus, you and the dazzling host that attended you."

"No. I…it wasn't…" Looking up, she shook her head and held out her arms as if to beseech their understanding. Couldn't they see how ordinary she was? She'd been a mere pawn in a greater game. It couldn't be as he said.

"Prince DeHelios called you a treasure. He did not go far enough," Ari asserted bluntly.

As always, when she most needed eloquence, the words flew away and left her mute. Adonia dropped her gaze and hid behind a fall of her hair, made awkwardly miserable by the esteem verging on reverence from those grouped around her.

Doral uttered a low sound and the left side of his mouth quirked upward. Was he amused by her tongue-tied misery? It seemed so. "You will be publically adored, Lady DeCorvus. Get used to it."

"She is not leaving Nyth Uchel," Hel warned, pulling her close to him.

Fleur smiled up at Adonia. "No, Prince DeHelios. She won't have to. Verdantia will come to her."

CHAPTER TWENTY-FIVE

L ife became surreal. Adonia had difficulty keeping track of days and hours following those tortured times high in Torre Bianca's keep. The heartbreaking number of sick and injured consumed almost all her energy as word spread throughout Verdantia that a powerful healer resided in Nyth Uchel and those suffering the aftereffects of the Great Deceiver converged on the fabled city. She spent all of her time healing but found to her fascination, that what had once been difficult was now as easy as breathing and she no longer needed Hel to anchor her.

The hours seemed to meld together and blend into days and those days into a week and then two and then three as all in Nyth Uchel labored to restore the city to her past glory. The defeat of the Great Deceiver combined with the resultant release of energy from three powerful combinations of highborn working the Great Rite, accelerated the transformation of Nyth Uchel begun by Adonia and Hel. The legendary place she'd found awe inspiring when frozen in ice burst apart with wonder after magickal wonder until she simply gazed about her with dumbstruck awe. How she wished her father had lived to see this.

In the sickroom, the heavy tapestries had been pulled back and floor-to-ceiling double doors had been opened outward onto an

enclosed garden. On the far garden wall, a small fountain danced
into a natural pool, sending liquid notes of delight cascading into
flower perfumed air. Adonia saw tiny jewel-colored birds flit from
scarlet trumpet flowers, white spider-lilies, and blue scilla, jousting
with fat bumble bees and pastel flutter-byes for the nectar. The
temperate air burst through the doors with the smell of new life.
Green foliage rioted everywhere.

The ornate gates of the Nyth Uchel stood wide in welcome
to the outside world and children ran laughing through meadows
of wild flowers where gravestones had once stood. One evening,
Adonia had even seen a shy mother fricki and her fawn at the
forest's edge, browsing on the new meadow grass. Constructed
entirely of diaman crystal, the very building stones of the city
glowed with a luminosity that softened the dark of night to
half-light for miles. The transformation of Nyth Uchel and its
surrounding forests and fields from an ice-bound prison to a
paradise made soft and new was jaw dropping.

Everywhere, people hugged their loved ones and rejoiced to be
alive. It was a time to share laughter and companionship with those
dear to you. Adonia ached to be with Hel. She missed Maddie and
Sara. Those attending Adonia now were attentive, but strangers,
and too much in awe of Nyth Uchel's healer for easy conversation.
Never good with words, she had not the slightest idea how to
begin with them. She would have welcomed even Bernard. She
missed her girl chats with Steffania, but like all those Adonia
had spent her former days with, some task elsewhere in the city
occupied Steffania. Adonia had lurked outside the family dining
room, hoping to catch some dinner companions but the room had
remained disappointingly vacant. After a couple of forlorn dinners
eating alone, she'd had all meals delivered to her in the sickroom.

The Second Tetriarch had set up temporary housekeeping
in the castle. The air rang with heralding fanfares as messengers

and dignitaries from all points of the planet thundered over the eastern bridge, up the broad boulevard and through the open gates of Castle Nyth Uchel at all hours of the day and night. A steady river of people flowed into the city from every corner of Verdantia, filling the streets with laughter and commerce. Even lacking its front window and part of its kitchen, the char-house where she and Hel had escaped the ghouls did a thriving business. The atmosphere throughout the great city was one of exuberant rejoicing. It seemed to a dejected Adonia that she was the only one not wearing a ridiculous smile.

She had a major complaint—the absence of her prince—well, that and the baffling reverence with which people approached her. She didn't know what they saw that caused such veneration. The mannish image reflected in her mirror had not improved; she still looked remarkably ordinary. She wanted Hel with an ever-present yearning. Through the sick room windows, she would catch glimpses of him with work parties, or hear his commanding voice in the halls, but of his company, the hard press of his body—she had a scant hour or two in the deep of the night. She crawled into their empty bed in the evening and sometime before dawn he would join her, pulling her to him with a soft murmur of love, but each morning she awoke alone but for her attendants. Early into the second week, she had tired of missing him and sought him out, finding him striding down a hallway with Ramsey, locked in argument. His clipped response, "Later, Nia," to her welcome greeting and smile had stopped her in her tracks, and she never looked for him again.

With a heavy sigh, Adonia rose from the patient she'd been attending. *I am simply lonely. It's nothing new, and it won't kill me. Get over it.* A warm tickle blossomed in her gut and spread up her insides, raising gooseflesh on her arms. Her nipples hardened into tight buds. Adonia recognized the feeling she'd been missing for the past three weeks, and she slowly turned, a brilliant smile growing on her lips. There, canted in the doorway, looking worn but incredibly handsome, stood Hel. A tender half-smile curled his mouth. His eyes held hers steadily, and he raised a beckoning arm. With a chirrup of joy, she ran to him, laughing when he picked her up and kissed her soundly. "I've missed you, my prince," she whispered against his lips, her arms wrapped firmly around his neck.

Still holding her, he backed out into the empty hallway and closed the sickroom door. "How I love you, Nia. I've stolen some time to spend with you." His eyes caressed her as he loosened his hold, and she slid down his front to the floor. "Behold a very impatient bridegroom. The arrangements to make you my wife were complete two weeks ago. I've been waiting for the witnesses from each noble house to arrive. The last appeared this morning." A contented smile tipped his lips, and he traced a gentle finger down her cheek. "So, my love, tomorrow at midday, with all due pomp and ceremony, I'm going to marry you. Afterward, the Second Tetriarch wants some sort of to-do announcing the defeat of the threat to Verdantia." He shrugged. "All I'm interested in is making you mine."

She blinked, owl-eyed, and then stared at his breastbone. This was really going to happen. She would publically and with finality, have her heart's desire. Her throat thickened and hurt with the intensity of her joy.

Hel chuckled. "Did you hear me, Beauty? We wed tomorrow." He leaned down to capture her gaze, and his eyes held hers expectantly. Second by second, pressure swelled within her to respond.

"Mmm-hmm." She cleared her throat and wrestled with her wretchedly inadequate tongue. She searched to find words to convey the depth of her rioting elation. Her mind clamored that she *must* tell him of the thousand ways she desperately loved and adored him. She *must* speak to him of the fulfillment he'd brought her, of the joy she experienced each time he ran his hand over the slight swelling of her midsection, of the unfailing wonder she felt that he had chosen *her*. She blurted out, "I need a dress."

She clapped a hand to her mouth and her shoulders sagged. *Ohhh…how could I? Of all the…I don't* care *what I wear.* Her crestfallen dismay must have been apparent, for his laughter rang in the vacant hall. "Yes. You will need a dress." He wrapped her calloused hand in his. "Come. Let's see what we can find."

"I hardly recognize you, Adonia." Eric admired her from the doorway to her bedchamber and offered an arm. "As instructed, I'm here to escort you to Torre Bianca and your wedding."

Sophi peeked at Adonia over his shoulder. "You look simply stunning, radiant. I don't need to ask if you are happy. Are you ready to join your bridegroom?"

Adonia nodded and smoothed the front of her elaborate gown. She had spent a light-hearted interval with Hel yesterday rummaging through closets and closets of women's gowns and accessories. The dress she wore now was the hands-down winner if she went by the look on his face when she slipped from behind the dressing screen to have him fasten it. The style was simple and the cut sophisticated. High necked and long sleeved, its iridescent panels of mother-of-pearl satin hugged her body in such a way as to make her look otherworldly and stunningly regal. Starting at her buttocks, where the skirt belled for walking, scrolls of gold, silver and amethyst beads, wrought in shapes of magical beasts, curled over her breast and shoulders and then down the free-flowing sleeves.

Her attendants had left her chocolate hair hanging free down her back, simply catching strands from the sides to sweep up into a basket weave braid ornamented with matching beading over the crown of her head. The final touch was a delicate tiara of filigreed gold—a statement of royal rank. She had protested. Hel had insisted. *Guess who won.* She rolled her eyes with a rueful huff and anchored the tiara more firmly on her head.

With a last smile of appreciation, Eric swirled a matching cape of the same iridescent cloth over her shoulders. He fastened the gold frog at her throat and then offered his arm. "Shall we, my lady?"

Adonia placed her hand on his forearm with a smile. "Gladly. Please don't abandon me until I'm safely where I need to stand. I could break my ankle." She held out her foot and showed Eric and Sophi the strappy gold and amethyst sandal with its tall, narrow heel and stacked sole. "I practiced walking in them last night, but I'm still as wobbly as a newborn fawn." She met Eric's admonishing gaze and winced. "Hel loves them. I can manage for one day." What she didn't feel the need to tell Eric was—at Hel's insistence—while practicing her walk she'd worn nothing *but* the sandals. He'd been an appreciative audience. She'd been wet with need when he'd called a halt.

"Tonight you sleep alone, Beauty. I want you well-rested for tomorrow." Hel had smiled as he'd swooped her up and laid her on the turned-down bed in the adjoining chamber. The desire in his eyes warmed her as he undid the straps to her sandals. "When I see you tomorrow in all your lovely finery, I'll be remembering how you looked in nothing but these." With a glint in his eye and her golden footwear dangling from his fingers, he sauntered out of her bedroom. She watched every step he took. The man had an exceptionally fine ass.

Now she stood beside Hel on the top step of the entrance to Torre Bianca and repeated the final words that would join her forever to her prince. Glorious blue skies created a sun-filled canopy and colorful flowers and greenery turned the unadorned patio into a floral arbor. The songbirds that accompanied their oaths were better than any hired musicians because they sang of returning life. No less than the stern High Lord of Verdantia administered their wedding oath while Fleur and Doral looked on, smiling. Eric and Sophi stood at her side, while Ramsey and Steffania stood at Hel's. When Hel took her in his arms and sealed their binding with a gentle kiss, the masses in the central courtyard around Torre Bianca erupted into cheers that grew in volume when she and Hel turned to face the crowd. The tumultuous celebration continued for some minutes. It was brought to a good-natured halt when High Lord DeTano addressed the crowd in a solemn voice that carried across the thronged space.

"People of Verdantia, these past weeks have seen our Great Mother restored to us in all Her verdant glory and all alien corruption wiped from our fertile world. We stand confident our way of life will continue and prosper. This incredible gift did not come without great cost. You cannot see the scars and you cannot hold the weapons in your hands, but a terrible battle was fought to bring this about—a battle whose outcome was uncertain, a battle that struck terror through the staunchest of brave of hearts. One of those hearts was mine and I tell you now—I have never felt such fear." Ari stood back and swept his arm in a gesture that included all those on the top step: Fleur and Doral, Eric and Sophi, Ramsey and Steffania, and finally Hel and Adonia. "You see before you your guardians, Her most earnest defenders and those beloved of our Great Mother. You know their mettle." Ari paused for a moment.

Adonia could hear birdsong and the drone of small insects

through the quiet that descended on the courtyard. Hel squeezed her hand, and she smiled at him absently. How long did High Lord DeTano plan to speak? She hadn't really been listening. Her feet were killing her, and she'd like to be somewhere she could sit, preferably sooner rather than later. She'd also like to be somewhere less public, away from the fascinated examination of everyone who was anyone on Verdantia. She longed for a less-open venue. *Ah well, it can't take much longer.*

Ari drew a deep breath and continued. "Yet, one stands here whose role is unknown to you and that must be remedied, for the fate of all rested upon the slender shoulders of this unlikely champion. It was she who ultimately defeated our foe when seemingly stronger hearts succumbed to the black void of despair.

"The First Tetriarch, in their prescient wisdom, foretold her coming. They engraved it upon the foundation stones of Torre Bianca to guide us. The Second Tetriarch has completed the inscription to ensure our posterity will never forget their debt to her. You can read it for yourselves on the stones, but I will tell you what it says.

Beneath her feet, the raven found them,
the mighty asleep from ages gone.
High in her keep, the raven bound them;
to evil's bane and a new light's dawn.
To our raven we bow with hearts overflowing,
for deliverance from death;
for love beyond knowing.

Adonia DeHelios nee DeCorvus,
our beloved raven and
Her invincible sword.

Dedicated this forty-third day, NTSD 4380, by

the grateful people of Verdantia"

The courtyard erupted in cheers and cries of "Goddess, bless you, Lady! Bless you, Princess Adonia!"

"What?" Adonia swayed painfully on her feet while her eyes sought Hel's, and she shook her head, not comprehending. "What did he say?"

Hel's solemn smile did little to enlighten her. Gradually, the meaning in High Lord DeTano's words struck her with the abruptness of a slap to the face. She no longer gave a moment's thought to her feet. She turned to Hel in confusion as first Fleur, then Doral and finally Ari, arrayed themselves before her. With solemn dignity, beginning with the queen, the three members of the Second Tetriarch went to a knee and bowed their heads before her. She gave a small cry of objection when Hel, love shining from his eyes, knelt and bowed his head.

Panic consumed her. "No! No. Get up. Please, get up. What are you doing?" She frantically tugged at first Queen Constante's arms, then Doral's and finally Ari's in a futile attempt to make them stand before turning in a complete circle and throwing up her hands in consternation at the sight unfolding. "Stop! All of you, stop! Please! Don't!"

In a wave that swept the courtyard, everyone sank to a knee and their cheering stopped. She realized with agonized discomfiture that amidst hundreds of the most illustrious people on her world, she alone remained standing in a courtyard suddenly hushed. Every upraised gaze focused solely upon her. Adonia covered her face, overpowered by awkward mortification. Finally, she dropped her hands and stood in the center of the top step, shoulders bowed. She took a deep, resigned breath. "Please, will you stand? I don't deserve this honor."

Fleur looked up. "Our Great Mother's fate, the fate of us all, rested on the courage and loving heart of one woman. You, dearest raven, decided the ultimate outcome of battle. How can we *not* honor you?"

Nia wrapped her arms around herself and looked at her feet, until as a signal to all, Queen Constante rose and hugged her.

On his knees like all those around him, Hel strained to hear the quiet words his Beauty and the queen exchanged. His heart ached with gratitude toward the Second Tetriarch for the very visible tribute paid to Nia, and he found himself clearing his throat and blinking to prevent an unmanly display of emotions. Representatives from all corners of Verdantia knelt in the courtyard. Hel had no doubt they would disseminate the Tetriarch's outward sign of acknowledgement until there was no one on the planet not aware of the contribution Adonia DeCorvus, now Princess Adonia, had made to their survival. Hel decided at that moment that his life's work would be to make Nia feel how loved and adored she was. Never again would she hesitate to raise her eyes to the world she had saved.

As the rustle of everyone rising to their feet replaced the former quiet, a rider pounded into the courtyard and pulled to a violent halt, slamming his mount back on its haunches. Hel recognized the rider and swore several vulgar oaths under his breath. Tristan's arrival could not have been timed to garner a more rapt audience, but then his younger brother had always had a knack for embarrassing him. He closed his eyes, stiffened his spine and waited for it. He hadn't long to wait. His younger brother's shouts carried clearly across the courtyard.

"Gurley! Gurley! By the Goddess, did I miss it? Did I miss your wedding?" The dark-haired male threw his reins to a bystander and began to shoulder his way through the crowd, waving.

Hel flinched, then sighed. His brother was his personal plague. He was certain of it. He'd sent him to the furthest corner of the planet. How had the man gotten back so quickly?

Ramsey nudged him with an elbow. "Who is that?"

Hel spoke through a clenched jaw. "My younger brother, Tristan."

An evil glint appeared in Ramsey's eyes. "He addressed you as girlie. Is that an insult to your manhood or is your real first name, Girlie?"

"Not 'girlie' as in g-i-r-l-i-e, but G-u-r-l-e-y as in Gurley, my mother's surname, you pestilent bastard."

"Girlie. Huh. No wonder you tell people to call you Hel."

Hel mistrusted the slow grin that crossed Ramsey's face. "Don't you have someone you need to rob, DeKieran? Some horses you need to steal? There's a very nice black in the stables you might be partial to. I know I am. He's yours if you leave. Now."

Ramsey's eyes widened in mock horror. "Leave? Oh no, Gurrrley. I'd never forsake a friend in need. This is your wedding day. We have a decanter of *Pottsdim Likor* crying our names. I wouldn't dream of abandoning you ... Gurrrley." Ram bestowed another wicked grin on Hel.

Hel turned away, grinding his teeth.

Close enough to overhear their interchange, Eric laughed and slapped Hel on the back. "Gurley, eh? Well, we all have our tribulations—at least you don't glow."

EPILOGUE

A fresh breeze flitted in through the open windows of their bedchamber and brought with it the green smells of renewal and the sounds of revelry in the streets below. The entire city celebrated their new princess and would for days to come. Hel knew exactly how he wanted to celebrate and none of it would be public. He stood for a moment in the doorway with eyes only for the pensive woman who stood gazing out into the night with a solemn expression. The air flirted with her wisp of a nightdress. The sheer material thinly veiled the slender elegance of Nia's body, teasing his eyes with suggestions of her nudity underneath. The sight of her stirred him, as she had always stirred him, and he moved to join her, wrapping his arms around her and pulling her to his chest.

She made a soft murmur of welcome, and he nuzzled a kiss into the crook of her neck. "Do you know what the people in the streets are calling you? Carissime Medica—Beloved Healer."

She shook her head, and for a moment, a bemused expression lightened her somber appearance.

"You look far too serious for a bride on her wedding night. What are your thoughts?" Nia turned in his arms and raised a reflective face to his.

"I came here to heal the people of Nyth Uchel. I never

expected Nyth Uchel would heal me."

He cocked his head. "Heal you of what?"

A glimmer of a smile traced her lips. "Self-doubt, a sense of not belonging. Before coming here, my past was a wound that bled daily. I had only my skills with herbs and an impossible dream. I didn't know where I belonged; it seemed I didn't fit anywhere." Nia nestled her cheek against his chest, and her words came out muffled. "I felt alone."

"Hmm. You belong in Nyth Uchel, and you fit in my arms very nicely." He raised his hand and stroked the back of her head. "Do you still feel alone?"

She drew back and looked up at him, her face radiant. "No." Warm pleasure ran through him at her obvious happiness, then a peaceful calm supplanted the open joy in her expression. "I saw Klaran … and he saw me. He stood among the crowd filling the courtyard at our wedding. I should have expected he would be here with Eric and Sophi."

The hot desire for vengeance flashed through Hel when he considered the lingering devastation the man's words had inflicted. "I'll give you his head as a wedding gift, if you like." Though he tempered his voice, he was deadly serious.

She laughed softly. "No. When I saw his face, heard him hailing me, I braced inside for the pain…" She shook her head in wonder. "It never came. I walked past him without a word, and I didn't care. I truly didn't care!" Her face lit from within, and her gaze captured his. "Your love has healed that wound. I am whole again."

Hel cupped her face in one hand and pushed words past a throat thick with emotion. "You are a light for my dark soul—a gift from our Great Mother. I had never thought to feel the love of a wife, to experience again the happy anticipation of a child. Thank you, Nia, for as much as you say I healed you, so your love has healed me." He took her hand and led her to their bed. "I don't have the words to tell you how much I love you, so I am going to show you."

Her glorious brown eyes flared, and she tossed him a seductive glance. "I hope you plan to take your clothes off."

He answered her with a slow grin. "Eventually."

~~The End~~

If you'd like to read more about the Verdantians (and many of the characters from past books) here's an excerpt from book five in the series, Hers To Captivate, a M/M/F, M/F, M/M story. Flip the page to read on.

HERS TO CAPTIVATE

CHAPTER ONE

The planet, Verdantia—spaceport city of Arkodaenia

Tristan DeHelios slouched against a tower of packing crates that vibrated from the ever-present rumble of arriving and departing starships and gazed off at a cluster of dockworkers busily unloading freight. In spite of his bored appearance, Tris listened carefully to the words of Lord Ramsey DeKieran, the gods-be-damned nanny inflicted upon him by his brother. Ramsey denied the accusation, but Tris knew better. Ramsey DeKieran was there to ensure Tris didn't screw up. Well… fuck Hel, and fuck the horse he rode in on. Bitter frustration seethed inside Tris. At thirty-two, he'd long outgrown the need for supervision, but Hel insisted on casting Tris as his heedless, immature, baby brother. Tris snorted.

"…and provide Dr. Giverny and our returning noblewomen with every possible protection and assistance." Tristan's former commanding officer and ostensible nanny stared at Tris with his eerie, indigo-ringed gray eyes. "Did you hear anything I said?"

Tris brought his hand to his forehead in a mock salute. "Yes, sir. Every possible protection and assistance, sir."

Ram straightened and uncrossed his arms with a sound of disgust. "Stick it up your ass, Tristan. I'm no longer your superior officer. For the last time, I'm in Arkodaenia because Steffania is here with her Blue Daggers, and where my wife goes, I go."

Tris arched an eyebrow. "You refused Gu-r-r-r-ley? I'm surprised he let you live." Tris supposed calling his illustrious brother "Gu-r-r-r-ley" instead of "Hel" when he'd crashed Hel's wedding was immature, but he couldn't help the delight he experienced when the arrogant ass squirmed with mortification as all the elites of Verdantia looked on—and it was Hel's given name. What had their mother been thinking? And why *hadn't* his brother invited him? Was he that ashamed of Tristan? It had been almost two years and the slight still smarted.

Ram choked down a laugh but quickly sobered. "Yes, I refused your pompous ball sack of a brother. You are technologically competent. You've an uncanny knack for getting people to do things for you, and I have no question you'll keep Dr. Giverny safe. You are the perfect man to smooth her way in setting up the neurological clinic and protect her in the process. I recommended you to High Lord DeTano and Queen Constante." Ramsey snorted in disgust. "Despite you showing up in Nyth Uchel obscured by so much hair even your mother wouldn't recognize you. I certainly didn't. What is it about House DeHelios? Your family averse to good grooming?"

Tris shrugged. "I shaved off my beard and cut my hair."

"Yes, and you still look like a roustabout." A humorless smile distorted Ramsey's mouth. He sniffed the air. "You smell like you spent the night on the floor of some dive."

"Julia would object to you calling her establishment a…" Tris paused mid-sentence when Ram waved him silent. He followed Ram's gaze. The man lifted his head and grinned broadly at a hulking giant of a humanoid male descending a nearby starship gangway. The metal plating rattled under each ponderous step. The giant's body obscured a petite beauty trailing him until the colossus stepped aside and ushered her forward with a delicacy at odds with his size.

"Verdantian," said the giant, a smile splitting his face.

"Khlossian," Ram acknowledged.

The behemoth strode up to Ram and slapped him on the shoulder in greeting. Ram staggered backward several feet then straightened. Tristan watched, bemused at the manhandling DeKieran allowed without protest.

His interest sharpened when the delicate beauty accompanying the Khlossian beamed up at Ramsey then dropped to her knees in front of him, placed her hands on her thighs, and bowed her head. "Dominus, I am very glad to see you."

Ram reached down and drew her to her feet. "Pansy... er... Dr. Giverny. We left that behind on Vxloncia. It's just Ram, or Lord DeKieran if you insist on formality. I'd like to introduce you to the man I mentioned in my communiqués."

Well... by *Her* ruby red tits. That tiny morsel of delicious female flesh was Dr. Giverny? Was that a look of adoration the good doctor lavished on DeKieran? "Dominus" she had called him. What was the story behind that? Furthermore, how did Ramsey's decidedly lethal wife feel about it? Tris chuckled to himself. This assignment promised to be far more entertaining than he'd thought. When Ramsey motioned him to join them, Tris sauntered over. The tiny beauty watched him approach then wrinkled her brow.

"Lord DeKieran, you are certain? The medical instruments I brought are irreplaceable. The equipment requires the most delicate handling." She lowered her voice to a murmur and turned away. "This man doesn't look... well... responsible." Despite her attempt to conceal her words, Tris heard her.

Tris ignored the wash of anger that accompanied her voicing

a sentiment he'd heard far too often. Instead, he slipped into the persona that had become his second skin, and put his head back and laughed. "Spend tonight with me, lovely, and you can decide for yourself how responsibly I handle delicate equipment."

Ramsey snorted. "Dr. Angelica Giverny, meet Tristan DeHelios—your new bodyguard and med-center liaison officer."

"Doctor." Tris tipped his head and acknowledged her blank, owl-eyed expression. "I take it you wish me to oversee the off-loading of your medical supplies?" The woman nodded. Her stunning violet eyes blinked up at him in the most humorous way. So… this was the body he was to guard day and night for an indefinite future. He'd pictured some wizened old biddy. How delicious to be wrong. Damn, but life was good. "I'll see to it, immediately. Oh, and Doc, about tonight—you can get back to me on that." He winked at her still immobile features, chucked her under the chin and turned to stroll up the gangway and into the depths of the starship.

***

The quiet hum of the air circulators for the starship, VNV *Revertar*, was the only sound competing with his footsteps as Tris strode down the narrow gray hallways of the vessel that had delivered forty genetically-priceless Verdantian noblewomen back to their home planet—in addition to the delectable person of Dr. Angelica Giverny and her sensitive equipment. Tris narrowed his eyes and straightened as he walked.

Since the trial of the Vxloncian slaver, Vittal Lontz, and his subsequent conviction—due primarily to the testimony of one Dr. Angelica Giverny—she'd been the object of several attempts to terminate her life. Vittal Lontz had been a mere planetary player. The task force set up by the Galactic Agency for the Protection of Sentients, or GAPS, was dedicated to shutting down the multi-galactic slavery cartel. From the repeated attempts on Dr.

Giverny's life, GAPS was getting too close to the serpent's head for comfort.

Dr. Giverny knew more than she realized. Whoever orchestrated those attempts had gone straight to the most elite and most expensive assassins in the known universes. Apparently, expense wasn't considered. The attempts narrowly failed. Tris was in Arkodaenia along with the Blue Daggers to ensure any subsequent attempts continued to be equally unsuccessful.

Not only did Verdantia need the neurological treatment center Giverny would set up in the spaceport, it seemed the luscious Dr. Angelica had a personal history with Ramsey DeKieran. After all the man had done for him, Tris would hate to let Ram down by not protecting someone important to him and vital to Verdantia. An ironic smile twisted his lips. Unlike most of the make-work jobs that his brother sent him on, this assignment held the certainty he was needed—and then there was the lovely doctor herself. He promised himself a careful pursuit of that delectable wisp of femininity. He'd enjoy putting the violet-eyed beauty on her knees in front of him. His groin tightened at the thought.

Tristan scanned the corridors as he walked. The payload commander had to be around somewhere. A tall, slim figure dressed in khaki fatigues turned the corner, head down, flipping fingers across the face of a compact tap-screen. His shoulder bars indicated the rank of captain. Tris had lucked out. He'd run straight into the ship's commanding officer.

"Captain, my name is Tristan DeHelios. I'm looking for the payload commander, I…" The man halted and raised his head. Incredulity flooded the captain's elegant, chiseled features and a pair of green eyes, once familiar, widened. The tap-screen slipped out of his hands and fell with a rattle to the deck. Tris knew how he felt. *By* Her *light. It couldn't be.* But… "Magellan DeLan? Mage? You're the captain on this ship?"

Tris grinned at the stupefaction covering the face of the male he'd known in Nyth Uchel. His advance toward the captain turned into a stalk as the man remained silently frozen in place. Tris prowled up to him, stepped him backward against the bulkhead and planted his outstretched arms on either side of the man's head. Not more than inches from the captain's face, Tris drank him in. The Magellan DeLan that Tris had known had been a pretty teenage boy—a tall, gawky youth with the promise of broad shoulders above his narrow waist and with an innocent, finely modeled face of shocking green eyes and topped by a mop of black hair. Now, the body beneath his fatigues had filled in and broadened with clearly defined muscle. Mage's pretty, boyish face had hardened and refined into that of an adult male. He exuded a sensual allure that was anything but innocent.

"Look at you. You're even more fucking beautiful." A surge of heat flooded Tristan. "You aren't sixteen anymore, Mage. You're a full-grown man. What's it been? Eight years?" Tristan's cock responded immediately to the lithe, muscled body of the ship's captain as Tris pressed him into the wall with his pelvis. "So... I'm free to do now what I wouldn't allow myself then." Tris held Mage in a steady stare and his face descended by fractions of an inch, his intention clear. Swiftly, Mage's hand wrapped his throat, halting his descent with impressive strength. "Fuck, Captain." Tris leaned into the man's steely grip, challenging him. "Do you really want me to stop?" The pressure against his larynx eased almost imperceptibly. It was enough.

Tris captured the man's head in his hands, sank his fists into Mage's thick black hair and devoured the full lips that had haunted him for eight long years—years of regret about what might have been—what *should* have been. After a moment of hesitation, the captain groaned, wrapped his hands around Tristan's waist and returned the kiss, giving back the same ferocious assault he received. Teeth bit and tongues explored. Hard cock ground into hard cock in a breathless explosion of lust. Too soon, footsteps and voices sounded from a nearby corridor. When Mage stiffened beneath him, Tristan swore and stepped back, wiping his mouth. His chest heaved and his cock begged for freedom from the constriction of his leather breeches. Their eyes stayed locked on each other. Some things never changed—his body's reaction to Mage DeLan was one of them.

The dark-haired, green-eyed captain straightened, licked his lips and swallowed heavily. "I thought you were dead."

Tris worked to control his breathing and appear normal as two crewmembers walked by and nodded respectfully to Mage with a murmur of, "Sir."

One leaned down, picked up the tap-screen lying on the deck and handed it to Mage. "This yours, Captain?"

"Yes, thank you, Evans. Carry on," Mage said. With curious glances at both of them, the crewmen continued down the corridor.

He shouldn't have put a starship captain in such a compromising position and particularly not Mage. A crooked grin pulled at Tristan's mouth and he kept his words low and intimate. "Sorry. Wrong time. Wrong place. That was not well-done of me."

Mage dropped his head and shook it helplessly before looking up with the light of laughter in his eyes. "If you'd been any better you could have had me on the departure deck of my own ship, crew be damned. Don't worry about it. They won't talk."

Tris chuckled but sobered on a wash of painful memory. "The way you left Nyth Uchel… What I allowed you to think." Tris shrugged and looked down the hallway as the crewmen vanished around a corner. "I couldn't let that stand."

The man regarded him with a crooked smile. "What? That you'd rather fuck my horse than a half-grown snot like me? I think those were your parting words."

Tris grunted softly. "Yeah… well… I lied."

The man, whose facial features had never failed to remind Tris of a fucking piece of art, cocked his head and shot Tristan a wry glance. "Evidently." Both men grinned at each other until Mage straightened and squared his shoulders. "So, Tristan DeHelios, what business brings you to my ship? Why are you in Arkodaenia?"

Tristan wanted certain details locked down before business distracted them. He held up a forefinger. "First, how long are you in port? Where are you quartered?"

Mage stood for a moment, a look of consideration on his face. "The *Revertar* is home for re-fitting. We're getting one of the new hyper-drive engines and some updated electronics for her nav system. As soon as we offload, she goes into stationary orbit for maintenance and an equipment upgrade that will probably take the better part of ninety days. I'd planned to stay onboard with the engineering staff and a skeleton crew."

Tristan crossed his arms and shook his head. "Negative. Unsatisfactory response, Captain DeLan." He held Mage's gaze steadily. "How can I see more of you if you are floating around somewhere among the stars? I do want to see more of you. I have an apartment in Arkodaenia with ample space." Tris paused and put his hands on his hips. "Spend your stay in port with me."

He waited with greater impatience than he wanted to acknowledge while Mage leveled a flat stare at him. Long seconds ticked away. Tris itched under the scrutiny of those intelligent green eyes. Disappointment bedeviled Tristan as the seconds accumulated. The man was going to refuse him.

Mage lifted a shoulder. "Sure. Chief Engineer Cox could do without me hanging over his shoulder and getting in the way. I need a week or so to get things lined out before I can join you, but… until then, how about dinner tonight? We can catch up."

Mage gave him a muted smile.

The degree of pleasure Tris felt at Mage's answer shocked him. He relaxed now that he'd received the answer he wanted. "I'd enjoy that. Do you know the Eight Bells on High Street? They serve a decent meal and the service is good." Satisfaction and anticipation warmed him.

"Yes." Mage nodded. "The Eight Bells it is. Now, you were looking for the payload commander. What can he and I do for you?"

Tristan laughed to himself. *More than you know, Captain, more than you know.*

Yes, this assignment had all the earmarks of becoming one hell of an entertaining ride.

Want to continue reading? Click https://geni.us/PAKHersToCaptivate to download Hers To Captivate

OTHER BOOKS BY PATRICIA:

The Verdantian Series
Hers To Command

Hers To Choose

Hers To Cherish

Hers To Claim

Hers To Captivate

The Heirs & Spares ~ Regency Romance
A Husband For Hire

A Destitute Duke

Lessons For A Lady

The Magic Series
Co-authored with Kris Michaels

An Evidence of Magic

An Incident of Magic

Standalones~Contemporary Romance
Undertow

Adam's Christmas Eve

ABOUT THE AUTHOR

Patricia A. Knight is the pen name for an eternal romantic and dyed-in-the-wool hermit who hides in Dallas, Texas with her horses, dogs and the best man on the face of the earth. With the BMOTFOTE as navigator, Patricia bombs down the highways of the United States in the Taj-ma-haul continuing her life-long search for the best chocolate cake recipe and new pictures of David Gandy. Look for her coming to your state! (Seriously, look for her. Her driving is very suspect.) When forced into it by her PA, Pam, she will actually write.

I love to hear from my readers and can be reached at **www.patriciaaknight.com**.
Or send me an email at **patriciaknight190@gmail.com**.
Join me on my private Facebook group
PAKS PEEPS at https://geni.us/PAKSPeeps, or follow me on:

www.amazon.com/Patricia-A.-Knight/e/B00D7GFZH2
facebook.com/patriciaromancewriter
twitter.com/patriciaaknight
bookbub.com/authors/patricia-a-knight
goodreads.com/author/show/7093656.Patricia_A_Knight
pinterest.com/patriciaknight190

If you would like to receive email notifications on my new *historical* romance releases, free short stories, personal appearances, etc., please subscribe to my ***Regency Readers***' Group. I send out, perhaps, three emails a year. This is a **separate** listing from those who read my erotic, gay, paranormal, and sci-fi, romance. You will **not** receive any information from me regarding those titles.

If you like your romance hot, sometimes kinky and definitely out of this world, please join the **PAK FANS** group. You may unsubscribe easily and at any time from either group with a simple click.

With many thanks.

Patricia

Join Patricia's *Regency Romance Readers*:
https://eepurl.com/dcJVCn

Join Patricia's **PAK FANS**:
http://eepurl.com/YqckL

And finally, please, leave a review.

Frequently interviewers ask, "What is your favorite part about being an author?" My answer is always the same, "My readers." I adore writing stories that resonate with you so greatly that my characters enter your life. You rejoice with them. You sorrow with them. *This* is why I write.

For readers, the ultimate reward is finding wonderful books—for authors, it is knowing readers love what they have written. Encourage your authors to write. Help your fellow readers find good books. Leave reviews.

Thank you!

GLOSSARY OF TERMS

Adalay—[a′ da lay]—high mountain range to the east of Sylvan Mintoth and part of the region considered under the governance of House DeHelios.

Aether—[ee′ thur]—The spiritual realm attained by highborn medical practitioners that allows them to address the seven centers of bodily life and by all other magistra*e* to communicate with the Great Mother.

Anima—[ah′ nee mah]—soul, spirit, internal essence of life.

Arcobaleno—[ark′ oh bah **lay′** no]—The color that the diamantorre in the sigil towers blaze indicating the highest amount of energy is being transferred, absorbed and transmitted. The color is a pure white at the furthest end of the light spectrum.

Ari—[ah′ ree]—Conte Aristos Camliel DeTano, Primo Signore of the Second Tetriarch, High Lord of Verdantia and the Queen Fleur de Luna Constante's husband and consort.

Bás dtost—[**bas′** toast] – "the silent death" Hel's nickname given to him by the Haarb.

Chambre Cristalle—[**shaam′** brah***kris**′tall]—the name of the ritual chamber in a sigil tower where the Great Rite is performed. This is the only place the Great Rite is performed. Every sigil tower in Verdantia has a Chambre Cristalle.

Chital—[**she′** tall]—a spotted antelope-like creature with lyre shaped horns. They travel in herds and occupy the open grasslands.

DeCorvus vs Corvus—In <u>Hers To Claim</u>, Adonia is introduced at various times with the last name of "Corvus" and "DeCorvus". In Verdantian society, the "De" prefix indicates the bearer is of one of the thirty-two noble houses originally founded. In the case of Adonia Corvus, her family dropped the "De" prefix when they joined the Mother's Acolytes. Hel introduces Adonia as "Adonia DeCorvus," properly giving her the aristocratic prefix.

Diamantorre **[Dee** ah mahn **tor]**—An immense block of diaman crystal that serves as the central dais in the Chambre Cristalle of each sigil tower. This block of crystal stores the energy of the Great Rite and releases it into the surrounding atmosphere. In an outward display of extravagance, the entire city of Nyth Uchel, its surrounding walls, and the white tower, Torre Bianca, were built of diaman crystal. As such, the overflow of energy is absorbed by the very building stones to the extent that all of Nyth Uchel is haloed with a soft, luminescent light giving the entire city an appearance of magickal enchantment.

Doral [Doh **rall'**]—Visconte Doral Celestia Agentio DeLorion, Segundo Signore of the Second Tetriarch, lover to Ari and Fleur. While neither Hel nor Doral realize it, they are distantly related. In fact, the entire Second Tetriarch is distantly related to Hel as their bloodlines cross repeatedly. This was not by accident. After the schism between Nyth Uchel and Sylvan Mintoth, the High Enclave Elders spent centuries quietly trying to duplicate the genetic makeup of the DeHelios line.

Fell **wolf**—A genetically engineered hybrid of a large, predatory canine and a giant lizard, similar to Earth's Komodo Dragon. They are the size of a large pony and have acute senses of smell, hearing and vision. At some point in time, someone added nano-bots to their genetic structure which makes them heal incredibly fast. It takes beheading or a shot to the brain to put one down. They are highly intelligent and controlled through the use of pulse collars which can be set in varying degrees of severity from mild to stun. They are a favorite of the Haarb.

Fleur—[Fler]—Queen Fleur de Luna Constante, supreme monarch of Verdantia. Her last name does not contain a "De" as she and her father and mother were of questionable nobility. It is the source of one of Hel's reservations about the legitimacy of the Second Tetriarch.

Fricki—[**frick'** ee]—an elusive, elk-like creature living in the mountain regions of Verdantia. They are snow-white in color and very rare. Lore has it that the sight of one of these exotic, shy creatures indicates the active presence of the Great Mother and is very good luck. To kill one is a criminal offense.

Magister—[ma **gis'** tur] – a High Enclave-bred and trained nobleman with a specific genetic link to "Her."

Magistra— [ma **gis'** tra] – a High Enclave-bred and trained noblewoman with a specific genetic link to "Her."

Magistra*e*—[ma **gis'** tray]—plural form of magistra or magister—gender inclusive. More than one magistra or magister.

Mela—[**may'** la]—a tart, lime green, oval fruit similar to an apple.

Nyth Uchel—[**nith'** oo chel'] – "High Aerie" – the DeHelios family seat – A large palace with a once-prosperous city below. Nyth Uchel was the original capital of Verdantia.

Plains of Vergaza—a vast open grassland west between Sylvan Mintoth and the desert wastelands of the Oshtesh.

Senzienza—[**sen'** zee **en'** za]—the Planet of Verdantia's sentience. Also referred to as *She* or *Her*

Signore, Primo—[**pree'** mo***sig'** nor eh] – "First gentleman" – the first male in the *Tetriarch*

Signore, Segundo—[**sah'** gun do***sig'** nor eh]—"Second gentleman" – the second male in the *Tetriarch*

Tetriarch— [**tet'** tree ark]—A trio of nobles formed by the Senzienza to rule Verdantia. They wield extraordinary mystical power with joined with Mother Verdantia. There have been only two in the five hundred year history of Verdantia.

Torre Bianca—[**tore bee'** ahn ka]—the "White Tower"—a sigil tower above *Nyth Uchel*. Torre Bianca is the first, and greatest, of all sigil towers in Verdantia. Her construction, as with all the sigil towers in Verdantia, was accomplished by the First Tetriarch, Hel's ancestors. She is the only sigil tower constructed entirely of diaman crystal.

www.ingramcontent.com/pod-product-compliance
Lightning Source LLC
Chambersburg PA
CBHW071049250626
47159CB00002B/418